* *

The moment she saw the flash and knew the MANED had exploded somewhere near Kierian, all vestiges of Emma Dareheart, daredeviless and graceful female adventurer disappeared. She was the Banshee now, death's handmaiden, and woe to those who got in her way.

Bright light beamed from her magnesium torch. She raced back through the Ironclad's lower deck, pivoting and leaping through the crimson carnage. She saw the stairwell, exchanged the torch for a pistol in each hand.

She rushed around the corner, taking two steps in one leap and collided into three river pirates.

The surprised pirates hesitated.

Banshee did not.

She stuck the barrel of her Colt into the guts of the first pirate pulled the trigger and gave him a second navel. Flames from the barrel set his clothes afire. Banshee spun to her right, shoved the barrel of her other pistol under the chin of the second pirate and painted the ceiling with his brains.

The third pirate leveled his rifle.

Banshee kicked it away, and roared with a shriek worthy of her name. Her Colts thundered .45-caliber death.

Banshee shouldered her way past the bullet riddled corpses and bolted up the steps. She dropped to one knee at the top of the stairs, reloaded and scanned the decks. Six pirates were climbing up the ladder that led to the Pilot House, screaming vulgar and vile oaths that involved cutting out someone's liver and frying it up in a pan for din-din.

Only Kierian could make someone that angry.

She raced towards the ladder. The last of the six pirates heard her footsteps. He spun leveled his pistol and fired all in one hasty motion.

His shot went wide.

Banshee's unflustered aim fired a single shot into the lake raider's head.

The other pirates spun to face her.

From the base of the ladder, Banshee's six guns spit out leaden death. Like wheat before the scythe, the pirates twisted and fell. Banshee climbed the ladder like a cat and made for the Pilothouse. A pirate groaned, and raised himself to his knees. Banshee shot him through the back and coldly stepped over his lifeless body.

She took up a position next to the door, careful not to charge in and create some God-awful tragedy.

The barrel of her smoking Colt rapped thrice

against the wall. "Knock, knock, knock, Mister Piper, I am home."

J.T. MURPHY

S.T.E.A.M.C.A.P.P.

THE ADIRONDACK AFFAIR

BOOK 1: THE RISING OF THE MOON

BY

J.T. MURPHY

Printed in the United States of America

This book is dedicated to my dad, who read me Treasure Island before bed when I was little and gave me my love of the Action Adventure story, be it on the Silver Screen or Printed Page.

J.T. MURPHY

CHAPTER ONE

Friday, August 24, 1901
Adirondack Forest Raquette Lake
New York State

Barnabas Blackwell gripped his Wycliffe electricity pistol tightly in his right hand and raced through the dig site's maze of trenches in order to save the man who would destroy America.

Barnabas had not expected to be thrust into action so soon. Once the temple's inner chamber had been breached, Sir John was to fire a green flare into the sky. Barnabas and his men would then move in, secure the dig and its workers, and proceed with the final phase of Operation Atlas.

But something had gone wrong.

As he had finished breakfasting, a *crimson* distress

signal had exploded in the sky indicating Sir John was in mortal danger and needed immediate assistance.

Cold talons of anxiety gripped his heart. He had promised Lilith he would protect Sir John. He had *sworn* to her that he would assure the success of Operation Atlas.

He touched a hand to his hunting jacket's left chest pocket where the tintype, with her elegant scrawl upon it, rested.

Lilith Grimm, the woman known as the High Priestess of the Labor movement, had beguiled his heart, mind, and soul. He had first heard her speak in the lecture halls. Her brilliance, the radiant glow of her beauty, the fiery passion and hypnotic sound of her voice had cast a bewitching spell over him and he had sworn his allegiance to her and her cause ever. Barnabas rounded a corner. A rifle cracked. Fragments of stone spit into his cheek. He spied a terrified worker fumbling with the bolt of his rifle, trying for a second shot. Barnabas aimed his pistol and fired. Pure electricity streamed from his weapon sending the worker into a convulsion of death. Barnabas leaped over the body and raced down a flight of stone steps. At the bottom lay two bodies, one atop the other.

He recognized the one on top.

"Sir John!"

Anxiety squeezed Barnabas's guts. Despair raked its cold fingers over his very soul.

I have failed her! I have failed Lilith!

Sir John stirred, rising slowly. He leaned back against the cold stone and cast desperate eyes at Barnabas.

"Wa-Water."

Barnabas ripped the canteen from his belt and handed it to the man he had sworn to protect. Sir John chugged the water down like he had just crawled across a desert. His bloody, blistered hand reached out and grasped Barnabas. "Blackwell! No one must escape! Not a soul! Do you understand?"

"What happened?" Barnabas's eyes quickly took survey of his charge. "Sir John, we must get you medical attention." Sir John's face was covered in dirt and muck. Cuts and scrapes peppered his face. His right arm was coated in blood.

"Misfortune has befallen us, Blackwell, misfortune and calamity. I was discovered, undone by that damn slip of a girl!" Sir John took another drink of water and wiped his face.

"Sir John, lie still. I will tend to your injuries." Barnabas knelt down and gently took hold of the injured man's arm.

Strong fingers, that felt more like claws, angrily closed around Barnabas's shirt.

"Damn you sir, listen! I will recover in time but you *must* act, now! Atlas is all that matters. We will never have another opportunity like this again!" Blazing eyes of zealotry glared up at Barnabas. "By the sacred stone, answer me, man!"

"You have my attention, Sir John," Blackwell said. "I am at your disposal."

Sir John released Barnabas and slowly stood. "The inner chamber of the temple cannot be breached at present. Yet all may not quite be lost." Frantic hands patted torn trouser pockets. Seeming to find what he was looking for, Sir John pulled out a notebook, ripped off the last page and handed it up to Blackwell.

"Take her alive and make sure no others escape! Atlas may yet be loosed!" Sir John gripped Blackwell's arm with surprising strength.
"Find her, Blackwell. Everything depends on it now!"

Barnabas looked down at the paper and read its contents. *Name: Gladys Gwynn Age: 15 Description: dark hair, dark eyes. Striking and intelligent face. A devil of a resourceful girl for her age. Real name –*

Blackwell looked up in astonishment.

"That is correct Blackwell. Now you see what leverage her capture will give us. Now you see why we *must* have her!"

* * * * * *

Die, you scabs!

Ezra Chaney squeezed the trigger of the Maxim machine gun. Bullets streamed out the barrel at a rate of six hundred per minute, felling the scabs like wheat before the scythe.

Barnabas had said to round up and secure the workers, and then he had darted off to find and save the high and mighty Sir John.

Sir John. Just another Goddamn tyrant, no better than the autocratic factory managers we are fighting against.

Round up the workers.

That had been the order and they had all agreed to follow Barnabas's orders but then he wasn't really disobeying was he? These were not workers. They were scabs, collaborating bastards, and class traitors.

So ,as soon as Barnabas had left, he had turned the habitation area around the dig site into a killing field.

Anarchy now reigned in the forest. Anarchy that Chaney had kindled. Scabs ran for their lives.

Chaney's union brothers gave chase, inspired by his

13

bloody act and releasing years of pent up rage in an orgy of brutality. Some scabs they shot, others they bludgeoned to death with axe handles and the butts of their British-supplied Martini-Henry MK IV rifles.

Chaney rotated the torso of the Gryphon, seeking new targets. There! Five scabs ran into one of the primitive log cabin dwellings. Chaney pulled the left hand trigger. A sheet of fire leapt from the flamethrower mounted in the Gryphon's left arm. Red-hot hell engulfed the cabin. Two flaming human scarecrows staggered from the inferno. Chaney gleefully gunned them down, the bodies jerking with the impact of each bullet.

Damn scabs! You reap what you sow, you traitorous vermin!

Orange flames consumed men and women still trapped inside. Their death howls burst through the view slot of the Gryphon's iron turret.

Chaney smiled. From inside his steam-powered Gryphon battle bot *he* was the master, not Sir John or Barnabas-fucking-Blackwell. Barnabas could shout orders and wave his electricity weapon all he wanted but the fact was that the Gryphon was the power of the small anarchist army, and *he* was the only one who could pilot the Gryphon. That meant they needed him, and that also meant he could do as he goddamn well pleased.

He throttled the Gryphon and its massive iron legs stomped forward. Inside the battle bot he was an avenging angel delivering leaden death to those who deserved it.

And these people damn well deserved it. They willingly took employment away from brave union men and women. They willingly bowed and scraped to the great Titan of industry, Vanderbilt just because he had funded their expedition and they willingly sat by as people like his Shirley were tossed aside like garbage on a heap.

Now, he would willingly kill them.

* * * * * *

Desperate legs propelled Gladys down the stony trail. Alfred had warned her not to go on the expedition. He had told her it could be dangerous, but her desire for learning, her passion to uncover the secrets of how ancient indigenous people lived before Columbus arrived, had caused her stubborn streak to dismiss his concerns. Alfred, as usual, could not refuse her, but he had insisted she take precautions. He had assigned an ex-marine officer by the name of Tyler to be her bodyguard, and she had agreed to use her mother's maiden name to hide her identity.

Still, she had paid no mind to his concerns. Even when she related her suspicions of that awful man to Professor Bridgewater, she had not given a thought to the danger in which she was placing herself and everyone else.

She had been naïve, and now, that naiveté could prove fatal.

Gunshots echoed. Screams and the pungent smell of burning wood and flesh blanketed the air. Urged by fear and terror her legs picked up speed. The workman's trousers she had chosen to wear today allowed her wonderful freedom of movement and the option of escape into the brush. There, she could let the thick Adirondack forest hide her from her murderous pursuers.

But her instincts demanded speed and screamed *escape*.

So she continued down the trail

She ran faster than she ever had before. Like two machine pistons at full speed, her legs carried her down the trail.

And promptly tripped her over a tree root.

Jagged stones sliced into her palms and legs. Pain streaked through her body.

Beneath her the ground suddenly shook. She spun her head about. Billows of black smoke hissed menacingly into the air.

The beast! That iron beast has found me! Get up! Get back up and run for your life!

* * * * * *

Chaney pushed the throttle forward. Pistons fired and gears turned. Coal transformed into a cloud of black exhaust that rose from pipes on the Gryphon's back. The Gryphon's massive legs marched onward through the forest, increasing speed and crushing small trees beneath its immense weight. Through the view port, he scanned the area for more targets.

There!

He saw her in the distance, limping down the trail. He pushed the Gryphon to full speed.

The girl zig-zagged from tree to tree, but always returned to the main trail. Chaney fired the Maxim, spraying a stream of bullets, downing branches and stripping bark from spruce, cedar and ash trees.

The girl ran.

Chaney pursued. Short bursts of hot lead ricocheted off stone and trailed her steps.

The bullets unnerved her. She stumbled, and

17

crashed to the ground. Chaney slowed the Gryphon, relishing the panic in the girl's face as she scooted away from his iron-killing machine. Powerful, sinister metal legs marched in for the kill.

Eyes, white with terror, gaped up.

Chaney aimed the flamethrower and smiled.

This one's for Shirley.

A stream of jagged electricity struck the girl searing her right shoulder. She convulsed and toppled over onto her back. Barnabas Blackwell darted out from the forest and stood over the girl. Chaney brought the Gryphon to a stop. Steam hissed as he popped the cockpit and stood up in the command turret.

"Damn it, Barnabas, what did you do that for? I was going to fry her like fish on a grill."

"We need her, Chaney! Sir John's orders," Blackwell replied.

Chaney scowled. He didn't give a damn about what Sir John ordered. He caught a better look at the girl and noted she was too pretty and too clean to be working–class.

He wanted to watch her burn, enjoy the crackle of her flesh and savor the aroma of her smoking bones.

Dr. Neil appeared and Blackwell took a few steps towards him, away from the girl.

18

Chaney moved his hand to the flamethrower trigger.

The black and yellow demon appeared out of nowhere, above his head. Toxic fear blazed through his veins, freezing him in place. One wrong move, one involuntary twitch that the demon might interpret as a threat and he knew he would feel its terrible sting, sealing his doom. The demon had stung him years before. What agonizing hell awaited him! Cheeks would bulge, breath would choke, and excruciating pain would race through him, paralyzing his entire body.

Members of the Brotherhood rushed down the trail and gathered around the fallen girl.

The bee flew off and Chaney sighed in relief.

One of the men dropped down and took the girl's pulse.

"Doctor? Is she alive?" Blackwell asked.

"She is merely stunned, Mr. Blackwell."

Blackwell smiled. "Brothers, our plans were momentarily undone by this girl! But now, she is in our power. Today, we have struck the first blow for the proletariat! But another will soon fall and when it does, the bourgeois titans will be recognized by all for the beasts they truly are!"

19

CHAPTER TWO

Monday, August 26, 1901
Above the High Falls
Rochester, New York

"Cavendish stop!" Freddie Paulson leaped for Cavendish's arm, but his large feet, swollen from a bout of the gout, became tangled with each other.

He crashed ingloriously onto the wooden floor of the observation platform.

Reginald Cavendish cackled as he pulled the trigger of Professor Shiverton's freeze gun. A cloud of liquid nitrogen streamed from the barrel enveloping the tightrope in a frosty shroud.

Emma Dareheart dashed up the steps of the one hundred foot high wooden observation platform. Freddie lay in a heap. He gazed up at her, embarrassed at his failed heroics.

Poor Freddie; he was a good man and a crackerjack promoter, but a portly body and lack of exercise made for a poor transition to a man of action.

Emma retrieved his bowler hat, offered him a hand which he reluctantly took, and helped her business manager to his feet.

Emma looked out and studied the tightrope spanning the Genesee River Gorge.

The rope was now coated in ice.

The Skywalk was always going to be dangerous but now it very well could be downright lethal.

Reginald Cavendish stood behind her. He slid the ice pistol beneath his cape and lit a big Cuban cigar. A Cheshire-cat grin stretched across his face. "Is there a problem Miss Dareheart?"

Freddie angrily dusted himself off and straightened his bowler atop his large head. "Of course, there's a problem. "You iced the damn rope!"

Cavendish cackled. "You can choose to cancel the Sky Walk of course, but if Miss Dareheart fails to meet her contractual obligations, you forfeit all the proceeds raised for the orphanage fund, as well as disappointing over twenty-five thousand of the good people of Rochester."

"Damn you, Cavendish! You have no right!"

Contemptuous eyes sneered at Paulson. "I have every right. The contract clearly states that any cancellation of the Skywalk within one hour of the event invokes a clause whereby the proceeds revert back to the sponsor of said event… which in this case, is me."

Emma turned her back on the two men and glanced across the city at the burned out shell of the Children's Orphanage Asylum. Fire had consumed it on 7 January during STEAMCAPP'S battle with the fiendish Ming Fang Fu and his deadly dragon airship.

It had been a horrifying scene. Children, their faces covered in soot, pressed their terrified faces against the windows of the west wing, screaming for help as the flames licked high into the night sky. Adult workers leaped from windows, accepting broken ankles and legs rather than death by flame, abandoning their tiny charges in the process.

The common firemen who responded had been brave but lack of proper equipment, self-interest, and utter contempt for the lower class children by their superiors, doomed their efforts to failure. Their new Webb Pump Engine, that could have been so effective in combating the inferno, was ordered to stand by in reserve and had been guarded by Auxiliary Company Seven of the Metropolitan Police Department, lest anyone should try to use it and make it unavailable to fight a fire at a residence of people who truly mattered.

God forbid some maid drop a burning coal on one of the Persian rugs in some wealthy elites mansion and start a small fire that destroys a painting or two.

Emma and her partners had managed to rescue fifty-two children from the conflagration. Kierian had rescued four by leaping out a third story window, with two tucked under his arms and suffering a separated shoulder, while RA-7, Dr. Waatt's Rescue Automaton, had saved forty-two himself. But Ray had paid a heavy price. The automaton, despite his hardy construction had been so badly damaged that Emma feared he was beyond repair.

Thirty-one children had perished; their small bodies, burned beyond recognition. They were buried together in a Mount Hope Cemetery grave, paid for by the Sisters of Mercy.

Immediately after the fire, there had been much talk of building a new orphanage, but business magnates, like Cavendish, had delayed the process for so long, with hearings and objections to the legal permits and zoning ordinances, that many lost interest.

Life went on, and the cares and concerns of the world crowded out the fading memory of the January tragedy.

How soon we forget.

Sister Mary Theresa of the Carmelite Order had approached her and her partners about a month ago.

"Winter will arrive before long and there is no housing for the orphaned and poor children. Please, help us," Sister Theresa had implored.

"I am not sure what we can do for you, dear lady," Dr. Waatt had replied. "Even if we had the money to pay for the construction, there is no place to build at present. Reginald Cavendish and his cronies have bought up most of the choice land."

Kierian, as usual, had been more optimistic. "Never fear; STEAMCAPP is always ready to lend a hand to the poor and needy."

"But as Dr. Waatt says, we have no money and no land," Sister Theresa said.

Kierian's blue eyes twinkled. "Yes, but I have a cunning plan. Banshee will raise the funds with one of her dare deviling do's," Kierian said, pointing to Emma and using her war-time code name, "While I shrewdly secure the deed."

So, here she was. about to skywalk across a tightrope, 100 feet above a gorge to raise the funds needed for the orphanage.

"So, what shall it be, Miss Dareheart? Are you canceling?" Cavendish asked.

Emma's upper lip curled in disgust. Cavendish was vermin. Vile, rotten to the core, vermin; the kind of person who deserved a bullet to the head as much as the poor people he exploited deserved food on their plates.

When the British, exasperated by the supplying of arms to Canadian rebels by American secret societies, had crossed the Niagara frontier in 1893, starting the four-year long British-American War, they had burned Buffalo, and occupied Rochester and other port cities along Lakes Ontario and Erie. Cavendish, along with many of the other wealthy elites, had fled pell-mell out of the city, stuffing the train's passenger cars with their baggage and valuables, while their guardsmen beat, kicked, and shot any common folk attempting to board.

Now, he was using his power to keep orphans from having a home.

What will be next? Buying up all the walking stick factories so the elderly have no canes to walk with?

"I will do it," Emma said

Cavendish's mouth fell open. Incredulous eyes stared at Emma. "What did you say?"

"I said I would do it. I'll walk the damn tightrope," Emma said.

"Miss Dareheart, I forbid it! It is too dangerous!" Paulson exclaimed.

"Listen to your manager, Miss Dareheart; plunging to your death before all these gawking fools will accomplish nothing! Nor shall I be held liable for death or injury that occurs to you. The contract clearly absolves me of all liability."

"Yes, yes, I know what it says." Determined brown eyes locked on Cavendish. "You are boot scum, Mr. Cavendish. You are a coward, a traitor, and a swindler."

"How dare you!"

"I am going to walk across your iced tightrope. I *will* walk across it and we *will* collect the funds raised for the new orphanage. I will not allow you to profit from the tragedy of that dreadful fire that killed so many last January."

"I'll enjoy watching you plunge to your death over children who will become nothing but criminals and whores!"

Emma smirked. She had rattled Cavendish.

"Mr. Paulson, if you would fetch me my oversized boots, please."

"Challenges are simply puzzles awaiting a well-executed and cunning plan. With Good Lady Fortune on one's side, nothing is impossible," Kierian always said.

Good Lady Fortune's intervention was Kierian's explanation for his astonishingly uncanny good luck.

Dr. Waatt often commented that he must have been birthed in a field of four-leaf clovers, surrounded by seven horseshoes, visited by a herd of rabbits who willingly gave one foot each as a birthday gift.

Emma looked out at the iced tightrope as Freddie ran off to retrieve the boots.

*Well, stone the crows, I have a cunning plan, all I need to do is execute it-*Emma pulled her airship helmet over her head and tightened the chin strap-*And hope Lady Fortune favors me as much as the old gal seems to favor Kierian.*

CHAPTER THREE

Colonel Richardson, late of the 1st Regiment of Foot, Northumberland Fusiliers, scowled as he sat at one of the Rochester Club's many coveted gaming tables.

"Bloody hell! Double sixes again!"

Kierian McKenna bore the checkers off his six spot on the backgammon board and grinned. "It's all in the wrist, Colonel."

The Colonel took a frustrated swallow of his Gin and Tonic. "I have never seen such damnable luck in my life, sir!"

Kierian projected his voice loud enough that the other guests, and he hoped one in particular, could clearly hear his words. "And yet you and your countrymen keep pressing yours. What is it now, colonel? Zero wins and three losses? One would think the British Empire would have learned their lesson about going to war with America by now." He took a puff of his Mozart cigar and blew a smoke ring past the left ear of the white-haired former British soldier.

"Gloating is unbecoming of a gentleman, sir. The war has been over for five years. No need to break open old wounds."

Kierian's blue eyes twinkled. He handed the doubling cube to the Colonel. "Be that as it may, I think I will press my own luck a bit further. Shall we double the bet? Say five thousand American dollars?"

Colonel Richardson studied the cube for a moment, shook his head and frowned. "No, sir, not with your damn good fortune. I shall not press the point. The game is yours."

Kierian smiled and reached to re-set the board as the colonel stood up to leave the table.

"I would have taken that bet had you offered it to me, Mr. McKenna," said a voice in a refined British accent.

Kierian looked up. A handsome, dark haired man dressed formally, grinned down at him. He wore a top hat, white waistcoat, with black dress coat and matching trousers. In his right hand, he held a cane crowned with an elaborately etched golden lion.

Kierian instantly recognized the clothing as coming from Grieves and Hawks, 3 Seville Lane London, one of the finest private tailoring firms in the world. He leaned back against the padded leather of the mahogany chair, rolled the doubling cube between his fingers and studied the John Bull.

The man had British Secret Service Bureau written all over him.

The Black Sheep are becoming more and more fashionable. Usually they send some thug of an assassin dressed in homespun wool and reeking of horses manure.

"Perhaps, you would like to take over the Colonel's game then, Mister...?"

"Stock, John Stock, and thank you for the invitation. I think I shall."

Stock sat down and grinned. He reached into his pocket, pulled out a gold-plated cigarette case and plucked out a Turkish Murad.

"Tell me, Mr. McKenna," Stock lit the Murad, "Are you not the same chap that blew up *HMAS Black Prince*?"

Kierian took a puff of his cigar. Stock knew the answer. The fact was public knowledge. He, Emma Dareheart, and what remained of their resistance cell had blown Lord Kitchener and his airship to kingdom come, 7 July 1897.

"It was war, Mr. Stock, and Field Marshal Kitchener

was Commander-in-Chief of your forces, here in North America. That made him a legitimate target."

"Yes, but it was not war on 7 July, was it ol' boy? That is the point. The Armistice was signed three days *before* your dastardly deed was committed." Stock picked up the dice cup. "Not quite cricket, at all."

Cold blue eyes glared back at Stock. "Neither is starving thirty-thousand American women and children in internment camps, Mr. Stock."

"An exaggerated number, repeated time and again by American propagandists."

Contemptuous lips smirked at the Brit. "I suppose Mr. Edison's moving pictures, which recorded the atrocities, were fabricated as well," Kierian said. Friends of his had died in Coldwater Internment camp. Others, mostly children, were mere skeletons by the time his cell and Roosevelt's Rough Rangers liberated them.

"An American inventor, recording the supposed state of American prisoners, and financed by the American government?" Stock shook his head, "Hardly an unbiased investigation, Mr. McKenna. In any case, if you and your merry band of rebels had not been attacking our supply columns, we could have fed and cared for our ... guests," Stock motioned for a waiter. "Gin and Tonic."

"I suppose that is one way of looking at the situation," Kierian said. He took another puff of his cigar. "The other, of course, would be to refrain from rounding up women and children, burning down their homes, and throwing them into the camps to begin with."

"Two wrongs do not a right make, Mr. McKenna," Stock said as the waiter returned with his drink.

Stock rolled the dice on the green felt of the backgammon board and came up with a six and a five. He grinned as he bore four checkers off his five spot. "Fancy that! Your good luck must be rubbing off on me ol' boy. That roll now allows me a fighting chance."

Kierian nodded, shook his dice cup, and tossed. Once again, double sixes came up. He bore off an additional four checkers, leaving only two on the board, both on his one spot.

"Consecutive double-sixes. What does that make it? Eight during the entire game you've thrown, ol' boy?" Stock took another puff on his Murad and blew smoke over Kierian's head.

"Something like that."

"That's more than natural luck, ol' boy."

Menace lined Kierian's voice. "Exactly, *what* is your

meaning, Mr. Stock?"

"Well, one might infer that a person who would kill two hundred and twenty-seven persons in a fiery explosion, when no state of war existed, might well be willing to palm loaded dice at the gaming table. One might further say that would account for such near supernatural luck. In fact, I would hazard a guess that the next roll from your cup will again, be double sixes."

Kierian picked up the dice and dropped his head to his chest, his eyes cast down at the backgammon board. He brought his hand to his stomach, a pained expression on his face, and ran a hand through his dark blonde hair.

"Suffering the torments of guilt, Mr. McKenna? I hear they are like a thousand knife points prickling all at once. They can haunt a person incessantly and cause all manner of maladies, even an early death."

Kierian dropped the dice in the cup. He finished off his glass of Thorton's Irish whiskey in a single swallow.

"I also hear, cheating at the gambling table is cause for expulsion from this club, Mr. McKenna," Stock continued. "As well as being illegal here in the Flour City."

"Are you making a formal accusation against me, Mr. Stock?"

Stock smiled, leaned back in his chair, and took a

sip of his G and T. His eyes locked on Kierian's dice cup. Slowly, his mouth stretched into a self-assured grin.

"I think not. Rather, I shall double the wager yet again. Shall we say, ten-thousand American dollars Mr. McKenna?" Stock said.

"You can only win by rolling double sixes, Mr. Stock. That is a bold bet indeed."

"Let us just say, I am feeling bold and lucky today, ol' boy."

"That wager is a tidy sum. As a guest of the club, it is required you post collateral for any bet over five thousand dollars. You do have collateral? Do you not, Mr. Stock?" Kierian asked

"As a matter of fact, I do." Stock pulled an envelope from his coat pocket and handed it to Kierian. "The deed to some choice property, on Pinnacle Hill in your fair city, recently sold to me by a certain, Mr. Cavendish. I believe it will more than cover the wager."

"Very well, then. The roll is yours, Mr. Stock."

A confident smirk played across the Brit. "Indeed and since we are playing by formal Rochester Club rules, I claim Player's Choice." Stock reached over, taking Kierian's dice cup in hand. He shook it twice and rolled the dice onto the board.

"Double sixes," Stock said. His face was a picture of smugness. He locked his eyes on Kierian, not even bothering to glance at the roll.

Kierian grinned from ear to ear and chuckled. "I am afraid your eye sight must be failing you Mr. Stock. Along with your luck."

Got you, you smug British bastard. You bit, hook, line and sinker!

Stock looked down at the dice. His jaw dropped in surprise.

"Double ones, or as we call it here in America, snake eyes," Kierian said. The grin disappeared from his face, replaced by blazing blue eyes of contempt. "You've been bitten, Mr. Stock, and never heard the rattle!"

Kierian replaced the dice into his cup, and rolled.

"Double ones again! Ha! What are the odds?" Kierian mocked. He removed the last two checkers, ending the game.

A white knuckled hand squeezed the lion head cane. Hate filled British eyes glared at Kierian.

Kierian casually slid his left hand to his right shirt cuff, where a small knife lay hidden.

"Mr. Stock, if there is a sword in that cane of yours, I would advise against drawing it," Kierian said.

Stock clenched his teeth.

"This is *my* club, and we are in *my* city, and these are *my* friends surrounding us. If by some unholy miracle I do not cut you down before the sword clears wood, there are a good many in here who had family in the camps and they are just looking for a chance to take legalized vengeance on some cocksure John Bull."

Stock glanced around the club. Realizing he was surrounded and outnumbered, the famous British self-control returned, and his hand wisely released the cane.

"I advise you to file that document quickly, Mr. McKenna." Stock said.

Kierian picked up the Pinnacle Hill deed and chuckled "Thank you for an enjoyable game, Mr. Stock," "perhaps I shall see you again sometime...ol' Boy."

Dagger eyes glared back at Kierian. "You may depend on it, Mr. McKenna."

Kierian backed away. Once a crowd was between them, he spun and strolled to the bar. Michael Mulcahy, a burly ex-army sergeant and the club's current Sergeant-at-Arms, stood behind the bar, a glass of whiskey in his hand. He pulled a bottle of Thorton's from behind the bar and poured a shot for Kierian.

"That Limey is not one to be trifled with, Piper,"

Mulcahy said, using Kierian's wartime code name.

Kierian nodded and threw down the shot. "It took him damn long enough to reach for the bait. I thought I'd have to start insulting the king himself to get him to take over the colonel's game."

"I hope it was worth it. He's SSB, sure. Heard he even has permission to kill whenever he deems it necessary to do so."

Kierian nodded. The British Secret Service Branch was one of the premiere foreign intelligence services in the world and they seemed to have more than a fair share of deadly and resourceful assassins at their beck and call.

"It was worth it, Michael," Kierian said.

"You realize he's probably here for you, or Emma, or the both of you. He probably planned on embarrassing you, then having you arrested for cheating."

"And then unable to bear the shame and disgrace, I would conveniently hang myself in my jail cell, I suppose."

"Sounds about right," Mulcahy replied. He took a rag from behind the bar and wiped down the oak wood to a shine. "It might be a good time for you to take Emma on an out of town holiday."

Kierian took the bottle and poured himself another

drink. "She's famous now, Michael. The Lady of Leaps, The Maiden of the Mist…"

"The Duchess of Danger," Mulcahy added

"I had not heard that one, yet. Though, I am not surprised. She seems to acquire a new title every fortnight," Kierian said.

"True enough. You know, she's Sky Walking the High Falls today. I'm surprised you did not attend."

"Well, I had business to see to, did I not?" Kierian snapped.

"That girl thought you hung the moon, stars and sun during the war, Piper. I never did understand why you left for Cuba without her, after all the shooting stopped."

"Maybe I was sick of her tagging along with me," Kierian snapped.

"If that's so you never showed it and you took a damn long time to cut the strings. Too long, if you want my opinion."

"Did you hear me ask for it?" Sitting through the revisionist balderdash of some Brit assassin was bad enough; he didn't need to hear Mulcahy's views on his relationship with Emma. Kierian threw down his whisky in one angry swallow.

"Best at least warn the lass, Piper. I'll say no more

than that."

"I will make sure she is duly notified, Michael."

"You were palming loaded dice. Were you not?" Mulcahy asked, suddenly changing the subject.

Kierian straightened his orange ascot, flipped open the cover of his silver pocket watch, and checked the time. Careful not to stress the stitching of his emerald green waistcoat, he returned the watch to his pocket, plucked a cigar from his silver case and lit it.

Mulcahy's question was indiscreet and with almost anyone else, Kierian would have just blown a smoke ring past the questioner's left ear and walked out, but Mulcahy had fought side by side with him against the John Bulls in numerous engagements. He had even taken a bullet in his right shoulder at the Inn-Between Tavern when the Black Sheep raided it in an attempt to capture himself and Emma. Mulcahy deserved a reply if not an answer.

But Mulcahy *was* an employee of the club and the question *was* still indiscreet. So he would receive that reply when Kierian was good damn and ready.

"You are acquainted with my derring-do's, Michael. What do *you* think?"

"I think you baited the trap with loaded double sixes. I think you had a second set of loaded serpent eyes

39

which you switched out when you had your...guilt pains."

Kierian nodded indifferently to Mulcahy's precise rendering of his actions. He took a puff of his cigar and blew a smoke ring a few inches over Mulcahy's head.

"And I think the Limey had it coming," Mulcahy said. The barman took a drink of his own whiskey and wiped off the condensation the glass had left on his bar. "Cocky lot the Brits are. Arrogance and over-confidence; it's always their undoing."

"Michael," Kierian began, the tension between the two now dissipated like the smoke from Kierian's Mozart cigar. He handed the property deed to Mulcahy, "See that this deed is delivered post-haste to Sister Mary Therese of the Carmelite Order. I believe Pinnacle Hill will be a most excellent site for the new orphanage."

Mulcahy grinned and nodded. "Mary and Joseph, bless you, Kierian. You're doing the Lord's work, to be sure."

"Let us hope then, that the Lord sees fit to keep Banshee safe and that now that we have the land, she can raise the money to begin the build."

"By the by, this came for you. I believe it is from Dr. Waatt." Mulcahy handed Kierian an envelope. It was inscribed in the impeccable hand of his business partner and genius inventor, Doctor Balthazar Waatt. Kierian slit the envelope open with a thin bladed knife. Inside was a train ticket and a note from Doctor Waatt. It read simply:

Mr. McKenna, we are needed.

CHAPTER FOUR

Freddie Paulson's baritone voice boomed through the brass voice trumpet. "Ladies and gentleman, boys and girls, young and old, may I direct your attention to the top of the High Falls."

The crowd of some twenty-five thousand Rochestarians gathered on the shores of the Genesee River, looked upward. Above the ninety-nine foot tall waterfall, Emma stood. A full-length bathing suit hugged her athletic form, a leather airship helmet crowned her head, and her right hand gripped a red, white and blue umbrella.

"In a few moments, you will see an extraordinary act of bravery as this tightrope is traversed by none other than the Lethal Lass, the Lady of Leaps, the Maiden of the Mist, our own Emma Dareheart!" The crowd cheered enthusiastically. Freddie raised his hand for quiet.

"This walk is to raise funds for the new orphanage, and I am pleased to announce that to date, we have raised over 100,000 dollars! Thank you all for your generous giving." Once more the crowd cheered, and again Freddie held his hand up for quiet.

"My good friends, you will note that the tightrope Miss Dareheart is about to walk, not only spans the High Falls gorge but also has been completely coated in ice!"

The crowd *oohed and aahed*. Ladies fanned themselves. Tense anxiety rippled through the crowd.

"Yes, coated in slippery ice! Miss Dareheart has agreed to attempt this extremely dangerous stunt only due to the fact that our sponsor, Mr. Reginald Cavendish has agreed to match the total donations raised for this event! Let us have a cheer for Mr. Cavendish!"

The people cheered Cavendish's name but he was not impressed. He scowled at Paulson. "I agreed to no such thing!"

"Fine. Tell them so, Cavendish," Emma said. "Tell them that they should not be cheering you. Tell them the lady who is about to do this foolhardy act on behalf of orphaned children, is a liar."

Cavendish ran a hand over his formerly smug face,

and looked out at the cheering throng. He slowly raised a hand and acknowledged their cheers, which also publicly acknowledged the new terms of her Skywalk. Emma smiled. Any attempt now to back out of the agreement would remind everyone how he spent the war enriching himself and selling supplies to both sides. It was a past he had worked hard to bury and one he most earnestly desired to keep buried.

Even if it cost him 200,000 greenbacks.

Of course, she still had to make it across the damn tightrope.

Emma reached down, toggled the switches on her boots, and popped open the umbrella.

I will cross this damn tightrope. I will not fall. No fear. I am the Banshee. I will complete the mission. The mission is all that matters.

She took her first step.

Foot over foot. No fear.

* * * * * *

Foot over foot. No fear.

The iced melted away under the intense heat of Dr. Waatt's Heat Optimized Treads, or HOT boots, as Kierian called them. Iron filings in the heel, super heated while a dissolving thermite tablet in the toe, powered a heat ray forward, providing purchase for Emma's next step.

Half way across the gorge, mist rose up from the falls below, and sprinkled cool water on Emma's bare calves, arms and face. Even with the HOTs, it had been slow but steady going. It was essential each step be as exact as the one before, lest the heat ray fry her stepping heel and send her plunging to her death.

The first few steps were the hardest, but after that it was simply a case of taking another one thousand steps in precisely the exact same manner.

Foot over foot. No fear.

Steam rose from the rope with each blast of the heat ray device. Exact repetition of her first step was easier said than done. The wind had picked up and constantly buffeted her to and fro, atop the tightrope. The umbrella however, helped to correct her lateral inertia.

Several times, she felt she had stepped wrong in some small way, from her previous step. Each time, she dropped to one knee and re-set her balance. It was a tedious process but better than being smashed to pieces upon the rocks one hundred feet below.

Foot over foot. No fear.

How sweet a victory over Cavendish this would be. Here he thought him self such a clever man, that he would either embarrass and discredit her or dispose of her permanently. In either case, he would abscond with a fortune.

Foot over foot. No fear.

Kierian would love her improvisation He would smile and his blue eyes would twinkle. Then he would say something witty and clever, and pat her on the head, which he thought she liked.

Well it makes me feel like a little miss, but I know he means it with affection. I wonder if he will still be dressed club formal. He looks so dashing in-

Emma froze.

What am I doing? Why am I thinking of Kierian when I am 100 feet high, walking on an icy rope over a river gorge?

Emma slowly dropped to one knee.

Focus. No more thoughts save for stepping thoughts.

She could hear the crowd below oohing, ahhing and shouting encouragements.

That was not good.

When her mind was focused, all she could hear was her own thoughts. She might hear the rush of air when a breeze kicked up, or the occasional *rheet-rheet* of a red tailed hawk, but even those sounds would be muffled due to her concentration.

Emma exhaled and slowly stood. She lifted her leg

and stepped slowly.

Good. Now do that again.

And she did.

Foot over foot. No fear.

Her mind locked on each tiny movement. Nothing existed except for her hands, feet and the feel of the rope beneath her boots.

Foot over foot. No fear.

One step after another, she moved at a steady pace across the rope.

Foot over Foot. No fear.

Her concentration intensified. She was almost across now. Just a little further... *Wait, where was the steam?*

Emma slowly lowered her chin and glanced at the HOTs. The red beam of energy was absent.

Immediately she stopped and dropped to one knee.

Were the HOTs malfunctioning or had she miscalculated how long the thermite reaction would last? No doubt Balthazar would insist it was the latter but what did it matter now? The cold hard reality was that she had no way of melting the remaining rope.

Improvise, and adapt, Banshee.

Kierian's words echoed in her mind. *Improvise and adapt eh? Very well, then. I still have a heat source but it is*

in my heel and that does me no good when moving forward.
Unless…

Emma raised her leg, pivoted and slowly turned. A gust of wind slammed into her side and unbalanced her. Deftly, she shifted the umbrella to her other hand and counteracted the lateral motion. She set her foot back down, inhaled a calming breath, raised her leg, pivoted again, and completed the turn. She now had her back to the opposite side.

The crowd below *oohed* and *ahhed*.

Foot over foot. No fear.

She stepped backwards. The ice melted from the rope as the heated iron filings did their job.

Foot over foot. No fear.

A heavy gust of wind struck her. Emma felt herself being picked up off the tightrope and pushed backwards. She focused her mind, resisted the urge to fight the squall, dropped the umbrella, pitched backwards, and spring boarded her hands off the rope, spiraling into a somersault.

Her first foot hit solid ground.

So did her second.

She stood and raised her arms heavenward.

The crowd below erupted in cheers and acclamation!

People rushed up to her and assailed her with back slaps and congratulatory handshakes. Someone threw a towel around her, and only then did she realize how wet the mist had made her bathing suit.

Her mind transitioned from its intense focus and relinquished control to her regular senses. She could hear Freddie shouting to the crowd through the voice trumpet. She caught a glimpse of Cavendish across the chasm, shaking his fist and shouting at her, his words lost over the roar of the Genesee Falls.

The crowd was escorting her, sometimes gently, sometimes a bit roughly, down the steps of the observation platform to the shores of the Genesee River. The band struck up *There'll Be A Hot Time In The Old Town Tonight*. Emma glanced back at the tightrope and smiled. Delight, exhilaration, and euphoria swept through her.

"Letter for you, Miss," a young voice said. A nine-year-old boy in a newsboy cap much too large for him, held an envelope out to her. She felt positively giddy and wanted to give the young lad a generous tip, but did not have any coins on her person.

"How about a trade?" She smiled and handed him her airship helmet. The boy could probably sell it for five to ten dollars at any pawnshop in the city. He

49

would be eating well for a goodly time.

"Lordy! Thank you, Miss Dareheart! Thanks aplenty!" The little urchin handed her his newsboy cap and dashed off.

Emma looked at the envelope. The writing, she noticed, was in the impeccable script of Doctor Waatt. She opened the letter. Inside was a single train ticket, an invitation from millionaire railroad and helium magnate, Alfred G. Vanderbilt, and a note from Doctor Waatt which simply read:

Miss Dareheart, we are needed.

CHAPTER FIVE

Tuesday, August 27, 1901
Garreth's Boarding House

"Mrs. Garreth!"

Emma stared into her empty armoire. Her clothes were gone, removed by someone for some unknown reason.

"Mrs. Garreth!" Emma shouted again. She moved to her dresser drawers and opened one after another.

Empty, empty, and empty.

She peered under her bed for the footlocker where she kept her weapons and gear.

Mother Freedom's bell!

"Mrs. Garreth!" She rubbed the sleep from her eyes. The answer to her shouts came in the form of the plodding footsteps of her middle-aged landlady as she climbed up the two flights of stairs that led to the third floor of the boarding house.

"What's all the noise about Miss Emma? No wonder that rogue, Mr. McKenna, calls you Banshee," Mrs. Garreth said.

"That's hardly why he-"

"Hooting and hollering enough to wake the sainted dead! You'll rouse the entire house with all your noise, and you know how Mrs. Nesbitt gets when she doesn't get her beauty sleep."

"If it is beauty Mrs. Nesbitt is attempting to acquire from her sleep, she needs to consider hibernation."

"Oh, Miss Emma! That is most unkind!" Mrs. Garreth shook her head in a most disapproving fashion. "Mrs. Nesbitt might be a bit ill mannered at times, but she is your elder. You should show her more respect."

"Mrs. Nesbitt could be Methuselah's elder, and she is about as pleasant as a bout of the clap."

"Oh, Miss Emma," Mrs. Garreth clucked her tongue and once more shook her head.

"Mrs. Garreth, can you please tell me why my belongings are not where they should be? I have a train to catch in an hour and one half's time, and I must be ready for travel." Emma rubbed her face. It had been a night of champagne and oysters at the Genesee Park Hotel, which overlooked the High Falls Gorge. She had raised the roof a little too much, come home late, collapsed on her bed, and fallen directly asleep.

"Why, I told you last night when you stumbled in, Miss Emma."

"I did not, *stumble in*, Mrs. Garreth. I tripped over that third stairwell step. The one that your husband was supposed to fix last week."

"Now, don't go blaming your failings on my poor Harold. I could smell the devil's brew on you when you walked in, I could."

"Billy Lush spilled his beer on me. That's all you smelled."

"Well, what do you expect when you spend time in the company of people named Billy the Lush? Drink and dancing never led to anything but sorrow and misery, Miss Emma, and that's the Lord's truth."

"Lush is his surname, Mrs. Garreth. He is a base ball player. He plays for the Bronchos."

"Making a living playing a game! What's the world coming to? Miss Emma, you're a pretty enough colleen, so you are. You should be in the company of men of more proper trades and more certain futures. Not carousing about with the likes of this... Billy the Lush, or that silver tongued rogue, Kierian McKenna."

Emma placed her hands on her hips, shifted her weight, and sighed.

"Mrs. Garreth, what about my belongings?"

"I told you last night."

"No, you did not. I would have remembered."

"I am sure I did, Miss Emma."

"Then please, tell me again."

"Dr. Waatt sent his metal man around while you were out. He said you were going on a trip, packed up all your belongings in trunks, and left in his steam carriage."

Mrs. Garreth shook her head. "Awful things those horseless carriages, with their puffing steam and smoke. Oh, and that soulless Metal Man? Oh, he gives me the frights, he does."

Emma sighed. Balthazar probably thought he was being both efficient and kind by sending his automaton to load her belongings, but his metal man had been too efficient. Balthazar probably said something on the order of: "Pack all of Miss Dareheart's belongings and take them to the train station." Of course, the automaton had done just that and not left her a single proper stitch in which to travel. All she had to wear now was what she had worn to the Skywalk: trousers, boots, shirt, and the newsboy cap she had traded for. Worse, her weapons had been in her footlocker. Now she was unarmed, except for the automatic double bladed knife in her boot, and while she was better than most with a blade, it wasn't going to stop a rush of lecherous men or vile villains.

For that purpose, the Good Lord allowed firearms to be invented.

Emma considered it sheer madness for a young woman, like herself, to walk about the city without at least a Derringer on her person; though she preferred a nice Colt single action Army revolver.

Miss Anthony and her Suffragettes could agitate all they wished for the vote, but in Emma's view, true equality had been achieved the day the first Colt revolver came into female hands.

She walked over to the armoire, reached in the back, and pushed open the hidden panel she had carved out, hoping....

Wonderful! It's still here!

She pulled out her steam pistol-an invention of Dr. Waatt's-unscrewed the nozzle, and shoved the weapon into her pocket.

"Here now, what did you put in your pocket, Miss Emma?" Mrs. Garreth asked.

"Just a tool Mrs. Garreth. It is nothing to concern yourself over," Emma snapped.

"Well, far be it from me to go poking my nose

where it don't belong," Mrs. Garreth replied. "I'm just a poor old lady trying to look out for your well being and passing on my life's wisdoms, I am."

Emma grinned. If prying and poking about were a profession, Mrs. Garreth would be its queen. Frequently, Emma had found signs that she had been searching through her drawers and armoire. More than once, the lock on her footlocker beneath her bed had been coated with chicken grease and pick marks.

"Is there anything else, you *told me*, that I *forgot*, Mrs. Garreth?"

"Oh, well now, there was the letter from Mr. McKenna."

"Mr. McKenna? He, was here?" Emma had hoped Kierian would stop out and celebrate with her after he finished swindling the Pinnacle Hill deed from whatever pigeon Cavendish had sold it to, but there had been no sign of him.

"Yes indeed. Himself dropped the letter off last night around the ninth tolling of the bells, and he instructed me to give it to you the moment you awoke." She reached into her apron pocket and handed a letter to Emma.

"It's a queer message to be sure," Mrs. Garreth said.

Emma took the letter, glanced up, and raised an inquisitive eyebrow.

"Oh, well, the sun struck it just so, and I could not help but see the words. Very queer, indeed."

Sure Mrs. Garreth, because there is so much sunlight at nine in the evening.

Emma looked down at the envelope. It had clearly been opened and then steamed shut again. She pulled her knife from her boot, pressed the button, and the blade sprang forth.

"Tsk, tsk, Miss Emma, tis a crying shame a young lady, like yourself, knows how to use such cutpurse cutlery."

Emma smirked and sliced the envelope open. It read:

Ba, Ba, Black Sheep, Banshee.

Piper

Emma folded the letter and stuffed it in her right trouser pocket. The smile dropped from her face. She walked to the window, moved the curtain back, and peeked out into the street below.

"Mrs. Garreth? How long has that hansom cab been sitting outside the boarding house?"

"Oh, all morning! And you know what's queer? He

won't take any fares at all."

"That is odd."

"Sure as sunrise, it is! Why Mr. Gould and Mr. Nichols both were ready to give him business, but he refused, and most enthusiastically too!"

"Really?" Emma said, half listening. She scanned the rest of the street. The usual hustle and bustle of Rochester street life had begun. Grocers, and assorted other traders, hawked their wares, men walked about with canes and women with parasols. A metropolitan Police officer strolled by, greeting those he knew and casting a wary eye on those of the neighborhood he thought might be up to some sort of mischief. He gave the hansom and its driver but a cursory glance, and walked by, probably figuring the man was waiting for someone within the bordering house.

He probably was, but not so he could earn a fare but rather, collect on a bounty.

"He did, sure! When Mr. Gould pressed him to take on his business he nearly gave poor Mr. Gould the back of his hand!"

Emma nodded and stepped away from the window.

Mrs. Garreth was as nosy as a newshound, and usually it was a bane to her existence, but the landlady did seem to care about her, and her curious nature had more than once alerted Emma to unforeseen danger.

"Is there trouble, Miss Emma? Should I call Sergeant O'Flannery 'round?"

"No, Mrs. Garreth, but if anyone comes asking for me, please do not tell them I have gone on a trip."

"This seems like one of your capers again, it does. Anytime that Mr. McKenna comes around, there's always trouble for you. But as you say, Miss Emma, I won't tell a blessed soul where you are,"

"Thank you, Mrs. Garreth."

"Since, I'm doing you a favor, can you at least, tell me what that queer note means?"

Emma glanced out the window again and took a good look at the driver of the hansom. No need to tell her landlady that Ba stood for British Army, or that Black sheep was code for the SSB, and that if Kierian was referring to her as Banshee, he was clearly warning her that trouble was afoot.

"Just Mr. McKenna having a bit of fun," Emma replied. "It is a private joke between us."

"You two and your jokes. Well, I cannot stand here talking away the morning when there's work to be done. I've got breakfast to cook and rooms to clean-"

"And steps to fix." Emma reminded.

Mrs. Garreth gave Emma a sour look. "Will you be

taking breakfast with us, Miss Emma?"

Emma tapped the letter against her chin and considered the situation. "Yes, I will be down directly. Thank you, Mrs. Garreth."

"You're welcome, sure, Miss Emma. I'll go set a place for you proper."

Emma waited until the landlady plodded back down the stairs. Dexterous fingers quickly untied her boot lacings. She padded quietly to her door, eased it open, and tiptoed her way across the hall to Mrs. Nesbitt's room. Freeing a hairpin from her brown mane, she dropped to one knee and began to work the lock.

She would not be taking breakfast.

Doing so would give the SSB agent a look at what she was wearing, making it useless as a disguise. However, if the agent was paying attention and saw Mrs. Garreth set a place at the table, it might keep him focused on the boardinghouse dining room and front door rather than its roof, which Emma planned to use as her escape route.

The lock clicked, and Emma quietly pushed the door open. Inside, old Mrs. Nesbitt laid snoring, her false teeth on the nightstand beside her. Soft steps silently traversed the wooden floor. Almost at the window, she took one long stride.

And stepped right onto a broken floorboard.

The crack echoed in the room like a sneeze in church. Mrs. Nesbitt bolted up in bed like someone had taken a cattle prod to her behind.

"Eh, who's there?" The old lady peered at Emma. "AHHHH! Get out, young man! Get out you devil!"

"Shh!" Emma brought her index finger to her lips and tried to quiet the old lady.

"AHHHH! Get out! You've come to ravish my body! I'll not let you have my virtue!" The old lady picked up a vase from her nightstand and heaved it. Emma dropped her boots, caught the vase before it smashed, and set it down on the floor.

"Mrs. Nesbitt, no one has come to ravish your body. It is Miss Dareheart from across the hall. See?" Emma removed her newsboy cap and let her brown hair fall mid-way down her back. "Please, calm down. I just need to use your fire escape."

Mrs. Nesbitt squinted hard at Emma. "Miss Dareheart, is it?"

Emma smiled. "Yes, that is right. I am sorry to disturb you. I just need to open your-" Emma tried to raise the window but it stuck- "window and then, I will be out of your hair."

The old lady stared at her for a peaceful few sec-

J.T. MURPHY

onds.

"Get out, you bitch!" She snarled suddenly. She picked up a water glass from her nightstand and flung it at Emma.

Emma ducked. The tumbler smashed against the wall littering the floor with shards of glass.

Damn, for an old gal, she sure can chuck!

"This is my room! Get out, you trollop!" Mrs. Nesbitt yelled. "You've come to rob me blind! I know about you! The Banshee! The Banshee! Come to kill me, like you killed all those British Tommies! Help! Help!"

Emma spun around and glared at the old lady. Up until now her screaming threatened to bring Mrs. Garreth plodding up the stairs, which would be an annoyance but not much more. However, yelling *Banshee*, would redirect the Black Sheep's attention upward.

Emma reached for her knife. Fear was driving the old lady's screams. Mrs. Nesbitt apparently knew her code name, and had at least had heard rumors of what she'd done during the war.

Fear can be your worst enemy or your best friend, Banshee. Control yours and prey on the fear of your enemy.

Kierian's advice during the Seldridge Affair rang through her head. She wouldn't hurt the old lady but she would damn well scare her into silence.

She flicked open the knife, took a step towards Mrs. Nesbitt, opened her mouth and made ready to lower her voice into a threatening hiss.

She stopped.

No. I broke into her room. Maybe when I'm one hundred and fifty-seven, or how ever old she is, I might react in the same manner. I don't need to scare her. This isn't the war. Just work the window. Get out of her room and she'll stop flapping her gums.

Emma turned around and used the knife to jimmy at the window.

"That's my window! You're going to break it. I'll make sure that idiot, Garreth, charges your bill for it, you'll see!"

Emma ignored her. *Work the window. Don't get distracted. Keep to your task.*

"Leave my window alone!"

Emma felt something wet and heavy strike against her back. She turned and saw Mrs. Nesbitt's chamber pot lying at her feet.

"That is disgusting, Mrs. Nesbitt."

"Not as disgusting as you, you Banshee bitch, you guttersnipe, daughter of a whore!"

Emma gave the top of the windowpane a hard punch with her left palm, placed both hands on the top, and shoved.

The window sprang open.

A satisfied smile played across Emma's face. She folded her knife, placed it back in her boot, and stepped one foot through and onto the fire escape.

"Toot-a-loo, Mrs. Nesbitt," Emma waved at the old lady. "I would say it has been a pleasure but," she put her other leg through the window onto the fire escape, "it has most definitely, been not."

* * * * * *

Emma stood in the New York Central Railroad's Passenger Terminal on St. Paul Street and held up a copy of the *Rochester Union and Advertiser*. "Extra! Emperor Custer takes Managua! Admiral Dewey throws out first pitch, as Senators beat Orioles 5-2! Get your copy! All the news fit to print for only 3 cents!"

After leaving Mrs. Nesbitt's, she had made her way up the fire escape to the top of the boardinghouse, leaped across three consecutive rooftops, shimmied down a water pipe, raced along Clinton Avenue, and hopped aboard one of the new electric trolleys headed for St. Paul Street and the train station.

When she'd arrived, she spotted Stinky Sadoti, a young newsboy with abominable hygiene, hawking the

U and A in the terminal. She slipped him a Lincoln fin, and he happily ran off, leaving her his stack of broadsheets. A little dirt and grease from the tracks rubbed onto her cheeks and forehead gave her a nice urchin glow. She pulled her cap down over her face, held the newssheets pressed against her chest, and grinned at her reflection in the terminal window.

The John Bulls would be looking for a woman in proper traveling attire, not one dressed in trousers, suspenders, and a cap.

The Midwest special out of Boston pulled in, disgorged its passengers, and took on coal, water, and other travelers. Emma remained alert and listened for any signs of a British accent among the terminal's denizens, including seventy persons she sold broadsheets to.

There was no sign of any Black Sheep.

"I'll take one of them there readers, boy!" a voice called.

Emma turned and handed a newssheet to a slender man with a Midwest accent. He was dressed in a bowler hat, black duster, and cowboy boots. Emma held out her hand for the pennies.

"Hold yer horses! There ain't nothin' here about good ol' Custer and his Mexes' whoopin' them boys in Nicaragua an' takin' their capital!"

"Sure there is! Are you blind?" Emma leaned toward the man and dropped her eyes to the paper.

His arm, streaked through the air. Too late, Emma realized her mistake.

She tried to pull back.

But the lead sap was faster.

CHAPTER SIX

Something heavy struck Emma's head. Dazed, she stumbled forward.

The man caught her under her left arm. A vice grip squeezed her forearm. A set of iron shackles slapped around both her wrists.

"You tryin' to hornswoggle me, boy? It's off to Johnny Law, with you!" yelled the man, loud enough to justify his actions to anyone taking an interest. He walked briskly, dragging Emma toward the front doors of the passenger terminal.

"Name's William Dunn, out of Pawnee, Oklahoma. Maybe you heard tell of me?" the man whispered.

Emma groaned. The name meant nothing to her. She tried to clear her head and focus. Until then, any attempt at escape would be foolhardy.

"No? Well, I'm a bounty killer and a damn good one. So don't go kickin' up a fuss, Miss Dareheart."

Emma felt the distinct pressure of a gun barrel pressed into her ribs as they walked out the doors of the terminal. "I'd hate to plug a lady, even one dressin' like a fella, but I'll damn well do it if you give me cause."

Emma groaned again and looked up. A black two-horse coach, separate from the long line of hansoms and hackney cabs, sat, waiting beside the roadside curb. Dunn pulled her close and headed directly for it.

"Calvin!" Dunn called up to the driver of the coach who was hunched forward, wearing a long black duster and bowler hat. "I got us the Lady Fair. Come on down and sit with her a spell, while I go help Bee, Dal, and George whoop that McKenna fella." The driver jumped down and Dunn opened the coach door.

"God Almighty!" Dunn screamed.

Emma peeked around his shoulder. Inside the coach was a dead man; his lifeless eyes stared at the coach ceiling.

Dunn shoved Emma away and spun around. He raised his pistol at the driver.

Like a cat, the driver sidestepped, chopped at Dunn's elbow, drove the pistol barrel skyward, and plunged his walking cane into Dunn's chest.

Strings of electricity sparked from Dunn's body,

sending 100,000 volts through the bounty killer.

Dunn convulsed. His finger pulled the trigger on his revolver, and fired a harmless shot into the sky. The bounty hunter toppled back against the coach, his lifeless body slumped down onto the curb below.

Emma leaned against the coach and exhaled. Her mind slowly cleared. The driver approached, reached down, and unlocked the shackles from her wrists. She sighed in relief and felt his soft leather gloved hand slowly raise her chin.

Blue eyes twinkled down at her.

Emma smiled.

"You know, Miss Dareheart, posing as a street urchin newsboy is a most God-awful disguise for you."

"Oh? Why is that, Mr. McKenna?"

Kierian brought his hand to her cheek and gently rubbed off some dirt.

"Because you're just too damn beautiful to pass for anything other than a lady."

Emma beamed.

"Let me take a look at your head," Kierian said.

Emma pushed his hand away and stood. She loved his charm, but did not want to be treated like Victoria Victim. "I am fine. There is no need to fuss, Mr. McKenna."

Kierian shrugged. He took off the borrowed duster and looked at it with disgust. "I suppose *this* is what passes for style out west." He unceremoniously tossed the duster inside the coach and covered Calvin Dunn.

"Oh, I don't know; I thought you looked rather raffish in it."

"That is because you do not have an eye for men's fashion." Kierian gently tapped Emma on the end of her nose with the silver four-leaf shamrock at the top of his cane.

He snatched his custom tailored, light brown, Hanlon Brothers frock coat from the driver's seat, slipped it on, and sighed in satisfaction.

Emma smiled. "How long were you out here playing driver?"

"About three quarters of an hour. Brother Calvin identified me as I arrived and decided apprehending me alone was a capital idea."

Emma stared at the corpse inside the coach, then back at Kierian. "Well, clearly that did not go well for him. Did you electrocute him as well?"

"No. Guess again." Kierian bent down and began going through Dunn's pockets.

"Chop to the neck?"

"Cane-sword through the heart." Kierian pushed

back William Dunn's duster to reveal a holster.

"So these two are brothers?"

"You have not heard of the Dunn brothers?" Kierian pulled the pistol from Dunn's hand, shoved it in the left pocket of his frock coat, grabbed Dunn by the shoulders, and pulled him up to the coach door.

"No, I have not." Emma grabbed Dunn's feet and together, they heaved him into the coach on top of his brother.

"There are five of them. Well, I suppose three now. They are bounty hunters out of Oklahoma. They killed Bitter Creek Newcomb and Charlie Pierce back in '97." Kierian dusted off his tweed coat and checked the time on his silver pocket watch.

"Who?"

"Miss Dareheart, you really need to read some of the western gazettes. They are full of fascinating events and colorful characters." Kierian pulled on the edges of his gloves and straightened his bowler. "Newcomb and Pierce were members of the Wild Bunch gang."

Emma leaned back, against the coach. Her silence invited him to elaborate.

Kierian sighed. "The Wild Bunch were a nasty, vile gang of outlaws. They robbed, killed, and stole in parts of Kansas, Missouri, Oklahoma, and Arkansas in the

71

'90s."

"Ah, I see."

"The Dunns' sister, Rose, was sweet on Newcomb. When he came courting her, her loving brothers shot him and Pierce dead, then collected the bounty."

"Lovely sort, these Dunns."

"Indeed, and if your head was not too scrambled for you to hear, William mentioned that Bee, Dal, and George were waiting to take me down."

"Well, at least the odds are close to even now." Emma reached into her pocket, assembled the steam pistol, and shoved it in her back waistband.

"Unfortunately, I do not think they are. You see, the man I cheated out of the Pinnacle Hill deed was a certain John Stock."

"I wager he is the head Black Sheep?"

"Correct, Miss Dareheart."

"How many do you figure are waiting for us?"

"I would hazard to guess a total of five are waiting for *me*. The three Dunn boys, Stock, and his henchman."

Emma nodded and held out her hands. "May I have the Dunn's pistols and ammunition, please?"

"You are not armed?"

"Only with my knife and steam pistol. RA-7 is apparently back in action. He stopped by at Balthazar's behest and packed all my gear. I wager it is already in the luggage car, by now."

Kierian shook his head "No wonder you are dressed in such a terrible state of dishevelment! Well, you are in luck. Both Dunn brothers were carrying Colt Peacemakers, which as I recall, is your favorite sidearm."

Kierian took the Colts out of his frock coat pockets and held them out, butt first. Emma smiled. It would feel good to have her favorite pistol back in her hands. She reached for the Peacemakers, but Kierian pulled them away at the last second.

"On second thought, perhaps you should sit this one out, Miss Dareheart, and wait here for the inevitable arrival of the Rochester Metropolitan Police Department. I can do my derring-do's solo."

Emma waited for him to grin.

Kierian did not. Sky blue eyes stared back at her without a hint of humor.

"What a thing for you to say, after all we have been through together, Mr. McKenna."

"You must admit, you did make a few errors. I mean, allowing an enemy, who clearly is not from around these parts, to get close enough to knock your noggin and scramble your sensibilities when you knew you were being hunted? And keeping all your gear in one place, so that when it was taken, you were damn near defenseless? I thought I taught you better. Let me guess where it was stored? The footlocker under your bed?"

Emma glared at him. She felt like someone had punched her in the gut and then tied her insides in a knot. He was talking to her like she was a damn civilian novice who didn't know the difference between a gun and a rifle, or between cover and concealment.

"You know they have wonderful things in banks called safe deposit boxes, these days," Kierian continued. "One can leave all manner of precious belongings within them that could aid them if matters took a nasty turn; say for example, a spare set of revolvers?"

Emma scowled. She had seen him turn his biting sarcasm and contempt on many enemies and annoying fools, but she couldn't ever remember him turning it on her as he was now. Her insides burned. Her heart ached.

"I imagine going over the falls in a thimble-"

"Barrel," Emma corrected.

Kierian waved her correction away with a gloved hand and continued, "-Or performing skywalks for the entertainment of the masses leaves one little time for trivial things like shooting practice. Eh, Miss Dare-heart?"

Emma said nothing. Part of what hurt was that he was right. During the war, they had squirreled away caches of supplies and weapons all over the area, to keep from ever being in the position RA-7 had placed her in today. Back then, she damn well never would have allowed someone like Dunn to get close enough to knock her silly when she knew she was being targeted. She *had* been sloppy.

But damn it all, he didn't have to be such a bastard about it.

"I am only looking out for your safety, Miss Dare-heart," Kierian said. He bounced the pistols up and down in his hands.

"Give me the damn Colts, Piper." Emma snatched the pistols out of Kierian's hands. "And stop being such a perfect ass."

Kierian grinned. "I see sass still flows out of that small, pretty mouth of yours, like the waters of the mighty Genesee rushing over the High Falls."

Emma clicked open the revolver's chambers to make sure they were properly loaded, and slid a bullet into the one chamber that had been fired. "It's apt to start flowing like the Niagara Falls if you don't stop talking to me like I am the horse dung you stepped in outside of the Rochester Club."

Kierian chuckled.

If he says I am adorable when I am angry I'll-

Kierian tipped his hat to her and bowed. "Miss Dareheart, the more you seethe with righteous indignation, the more adorable you become."

Emma shook her head. It was a damn trial and a half, to remain angry at Kierian. Even when he was being dismissive, he did it with such flare and grace that you wanted to curtsy and thank him for it.

"Just call the damn tune, Piper," she said, resisting the temptation to acknowledge his bow with a smile.

Kierian shrugged. "Have it as you will, my lady." He reached into his coat pocket and pulled out his silver cigar case, plucked a Mozart from it, lit it, and took a few short puffs.

"They, most certainly, will not let us reach the train. Judging by their actions towards you, they will probably try an abduction, rather than just shooting us down."

"Well, that is comforting." She glanced around. No one seemed to be paying any attention to them. Was it because of the isolated location the Dunns had chosen for the coach or Kierian's ever present good fortune?

Probably a little of both, she decided.

"We will be outnumbered," Kierian said, "nothing new for us, of course."

Emma nodded. "Maybe, but they'll still make the play. I imagine Stock has offered them a tidy sum to abduct and transport us to London via Toronto." She carefully placed the two Colts in her front waistband and pulled her shirt over them.

Kierian nodded, and took another puff on his cigar. "Indeed, but William's absence will cause them some trepidation. He was always the leader of the brothers. They'll be hesitant to move without him." He puffed on his cigar, gazed towards the terminal, and continued speaking with such confidence, it sounded like he was delivering a prophetic vision from on high. "One or more of the brothers will become impatient and move without warning, so look sharp. Almost certainly, they will make their move at the last second, as I approach the train."

"Knowing when and where you will be hit does give us an edge."

Kierian nodded and took another puff from his cigar. "All things considered, I think we shall implement the 'Tiger and The Fox'. You do remember that stratagem, do you not Miss Dareheart?"

"Indeed, I do. Lure the enemy hunting you-the tiger-into your trap with someone as bait. Then turn the tables on them. However, as I recall, the bait was known as the goat."

"Yes, well that was when someone else was the bait. When it is me," Kierian took a final puff of his cigar, dropped it and snuffed it out beneath his leather Bronnigahn boots, "we call it the fox."

* * * * * *

"Where in tarnation is Bill?" Bee Dunn asked.

"Probably still inside, watchin' the front lobby for our bounties. Now stop fidgetin' Bee. You'll draw attention," Dal Dunn said. He rolled a cigarette, leaned against the outside wall of the passenger's terminal building, and glanced up at the clear blue sky.

"I hate these city slicker duds, Dal. They make me itch somethin' awful."

"Brother Bill will clean your plough line, fer sure, if you make a mess of this bounty, Bee. Best stop worrying about your itches and keep your eyeballs peeled for that McKenna fella and his lady friend."

Bee looked inside his hat. A photograph of both bounties lay on the cheap felt lining of the bowler. The man and young miss were dressed formally, and smiling sweetheart smiles at each other, probably at some fancy dress ball.

"They don't look like much to me," Bee said.

"Bill said that McKenna fella is quick like a jackrabbit and twice as deadly as a Texas rattler."

"What about the girl?"

"Word is, she's a regular she-wolf. The Limeys even got a name for her. They call her the Banshee."

"Banshee? What in tarnation is a Banshee? That some kind of eastern coyote?"

"It's a ghost. The kind them shanty Irishmen have back in Ireland."

"So, the girl is Irish?" Bee asked.

"No, she ain't Irish. Her name is Dareheart. Does that sound Irish to you?" Dal shook his head, licked the cigarette paper, folded it, and popped the cigarette into his mouth.

"If she ain't Irish then why in hell do they call her the Banshee? Why not call her the ghost?"

"On account of, once you hear a banshee's croon, you're a dead man. Mr. Stock says it's the same with the woman; you never see her comin' and once you get the knowin' of who she is, it's too late. You best be ready for 'em both, Bee." Dal struck a match off the sole of his boot and lit his cigarette.

"A fancy pants and a petticoat Polly. That's all I see in this here photograph." Bee watched the passengers as they exited the terminal building and walked towards the Mohawk Special. None looked like the bounties.

He tapped his fingers against his holstered Colt Peacemaker, hidden beneath his frock coat. "Bill and Cal should be down here. If the Fancy Pants is as tough a cob as you say, then they should be giving a hand rather than lollygagging in the damn lobby."

"I told you, Bill is watchin' the lobby for the bounties. Hell, he might take one or both of them himself and save us the labor, if'n he has a mind to, so stop your complainin."

"Bill's the fightinest rooster ever I did see, but Cal should be-"

"Cal is driving the stagecoach. Once we put the hood on these two, we're gonna need to hit the trail, lickety-split for Canada." Dal took another puff from his cigarette, "Can't do that if there ain't no driver. Besides, George is over yonder by that newsboy. He'll-"

"There he is!" Bee said, and pointed toward a well-dressed man in a bowler hat and tan tweed frock coat. "That's him! That's the Fancy Pants!" He started to move towards the man but Dal grabbed his arm.

"Hold your horses, Bee. I gotta give George the signal, and I reckon we should wait on Bill. I doubt McKenna slipped by without his notice, so he should be along directly."

Dal looked over at his brother George. George was saying something to the newsboy. He waited until George was done chatting and was a looking his way. Dal stretched, yawned, looked at McKenna, tossed his cigarette onto the ground, and crushed it out beneath his boot.

George nodded in understanding.

"I don't see Bill no wheres, nor Miss Banshee, and that McKenna fella is strolling without nary a care in the world, towards the train. I say we pull our horns out and take 'em."

"You change your tune quicker than a politician's preacher, Bee. A moment ago you wanted to wait for brother Bill, now you want to kick up your heels, grab the fiddle, and start the dance without him."

"Yeah, well, now my blood's up, brother Dal, and it's certain we can't let Fancy Pants get on the train." Bee nervously tapped the Peacemaker with his fingers. He locked his eyes on his target, licked his lips and flexed his fingers in anticipation.

Dal looked back at the door of the terminal. "It ain't like Bill to tarry, and I don't like that we ain't seen Miss Dareheart. Remember what Mr. Stock said? By the time you recognize her, you're already a dead man."

"I don't give a hoot nor holler about that Petticoat Polly. My blood is up and my trigger finger is itchy, brother Dal!"

Bee was trembling now, like a drunk at a saloon bar, anticipating a drink of whiskey. He could feel the exhilaration of the anticipated conflict racing through him.

He wanted blood.

"Just hold your hor-" Dal began.

"I can wait no longer brother Dal! The Killin' time's a come! Let's get the party started!" Bee took off his hat and waved it frantically in the air, to brother George.

George produced a lariat from under his long frock coat and began to swing it in the air. Bee grinned. This would be easier than when they killed Bitter Creek and Charlie Pierce while they were dismounting. Fancy Pants had his back to them.

He would never know what hit him.

CHAPTER SEVEN

Emma tossed the newspaper aside, dropped to a squat and swept her right leg in a semi-circle cutting the legs of the man swinging the lariat. He collapsed just as he made his throw.

The rope loop missed Kierian; instead it lassoed a middle-aged man in business attire.

As George Dunn crashed to the ground, he pulled the lariat knot tight, cinching the loop around the bewildered and terrified man.

The lariat sparked with electricity, the businessman convulsed, and fell to the ground.

Emma drew one of her Colts, but quick as a cat, George Dunn sprang to his feet and cocked the hammer of his revolver.

Emma leapt hard to her left.

Dunn fired.

His hurried shot went wide.

Emma fanned the hammer of her Peacemaker. The pistol sparked forty-five caliber death. Four bullets rocketed out the barrel. Dunn crashed to the ground, a pool of crimson seeped out from under him.

Emma spun, old instincts no longer dormant. She anticipated incoming fire and ignored the desire for self-preservation.

The best way to save your own skin is to eliminate the threat, as quickly as possible.

The remaining Dunn brothers brandished their six-shooters and advanced at a run. They raised their weapons, cocked the hammers and took aim.

But Kierian was faster. He raised and fired his Colt M1900 in one smooth action, the pistol booming three times in his hand.

One of the brother's face contorted in pain. He crumpled to the floor; blood darkened the fabric of his shirt.

Panic spread like wildfire. People darted for the safety of the passenger terminal building, colliding with one another, as they attempted to squeeze through the door. Women screamed; their men tried to shield them from danger. Mothers hugged their children tightly and ducked behind benches, train cars, and unlit gas light poles, or unable to find cover, threw their own bodies on their little ones to protect them from the violence that swirled around them.

Emma tried to draw a bead on the Dunns. Civilians ran in front of her gun sights.

Get clear peoples or just hit the damn deck, already!

"You shot brother Dal! I'll kill you, Fancy Pants!" Bee Dunn yelled. He fanned his own pistol, firing six times.

Kierian staggered back and clutched his right shoulder, then leapt behind a light post. Behind him, a woman cried out and fell. Blood seeped out from under her. Another round struck a man in the head, bone and brain exploded and he tumbled back against the side of the second-class passenger's car of the Mohawk Special.

Emma stepped left, dodging a fleeing bystander, to get a better angle on the Dunn brother, reloading behind a bench.

Kierian squeezed the trigger of his pistol four times in rapid succession, reloaded the M1900 with a fresh magazine, and fired one shot after another at an expeditious pace.

Good! Covering fire. A few more steps and I'll have the shooting angle.

A heavy shoulder slammed into Emma's left side. The air whooshed from her lungs, and the revolver fell from her hand. She tumbled forward, but still in control of her body, executed a somersault, coming up on one knee on the edge of the curb, just in front of the caboose of the Midwest Special.

A large bearded man, dressed in a flannel shirt, and brandishing a double-headed axe in one hand bounded towards her. Emma drew her remaining Colt, cocked the hammer, and fired directly into his chest. The man wobbled but continued his advance. Tree trunk arms slashed the axe at Emma.

The Banshee leaped back.

The honed axe edge tore through her shirt, seeking to find the flesh beneath.

It missed her stomach by inches.

She stepped back onto the train tracks, fired, retreated, cocked the hammer, fired, and retreated again. Each shot struck the man's chest, each time he staggered but refused to go down.

Damn it! Is this guy's chest made of iron? Well, time to turn off all the lights.

She cocked the hammer again, raised the gun, and aimed for the Bearded Man's head.

The Bearded Man's axe chopped through the air

and cleanly severed the barrel of the Peacemaker. He pivoted, and punched the axe handle into Emma's stomach.

Emma doubled over. Beardy's powerful paw slammed her against the Midwest Express's wood car.

"There's no where to go, Miss Dareheart and you can quit with the gun play, if'n you have any others on ya person, that is." He pulled back his flannel shirt to reveal an iron chest plate and laughed, a deep cackle.

Emma raised an eyebrow, as she took advantage of the break to get her wind back.

The weight of that thing must be enormous. How in hell does beardy even walk around in that much less move, as quickly as he does?

"My name is Caribou Jack, leader of the Lumber-jack Nine from New Brunswick province, and this here," he held up his axe and smiled, "is Mr. Choppy."

Emma raised an eyebrow. "Mr. Choppy? You named your axe, Mr. Choppy?"

"Damn right I did. Mr. Choppy and me been through the hells and high waters together. We done out fought bears, moose and men, chopped more trees, drank more whiskey and poked more whores than your Mr. Bunyan ever dreamed of! I keeps Mr. Choppy sharper than a Bull Moose's antler points, and he keeps

87

me breathing."

Emma inched her left hand to her hip and towards her back. "I do not suppose we can sit down and settle our differences over a mound of flapjacks, Mr. Caribou? I'll even provide the syrup, New York State's finest."

"Tempting as that offer is, Missy, and it *IS* tempting, I needs decline, and so you knows, Mr. Choppy has felled just as many Yanks as he has trees, so you best show him and me some respect." Caribou Jack gave Mr. Choppy a little kiss and cackled again.

The Mohawk Special blocked any view of what was transpiring, but Emma could hear the occasional report of a Colt revolver and the distinctive sound of Kierian's semi-automatic.

But Kierian's shots had slowed, and it sounded to her like he was running low and conserving ammunition.

She had to get back to him. Time was no longer their ally.

"The Lumberjack Nine you said? Who the hell are they?" Emma asked. She again, inched her hand past her hip and toward her back.

"We're the ones who hacked through your Maine boys during the Battle of the Caribou. That's where I got my name," Caribou Jack said proudly.

88

"Ah, and here I thought it was because you *smelled* like a caribou." She inched her left hand to her back.

Almost there.

Caribou Jack's hairy hand wrapped around her neck and pinned her against the train car. Steam hissed into the air from the Midwest's engine.

"Mr. Stock said you was a sharp tongued doe. I don't want to kill you, Miss Dareheart. Mr. Stock wants you in Toronto alive and what Mr. Stock wants, Mr. Stock gets, but throw any more of that Yankee sass my way and I'll carve your tongue out, turn it into a flapjack, and feed it to my wolves." Caribou Jack cocked his head back and cackled once more.

"If you do not care for Yankee sass how about a little Yankee steam!" Emma drew the steam pistol from her back waistband, elevated the funnel shaped barrel, and pulled the trigger. Inside the weapon, sodium dropped upon the first thermite tablet, the tablet dissolved, released its heat, turning the water in the tiny holding tank to gas.

Scalding steam seared Caribou Jack's Face.

The lumberjack screamed and clutched his blistered face. Emma raised her steam pistol.

But Caribou Jack was quicker.

The lumberjack growled and raised his axe to the

clear blue sky.

Mr. Choppy screamed downward hungry for blood.

Emma sidestepped.

The axe crashed into the wood of the train car, sending splinters and slivers flying. The Midwest Express hissed steam, a billow of black smoke rose into the air, wheels moved, and the train began to pull out of the station.

"Mr. Choppy, get free!" Caribou Jack yelled. He pulled hard, but the axe was embedded deep in the wood.

The train chugged. More smoke billowed from the stack and it picked up speed, but the lumberjack held fast to his axe.

"Mr. Choppy!" He ran along the side of the train, holding the axe with both hands.

Emma watched amazed. The big Lumberjack vaulted one leg over the side of the wood car, hugging it as it sped down the tracks.

"Mr. Choppy! Don't ya worry. I won't leave ya!" The Midwest Express picked up steam and chugged away. Caribou Jack flung himself into the wood car. The train rounded the corner and disappeared from view.

The gunfire had stopped.

Emma dashed back to the Mohawk Special's caboose and peeked around the corner.

Kierian stood, his frock coat balled up behind a light pole. His green Madrona vest was speckled with blood about the shoulder, and his pistol was raised and aimed at one of the Dunn brothers, who was breathing hard, his own Colt Peacemaker, held down by his leg.

For a second, she wondered why Kierian did not empty his pistol into the Dunn brother's chest, but then, she saw the other brother off to Kierian's left, the one he had first shot. He stood, holding a large Bowie knife to a young girl's throat.

"The dance is all over, McKenna," said the Dunn with the knife. "You drop your weapon and come along quiet like, or I'll slit this girl's throat like I'm slaughtering a hog for Sunday supper."

"NOOOO!" The girl's mother screamed, tears coursed down her face. "Please, sir," she said to Kierian, "do as they ask. Don't let them hurt my baby, she's all I got!"

"Shut your mouth, and keep your place, Lady!" Bee Dunn said. He turned and addressed his brother, "He ain't comin' along no wheres but to a shallow grave, brother Dal. They done kilt brother George. They's got to pay in blood!"

91

"Actually, I killed big brother William *and* brother Calvin, as well." Kierian corrected.

"The hell you say! I'm gonna gun you, gut you, and chop you into little itty bits, Fancy Pants."

"Bee! Let me handle this," Dal Dunn yelled. He turned and looked at Kierian. "McKenna, drop your weapon, or I'll slit this girl's throat. I'm shot full of holes, and I ain't got time to parlay. Now, you do like I say."

Quietly, Emma came out from behind the caboose, picked up the pistol she had dropped earlier, and confirmed it was loaded with the remaining two shots.

Dal Dunn's head was just over the girl's left shoulder. It would be a tough shot, but one she had made before. She raised her pistol and stepped forward.

"Ah, Miss Dareheart," Kierian said. "I wondered where you had tumbled off to."

"I had to deal with some crazy lumberjack and his axe, Mr. Choppy."

"Mr. Choppy? Really?"

"Indeed. I'll regale you with the tale, later."

Dal Dunn looked white as death. He'd probably faint if they could delay things long enough. It made sense to keep the chit-chat going as long as they could.

"You take a shot at me, Missy, you better damn well

not miss cuz I aim to cut this girl just out of spite, even it be with my last dyin' breath," Dal Dunn pushed his Bowie knife against the terrified girl's throat. A crimson droplet rolled down her neck.

"Hiding behind a child," Kierian shook his head. "Is that really the way you want to go out, Dunn?"

"I ain't proud of what I'm doing. I won't deny that, but it's a hard testin' that's come our way this day, and that calls for hard doings. Now, for the last time, drop your weapon, and you too Miss Dareheart."

"I could do that," Kierian said, "or I could shoot your brother Bee over there, then walk over and shoot you through the head. As for the girl? I'm not aquatinted with her or her family. Why should I care what you do to her?"

"You're a ruthless bastard, McKenna, or so I've heard tell, but that's too thin for my likin'. All my chips are in the pot already, so I'll call your bluff and see your cards," Dal replied. "I'm aiming to count to three and when I do, I'm cutting this girl, sure. One-two-"

Kierian sighed and shoved his pistol in his shoulder holster. Bee Dunn smiled and began to raise his pistol. Emma immediately changed her aim from Dal Dunn to Bee.

"Drop your weapon, Miss Dareheart! Be smart like

Mr. McKenna." Dal said.

"The deal was we come along, not that we let brother Bee, gun us down."

"Bee, holster your damn Pistola," Dal said to his brother.

"No, sir. I will not. I'm notchin' my six-shooter for the Fancy Pants," Bee licked his lips and stared hard at Kierian.

"Actually, they are Franklin trousers, tailor fitted of course," Kierian said.

"They gonna be bloody trousers in a second, Fancy Pants!"

"This really is tiresome. You already speckled my vest with blood. It'll be a damn hard time for certain, for Saul to get the stains out! " Kierian dusted off the sleeves of his dress shirt. "And Saul does not work cheap. That alone earns you a bullet. Now, you wish to ruin another part of my dashing apparel?" Kierian shook his head with disgust.

"What *is* the world coming to?" Emma remarked.

"Exactly, Miss Dareheart! A man can't even have a good morning shoot-out without someone threatening his stylings, these days."

"Bee-"

"Ain't no use tryin' to dissuade me, brother Dal. I'm

94

getting me a Fancy Pants notch and that's the end of it."

"Well, Mr. Dunn, if that's the way you want it, let's get to it." Kierian opened up his silver watch and turned a dial. A melody began to play.

"Holster your pistol and when the song ends, we'll draw and blast away until one of us is dead."

Bee motioned towards Emma. "What about Petticoat Polly, yonder?"

"Petticoat Polly? That's an absurd name for Miss Dareheart."

"Indeed, especially since I am wearing trousers," Emma replied.

"Right. Trouser Tess, or News Cap Nancy would be more appropriate," Kierian replied.

"Petticoat Polly was a saloon whore, that liked her shooting irons more than her customers. She got beat blue and black for sassin'. Should've kept her place and seen to her craft, like a whore's supposed to," Bee explained while looking directly at Emma. "Now, tell your Polly to drop her shootin' iron, Fancy Pants."

Kierian nodded. "Miss Dareheart, lower your weapon after Dunn holsters his, please."

"Are you serious?"

"Dammit! Do like I tell you! Lower your weapon

and next time, stick to your cross-stitching," Kierian commanded.

His watch continued to play its melody.

"That's telling her, Fancy Pants."

Bee Dunn holstered his Peacemaker and Emma lowered her weapon to her side.

She suppressed the urge to grin. Cross-stitching meant to cross shoot, and take out the enemy facing Kierian and away from her.

"You really wanna High Noon it, Fancy Pants? You wanna try your luck quick drawing on ol' Bee Dunn, the fastest gun in Oklahom-ey? Well, you got it, boy! When that music stops I'm gonna fill you with hot lead." Bee flexed his fingers, ready to draw.

Kierian smiled and looked down at the watch. He moved the hand holding the watch slightly, in Dal Dunn's direction.

"Gonna hang your fancy dancy duds in my trophy room, right next to the big horn elk I shot last winter," Bee added.

Kierian nodded, but his attention was on the face of his watch.

"That sure is a purty tune coming from your pocket watch, I have to admit. What's it called, Fancy Pants?" Bee asked.

Kierian kept his eyes on the watch face. He adjusted his hand, ever so slightly, and grinned. "It is called Dr. Waatt's Third Symphony but you might as well call it, Welcome to The Twentieth Century." He pressed a small, concealed button on the bottom of the watch. A beam of pure energy sliced through the air and struck Dal Dunn's knife.

Instantly, the knife superheated and sizzled skin. The girl screamed.

Dal Dunn dropped the knife.

And Bee Dun drew his Peacemaker faster than greased lighting.

* * * * * *

Kierian and Emma drew their weapons and fired simultaneously. The reports of their pistols echoed together.

Kierian's first shot caught Dal Dunn in the shoulder and spun him back. The screaming girl darted for her mother. The M1900 boomed again, and punched a third eye in Dal Dunn's head.

Bee Dunn was fast, but he had to make a full draw, and Emma only had to raise her pistol. With no human shield to contend with, Emma fired center mass. The first round slammed into Bee's chest, while his shot missed over Kierian's right shoulder.

97

Cool, emotionless hands hammered a second shot into his chest, a half-inch to the right of the first shot.

Bee Dunn was dead before he hit the ground.

Emma walked over, and looked down at the two dead Dunn brothers.

"Very, well...done, Mr. McKenna."

Kierian chuckled.

"I guess this fight is all... done."

Kierian looked over at her, smiled, and nodded. "Yes, I understood it the first time, Miss Dareheart, very clever."

Emma chuckled. She reached up and touched Kierian's shoulder.

"I swear by Mother Freedom's bell, I saw you take a bullet to the shoulder. Did Balthazar invent a bullet-proof dress shirt as well as a heat-ray watch?"

"Ha! If only he would! I have persuaded him to make his inventions more stylish, hence my stun cane and weaponized watch, but he has yet to dip his genius into the fashionable garment industry. As for why I am not bleeding profusely from Bee Dunn's gun shot to my shoulder..."

Kierian reached down and retrieved his frock coat, pulled out his silver cigar case, and held it up. A Colt . 45 slug was halfway embedded within it.

98

"And the Decency Society says smoking is bad for you," Emma said.

Kierian chuckled.

"Lady Fortune smiles on her favorite son, once again," Emma said.

Kierian beamed. "Of course she does! And now, rather than test the good Lady's patience, I suggest we board Vanderbilt's private car and be on our way."

"Should we not render assistance?"

People all around them were just now recovering from the shock of what had transpired; women and children sobbed. The injured moaned and pleaded for help.

Kierian slipped his frock coat back on, retrieved his cane, straightened his dark blonde hair, and carefully donned his bowler.

He shook his head, "Panic is still in the air, Banshee."

Emma nodded. They had danced to this tune before. Victims of a traumatizing attack were just as likely to blame you for the injury to a loved one, as they were to thank you for saving them.

Piper is right. The best course of action is to walk away, board the Mohawk Special, and be on our way to Sagamore, to see what the hell Alfred Vanderbilt wants.

CHAPTER EIGHT

"A watched pot never boils, Mr. McKenna," Emma said.

Kierian sighed. He checked his silver fob watch and glanced down the road for a carriage.

They had made excellent time on their journey from Rochester to Thendara Station, but once they arrived, their journey stalled. A line of elegant horse-drawn carriages awaited the passengers of the Vanderbilt private rail car, and Emma was confident that at least, one of the carriages was there to deliver them to their meeting with Alfred Vanderbilt. One by one, however, the carriages pulled away, including the hackney cabs, leaving Kierian and Emma abandoned at the station.

At first, the delay was not much of a bother. The inner rooms of the station included private dressing rooms for both lady and gentleman travelers. Kierian took the opportunity to engage in a change of clothing, and was particularly happy to replace his blood soaked Madrona vest with a fresh one. He even convinced Emma to change into more appropriate women's attire. Emma chose a brown dress with a basque that tightly hugged her slender frame. Five black buttons ran down the center, tying it together, and a high cotton collar rose up to cover her neck. A black parasol rested against her left shoulder Concealed within, was an air cartridge that fired a single .22 caliber bullet out the tip. Gloves, a black riding hat with a red band around it, and a pair of goggles hanging around her neck, completed her formal wear.

Kierian tipped his hat. "I unequivocally approve of your transformation, Miss Dareheart. You look absolutely beguiling."

"Why thank you, Mr. McKenna."

"I would advise you to lose the red band that circles your riding hat, but I suppose it has practical usage and hides a small Derringer, or another such weapon."

"Heavens no, Mister McKenna," Emma paused, twirled her parasol, leaned forward, and whispered in Kierian's ear, "the Derringer is in my garter. A dagger is under the sash."

Kierian grinned. His eyes twinkled with approval. "I tip my hat to your preparedness, my lady." He placed his watch back in his vest pocket. "You would think, Miss Dareheart, that if one sends a personal and urgent request for another's presence, the writer of said letter would make damn sure their transportation is punctual."

"Perhaps something happened to cause their delay."

"If that is the case, then alternate transportation should have been provided. I mean-"

A horse whinnied, and the sounds of thundering hooves and clattering metal, echoed from down the road.

Emma glanced towards the sound. A team of eight magnificent champagne colored horses trotted down the road, pulling a fully armored hearse. Small slits on its armored side panels were the only signs of any windows. Rising up from the center of the vehicle, was a cheese-box shaped gun turret, with an eight-barreled Gatling gun protruding from the center. Even the driver was enclosed behind armor, as he held the reins through a large slit in the iron plating.

"Perhaps that is our transportation," Emma suggested.

Kierian raised an eyebrow, "To where exactly? The graveyard?" He pulled his brown derby tight over his forehead, lest it fall off in the midst of a confrontation. "We had best take to cover until we are sure if they are friend or foe."

Emma nodded. They both slipped inside the empty train depot, and took up positions on either side of the front window.

She pulled her Colt Peacemaker Store Keeper model with its short four-inch barrel from her handbag and glanced over at Kierian. His gloved hand wrapped around a brass handgun. Three concentric rings circled the barrel and a pressure gauge was attached to its side. "Doctor Waatt's heat-ray pistol?" Emma asked.

Kierian nodded. "The watch's bigger brother. After nearly running empty during our battle with the Dunns I thought it best to augment my armaments with a weapon that does not require ammunition."

"A wise precaution. However, it doesn't blend in very well with your dashing apparel. How ever can you stand it?"

"It is, to be sure, a trial. It has no aesthetic beauty or elegance whatsoever. How can I be expected to arm myself with such a weapon on a regular basis?"

"I think Balthazar was more concerned about its functionality than the refinement of its appearance."

The horse drawn fortress approached.

"Functionality? It is deadly up to thirty feet, to be sure, but after that, it's a damn nuisance! Still, I suppose if we need to engage this iron behemoth, having a weapon that can burn a hole through the armor plating will come in handy."

"Quite handy, indeed."

The iron coach came to a halt in front of the station and the door of the vehicle opened. A well-dressed middle-aged man with graying sideburns and a gray bushy mustache stepped out.

The Gatling gun in the turret swiveled, menacingly scanning the surrounding area.

"Mister McKenna? Miss Dareheart? Are you within?" the middle aged man yelled.

"Who is inquiring?" Kierian said. He stepped only half way through the depot's door, the heat ray pistol discreetly held behind his back.

"I am Ambrose Russ, the Vanderbilt's' family lawyer, and a mentor of sorts to young Alfred, as he adjusts to being the head of his branch of America's first family."

"Is not President McKinley's family, the first family, sir?" Emma asked, as she followed Kierian out the door.

Russ laughed. "If you say so, Miss Dareheart."

Kierian placed the heat ray pistol in his coat pocket, walked towards the carriage, stopped, and examined the vehicle.

Russ grinned with pride. "Never seen the like of her before, I wager, Mister McKenna? We call it the Combat Coach."

"Actually, Dr. Waatt has a steam-powered version he calls the Juggernaut."

Ambrose Russ scowled. Disappointment, and a flare of jealous anger played across his face.

"However, I would rate yours more pleasing to the eye," Kierian encouraged.

"I think it is the horses that give it a more eloquent appearance," Emma said and ran her hand softly along one of the champagne manes. "They are quite beautiful."

"They are part of a new American breed of draft horse, Miss Dareheart. The British have their Shire horses and the Scots their Clydesdales, but now we're developing our own. The American Cream Draft," Russ said.

"They are very beautiful, Mr. Russ," Kierian said, " but are they strong enough to pull a coach this heavy, for any length of time?"

"This team is incredibly powerful and their stamina

105

unmatched, Mr. McKenna. They are able to trot all day and are surprisingly fast, too. One of Mr. Vanderbilt's… er- more portly guests- took Prince here, hunting last season and he was able to keep up with the field. And they are quiet as lambs. So much so, that my five year old niece drives them."

"What of your armored coach?" Kierian asked, and tapped the armored plating with his cane. "Has it ever seen action?"

"No sir. Its mere appearance has deterred any ruffians from attempting an attack on those within its armored bosom."

Kierian nodded and held the door open for Emma. Emma climbed in and Kierian followed. Ambrose Russ took a seat across from Kierian. He tapped his cane on the roof of the carriage, and they began their journey to Sagamore.

"Impressive as this carriage is, Mister Russ, it seems a bit…excessive. I mean, we are not in a war zone after all," Emma said.

Russ looked first at Emma, and then at Kierian, before sitting back in his seat and crossing his arms over his chest.

"These are dangerous times, Miss Dareheart. President McKinley made the courageous decision to put our country solely on the gold standard, and while I completely support his action, those who were invested in silver took a tremendous financial blow."

"Large enough of a blow for acts of violence to be perpetrated against those who profited from the President's decision?" Emma asked.

"Indeed, Miss Dareheart. The discovery of silver throughout the Adirondacks created many boomtowns; fortunes were made and employment created for the masses. Now, that silver is no longer legal tender, the boom is going bust, those fortunes are lost, and the masses are now unemployed."

"Angry, unemployed workers harboring a grudge is never a good situation," Kierian remarked.

"Angry, unemployed, ARMED workers harboring a grudge is even worse," Russ replied.

The carriage rolled along the dirt road and Emma could not help catching wafts of the strong pungent smell of pine in the air every time a breeze kicked up. "And I suppose there is no end to the rabble rousers ready to take advantage of these armed masses?"

"Indeed there is not, Miss Dareheart. Whether it is the Brits in Upper Canada, looking to chop off the Adirondacks to add to their North American Empire, or our own homegrown anarchists, demanding a return to

Bi-Metalism and the confiscation of private property, the undeniable fact is, that this area has become a powder keg."

"Not the best spot then, for Alfred to have purchased a vacation home," Kierian said.

"I warned him against it but well, you know Alfred. He is young, impetuous, and was enchanted by the beauty of the forest streams and mountain peak visages. In the end, what Alfred wants, Alfred gets," Russ replied.

"Still, nothing has happened as of yet, I wager. If it had, I would have expected all your guests to have been escorted from Thendara in armored carriages," Kierian said.

Russ frowned at Kierian.

"Alfred's younger sister, Gladys, was abducted this past Friday. She has a fascination with this region and with the science of archeology, and so not only financed the expedition of one Professor Bridgewater, but insisted on going along on it as well."

"Good heavens! Do you have any idea who abducted her?" Emma asked.

Russ sneered as he spit the word out. "Anarchists. Loathsome, damnable, anarchists. They reportedly slaughtered everyone besides Gladys, Professors

Bridgewater and his assistant, Professor Boaltt."

"How many persons were on the expedition?" Kierian asked.

"One hundred and twenty seven souls, Mr. McKenna. Most of them from the laboring class; thank heavens."

"I do not see why the class of a person makes it any less a tragedy, Mr. Russ," Emma retorted. "In death, we are all equal before the Lord."

"Yes but not in life, Miss Dareheart. It is a fact that society is hit much more harder as a whole when men of capital, those who make the trains run, the factories produce, and who allow the builders to build and the laborers to labor, are removed from the chessboard of life."

Emma leaned back in her seat, crossed her arms, cocked her head to one side, and was about to tell Russ that life was not a game for most but a hardscrabble day to day struggle, and that laborers were not pawns, and the wealthy not kings. Before she could speak, however, she felt Kierian's hand give hers a pre-emptive squeeze.

She let out a calming breath. Informing Russ he was an insufferable snob, whose attitude and disregard for the lower classes actually helped create the anarchists would accomplish nothing. Gladys Vanderbilt had been abducted and over a hundred people slain. Recovering her was the mission and the mission had to come first before anything else, including personal differences with the client.

"Did Gladys have an escort?" Kierian inquired.

"A man by the name of Jerome Tyler. He was formerly a Captain in the United States Marine Corp."

"Never heard of him, and if he was any good I would have," Kierian replied.

"He came highly recommended, Mr. McKenna. I assure you, his credentials were impeccable."

"By credentials, do you mean he knew the right kind of people, and came from the right kind of family?" Emma asked.

Russ glared at Emma. "We could not very well, place young Gladys's safety in the hands of…common folk." Russ pulled down on his vest and straightened his tie. "It was crucial we choose someone who would behave as a gentleman."

"Bullets are no respecters of status, Mr. Russ," Kierian admonished. "When they start flying it is best to have those about you who know how to stop those firing them, rather than those whose expertise is knowing the difference between a table spoon and a bouillon spoon."

"Gladys was traveling under her mother's maiden name: Gwynne. No one knew her identity and therefore, there was no reason to think any bullets would be flying, as you put it, Mr. McKenna."

"Clearly, someone knew her identity, Mr. Russ," Emma remarked.

"Or discovered it," Kierian added.

"What's done is done, Russ said in a firm voice. None of us can rewind the hands of father time. This matter has nearly ruined Alfred's health, so please, I ask you to desist with your recriminations, and proceed to developing some stratagem to rescue his beloved sister."

"Very well. What was the expedition's mission, exactly?" Kierian asked.

"Those details must wait for now. I am not an expert in the field of archeology, and so it is best that we wait until Doctor Waatt and Professor Stonechat have arrived."

"Professor Stonechat? Who is he?" Kierian asked.

"He is a she, Mr. McKenna. Professor Veronica Stonechat is a member of the American Institute of Archeology. She was to be a member of the Bridgewater expedition, but was delayed.

111

"How fortunate for her," Kierian said.

" I take it from your tone, Mr. McKenna, that you find her delay suspicious. I must disagree for I sincerely doubt a member of the weaker sex would have the fortitude and mettle to conspire in such a bloody affair. In any case, she will meet us at Sagamore and will answer any questions you have regarding the expedition's mission. Until then, Alfred has insisted that we act like nothing is amiss, and I am in agreement with him on that request. "

"I see. I suppose a considerable ransom has been demanded. If that became public, it could cause all manner of complications," Kierian said.

"Indeed, it would. Nor would those jackals in the press care if their meddling did create such complications. Therefore, it is of the utmost importance that we be discreet about poor Gladys's abduction."

"Am I correct then, in assuming that the authorities have not been notified?" Kierian asked.

"The villains made clear that they were not to be alerted and implied they would know if we attempted such. That is why we sent for STEAMCAPP, Mister McKenna."

"Ah, so if anyone is watching, they would simply see a lady daredevil invited to provide entertainment and her escort," Emma said.

"Precisely so, and Doctor Waatt is famous for his airship, his inventions, and … his tinkering. He will just be one more of a great number of illustrious guests in attendance, to celebrate the inaugural opening of Great Camp Sagamore. No one will suspect we have brought in a team of operatives," Russ replied.

The carriage lurched suddenly as it turned, tumbling Emma into Kierian.

"Really, Miss Dareheart, you must stop throwing yourself at me." Kierian grinned.

Emma smiled and straightened her hat. The carriage came to a stop in front of a church.

"Ah, we have arrived," Russ, said.

"I was expecting a few more buildings," Kierian said, as he stepped out of the carriage.

"Oh, this is not Sagamore, Mister McKenna. There was no open field large enough to accommodate the landing of Doctor Waatt's airship at the Camp. Father Doyle, the pastor here at the Twelve Apostles Church, however, was kind enough to lend us the use of his church fields."

Kierian nodded. He and Emma followed Ambrose Russ behind the church.

A large crowd of guests gathered around an immense field covered in dark red flowers, about a foot and a half tall. Several large telescopes were set up and aimed skyward, so the guests could get a fine look at the *Excelsior*, the airship famous for its major role in the destruction of the British fleet at the Battle of Ontario, which had brought a swift and brutal end to the British-American War.

Servants bustled around with trays of champagne and hors d'oeuvres, as Ambrose Russ introduced them to several illustrious guests. J.P Morgan, Andrew Carnegie, John Rockefeller and many other captains of industry were among those she met. Many other occupations were represented as well: baseball players, politicians, entertainers, military figures and dignitaries from several countries, were also in attendance.

"Kierian! Kierian McKenna! Ha! Whatever are you doing here, you rogue?" Emma snapped her head around at the distinctive voice of Theodore Roosevelt. The Vice President of the United States stormed through the crowd, his powerful legs pumped quickly, while his entourage struggled to keep up.

Kierian tipped his bowler. "Mr. Vice President, it is good to see you too," Emma stepped away from board game inventor George Parker who had been telling her how his new game, Rook, would revolutionize card

114

playing for the religious folk, who viewed face cards as inappropriate. She smiled at the Vice-President and curtseyed.

Roosevelt's voice boomed over the distance, still separating them "Emma Dareheart! I did not see you back there. My, how you have blossomed. Why, you are near as pretty as my own Alice.

"Thank you, Mr. Vice President," Emma replied when Roosevelt reached them.

"Oh, no need for such formalities between us old soldiers. It is good to see you both, damn good to see you." Roosevelt inverted his left hand and still managed a hearty handshake in Kierian's right.

"Does Dr. Watt's robotic arm still give you trouble?" Kierian asked, and motioned with his cane to the mechanical right arm hidden beneath Roosevelt's finely tailored day suit.

The Vice-President shook his head, laughed, and flexed the mechanical hand. Gears whizzed and pistons pumped beneath the suit coat.

"No. It does not give me trouble. However, I am still unfamiliar with the power of the thing. I do not believe I exaggerate when I say I now possess the strength of ten adult grizzly bears in my right arm!"

Kierian grinned. "Then I thank you for not crushing

my hand in your powerful paw."

"I will forever be thankful that Dr. Waatt replaced my ruined arm after it was near blown off, when the Rough Rangers and I charged up Cobb's Hill."

"Indeed, you should feel very thankful as the good doctor does not usually part with his technology so freely," Kierian replied.

"I do not understand why that is so! In fact, I have, on several occasions implored Dr. Waatt to make this fantastic invention available to all our men-in-arms."

Kierian opened his mouth to speak, but Teddy thundered on with his little speech.

"Imagine if we could augment our fighting men with enhanced robotic limbs. Not just the wounded, mind you, but a whole division of super soldiers, spreading the God given gift of Capitalism and Democracy throughout the earth, while fighting in the just cause of the United States of America."

A spattering of applause issued up from the Vice President's entourage and the nearby titans of industry.

Emma smiled. Teddy sure had a gift for oration. He could make ordering food off a menu seem inspiring. In fact, it had been largely because of his slogan of, "Dareheart and McKenna acquire acquits and to hell with the Brits!" during the Presidential campaign whistle-stops of the previous year, that she and Kierian had received their Presidential pardons.

"So, Dr. Waatt has refused to share his robotic limb technology with you?" Kierian said.

"Indeed he has! I do not understand why he insists on hoarding his knowledge rather than sharing it with his own country, as Mr. Edison over there has done," Roosevelt motioned to the famous inventor who was peering through a telescope into the sky, "or Mr. Tesla has, for the Austrian-Hungry Empire."

"Perhaps, he lacks the materials to mass produce a sufficient quantity," Emma offered.

"Bunkum and balderdash, Miss Dareheart! Why, Dr. Waatt would have the full backing of the United States Government behind him! He would be rich, with enough funds to purchase whatever materials he needed. Lady Capitalism would compensate him well and the service he would provide to his own country would be immense. Kierian, you truly need to—"

"Bullying your guests again, father?" a female voice interrupted.

Emma laughed as the beautiful Alice Roosevelt, pushed through the crowd and joined the group. Her blue day dress and wide brimmed hat were paired with a green boa constrictor. The snake draped around her shoulders, like the exotic living ornament it was. Her long-haired Chihuahua followed behind on short legs.

At twenty-two years old, Alice was only two years younger than Emma. They had met just after the war ended and formed an almost sisterly bond.

"Alice, I have told you before, it is impolite to—"

"Interrupt," Alice said, and smiled. "But, father, you suck the oxygen out of every room you are in. How else will anyone get a word in if I do not inter—" Alice's eyes fell on Emma and the desire to chide her father disappeared. A huge smile spread across her face. "EMMA!" she ran and threw her arms around the daredeviless and embraced her tightly. "I am ever so glad to see you! I had no idea you were going to be attending this forest festivity!"

"Our invitations arrived at the last moment," Emma explained.

"I am ever so glad you are here. I have followed all your sensational and outrageous acts. Every one!"

Emma grinned. "I heard you have engaged in a bit of outrageous activity yourself."

"Have I?" Oh, you mean, Emily Spinach here?" she tapped her snake gently on its head. "Having a Boa as my boa?" Alice chuckled.

"Miss Dareheart is no doubt, referring to your out-

118

rageous antics on board the steamer *Manchuria* before the Crown Prince of Japan," Theodore Roosevelt replied.

Kierian smiled and tipped his hat to Alice. "I missed that one. What did Miss Alice do that was so outrageous?"

Alice smiled back and batted her eyes at Kierian.

"She yelled like a savage and leaped into the ship's swimming pool, fully clothed!" Theodore Roosevelt replied. "Outrageous, simply outrageous."

Alice stroked her fingers down the scaly skin of Emily Spinach. "Oh, father, it would only have been outrageous had I been *un*clothed."

Emma laughed.

Kierian had once remarked how alike she and Alice Roosevelt were. *"Two beautiful blossoming roses from two very different gardens,"* he had said.

Emma had to agree. Alice knew how to shoot, ride, and like herself, excelled at all manner of athletics and activities, even those reserved strictly for men like, boxing, snooker, and nine-pins.

But Alice still came from a wealthy sheltered background and never had to worry about want of food or shelter. Five Tommies, never violently forced themselves upon her and she had not been forced to fight for her very life in kill-or-be-killed situations, almost every,day for three years.

It was queer how life's events directed such similar spirits to such different paths. If their family situations had been reversed, Alice might be the one adventuring with a solider of fortune, and Emma would be the one jumping into swimming tanks before heads of state just to break up the monotony of daily upper-class life.

Alice grabbed Emma by the arm and led her away as her father shook his head, and Kierian smiled at them both.

"I just read the afternoon edition of the Adirondack-Observer," Alice said in a hushed tone. She smiled with glee, as she rummaged through the small pack she wore on her hip and pulled out a clipped newspaper heading.

The Great Rochester Train Station
Shootout!
Daredeviless Guns Down Bounty Killers
In Western Gunfight.

Emma rolled her eyes.

"Did you really outdraw four gun fighters, wearing a full length dress and a cowboy hat?" Alice's eyes shone with glee. "Can I see the hat and wear it to dinner?" Alice rubbed her hands in anticipation. "It will shock and outrage everyone. Father will be ever so exasperated with me, but he always is these days."

"That is not exactly how it happened." Emma shook her head at the press's exaggerations.

"It was not?"

"There were five Dunns, not four. I was wearing trousers and a news cap, not a dress and a cowboy hat, and Kierian killed three of the Dunn's. I only shot two."

"But they have an artist's rendition." Alice handed the clippings to Emma.

The drawing was absurd. It pictured Emma in a full ballroom dress and a cowboy hat. The image brandished a revolver in each hand, while four Western dressed outlaws fell backwards from her blazing guns. The caption below read:

Lethal Lass Does In The Dunns!

"Oh, good Lord."

"Were you hunting the outlaws to collect the bounty on their villainous hides?"

"It was the other way around. They came after us. We were just defending ourselves."

"Oh." Alice sounded disappointed, then suddenly, brightened all over again. "Well, I still think it is wonderful that you can fight, shoot, and defend yourself and you don't care a whit about what everyone says about you!"

"What *do* they say about me?"

"Oh, you know, what they say about me: That you're scandalous, a disgrace to your family, a blot on all womanhood, a slut, that you should be jailed for dressing so obscenely, that…"

Emma held up a hand. "I get the gist of their comments, Alice." Emma smiled, as a thought raced through her mind. "Alice may I borrow the clippings? I would love to show Mr. McKenna what the press said about his daring Dunn fight."

"Dunn fight!" Alice squealed with laughter. "Oh Emma, you are ever so clever." She handed the clippings to Emma. Emma walked towards Kierian.

"…It is absurd and I am damn glad it is NOT working out in the manner you wish it to, Kierian!" Emma heard Theodore Roosevelt say. He held a folded sheet of paper in his left hand and slapped it into Kierian's right.

"I got her into this life, Theodore. It is my duty to get her out of it," Kierian replied.

Roosevelt saw Emma first and both men stopped talking. Kierian followed Roosevelt's gaze. He smiled

122

and slipped the paper into his inner coat pocket.

"Oh, please, do not stop talking on my account," Emma said. She cocked her head to one side and spun her parasol. "Unless, of course, the conversation *is* on my account."

"Just men talk, my beautiful Banshee, nothing more." Kierian smiled again, and his blue eyes twinkled.

Emma scowled. Kierian was a charmer and smooth as butter, almost every second of every day that he drew breath. However, on the few occasions he chose to lie to her, his eyes twinkled just a bit more than usual, and his speech was peppered with more flattery than usual.

It exasperated her to no end.

"Well, you know how I enjoy 'men talk.' Please include me. Who was the 'she' you were talking about?"

"Miss Dareheart, there is no call for you to alter your gorgeous visage with a scowl and a tone of suspicion. We were merely — "

"Evangelina Cosio," Theodore Roosevelt said.

"What?" Emma replied, taken back by the name.

"Surely, you have heard of her, Miss Dareheart. The beautiful, young, Cuban revolutionary rescued from a Spanish prison cell in Havana and smuggled back to

123

the United States?"

"I…yes of course. I know who she is…it was in all the broadsheets, but what does that—"

Roosevelt chuckled. "Well, you did not really think she was rescued by some New York Journal reporter, did you?"

Emma turned and looked at Kierian. "You were the "swashbuckling man of action," the Journal spoke about?"

Kierian smiled. "Guilty as charged."

"I would not have thought you would have allowed someone else to take credit for one of your derring do's," Emma retorted.

"Normally, I would not, but I figured one European power seeking my apprehension was enough." Kierian's blue eyes twinkled.

Emma locked eyes with him. She still felt he was deceiving her or maybe her rising blood pressure was because Evangelina Cosio was nineteen, a fiery revolutionary, a fighter, a woman of action, and if the pictures in the magazines had not been altered, one of the most beautiful women she had ever seen in her life.

Just the kind of woman Kierian seemed drawn to.

"Why is it that you always risk life and limb to rescue *beautiful* women, Kierian," Emma said out loud, when she meant to only think the statement.

Kierian and Roosevelt chuckled in the manner men do when they are being dismissive of the "overly emotional female." Emma's cheeks burned hot at the disrespect and she cursed her indiscreet words.

A shout came from the front of the crowd, near the telescopes. Kierian turned to look. People were pointing into the sky in astonishment and wonder. Emma pulled her goggles over her eyes and began using the small switch on the side that increased the lenses to maximum magnification. She peered through the Binoggulars and smiled, glad for the distraction.

Good timing Balthazar.

The *Excelsior* had arrived.

CHAPTER NINE

Theodore Roosevelt gazed proudly through the telescope at the approaching airship. "Magnificent! A most unconventional design and a remarkable example of American engineering."

Commodore Moffit, commander of the American Air Corp, shook his head and scowled. "Unconventional is an understatement, Mr. Vice President. It looks like a damn flying whale!"

Emma smirked at Moffit's remarks. The *Excelsior's* elliptical shaped hull had been variously described as a floating mound, a flying manatee, and resembling the capsized hull of a sailing ship. It's odd appearance had even caused it to be mistaken for an otherworldly vessel, one August evening in 1899, after a malfunction during a nighttime flight had necessitated an emergency decent.

MOON MEN INVADE!

Alien Ship, Seen Over Dayton, Ohio!
Governor Bushnell Calls Out Militia!

The *New York Journal's* headline had hysterically declared.

"Unconventional or not, she is truly impressive," Roosevelt replied.

"She doesn't look that impressive to me, Mr. Vice President," Moffit, said. He peered through an identical brass telescope, a few feet to the left of the Vice President's. "I estimate her hull length to be only around 250 feet."

"266, to be exact, Commodore," Emma corrected.

The Commodore ignored the correction. "The *Bunker Hill* and the *Constitution* are nearly two and a half times her size, and the Brits' *HMAS Majestic* and the German's *Bismarck* probably three times as big."

"Good things come in small packages, Commodore," Emma reminded.

"Perhaps Miss Dareheart, but in war, small packaged things often get blasted to pieces, by larger packaged things." Moffit waved towards *Excelsior*. He kept his eye to the lens of his telescope. "The *Excelsior* is very lightly armored, and I see not a single cannon on her, just ten or so Gatling guns."

"She did alright against the British at Ontario," Emma replied.

"Yes, but that was before anyone else had any heavily armed airships. In a battle amongst the clouds today, I doubt she would last half an hour."

"Commodore, do you see those three armored rotating ball turrets, on the top, nose and belly?" Roosevelt asked. "I am almost certain those contain heat-ray cannons. And look at the flame coming out the twin tailpipes. That must be rocket power propulsion. She'd run rings around anything we or anyone else has at present. I am sure of it!"

"If what you say is true, Mr. Vice President, she might be able to run from a fight well enough, but as for engaging in battle?" Moffit shook his head. "She is too lightly armored. Before she can get close enough to use her heat-ray weapons, the Brit's, or any other major power's airships, would blow her to kingdom come."

"What is that dish shaped array atop the vessel?" Roosevelt asked.

"I do not know," Commodore Moffit said. "Possibly, it is some type of weather gauge or other scientific tool. I cannot think, however, it would have any military application."

Emma smiled at the incorrect guess.

She did not understand the science behind the Spectrescope, but Balthazar had explained that it sent out radio waves that bounced off objects and when they returned, they revealed on the scope, the exact location of any near-by air and naval ships.

Excelsior was now directly overhead and beginning its vertical descent. Its nose pointed at the crowd.

The crowd's cheers suddenly faded. The airship's downward pitch accelerated. The elites looked around, with increasing trepidation, as the *Excelsior* dropped towards them.

Commodore Moffit's eyes darted back and forth between the airship and the flowered covered field. "Where are the mooring lines? Why isn't she releasing her mooring lines?" His eyes pitched about again and his voice betrayed a tone of panic. "Where is the docking tower? I do not see one. How can she land without mooring lines and a docking tower? My God! She is going to crash!"

Excelsior continued her rapid decent. The Commodore's words, heard by a few guests behind him, quickly spread, morphing from loud mutterings throughout the anxious crowd into exclamations of panic.

Champagne glasses and plates of hors d'oeuvres

dropped from white-gloved hands. Feet shuffled rest-lessly backwards, pushing against each other like a herd of cattle about to stampede.

Without warning, *Excelsior* pivoted in mid-air, and with her starboard side facing the crowd, resumed its downward climb. A loud hiss escaped from its belly and four massive cylinder air bags emerged, as it provided its own landing pad. The airship gently touched down and a collective sigh of relief rose from the crowd.

The *Excelsior* had landed.

* * * * * *

The relieved guests of Alfred Vanderbilt applauded with great enthusiasm, as Doctor Balthazar Waatt disembarked from his airship. Long, shoulder length, snow-white hair fluttered in the late summer breeze beneath a weather worn top hat. His tall, slender frame limped down the airship's stairwell, past *Excelsior's* Sikh security force, resplendent in their blue turbans, and the formidable Tulwar swords at their sides.

Emma linked her arm through Kierian's, and they strolled to greet their partner.

"Good day to you, Doctor," Kierian said, and extended his hand.

"Is it, Kierian?" Dr. Waatt said, leaning heavily on his silver headed cane. "Tell me sir, exactly how is it a *good* day?"

Kierian smiled and motioned about with his walking stick. "The sun is shining, a crowd of enthusiastic onlookers applauds your every step, I have this beautiful lady daredeviless on my arm, and we are all still breathing. That qualifies as a good day in my ledger."

"Indeed, but your last point was in question for you both, a few hours ago. Was it not?"

"Ah, you heard about our train station troubles in Rochester, I see."

"You are correct, sir, I did. It made the front page in the early edition of the *Times–Union*, and probably every other paper in the state!" Dr. Waatt locked his cold dark eyes on Kierian.

"No need for anxiety, Doctor," Kierian grinned and twirled his walking stick between his fingers. "As usual, we were able to turn the tables on our adversaries and snatch victory from the gaping jaws of utter defeat."

"Indeed, but according to witnesses, you barely made it out alive. Further, you were about out of ammunition at the end. Were you not?" Doctor Waatt poked Kierian with the end of his cane.

"True, but you know the saying: Necessity breeds improvisation and I improvised brilliantly." Kierian smiled. His eyes twinkled.

"You would not need to improvise if you properly used the weapons and equipment I provide, Kierian! Where was the Maser gun I gave you? In your luggage, I wager!"

"The Maser? You mean the heat-ray pistol?"

"How many times must I tell you it is not a *heat-ray* gun. It is Molecular Amplification by Stimulated Emission of Radiation weapon. A Maser, if you will."

"I pull the trigger, and a beam of heat blasts out the barrel. Heat-Ray seems a fitting name for your wonder weapon, Doctor."

"Heat is only a property of the excitation of the molecules in the path of the radiation beam. In fact, the radiation is not actually heat it is—" Dr. Waatt shook his head and pounded his cane down upon the ground. "It matters not. My point is you did not use it and thus, found yourself in the most dire of circumstances."

"The heat-ray pistol, was not on my person, but I did use the watch."

"And what if you had missed? That device only has enough power for a single firing!" Dr. Waatt shook a boney finger at Kierian. "Had you not stowed away the

132

pistol you could have fired away to your hearts content. At least until the battery ran out."

"Doctor, there is no reason for recrimination," Emma soothed. "Both Mr. McKenna and I came through the matter unscathed. All's well that ends well, as the saying goes."

Dr. Waatt turned his gaze upon Emma. "You do no favors taking up for him as you do, my dear. Nor am I particularly pleased with the risks you took, sky walking on that icy rope." He turned his head, locked his eyes once more on Kierian, sighed, and leaned both of his gloved hands on his cane. "Dash and daring will only get you so far, Kierian. We have serious work to do. Our enemies continue to refine and improve their weapons and equipment all the time. We must adjust our tactics accordingly."

Kierian smiled at Dr. Waatt. "Yes, but their armaments and tactics are no match for my good fortune, which is a family inheritance and thus, always with me and can never be lost as some wonder weapon may be."

Dr. Waatt stared coldly at Kierian. His left cheek twitched.

Rather than looking away or redirecting his attention elsewhere to diffuse the situation, Kierian simply grinned and kept his twinkling blue eyes on Dr. Waatt.

Emma shook her head.

Men and their pissing matches.

"How is the *Excelsior*, Doctor? You seemed to perform a perfect landing, to the amazement of all assembled," Emma said.

"These people would not know a perfect landing from a crash landing unless the ship burst into flames! As for the *Excelsior* she is not well at all!"

"Problems with your beloved technology, Doctor?" Kierian asked.

"Problems tend to arise, Kierian, when scorching heat of The Lake of Fire itself, is flayed across your air ship! It has been five months now since we battled the fiendish Ming Fang Fu and his dragon airship, yet the *Excelsior* still is not fully operational!"

"What exactly are the problems, Doctor?" Emma asked in a gentle voice.

Now we come to the real reason Balthazar is being such a pip. Hopefully, Kierian will let sleeping dogs lie from this point forward.

"What are not the problems is a better question, my dear."

"Are there still so many?" Emma asked.

"The Spectrograph's performance is erratic at best;

134

we have only two functional heat cannons; the rocket pods keep jamming and will not deploy as they should; the Data Repositor continues to shut itself off, usually when I am in the middle of research, and the Invisibility Veil tests have been miserable failures!

"So, that is why you did not heed my suggestion," Kierian said.

"Even if the Veil functioned, Kierian, I would not have done as you suggested."

"It would have amazed the onlookers, as you appeared like magic, and would be certain to have attracted business for STEAMCAPP."

"And exposed a key strategic advantage we hopefully will soon posses, to anyone in attendance with a brain in their skull. Which admittedly might not be many with this lot."

"Well, I doubt they are as brilliant as you, Balthazar. I am confident that even if they knew the what, they would not discover the how."

"Perhaps so, Kierian, but I am not about to provide them with the opportunity to try." The Doctor peered over Kierian's shoulder and scanned the crowd who were awaiting his presence.

"Is that Mr. Edison back there?"

"Yes. He will be showing several of his new moving

pictures over the next few days," Emma said.

"Teddy says he has even perfected sound to accompany them. He calls them Talkies," Kierian added.

"Indeed? How so?"

"A cylinder disc is played on his phonograph and synchronized to the speed of the film," Kierian explained.

Dr. Waatt folded both hands on top of his cane and pursed his lips, pondering the information for a few moments. "No, No, that is all wrong. That will never be commercially viable. Edison is a good egg. I will perhaps, give him a shove in the right direction."

"Which direction would that be?" Emma asked.

"Sound recorded directly to film via translating the sound waves into light waves."

"Ah, a very clever solution, I am sure," Kierian, said.

Emma rolled her eyes. The only thing Kierian was sure about was that he did not understand what Balthazar had just said. Of course, neither did she. She wanted to ask Balthazar how such a thing was possible, but his explanation would most likely also be beyond her understanding; so she chose to just nod and remain silent rather than bluff as if she understood as Kierian had done.

"Teddy? You mean Theodore Roosevelt?" Dr. Waatt suddenly asked Kierian.

"Yes, and the Vice President would like a word with you. He wants you to sell some of your robotic limb technology, so he can create an army of super soldiers."

"You see?" Doctor Watt wagged his index finger at Kierian, his irritability freshly rekindled. "Had I emerged "like magic" as you say, that bull moose Roosevelt would be demanding I hand over my Illumination Curvature research as well!"

"Perhaps we could convince him that you had mastered black magic of some sort," Emma said and chuckled. She moved her fingers about wildly, as if she was casting a spell.

Kierian glanced at her and chuckled.

Doctor Waatt did not join in with their jocularity. He looked from Kierian to Emma, with a stern visage.

"You two are well matched. You should add him to your shows, Miss Dareheart. You can both extoll wit and witticisms to the ignorant masses, as the world burns around them!" Doctor Waatt pushed past Kierian, bent over, plucked a red flower from the field, and placed it in Kierian's lapel.

"There! That is a gift, which truly becomes you, Kierian. Enjoy it. It has nothing to do with technology;

it is stylish and if legend is correct, magical. Maybe it will keep you alive past your thirty-fifth birthday, and grant you a modicum of wisdom." Doctor Waatt turned his back on Emma and Kierian and limped away from them toward the awaiting crowd.

"What legend?" Emma asked. She looked over the flower in Kierian's lapel and judged it as a good addition to his apparel.

"It is a Red Shamrock," Doctor Waatt said, continuing to limp away. "Legend says it protects the daring and grants wisdom to fools."

* * * * * *

Camp Sagamore was breathtaking. Each of the many buildings was well constructed with splendid native timber; the sides of each were paneled with gray cedar bark; the shutters, and doors of the cabins, were painted in a dark forest green. Massive evergreen trees rose majestically into the air, encircling the cabins, and a small babbling brook ran through the entire property.

"What an enchanting place," Emma said.

I agree it is indeed, magnificent," Kierian replied, "but I am surprised Alfred and his friends would wish to reside here. After all, enchanting or not, the cabins are rather small compared to the Fifth Avenue man-

138

sions they call home."

"True, Kierian, but we have only seen the exteriors of these fine buildings," Doctor Waatt said, as he limped along the path. "The interiors may, indeed, consist of all the amenities our hosts are regularly accustomed to."

Dr. Waatt was correct. Each cabin contained running water, chandeliers with new electric lighting, hot showers and baths, beds with silk sheets, goose feather pillows, and hand built, stone fireplaces so large, a full grown man could stand within them.

Five years ago, as Emma and Kierian dodged British Army patrols and Special Branch agents, she would have considered sleeping on a hay pile, in an empty barn absolute heaven. Now, she would be slumbering under silk and resting her head on pine-scented pillows.

She changed into a green brocade dinner gown. This time, she could not even wear a hat, though she was still able to slip the derringer under her garter.

Dinner was wonderfully delicious and elegant, the conversation, very pleasant.

This ended with dessert.

Kierian and Balthazar retired, with the rest of the men, to the Playhouse where they would play cards,

139

backgammon, chess, billiards, talk about politics, drink brandy, and smoke cigars.

Even Alice deserted her. She waved to Emma with a naughty grin on her face, as she snuck out the door with some handsome young thing. Emma was left to suffer insipid conversations about who was to marry whom, whether the next party in the social calendar would be a huge success or an utter disaster, and what new dressmaker was to be all the rage in New York City this summer.

Mostly though, she was ignored

She might be a guest of Alfred Vanderbilt's, but so were the rest of the Fifth Avenue clucking hens surrounding her. They were politely, but perspicuously, making it known that a woman who made her living jumping off cliffs into gorges, doing the Loop — de-Loop on a bicycle, or going over the Falls in a barrel, was not worthy of their notice.

The grandfather clock tolled the hour. Emma took a sip of her champagne. The front door opened, and Ambrose Russ hurried past her to a tall, golden haired lady a few years older than herself. The lady sported an athletic frame, an engaging face, and radiated intelligence and competence over beauty and grace. The purple evening dress she wore seemed out of place, and there was restlessness of spirit about her as her slender fingers nervously tapped the stem of her long, full champagne glass. Russ whispered into the lady's ear and she nodded. He turned and without delay, walked over to Emma. The blond lady followed.

"Miss Dareheart, this is Professor Veronica Stonechat. Would you please follow us to the Playhouse."

Emma tossed the remnants of her champagne into the fireplace. All at once, the flames flared upwards, unsettling the hens, and causing them to cluck their most ardent disapproval.

* * * * * *

The eight ball kissed off its third cushion and rolled slowly, across the burgundy Worston wool surface of the Playhouse's billiard table. The english on the ball spun it towards the leather mesh corner pocket. The two ball, the last of the solids on the table, sped on an intersection course towards the eight, missed it by less than a quarter inch, and headed for another corner pocket. The eyes of a swarthy dark-haired man flitted back and forth between the rolling billiard balls. If the eight dropped into the pocket first, he would be five hundred dollars richer and Kierian that much poorer. It

141

seemed a sure thing. The eight was ahead of the two ball and would reach its pocket first.

It did.

But it rattled between the corner of the two cushions, and while it rattled, the two ball rolled into its pocket. A half second later the eight dropped.

"Madre de Dios! I have never seen such...such luck!" The dark-haired man said and threw his arms wide in exasperation.

Kierian laughed boisterously and collected the pile of money from the side of the billiard table.

Emma smiled. Kierian was a damn shark at the pool table and she always enjoyed watching him play. In truth, he was not skilled enough to defeat a world champion like Alfredo De Oro, but whatever patch of four leaf clovers he was conceived in, once again, afforded luck enough for the day to be his.

Kierian raised his eyes, noticed her for the first time since she had entered the playhouse, inclined his head, smiled, and bowed to her.

"Senor McKenna," the man continued, "I do not mean to be impolite or disparage your skills, but you must admit, sir, those last few shots were more good fortune than good shooting."

"Good fortune or good shooting, the victory is still

142

mine, Mr. De Oro, as is your money." Kierian grinned folded the bills with a neat, crisp crease, and added them to his billfold.

Glass thudded against mahogany, drawing Emma's attention to the table where Dr. Waatt and Theodore Roosevelt sat playing a game of chess. "No, Non, nie, nai, niet, nein, Mr. Vice President," Doctor Waatt said. "How many ways must I say no to you, sir?" He moved his knight on the chessboard eliminating another of Theodore Roosevelt's pawns.

"Doctor, it is unpatriotic to withhold one's gifts when they could truly benefit one's country. Your inventions and genius could help create an American Empire that would rival, nay, even surpass, the British Empire."

"That is exactly what I fear, sir. No empire, no matter how benign its intent when founded, ever leads to anything but injustice and oppression."

"And yet you intervened on behalf of America when you destroyed the British Great Lakes Fleet."

"Of course I did! I love my country Mr. Vice President, and thus, I acted to save it when it was in peril. Likewise, because I love it, I will not feed the beast and allow it to turn, as Rome did, from a free republic into some bloated, oppressive empire!"

"An American empire would be a God-given blessing to the entire world, Doctor. Our chief exports would be capitalism and freedom, not tyranny and oppression."

"Indeed, and how would you go about that? If you model yourself on Rome or Britain, it will be by conquering others with the excuse that it is for their own good."

"America will be different, Doctor. We will not oppress. We will liberate."

"Different? Ha! Man's nature does not change, Mr. Roosevelt. You proclaim an American Empire would be a blessing from the Lord Himself, correct?"

"Indeed it would, sir."

"Very well. Let me then, explain to you the danger of that thinking. The empire is a God-given blessing. Therefore, those who oppose that blessing are fighting against God Himself, and are obviously wicked. Therefore, it is right and just for us to do our utmost to maintain the empire by whatever means are necessary." Dr. Waatt shook his head, a stony expression directed at Theodore Roosevelt.

"The British have been saying that for decades," Kierian said, retrieving a fresh ale from the barman.

"Indeed," Dr. Waatt said, "and it has enabled the

144

leaders of a strong and virtuous people to justify tyranny and oppression on whomever they conquer, whether they are Irish, Indian, Canadian, Boer or Americans."

"We are different, Doctor. This country was founded on freedom and liberty. Britain and Rome were not," Roosevelt said.

"Indeed, and so long as the Lord God allows me, I will make sure we remain a country of liberty and freedom. I will not, sir, be a party to my country's corruption!"

"Dr. Waatt, I must be forthright with you and tell you, there are some, 'voices,' in the government, who have advocated the seizure of your airship in the name of national security. I am not one of them, of course, but your continued refusal to share your inventions and knowledge, on any scale, give power to those voices."

Roosevelt kept his eyes on Dr. Waatt, moved his bishop, and took the Doctor's knight.

Balthazar Waatt slowly raised his head. The cauldron of his eyes burned with scalding fury at the Vice President of the United States. Neck veins rose tight against skin.

Emma rushed towards the table. The blazing eyes, the stern look, and the eerie silence signified a giant emotional volcano, grumbling for days and suddenly going quiet. Once it erupted, it would destroy all in its vicinity.

Dr. Waatt leaned forward; palms pressed against mahogany, knuckles knotted with anger. He rose slowly, his gaze never leaving the man who had just issued a veiled threat against him. Snow-white hair fluttered beneath the electric ceiling fan. A boney finger rose and jabbed like a dagger at Theodore Roosevelt.

"THE *EXCELSIOR* IS MY AIRSHIP AND MINE ALONE!" The blow his right fist delivered to the table echoed powerfully throughout the room. Heads turned and conversation stopped. A whiskey glass dropped and shattered.

Emma rushed up beside him, placed a hand on his fist, and gently patted it. Balthazar snapped his head around and glared at her.

Emma's eyes met his and offered supportive comfort. She tapped his hand again and smiled.

Doctor Waatt turned his gaze back to the Vice President and slowly descended into his chair.

"The *Excelsior's* secrets will remain known only to myself and to those I judge worthy to share them with," his voice became ice, cold and sharp as a scalpel, "and you may assure those 'voices in the government'

146

that *any* attempt to seize the *Excelsior*, or any of my personal property will have very grave consequences for those attempting such." Doctor Waatt moved his queen. "Very grave consequences, indeed."

CHAPTER TEN

A stony silence filled the room.

"By the by, I will checkmate you in three moves," Dr. Waatt said, breaking the silence.

"What? How can that be?" Theodore Roosevelt looked down and studied the chessboard.

"Don't feel bad, Theodore," Kierian encouraged. "You lasted longer than most."

Kierian walked past the Vice President. His polished dress shoes echoed on the cherry wood floor. He leaned across the mahogany billiard table and placed six billiard balls in set positions as the rest of the room returned to their conversations and activities.

"What about you, Kierian? Have you ever emerged victorious against Dr. Waatt in a game of chess?"

"Of course I have!" Kierian said, a smug smile on his face. He picked up his glass of beer, took a sip, and placed it on the pool table in front of the nine ball and the right corner pocket.

148

"You defeated me once, Kierian, and with that ridiculous Celtic gambit of yours! By my calculations, your record stands at one win and one hundred and seven losses. That is certainly nothing to be gloating about," Doctor Waatt snorted.

"It was Uncle Seamus's Irish Gambit, Balthazar, and the fact it was my singular victory does not detract from the cunning and spectacular way I achieved it."

"A win is a win, Kierian, and a loss is a loss. No extra points are awarded for style," Dr. Waatt said.

"I must agree with Dr. Waatt, Kierian," Roosevelt replied. "Have you not heard the saying that winning isn't everything, it is the only thing?"

"I have a saying too," Kierian said. He chalked his cue stick and lined up his shot. "The thrill isn't in the winning..." he pulled back his cue stick and drove it forward. The billiard balls scattered across the table, each ball plunging into a different pocket. The cue ball struck three cushions and slowly rolled towards Kierian's beer..."It's in the doing."

He picked up his glass just before the cue ball reached it and smiled as the cue ball gently kissed the nine, knocking it into the right corner pocket.

"Bravo! Bravo, Mister McKenna!" Emma said. The other men in the playhouse applauded. Alfredo De Oro

149

shook his head with contempt.

"Kierian, do you know the chances of finding balls in those exact positions for a shot, during an actual game?" Doctor Waatt said.

"No, I do not, but I think the chances of impressing the hell out of people with it is approximately one hundred percent!"

Emma laughed and walked over to stand by Kierian, confident the explosion of Mount Waatt had been averted.

"Dr. Waatt, Mr. McKenna, may I introduce Professor of Archeology, Miss Veronica Stonechat," Ambrose Russ said abruptly.

Dr. Waatt rose to his feet and bowed to the tall, blonde lady. "It is a pleasure to meet your acquaintance, Miss, er-Professor Stonechat. I am Doctor Balthazar Waatt."

"The honor is all mine, Doctor Waatt," Professor Stonechat replied, "I observed the *Excelsior* land earlier. It is a most impressive airship, to be sure."

"Perhaps you would like a tour sometime, under my personal direction," Doctor Waatt said.

"Now, why would he give her a tour and not me?" Theodore Roosevelt said, in protest to no one in particular.

"When you can fill out an evening dress just as well, I am sure Doctor Waatt will oblige you," Emma said.

"Ladies and gentleman," Russ announced to the entire room, "if you would follow me into the adjoining room, Mr. Edison will exhibit for us, several of his new moving pictures-with sound!"

Murmurs of excitement filled the playhouse.

Russ led the way into the next room where Thomas Edison stood fiddling with his projector and the attached phonograph. Several cans of film were stacked on a nearby table. Once everyone had taken their seats, the lighting was diminished, and Edison started his first film, *The Great Train Robbery*.

Emma marveled at the film, and was so engrossed she jumped when Kierian touched her shoulder, and motioned his head, indicating it was time for them to make a discreet exit.

They walked out of the room, following Ambrose Russ to an office. "Couldn't we have waited until the second film began?"

Kierian smiled. "Duty calls, I am afraid, Miss Dareheart, but I promise to personally accompany you to a nickelodeon for a private viewing when all is said and done. I'll even provide the drinks and purchase the

151

cracker jacks."

Emma's cheeks glowed. "I will hold you to that promise, Mr. McKenna."

* * * * * *

The last time Emma had seen Alfred Vanderbilt, he was every bit the youthful playboy with a constant smile on his face and nary a care in the world. Now, he stood in front of an enormous, green-oak desk in his study, pale and gaunt, wearing a world-weary frown.

"Kierian, thank God you are here," Alfred said, and pumped Kierian's hand several times. "And Emma—" Alfred walked over and kissed her hand. "Dear Emma, thank you for coming to my aid with such haste. I apologize for all the cloak and dagger, but I could take no chances with Gladys's life."

"No need for apologies, Alfred," Kierian said.

"If word of her abduction had leaked to the press and something dreadful had befallen her, I could never have forgiven myself." Alfred leaned back against the desk, brought a hand to his forehead, and sighed.

"All will be well, Alfred," Emma said. "Worry not."

"STEAMCAPP, is not without experience in these situations," Kierian said. "We will return your beloved sister to you, safe and sound."

"STEAMCAPP?" Professor Stonechat asked.

"It is an acronym," Dr. Waatt explained, "for the name of our business. Mr. McKenna conjured it up with his over-active imagination."

Kierian smiled with pride. "It stands for Special Tactics and Extraordinary Adventurers Management Consultation And Protection Partnership."

"I see."

"And I trust you will agree, it is a much more attractive moniker than the American Adventurers Association, which was what the good Doctor had proposed as the initial name for our partnership."

"It would have placed us first on the list of *every* business directory, Kierian. Your predilection of appearance over practicality will cost us customers; mark my words."

"In any case," Emma said, casting a disapproving look at her quarreling partners, "There is no cause for anxiety, Alfred."

A gruff voice interjected from across the room. "That is too much confidence, when you do not know the situation, Miss Dareheart."

Emma turned her head and followed the voice. For the first time she noticed a man stretched out on a black leather couch, his head propped up by a pillow. He was middle aged and attired in an exquisitely tailored evening suit. His skin was pale. He wore a bushy mustache with a thin, pointed beard on his chin. His left arm was bandaged and rested in a sling. His brown eyes were captivating and strangely compelling. So much so, that Emma found it difficult to avert her gaze.

"Suppose you enlighten us on exactly what the situation is Mister...?" Kierian said.

"Boaltt. Professor S.J. Boaltt. I was with the expedition when it was attacked by the anarchists." Boaltt pushed himself up to a sitting position.

"Professor," Kierian said, "before we continue, I must say, that is a beautifully tailored set of clothes you are wearing. Grieves and Hawks, One Seville Row, London, if I am not mistaken."

Ambrose Russ chuckled. "Indeed, you are mistaken, Mr. McKenna. The Professor's clothes are from Beck And Stien Bespoke on West 39th street, New York City."

Kierian shook his head. "No, I do not think so. The stitching, material, and cut of the trousers, clearly is from Grieves and Hawks. I may be less than expert about a few things, but men's fashions is not one of them."

"Mr. McKenna, you are embarrassing yourself, sir," Ambrose Russ chuckled. "Professor Boaltt emerged from the forest with a pack over his shoulder, and his clothes in tatters. I lent him the suit he is wearing, and I know where I had it fitted."

"He is right, Mr. McKenna," Professor Boaltt replied. "This is the same suit Mr. Russ gave me. If he says it is from New York City then so it is."

"Is that a fact?" Kierian said. He pulled a cigar from his silver case, cut off the end, and lit it.

Emma watched Kierian take a puff from his cigar. Clearly, he felt he was being both lied to and insulted, possibly by someone trying to hide his British affiliation.

And she knew he was not about to let that stand.

A smoke ring blown just over your right ear, professor, is on the way.

Kierian pursed his lips.

"Mr. McKenna!" Dr. Waatt said. Kierian turned towards Balthazar, who shook his head ever so slightly, discreetly discouraging the act and the more aggressive stance Kierian was about to take. "We have more important things to discuss than what tailor the Professor uses."

Bright orbs of aggregated blue glared at Dr. Waatt momentarily. Kierian raised an eyebrow, dispatched a smoke ring past his partner's left ear, turned to the bar,

155

and poured himself a glass of Thorton's Irish whiskey.

Dr. Waatt crossed the room and shook Boaltt's hand.

Boaltt winced at the pressure of the handshake.

Dr. Waatt turned the man's hand over. Blisters blanketed the lower palm to finger joints. "Goodness, your hand is thoroughly blistered."

"An occupational hazard when one is working at an archeological dig site, I'm afraid."

Dr. Waatt nodded. "Of course, of course. I presume you injured your arm during the attack?"

"Indeed, one of the blackguards stabbed me with a bayonet as I tried to protect Miss Vanderbilt."

"A most valiant effort, to be sure." Doctor Waatt gently touched Boaltt's injured arm. "May I, Professor?"

"I would rather you not, sir. I—"

Doctor Waatt unwrapped the bandage with care, removed Professor Boaltt's arm from the sling, and peeled back the bandage.

"Sir, please—"

"Tut, tut, sir, worry not. I am a doctor, after all."

He retrieved a magnifying glass from his coat pocket and examined the wound for several seconds.

Boaltt snatched a glass of water from an end table

and chugged it empty. "Your reputation as a genius and inventor precedes you, Dr. Waatt, but I was not aware you were a medical doctor."

"I am not. My formal degree is in engineering, but I am schooled in many subjects, well beyond the knowledge of any presently in this room."

"I would not trust a medical doctor to design a machine. Why should I trust an engineer to examine my wound?" Boaltt asked.

"Because the human body is nothing more or less than a marvelously designed, complex biological machine."

"Designed Doctor? Mr. Darwin would disagree with you, sir," Ambrose Russ said, from across the room.

"Mr. Darwin's theory is incorrect. For it is founded on the principle that the single cell is a simple machine, when in fact, it most definitely is not."

Doctor Waatt continued to peer at the wound, nodded, re-wrapped the bandage, and placed the professor's arm back in the sling.

"That is a nasty wound, to be sure. Be certain to keep it clean and change the bandages daily. Now sir, pray, tell us your tale, and enlighten us as to the situation as you know it."

157

Doctor Waatt sat down in a leather chair, pulled out a small notebook, a pencil, and gave his full attention to the only witness of the abduction of Gladys Vanderbilt.

"Very well, Doctor. I was conferring with Professor Bridgewater at the dig site, when there was a sudden tumult. The ground trembled beneath our feet. There were cries of distress from the workers and then, the unmistakable sound of gun shots." Professor Boaltt paused and held up his empty water glass. "May I have another, Mr. Russ, I have a terrible thirst."

Russ poured another glass of mineral water, and handed it to Boaltt, who drained the contents before continuing.

"After the shots were heard, Miss Vanderbilt ran to us for succor and then… it appeared."

"What appeared, Professor?" Dr. Waatt asked.

Professor Boaltt leaned forward, and locked his eyes on Dr. Waatt.

"An iron beast! The likes of which, I wager, you have never seen before, Dr. Waatt. It had the appearance of a man and walked on two legs, but was built of iron. Steam rose into the air from its back, on its left arm was a large Maxim machine gun, and from its right arm a Livens flame projector blasted great sheets of hellfire. It killed all who opposed it."

158

"But yourself, Professor Bridgewater, and Miss Vanderbilt survived?" Dr. Waatt asked.

"Professor Bridgewater and I offered no resistance. Miss Vanderbilt fled but was hunted down and captured by the iron beast."

"What were the attackers' numbers?"

"I would say about two dozen. They were armed with rifles, pistols, and an assortment of other weapons."

Dr. Waatt made a few notations in his book. "I see, pray continue your narrative, Professor."

"After her capture, one of the villains seized Miss Vanderbilt in a most violent manner, and I sprang to the young Miss's defense. It was then I was knocked to the ground and stabbed."

"A truly horrifying ordeal," Emma said.

"Yes and it was not over, Miss Dareheart. Our hands were bound and we were force-marched, about three miles through the forest to their campsite. After a few hours, their leader, a man who called himself Blackwell, approached me. I was then separated from the others, so I could deliver their ransom demands."

"Which you did, and presumably, that hazardous hike is what tore your clothes to tatters?"

"Yes, doctor. I became lost several times and had to

159

bushwhack my way to the main trail. The thick under-brush of the Adirondack forests will cut anyone's clothes asunder in such circumstances."

"Unless, of course, they are competent and know what the hell they are doing," Kierian said.

Dr. Waatt glared at Kierian. The dapper soldier-of-fortune shrugged and sipped his whiskey.

"What are the ransom demands?" Dr. Waatt inquired. Alfred Vanderbilt handed a sheet of paper to Dr. Waatt. "One million dollars in silver and the presence and assistance of Professor Veronica Stonechat."

"Good heavens! What ever do they want with me?" Professor Stonechat asked.

"They have what appears to be an ancient artifact, with Algonquin symbols upon it," Boaltt replied. "Blackwell demanded Professor Bridgewater translate the symbols but alas, he could not. They tortured him in unspeakable ways, trying with the most devilish intent, to persuade him to translate the symbols, all to no avail. Finally, he revealed that Professor Veronica Stonechat could interpret the symbols, and that she was due to join the expedition in a few days time. I was instructed to return personally, with the silver and Professor Stonechat no later than the 29th of August."

"That is two days from now," Emma said.

Dr. Waatt nodded and jotted down a few more notes. "What, pray tell, was the focus of Professor Bridgewater's expedition?"

"He was investigating the possibility that Europeans had reached America hundreds of years before Columbus."

"Indeed. What was his theory, exactly?"

Professor Boaltt hesitated for a brief second, readjusted his position, cleared his throat, and pulled down on his dinner jacket. He opened his mouth to speak, but it was Professor Stonechat who answered.

"He was following up on the legend of St. Brendan the Navigator, Doctor."

"St. Brendan?" Emma asked.

"Yes, Miss Dareheart; there are several ancient texts that record a voyage made by an Irish monk named Brendan to 'The Island of Paradise' hundreds of years before Columbus made his famous voyage of discovery."

"New York State is not an island, Professor Stonechat," Dr. Waatt replied.

"True, and much of the text has been dismissed as fanciful. However, Professor Bridgewater held to a theory that while the 'island' most likely was a myth, the discovery of unknown lands was not, and there are

161

several intriguing descriptions within other texts that may support his theory."

"Like what, exactly?" Emma asked.

"Columbus himself marked Brendan's Island on his maps, and the Norse, who we know were in New-foundland around 1000 A.D., referred to lands south of their settlement in Vinland as 'Irland it Mikla' or 'Greater Ireland.'" Veronica Stonechat's cheeks flushed with excitement. She glanced around the room before continuing her lecture.

"Further, the amazing wonders described in the text, though almost certainly exaggerated, could be sign posts of a route between Ireland and North America; a route very similar to the one the Vikings took. For ex-ample, the crystal pillars in the ocean could refer to ice bergs, the giant sheep he mentions could be the large breed of sheep that have been discovered on the Faroe islands, and the fireballs thrown by giants that smelled like rotten eggs may refer to sulfur dioxide from Ice-landic volcanic activity. Also…"

"Professor Stonechat!" Alfred Vanderbilt interrupt-ed. "Professor Stonechat, please! While I am sure this is a fascinating topic of study, I fail to see how it aids in the recovery of my sister."

"I must disagree, Mr. Vanderbilt," Doctor Waatt

said, "According to Professor Boaltt, the men who abducted your sister are in possession of an artifact that is so important, they included bringing Professor Stonechat to them in order to translate it, as a ransom demand. A demand on equal footing with their demand for one million dollars in silver."

Vanderbilt tapped a pencil atop the enormous desk. After a few moments, he nodded. "Perhaps you are correct, Doctor."

Doctor Waatt nodded. "I am. Every detail we can glean regarding the situation may prove critical in the success of our mission." He paused and drained his brandy. "However, perhaps it would be best, Professor Stonechat, if we moved forward to the part of Professor Bridgewater's theory that you were to aid in proving."

"Very well, Doctor, as you wish. My expertise is in Pre-Columbian Indigenous cultures and ancient Celtic languages. Professor Bridgewater was investigating Algonquin symbols that may indicate that the Algonquin, near what is now the Canadian border, captured Europeans. The semi-nomadic Algonquians or so Professor Bridgewater's theory went, transported the captives to a location, which the Algonquin called 'Makwa Inin Machicomuc.'"

"Indeed. I was not aware the Algonquin or the Iroquois settled in the Adirondacks. Rather, I was under the impression it was largely used as a hunting ground."

"You are correct, Doctor. However, "Makwa Inin Machicomuc" translated into English means: Temple of the Bear. Therefore, it was most likely not a settlement but a ritual site."

"I see."

"This would have occurred during the time of St. Brendan's voyage based on the seriation of artifacts identified in context with a certain remarkable stone tablet. The tablet in question apparently contains inscriptions that tell a strange tale involving blue-eyed, white-skinned people. I haven't seen it myself yet to verify its authenticity, or to translate the symbols, but when Professor Bridgewater wired me, I felt I had to come see it for myself."

"I see, and when exactly did Professor Bridgewater wire you?"

"August 21st."

"Indeed? Yet, you were still not present five days later when the exhibition was attacked?"

"I was delayed due to a...personal matter. When free to finally travel, I was intercepted by Mr. Vanderbilt's people and escorted here."

Dr. Waatt nodded. "Professor Boaltt, at what point did you become aware of Miss Vanderbilt's identity?"

"Oh, I was aware from the beginning. Professor Bridgewater confided her secret to me at the start of the expedition."

"I see. Thank you, Professor Boaltt. Mr. Vanderbilt, I trust you were able to raise the ransom?"

"It was not easy, Dr. Waatt. One million in silver is harder to come by now that we are solely on the gold standard," Alfred Vanderbilt said.

"Surely, you had reserves you could transport here by rail," Emma said.

"Professor Boaltt pointed out that any mass transport of silver would attract too much attention and put the news hounds hot on our trail," Alfred replied. "He also cleverly suggested we melt down every last silver object we possessed here at Sagamore. Fortunately, we had just enough to cross the million dollar threshold and pay for Gladys's release."

"Why did they ask for payment in silver when it no longer can be used for currency?" Emma asked.

"I am afraid you are in error, Miss Dareheart," Kierian said. His voice was somber, and lacked the usual charming lilt. "Silver still can be used for currency." He took a puff on his cigar and exhaled. "...In British

165

Canada."

A grim silence filled the room, as everyone took stock of the implications Kierian was suggesting.

It was one thing for the SSB to take a stab at abducting two recently pardoned freedom fighters.

It was quite another matter altogether, to abduct and hold for ransom, the fifteen-year-old sister of the wealthiest man in America. The same man who owned one hundred percent of the world's helium, and who provided it exclusively to the American Air fleet. Tensions were still high between the two countries; there was deep bitterness on both sides of the border, especially in New York, and other northern states that had felt the British Lion's vicious bite.

Both sides of the border were heavily armed. Forts and coastal defenses dotted Lake Ontario and airships patrolled their respective air spaces aggressively.

"If this was a British assisted operation, it would surely lead to intense saber rattling between both sides, at the very least," Russ said.

"Saber rattling often produces sparks, Mr. Russ. The kind of sparks that lead to war," Emma added.

"Let us hope not, Miss Dareheart. For I fear this time, it would not just be an America and British affair," Russ replied.

"What do you mean?" Professor Stonechat asked.

"We are close to a mutual defense pact with Imperial Germany. The Kaiser would no doubt come to our aid if hostilities are renewed, especially if we offered to lease them helium for their own airship fleets," Russ explained.

"And then the John Bulls would call in their alliance with France, and Russia," Kierian explained.

Russ nodded. "The entire world would be at war."

"Good Lord! A world at war!" Professor Stonechat exclaimed. "What a ghastly thought!"

"Let us pray it does not come to that," Dr. Waatt said. "Mr. Vanderbilt, if you will be so kind as to bring us the most accurate topographical maps you possess and place them on your desk."

"I have them right here, Doctor." Alfred Vanderbilt unrolled the requested map, spread it across his desk, and anchored the corners with four gold paperweights.

"Professor Boaltt, if you would be good enough to show us on the map, the area where all this took place," Doctor Watt said.

Professor Boaltt stood, walked to the desk, leaned over the map for a moment, and placed a long index finger near a large round body of water.

"That is it. Reese Lake. There is an island in the cen-

167

ter of the lake and that is where the exchange is to take place. "

"And the abductor's camp and the dig site?" Doctor Waatt asked.

"The Anarchist's camp is about three miles north of the lake, and the dig site, three miles north of that."

Doctor Waatt nodded, looked over the maps and rested his chin atop his cane for several seconds in contemplation.

"Thank you both. That is all the questions I have for you at present," Doctor Waatt said abruptly. He waved his hand in the air. "You are dismissed."

"Now, see here Doctor, I am not some servant who may be ordered to come and go at your good pleasure!" Professor Boaltt replied.

"I must agree, Doctor," Professor Stonechat said. "Since we both will be coming along on the journey, I think we should share in the planning of it."

"Professor Stonechat, Professor Boaltt," Emma said, her voice soft and disarming. "Doctor Waatt meant no disrespect. I am sure your input will be crucial to our success, and we certainly will not hide our plans from you. However, the three of us have a routine that we are accustomed to when planning operations, and there are certain details about equipment and technology

168

that must remain undisclosed."

"I suppose that is understandable," Professor Boaltt said. Emma held her smile at his words, even though by his tone she doubted he was completely mollified.

Professor Boaltt slowly stood and made his way out of the study, followed by Veronica Stonechat.

"Is there anything I can get you, Doctor?" Alfred Vanderbilt asked.

"Indeed. If you will be so good as to bring a pot of your strongest and most excellent coffee; Mr. McKenna, Miss Dareheart and I will develop a sound stratagem to deal with the abductors, their mechanized monster, and most importantly, bring about the safe return of your sister Gladys."

CHAPTER ELEVEN

Wednesday. 7:30 AM

August 28 1901

Anarchist Camp

3 miles northof Reese Lake

"What's the matter, Duchess? The grub not to your liking?"

Gladys Vanderbilt looked up from her tin plate. The rich red glow of embers, mixed musky, with the sweet scent of fresh pine needles in the morning air. "I am not hungry at present, Mr. Chaney."

"*I am not hungry*," Chaney mocked. The brutish pilot of the iron beast sat by the campfire. Aimlessly, he whittled a piece of wood.

"Brothers, the Duchess over here deigns not to eat our food. She says she is 'not hungry!'"

The anarchists around the camp responded with

quiet cackles.

Chaney stood up, walked around the fire, and dropped to a squat in front of Gladys. Filthy, aggressive hands tapped out hate upon her tin plate with the point of his blood stained hunting knife. "You know what this meal is called, Duchess?"

Gladys smelled danger as clearly as she smelled the rotgut hooch on Chaney's breath. She looked down at the beans, rice, and biscuit on the plate. "I would assume from the time of day, it is called breakfast."

Chaney scowled at her. "You assume wrong, Duchess. It's called the workman's feast. Beans, rice, and a biscuit; that's a goddamn feast to the laborers that toil away in the factories and mines, you and your family own. None of them ever have the luxury of saying: *I am not hungry*." Chaney waved the glistening crimson stinger in Gladys's face. "The working man is hungry all the time and you know why that is?"

"I assume, from the lectures I have previously received from you, through some fault other than their own?"

Chaney's eyes grew hot with hate. His face reddened, his lips curled in contempt.

Gladys returned the hard stare, swallowing the fear that her remark might bring, yet another slap across her

171

face.

For five days now, she had been a prisoner. For three of those days, she had played it safe, keeping her mouth shut as these hard, violent men raged on about how justified they were in the slaughter of innocents, and how all the ills of society were the fault of the "titans of industry."

By the fourth day, she had swallowed all the pride she could and sparked back with arguments and words that they did not wish to hear. The backhands and cuffs to her face and ears were painful but less so than remaining quiet, while her family was shamefully disparaged.

She was a Vanderbilt after all, and young though she might be, Vanderbilts did not remain silent in the face of adversity.

Chaney whittled deep into the wood with his knife. Splinters flew into her face.

"The slave wages your family pays are not near enough for the workers to live on. You buy what you can from the company store because you aren't allowed to buy from nowheres else. You feed the wife and kiddies first and then, eat what's leftover, which is never enough."

"Why take the job if the wages do not pay enough

to even subsist upon? That seems most unwise."

"Because if you don't take it, someone else will. Because the little ones are crying at night, and the wife looking at you with pleading eyes, expecting you to provide. But you and your family wouldn't know anything about that. Would they, Duchess?"

"My family," Gladys said, her voice becoming louder and more defiant, "created its wealth through hard work, Mr. Chaney. My great grandfather borrowed one hundred dollars to start his first ferry business. He transported passengers and cargo between Staten Island and Manhattan, and worked sixteen hour days."

"Well bully for him!" Chaney whittled intensely. Each stroke of the knife cut deep into the wood, sending larger splinters in Gladys direction.

Gladys dodged two of the large chips. "It was through his energy and industriousness that he made his fortune. My family's wealth was not inherited, Mr. Chaney, nor was it found at the end of a rainbow, nor did the stork bring it."

"Industriousness, huh? What are you saying? The working man is a lazy lout?"

"I said nothing of the kind, Mr. Chaney. Indeed, I think it was YOU who implied my family was such."

173

Chaney scowled. Hate reflected off him in waves. His knife cut hard into the wood and he muttered something under his breadth. Violent hands tossed the branch into the campfire.

"My wife was industrious, Duchess. She worked in a shirtwaist factory making blouses. The boss man demanded she work twelve-hour days with no breaks, and at hell for leather speed at the sewing machines. Poor Shirley did as she was told, and tired with exhaustion one day, she sliced two fingers clean off!"

"How awful!" Gladys reached down, picked up her plate, gripped the two-pronged fork, and held it discreetly at her side.

"You know what those bosses did, Duchess?" Chaney pointed his knife at Gladys. "They fired Shirley. They said a worker minus two fingers weren't good for nothing! So they fired her and hired another. Just tossed her aside like a disposable part of a machine and replaced her with a new one."

"I am sorry such injustice was visited upon your wife, Mr. Chaney."

"Sorry? Yeah. I bet you're real sorry. Maybe if I slice a few of your fingers off, you'll be even sorrier!"

Chaney lurched forward, grabbed Gladys's wrist and brought the knife to her middle finger.

174

With all her might, Gladys drove the fork into the brute's meaty shoulder, and immediately ripped it free.

Chaney bellowed in pain and lurched towards her. Gladys slammed the tin plate of food into his face and pushed her attacker hard in the chest, unbalancing him.

Unsteady legs stumbled backwards, tripped over a log, and fell into the fire. Two men rushed to prevent Chaney's conflagration and patted out the flames.

Brutal hate and bloody intent blazed in Chaney's bloodshot eyes. Spittle flew from his mouth with every word. "You stabbed me! You little bitch! You stabbed me!"

Gladys gripped the fork tight and held it high at the ready. "I grew up with several brothers, Mr. Chaney, and they taught me painfully well, how to play rough with the boys!"

"I'll kill you, Duchess, and I'm going to do it slow-like, too. I'll bleed you out like a stuck pig!"

"Chaney! Stand down!" The voice was from Barnabas Blackwell. Chaney spun his head and glared at his boss. Blackwell held his electricity pistol pointed at Chaney's chest.

Chaney licked his lips. Cautious eyes stared across the fire at the deadly device.

"The bitch stabbed me, Barnabas!"

175

"Good thing she did, otherwise, I would have had to shoot you with Ol' Sparky here."

"I wasn't going to kill her, just do a bit of…of carving. Make her feel what Shirley felt. Give her some education."

"I said, stand down, Chaney! There will be no carving. We need Miss Vanderbilt in one piece right now, and I'm not going to lose a million in silver for the Brotherhood because you want to sate your blood lust. Now, go get your shoulder looked at by Doctor Neil."

Chaney picked up a clump of dirt, and threw it at Gladys. "You'll get what's coming to you, Duchess, once the ransom's paid! You and all your kind! We got a plan that will fix you all, and soon enough too!" Chaney spit at her and stormed away.

Blackwell watched Chaney make his exit; his pistol covered the angry anarchist, until he was out of view.

"You shouldn't argue with Chaney, Miss Vanderbilt. He has less self control than most."

Gladys sat back down and set the fork on the log next to her. "I do not think any of you have any self control, Mr. Blackwell. I saw what happened. You butchered over a hundred and twenty innocent men and women."

Blackwell holstered his pistol. "There are no inno-

176

cent bourgeois, Miss Vanderbilt. Those who do not stand up to elites, stand with them. Soon, everyone will understand that fact. The days of the working class lapping up the crumbs you elites throw to us are over."

"You sound no different from Mr. Chaney."

"Why should I? We are both part of the Brotherhood. The difference is that I understand that your well being at present is paramount to the success of my part of the mission. One million in silver will buy a lot of guns and dynamite."

"I see, and so that is what you will purchase from British Canada; bullets and bombs? What of all this grand talk of helping poor starving families? You could relieve so much of their suffering, rather than spend it on implements of violence and destruction."

"That is just the kind of short sighted thinking that has hampered our movement for years. Fortunately, we now have new leaders, men and women of action! We are at war, Miss Vanderbilt, and in war, sacrifices must be made."

"I suppose then, I shall be one of those sacrifices, and you shall kill me after you have the ransom you have demanded."

Blackwell smiled. "That depends."

"Depends on what?"

"On how cooperative you are. In the meantime, I'd suggest you cease with your elitist propaganda when arguing with the brothers, because as of right now," Blackwell grabbed the fork off the log and sneered at Gladys. "Once that ransom is paid, they'll tear you apart and leave your prissy little body for the wolves to chew on."

* * * * * *

Wednesday, 8:30 AM
August 28th
The Church Of The Twelve Apostles

Ambrose Russ stood in the back of Twelve Apostles Church, flipped his gold pocket watch shut and frowned. Manicured fingers gestured towards the front pew where Dr. Waatt knelt, his white-haired head bowed in solemn prayer.

"This is intolerable, simply intolerable. How long is he going to remain in that damn pew?"

"A man's time alone with the Lord, should not be hurried, Mr. Russ," Father Doyle said, in a practiced and patient voice.

"In this case, it damn well should be! We are embarking on an important mission. Lives are at stake,

178

Father! The later we get underway, the more those lives will be imperiled."

"The Lord honors the ways of a man who honors Him, Mr. Russ. Would it not profit the mission to have the Lord on your side?"

Russ rolled his eyes. Religion certainly, had its place in society. Dosages of spiritual laudanum did well to dull the pain of the beasts of burden that had not the intellectual capabilities or the breeding to keep the world's wheels of progress in motion, but applying its principles to affect actual daily life was dangerous and absurd.

"He's been in there for twenty-five minutes and has been as still as these two statues." Russ motioned to the two marble angels holding basins of holy water in their hands. "Perhaps, he has fallen asleep. You should go rouse him, Father."

"Dr. Waatt gave explicit instructions that he was not to be disturbed, Mr. Russ. I must honor his wishes."

"I would do it myself of course, but I am unsure of how his...metal man will respond." Russ pointed with his walking cane to the bronze robot that sat in the pew behind Dr. Waatt. "Miss Dareheart said it literally has a mind of its own."

Father Doyle nodded. "I must admit that its pres-

179

ence is a bit disconcerting to me as well, but Dr. Waatt assured me there was nothing to fear, and that his robot is a Rescue Automaton. He apparently built it to aid people not harm them."

Russ tapped his ringed finger on the top of his cane. "Then perhaps, I will risk it. If Waatt has fallen asleep who knows how much time we will waste standing here."

Russ walked with a brisk, confident gait, into the main sanctuary and approached Dr. Waatt from behind. The robot's head suddenly rotated one hundred and eighty degrees and stared at Russ. It stood. Its heavy metal feet stalked to the aisle, paused, and brought its body into alignment with its head. The robot clunked toward Russ and blocked his path.

Russ squeezed a worried hand tightly around his walking stick. The robot stood seven feet in height. His head was oval, bronze, and it wore finely tailored buck-skin leggings, a blue western style scout shirt, buckskin coat and a silk red bandana around its neck. In its hand, it gripped a pith helmet, while around its midsection, sat a black equipment belt. An enormous backpack completed its outfit.

"Stand aside, robot," Russ commanded in the same tone he used when ordering servants out of his way.

The robot blinked its round yellow metal orbs at Russ and stood its ground.

"I said, stand aside. I would have words with your Master."

The robot did not move. It stood in the aisle and blinked at Russ.

"Impertinent metal man! If you will not move out of my way, I shall move out of yours." Russ took a step to the robot's left, but the robot sidestepped, blocking Russ's end around.

Russ moved back to the right.

The robot blocked again.

Back to the left.

The robot sidestepped and blocked.

"Stop that!"

The corner of the robot's lips turned upward into a smile. It pulled a yo-yo from its equipment belt and began to bob the toy up and down.

Russ's face reddened. "Now, see here you, arrogant automaton! I am Ambrose Russ. I come from one of the finest families in New York. I am the Vanderbilt's family lawyer and I will not be ignored. I insist that you step aside!"

The robot smiled, stepped back, and hurled the yo-yo, at Russ's face.

Russ's eyes went wide as saucers. He flung his hand up, like a fan, to shield himself. When the yo-yo was less than an inch from his face, the robot pulled it back into his brass hand, opened his mouth, and bobbed his metal jaw up and down in a silent laugh.

Deep, crimson anger overlaid the well-bred face of Ambrose Russ. "Why you, piston-powered prankster! Dr. Waatt! Dr. Waatt! Will you please tell your mechanical manservant to get out of my way? I would have a word with you."

Dr. Waatt remained motionless, his head bowed and fingers locked together.

"Unacceptable! Completely unacceptable!" Russ said. He glared up at the smiling robot, shook his head, spun on his heels, and stormed back to Father Doyle at the back of the church.

The robot waved to Russ and resumed his place in the pew, behind Dr. Waatt.

Five minutes passed before the sound of the great hymn, *Nearer My God to Thee,* emanated from Dr. Waatt's watch. At once he rose, took up his cane, and glanced around the sanctuary. He limped around the pews and studied each of the magnificent stained glass windows, before joining Russ and Father Doyle at the back of the church. The bronze robot dutifully followed behind.

"Finally!" Russ said.

Dr. Waatt cast an annoyed eye at Russ.

"Reverend Doyle," Dr. Waatt began, "I am intrigued with the stained glass windows of your church. They seem to portray twelve different men who I assume, based on the name of your church, to be the Twelve Apostles of Christ, but I have never seen them portrayed as they are in your windows."

Father Doyle smiled. "I am glad another besides myself, has noticed. I have often found it strange that not only are there no names upon the glass to identify each individual apostle, but all lack the traditional identifying attributes usually portrayed with them in western art."

Dr. Waatt nodded. "Indeed, the Apostle I surmise to be Simon Peter, has not the keys to the kingdom he is normally portrayed with; instead there is a picture of a boat in the right corner, no doubt a reference to his occupation as a fisherman."

"I agree, and the window portraying St. Paul, shows a ship wrecking upon rocks. While the Bible does indeed, speak of Paul being shipwrecked, I have not known it to accompany any portraits of the Apostle to the Gentiles," Doyle said.

183

Dr. Waatt nodded. "What does the cow represent in the second window? The one with the man playing the harp?"

"I believe the harp represents the Apostles' entrance into heaven as a martyr. As to the cow?" Father Doyle shrugged. "I really cannot say."

"Have you any theories as to why the artist deviated from the traditional portrayals?"

"Only that the artist was, perhaps, not himself Catholic and choose not to include any references to Catholic tradition."

Dr. Waatt tapped his index finger against his boney chin and pondered the priest's words. "Exactly how old *is* your church?"

"Very old. Tradition says, it was originally a missionary camp for French Jesuits in their attempt to convert the Algonquians, but how old it actually is I cannot say. About seventy-five years ago, a fire destroyed most of the early church records. Only a silver tipped arrow and few pages of an anonymously authored journal, written in an unknown language survived."

"A silver tipped arrow? How odd."

"It is thought to be a gift from an Algonquin Chief, who converted to Christianity.

"In regards to the unknown language of the journal,

have you considered it may be a code?

Father Doyle nodded. "I used to think it was too, but Professor Bridgewater, the noted archeologist, was certain it was a language. He seemed quite exhilarated when I showed him the pages."

Dr. Waatt raised an eyebrow at the mention of the archeologist's name. "Professor Bridgewater was here?"

"Why, yes. He is conducting a dig north of here and stopped by the church on his way."

"Intriguing. Was there anything he took an interest in, besides the journal?"

"As a matter of fact, there was. Like you, he was fascinated by the unorthodox symbols on the stain glass windows, as well as the field of Red Shamrocks, surrounding the church." Father Doyle motioned toward the flowers, "You know they are not native to the Adirondacks."

Dr. Waatt nodded.

"Dr. Waatt," Russ began, "if you are finished with the church history lesson and your communing with the Almighty, I would suggest in the strongest of terms, that you get on with your mission."

Dr. Waatt turned and locked eyes on Russ.

"Mr. Russ, I find your impatience and lack of faith

185

most distressing."

"It distresses me that a man of science like yourself, still believes in these ancient superstitions," Russ retorted.

Dr. Waatt reached into his coat pocket and pulled forth his watch. "Mr. Russ, is this man-made, or did it bloom from nature?"

"Clearly, it is made by a watchmaker." Russ replied.

"Correct and yet, you would have me believe that this entire planet, and its eco-system, and the laws of gravity and thermodynamics, for example, that we find in science just bloomed into being on chance?" Dr. Waatt shook his head. "No, Mr. Russ; it is precisely because I *am* a man of science that I must follow the data and believe the evidence for a creator when I encounter it. Yesterday, I landed my airship in that Creator's church field. The least I can do is spend half an hour paying my respects."

Dr. Waatt pushed past Russ, and exited the church. His bronze robot followed. It stopped on the church step, spun its head around, and stuck out a metal tongue at Ambrose Russ.

* * * * * *

Emma sat at the picnic table and checked he face in the mirror of her theatrical make-up kit. *Excelsior* loomed majestically in the background; its Sikh security detail, still holding their security perimeter.

She deliberately avoided looking at the mirror's left side where the letters J.P. were monogramed, the initials of the case's former owner, Emma's friend, and a fine actress, Josephine Prinze. Emma had always admired the way Josephine used the paints, powders, and the odd little pencil that she lined her eyes with, to transform her face. She could become the beauty of the ball, or a convincing toothless West End hag, just by applying the paints. To the fifteen-year old Emma, who had never even seen cosmetics applied before, it was like magic. She would sit and watch for hours. Josephine would smile at her, speak to her with genuine tenderness, and even show her how to paint and transform her own face. She had been the first woman who ever showed Emma any affection, any kindheartedness, or anything approaching friendship and Emma had loved her for it.

The case had come into Emma's possession after Josephine was put up against a wall and shot for spying. Sir Henry Perceval Blye, the John Bull colonel in command of the occupying force's Black Sheep, didn't even bother to charge or try her. Instead, he tortured her for hours in a vain attempt to rip information out of her and executed her, before Kierian and the others could mount a rescue mission.

Emma sighed. The Tree of Liberty must be refreshed from time to time with the blood of patriots, Thomas Jefferson had said. Well, that tree had to be about as refreshed as it ever would be, after damn well gorging itself on her friends, and those she considered family.

So many have died. So few of us left.

They had won in the end, and drove the tyrant John Bulls back, across the Lake. But the price to her friends and the brave civilians, who had fought the British prior to then-Governor Roosevelt and his Rough Ranger's liberating the city, had been tremendously high. Kierian's Empty Chairs Toast at the Liberty Tavern, after the armistice echoed in her head:

"For us, no statues of marble. No ticker-tape parades. Just glasses held in toast to the brave who fought and stayed."

"Good morning to you, Professor Stonechat," Kierian called cheerfully from across the picnic table.

Emma broke free from her memories and glanced up above the top of the kit.

Professor Veronica Stonechat walked across the fields of the Twelve Apostles Church. Golden locks of hair fluttered in the morning breeze, from beneath the back of her pith helmet.

The archeologist waved her hand in greeting. "And to you Mr. McKenna. Tending to your gear, I see."

In addition to Emma's kit, the picnic table was covered with both her and Kierian's equipment.

"It is a poor operative who does not check his weapons and wares daily." Kierian closed one eye, looked down the barrel of the pump action shotgun he was cleaning, and examined it for any dirt or grime. Experienced and dexterous hands reassembled the weapon, once satisfied with its cleanliness.

"Miss Dareheart would seem to disagree with you, and is putting fashion first," Professor Stonechat said, gesturing to Emma.

Emma raised her face above the kit. "That will be the day." Her face was colored in green and brown shades of face paint, similar to the colors of the Adirondack forest.

"Amazing, Miss Dareheart! You look like you have been birthed from nature itself!" Professor Stonechat said.

"Dr. Waatt calls them Chameleon Colors. Another of his inventions."

"Best if we blend in with our surroundings and see the enemy before they see us," Kierian explained.

"Yes, but, not all of us will be so concealed," Professor Stonechat replied.

"Worry not, Professor. The enemy who does not see Kierian and I before we see them, is a dead enemy," Emma replied. "We shall put them down before they can do you civilians any harm."

Emma finished applying the face paint, and put on her Balmoral cap; stitched on its back and side, were the words *American Maid* and *Banshee*. She next inspected a large device, with two large cylinders attached to a metal frame.

"What manner of device is that, Miss Dareheart?" Professor Stonechat asked.

"That is the famous rocket pack that carried her over Letchworth Gorge," Kierian replied.

"Fascinating. How tall is the gorge?"

"550 feet," Emma replied.

"So you can fly with that device?"

"I can fly vertical about 700 feet, and looping into an arch is not too difficult, but moving horizontally, is a bit trickier."

A thundering of hooves drew Emma's attention away from the rocket pack. The combat coach raced to a stop in front of them. The driver dutifully climbed down and opened the door of the carriage. Alfred Vanderbilt, Ambrose Russ, Professor Boaltt and three other men, climbed out. The last three were dressed in red shirts, blue trousers, and brown hunting coats.

"Where is Waatt?" Boaltt demanded moments after his feet touched ground. "I want to know what this damn secret plan you three cooked up is and I want to know now!"

"After returning from his morning prayers, he ascended into his airship, like Hermes rising to Mt. Olympus," Kierian replied.

"Good morning to you, too, Professor Boaltt," Emma said.

"Does my forthright manner bother you, girl? Well, that is too goddamn bad! You, Waatt and McKenna, summarily dismissed myself and Professor Stonechat last night like we were Vanderbilt's servants and now, you expect pleasantries and civility?"

"Professor Boaltt, as we told you last night, no offense was intended," Emma replied.

Professor Boaltt took a big gulp of water from a canteen he was carrying.

"Your secrecy is damn offensive, girl. In truth, I see no reason why any of you are needed on this trip, least of all you, a female daredevil trollop."

"Professor Boaltt," Kierian said, as he casually loaded five rounds into his shotgun. "You need not care for our company, nor approve of our decisions." He worked the action of his shotgun sending one shell into the firing chamber, and then casually loaded another round into the tubular magazine. "But if I ever hear you talk to Miss Dareheart in that manner again, you will have a broken jaw to go along with that broken arm of yours."

"Oh, will I?" Boaltt growled. He moved with surprising quickness to Kierian's side. Kierian placed the shotgun down on the table, freeing both hands for use. He turned, and squared himself to Boaltt.

Boaltt clamped his good hand around Kierian's wrist and violently pinned it to the table.

"Take heed, Mr. McKenna, and do not under estimate me. I'm a different breed than the usual intellectual you come across and not one to be trifled with. If you choose to cross swords with me, you'll find more than you bargained for, I assure you."

"Gentlemen, please!" Alfred Vanderbilt said. "Your personal grudges can wait until after you have completed the task of recovering poor Gladys."

Whizzing and grinding metal gears signaled the lowering of the *Excelsior's* ramp. Boaltt turned to look and released his hold. Doctor Waatt descended down the ramp. He had discarded his top hat in favor of an olive drab, wide brimmed campaign hat, with a Montana peak-high crown in its center. The robot dutifully followed.

Professor Stonechat gasped in amazement at the site of the robot. "Oh my word!"

"RAY!" Kierian shouted. "It is good to see you back in working order. I thought we had lost you in the battle with the fiendish Ming Fang Fu!" Kierian strode quickly to the automaton and shook the robot's hand warmly.

"I was severely damaged but not beyond...re-pair," the robot replied in a mechanical voice, returning Kierian's handshake.

"Good Lord, it talks!" Professor Stonechat said.

The robot turned and looked at Veronica Stonechat. Its mouth broke into a smile. The robot sauntered over to her, with the confident gait of a man-about town.

193

"I speak over fifteen languages fluently including the language... of love." The robot once again, paused at the end of his sentence, speaking the last few words in a singsong tone. He took Veronica's hand, brought it to his metal mouth, and applied a soft kiss before releasing her hand.

"Now, he speaks!" Ambrose Russ said. "Why did it not speak before when I addressed it in the church?"

"Speaking in the house of God is... disrespectful."

"I suppose since I spoke in the church, you think I was disrespectful, Robot?"

"I do not think...I know." The robot grinned, opened his mouth and slowly turned his head, looking at each person. Emma laughed. It was RAY's way of seeking approval for what he hoped was a witty retort, not unlike a precocious child who had just gotten off a zinger of a reply.

"Why you... you bellicose bag of bolts!"

A razor sharp blade sprung up out of RA-7's middle finger. He smiled at Russ, bent over and with expert precision cut a bouquet of Red Shamrocks. "Mr. Russ, my name is Rescue Automaton...Seven," the robot said. "You can call me...RA-7." The automaton turned, and smiled again at Veronica Stonechat. "And you can call

194

me...anytime." The robot smiled out of one corner of his mouth and handed the archeologist a flower.

"My, oh my, Doctor Waatt, your robot is quite the charmer," Professor Stonechat said.

"That is not my doing, I assure you," Doctor Waatt replied.

"Not your doing? It is your damn creation sir," Russ said. "How can it not be your doing?"

"Indeed, it is my creation, but just as the good Lord gave his creation free will, so I have followed His lead and granted such to RA-7."

"And after spending a month with Mr. McKenna on a mission, he chose to use that free will to duplicate his style and wit." Emma explained.

"Shame on you, Miss Dareheart. No one can duplicate my style and wit."

Emma curtseyed, gripping the sides of her green canvas trousers in place of the frills of a dress. "All too true. I stand corrected, Mr. McKenna."

Kierian grinned. He picked two flowers from RA-7's bouquet, placed one in his lapel, and handed the other to Emma.

Emma smiled.

Flatter Kierian by morning, Villains take warning.

"Dr. Waatt, if the introductions of your automaton are finished, I would make a few of my own," Alfred Vanderbilt said. He stepped forward and the three men from the carriage followed behind him.

"This is Mr. Leslie, Mr. Kaplan and Mr. Henroff. They are all skilled Sportsmen and members of the Adirondack League. They will help you navigate to Reese Lake."

"The Adirondack League?" Emma asked. She looked the three over. Kaplan and Henroff had the look of old grizzled local hunters about them. Mr. Leslie, however, appeared to be around her own age.

"The League is an organization dedicated to the teaching and preservation of hunting, fishing, and forest craft; skills that though once were quite common, are fast disappearing," Mr. Kaplan said.

"The price of Industrialization," Russ said.

"Some would say the curse of Industrialization, Mr. Russ," Henroff replied.

Kierian put on his slouch hat. The right side brim was pinned to the crown, so as to not interfere with his aim when shooting. Fashion conscious as he was, there was a deadly pragmatism to Kierian when he was on mission. "Thank you, Alfred," Kierian said, "but we will be fine without them. Not all of New York State is

196

like New York City, you know. We do have forests up-state."

"Mr. McKenna and I are experienced in moving through the wilderness, Alfred. So is Dr. Waatt," Emma explained.

"You might be experienced in moving about the forests of Western New York, Miss Dareheart," Kaplan said, "but navigating the wilds of the Adirondacks is a horse of another color altogether."

"A forest is a forest, Mr. Kaplan. I am confident we will be successful without your assistance," Kierian said.

Mr. Leslie shook his head at Kierian. "Mr. McKenna, you don't understand. The terrain can change from grassy plains to thick brush without warning. There are boulders the size of houses throughout the forest, and the massive trees are hundreds of years old," Henroff said.

"Big trees, big boulders, diverse terrain. Understood and thank you," Kierian replied.

"Mr. McKenna," Kaplan began. He rubbed a hand over his grey stubble. "Henroff and myself know every back trail, bushwhack, and bear den out there, and young Leslie is a crack shot. You will find us handy to have around. That I can assure you."

197

"Fifteen people, over the last three months have been attacked and killed by bears here abouts, Mr. McKenna," Leslie said. "You'd be a fool to turn us away."

"Fifteen people?" Dr. Waatt said in alarm. "That is quite a high number, particularly since black bears are not generally hostile."

"Some say it's Horribis Ursus Arctos," Kaplan said.

"The Horrible Bear-Bear?" Kierian replied.

"Your direct translation of the Latin is accurate, Kierian," Dr. Waatt said. "Someday I must find the Jesuit priests who had the unenviable task of educating you and compliment them on a job well done."

Kierian smiled with pride.

"However, I believe the meaning is the Horrible Bear of All Bears and is, in fact, the scientific name for the Grizzly Bear."

"You'd be correct, Doctor," Kaplan said.

"Yet, the Grizzly is not native to the Adirondacks, and is found almost exclusively on the western part of the continent."

"True, but the few eyewitnesses who survived spoke of a ferocious brown-colored bear. It's not impossible that one migrated up here. In any case, your people would find us helpful to have along," Mr. Leslie replied.

"Were we hunting moose or bear," Kierian said. "I am confident you three would be my top choice to hire on, but this is no big game hunt. Bears, ferocious as I am sure they are, do not shoot back. This is life and death, kill or be killed, and I wager none of you have ever spilled blood before."

"You'd wager wrong, Mr. McKenna," Leslie replied.

"Human blood, he means," Emma added. "Have you seen the elephant, Mr. Leslie?"

"Not exactly, but I'm sure we'd do as well as you, Miss, if the bullets start flying."

Emma shook her head but knew argument would be fruitless. Men always figured they'd rise to the occasion if they ever had to fight and men who hunted and knew guns, all the more so. To be sure, local hunters and guides were wonderfully, self-reliant people, and they often did indeed, possess forest craft superior to Kierian's; but far too many who had never experienced the butcher's field of battle, held much too high an opinion of themselves in an area they knew nothing about. They were often decedents of old Indian fighting pioneer families and assumed combat was in their blood.

That assumption was false.

There was no substitute for combat experience. More than once she and Kierian had lost friends to a bullet in the back because some inexperienced civilian hunter panicked during combat and started firing without regard to friend or foe.

"Kierian, perhaps they would be an aid to us on this mission," Dr. Waatt said. "Once we rescue Miss Vanderbilt, it would be useful to have knowledge of alternate trails of escape."

Kierian glanced at Dr. Waatt, shrugged, and turned back to the three hunters. "Very well, but I do not wish to hear any bellyaching when I deploy you forward. At least then, if you panic, RA-7 will only have to dig *your* graves, instead of having to dig a bullet out of *my* back."

Awkward silence fell like a shroud, over the group.

Dr. Waatt coughed, dispelling the uncomfortable quiet. "Mr. McKenna, Miss Dareheart, if you are finished checking your gear, may I have the table please," Dr. Waatt said.

Emma and Kierian nodded and removed their equipment from the table.

200

"RA-7, the maps if you will." The automaton retrieved the maps from his large backpack and rolled them out, over the table.

"Now that our team is formed, it is time we revealed to all of you the plan we have devised to rescue Miss Vanderbilt." Dr. Waatt pointed to two spots on the map. "Here is where we are and here is where the exchange is to take place. Now, this is what we shall do…."

CHAPTER TWELVE

Henroff and Kaplan paddled down the calm waters of Raquette Lake, oblivious to the danger ahead.

"We are gaining on them. Keep the pace, my friends," Dr. Waatt encouraged.

Emma dug the paddle into the water, matching Kierian and Dr. Waatt, stroke for stroke. "How do you suppose, two experts in forest craft did not see the reflection of signal mirrors among the trees?"

"Because they were looking at the shoreline, like hunters do, for signs of game," Kierian said. "I told you they would be a hindrance."

Emma nodded. Kierian, Balthazar and herself had been watching the tree-covered mountains for spotters, precisely because that is what they would have done if they were the anarchists: post scouts to warn of approach from an unexpected direction.

"Why they did not, is unimportant, at present, Kierian," Dr. Waatt said. "What is important is that we catch up to them and inform them we have been spotted."

"Preferably before they paddle around that bend in the Lake," Kierian said. He pointed to the upcoming right hook in the water. "If I was going to ambush a rescue party on water, that is where I would lie in wait."

Emma glanced behind her. The third canoe, helmed by Mr. Leslie, with Professor Boaltt, his rapidly healing injured arm in the center, and Professor Stonechat in the stern, had fallen well behind.

Just above the water, next to the canoe was RA-7's periscope.

"The professors are not keeping pace," Emma said.

"Good! When we round the bend, we will not have to play nanny to them while bullets are flying at our heads," Kierian said over his shoulder.

"It is premature to conclude we will be in a firefight Kierian," Dr. Waatt said. "Those who watch us might simply be signaling to the others that we chose to take a water route rather than hike the longer overland trail Professor Boaltt was instructed to take, that I recommended last night, and, as you will recall, you rejected."

"Well, excuse all hell out of me, Balthazar, for not doing precisely as vile kidnapping anarchists wish me to do."

"There is no need for cussing, Kierian. I was not assigning blame, simply reminding you of the facts; though had we taken the land route, we could have brought horses and more equipment."

Emma rolled her eyes. It was the same argument to one degree or the other, every time they planned an operation. Balthazar wanted to play everything safe, take as few risks as possible, and bring as much of his high tech gear as he could.

"Risks usually lead to error, so let us take as few as possible, and allow the enemy to take and make them instead," Balthazar would say.

Kierian, on the other hand, wanted to travel light, move fast, and do the unexpected. If that meant taking a few calculated risks, then so be it. It had kept them alive for four years, while fighting the John Bulls, and Kierian saw no reason to alter what he considered a tried and true method.

Kierian's paddle hit the water hard, splashing lake water upon Emma. "If you had consented to bringing Mr. Singh and his men along, we wouldn't have to rely on these sports."

"Mr. Singh leads the *Excelsior's* security force, Kierian, and their job is to protect the *Excelsior*, not augment

STEAMCAPP's missions."

In perfect rhythm, their paddles cut through the lake water. Emma stole a glance forward. Little by little, they were making up the distance between their canoe and the sports. "I sincerely doubt anything will happen to the *Excelsior* while it is on the ground, Balthazar."

"I did not like what Roosevelt said to me, my dear. He is a man of rash and unpredictable action. The perfect time to board the *Excelsior* would be while we and the security personnel are away on a mission." Dr. Waatt shook his head. "No, I will take no chances with that Bull Moose around."

"At least, we have RAY along with us," Emma said.

Kierian cast a vigilant gaze along the shoreline. "I like RAY, but he's fairly useless in a firefight."

"That is because he was created to be a Rescue Automaton, not a Battle Bot as should be obvious from his name," Dr. Waatt said.

"You built him with the ability to learn. He should have learned a thing or two about combat by now."

"Whose fault is that, Kierian? He spent three weeks with you on a mission and all he learned, was how to dress like a dandy and spout those witticisms you seem to think pass for charm."

Emma chuckled. RA-7's first mission had been with

Kierian down in Mexico, to free some miners. It was supposed to be an in-an-out job, but something had gone wrong and they had spent three weeks on the run, alternately avoiding banditos and Emperor Custer's Federales.

By that time, RA-7 had taken on many of Kierian's mannerisms, and considered himself a ladies' man, or ladies' bot, as the case might be.

Kierian set his paddle across the gunwale of the canoe, and cupped his hands around his mouth. "Henroff! Kaplan!"

No response.

"What is the matter with those sports? You would think they would turn around and glance our way now and then."

"Perhaps, *that* is what has drawn their attention, Kierian. Look!" Dr. Waatt pointed up into the sky. Two trails of black smoke rose into the air.

Around the bend, steamed an ironclad. Two cylinder stacks puffed black smoke into the sky and rifle barrels bristled out gun ports on both sides of the armored citadel, in the middle of her upper deck. A black skull and crossbones flag, flew from atop a wooden pole at the stern of the boat and an enormous cannon was positioned forward on the bow.

Emma swept her paddle through the water, initiating a turn. Kierian and Dr. Waatt did likewise. They had to make shore, and fast, before —

Kash-boom!

The massive cannon thundered. The front of the canoe ripped away. Kierian fell head first and hit the water hard. Dr. Waatt toppled over the side, the paddle still gripped in his hand.

Emma knew she was going into the water.

Best to enter under control and on my own terms.

She leaned back, held her nose, and rolled over the side of the canoe, plunging below the surface.

Kierian sank past her, his pack still attached to his back and pulling him down. Emma pivoted under water, pulled her knife from its sheath and swam towards him.

Something hard hit her head. Her skull seared with pain and the crystal clear lake suddenly turned murky and then, black.

* * * * * *

Veronica Stonechat gasped. Green eyes widened in horror. "They have not surfaced! Oh Good Lord! They have not surfaced!"

"Professor Stonechat, we must paddle for shore!" Mr. Leslie said.

207

"Don't be a fool boy!" Professor Boaltt yelled. "We'd never make it!"

Veronica stared at the capsized canoe. How could this have happened?

After being summarily dismissed the previous night, she had sent a cable to the Institute requesting information on STEAM CAPP and Professor Boaltt. She knew the Colonel did not like to be woken but fortunately, Oscar had been manning the Wheatstone teletypewriter, and she had received an immediate response.

The information on Boaltt was general and unremarkable. Dr. Waatt's had been surprisingly sparse. Kierian McKenna and Emma Dareheart's files, however, had been extensive, and both unnerving and comforting. Unnerving, because despite their seemingly affable nature, the pair seemed to be ruthless and remorseless killers when they chose to be. Comforting, because at present they were just the sort of person you needed on such an adventure.

All three had seemed both on paper and in person, extremely competent and impressive.

Yet now, with a single shot, they were gone.

"We must render aid to Dr. Waatt and his friends," Veronica said.

Taka-taka-taka-taka

The river pirates' Maxim machine gun made its deadly introduction. A parade of rippled water splashed near the front of their canoe.

"Ahoy! Place your paddles on your gunwales and stay where you are, or the next burst will turn you into fish food like your friends," a pirate bellowed through a brass voice trumpet.

Veronica placed the paddle down as directed. The ironclad chugged slowly forward, and collected Kaplan and Henroff from their canoe before steaming to her location.

Savage looking men, pierced and tattooed, pulled her canoe to their vessel's side. Filthy crusted hands roughly pushed her and her companions on deck.

"You have our gear, let us go. We're on a mission of mercy," Leslie said.

"Shut your mouth, boy!" The pirate captain brandished a cutlass and struck Leslie hard in the mouth. The young hunter crashed to the ironclad's wooden deck.

"You brute!" Veronica said. She placed her arms under Leslie's shoulders and helped him back to his feet.

"That's right, lady, I am a brute. We're a boat of

209

brutes and it's good that you know so," the pirate captain announced. "Any of you who decide to give me sass, will get the same treatment as this pup, here." The captain drove his fist into Leslie's gut, instantly doubling him over. "That's a promise."

"Who are you?" Henroff asked.

"I'm Captain Bully Browne," Bully waved his cutlass towards his crew. "And these are the Ninety-Niners

"Ninety-Niners? That's the compliment of your crew, I suppose," Kaplan said.

"We ain't named so, because there's ninety-nine of us. We're the Ninety-Niners on account of this lake is ninety-nine miles long and we own every damn bit of it."

"What do you plan to do with us?" Veronica asked.

"The men we'll sell for ransom, unless they want to join us, as for you..." Bully smiled, licked his lips and looked Veronica over like a dog eyeing a sirloin steak. A blood stained hand slithered through Veronica's golden locks.

The archeologist slapped the pirate captain's hand away. "Take your hands off me, you fiend!"

The back of Bully's hand cracked across Veronica's face, snapping her head to the side. Fear spilled from her eyes, blood from her lips.

Kaplan, Henroff and Leslie surged forward. Leveled, pirate rifles promising certain and bloody death halted the sportsmen in mid stride.

Bully sheathed his cutlass. Rows of darkened yellow teeth gloated in victory. "I trust it is clear to you all, that I am in control. I have the goddamn guns, which means I have the goddamn power! That means I can do anything I goddamn like!" He grabbed Veronica roughly. Chapped lips and foul breath pressed hard against the waxy gloss she had applied only hours before.

Fear knotted inside her. She pushed back, but he was too strong. Bully grasped her wrists in an iron grip, holding them in place as he continued with his pleasures. Veronica pulled her head back and spit into the lake in disgust.

"That's what I call the Bully buss," Bully crowed, "And Blondie, you can be goddamn sure there'll be more bussing and less fussing once I get you below decks."

Bully sneered and the Ninety-Niners cackled their approval. Bully's eye fell on Professor Boaltt, who had not said a word or made a single move since coming aboard.

The captain looked him over, and curled his lip.

"Now, here is a smart man. He knows he is in my power, and at my mercy, so he keeps his damn mouth shut and minds his own business." He slapped Boaltt on his injured arm and laughed.

"You were not too smart yourself, Captain," Veronica said, wiping away whatever filth Bully Browne had deposited in her mouth. "The canoe your man destroyed had the most valuable treasures of all in it. Now, they are at the bottom of the lake!"

"Is that a fact?" Bully gazed back at the remains of STEAMCAPP'S canoe and scowled at his gunner. "What kind of treasure?"

Veronica hesitated. Boaltt spoke.

"The man in the center of the canoe was Dr. Waatt."

"Dr. who?"

"No, Dr. Waatt. He is a famous inventor and was in possession of advanced weapons and supplies when the canoe sunk."

"Tech gear huh? That always sells for a high price," Bully mused. "You hear what he said, Merckle? I told you to fire a warning shot across that canoe's bow, not sink it. You cost us some high selling bobbles, sure."

"Sorry, Bully," Merckle replied.

"Sorry don't get it done, Merck! You and your gunnery crew get out the diving gear, get in the goddamn

212

rowboat and start fishing out whatever sank out of that canoe you blew to holy hell! We'll meet you up the lake at Raider's Roost."

Merckle's jaw dropped. "You're leaving us here, alone?"

"Damn right I am!" Bully scowled. "Someone might have heard the shooting and come back with the law. They'll be armed and ready for a fight, not like these civilians we took unawares."

"All the more reason to stick together, so as you can protect us," Merckle said.

"Oh hell, you all can say you are just out fishing if anyone comes along, but the *Vulture* here would be a bit harder to explain away." Lust filled eyes gazed at Veronica. "Besides, I want to have a taste of this one somewhere proper, where the bullets ain't a flying."

Merckle, scowled, shuffled his feet and rubbed his bearded face. "Hell, Bully, we want a taste too."

Bully Browne drew his revolver, whirled and fired. The bullet slammed into the deck, an inch from Merckle's foot sending the pirate into a two-step. "The only thing you'll be getting a taste of is hot lead, if you don't do like I say! Now, get in the goddamn rowboat and fish out what you sunk!"

With the enthusiasm of children ordered to clean

213

their rooms, Merckle and his gunnery crew retrieved the rebreathers from the lower deck, climbed into the rowboat and rowed towards the floating Balmoral cap.

* * * * * *

Merckle sat in the center of the rowboat and watched the *Vulture* steam out of sight. "It ain't right Bully abandoning us and blaming me for sinking that canoe. Shooting a cannon ain't like firing a rifle. Sometimes, close is gonna be too close."

"No reason to begrudging Bully, Merck," Dangerous Dan, the pirate sitting at the stern of the rowboat said. "He just wanted to start working on Blondie is all; but I'll tell you this: if Selvin and Miller find gold or silver at the bottom of the lake, I don't see any damn reason we should have to share it with Bully."

Merckle nodded. "Hey, they're coming up," Dangerous Dan said. Their two pirate companions, both wearing the rebreathers, broke the surface of the water and held up two backpacks.

"Ha! They got something!" Dan rubbed his hands in anticipation and extended a long pole out for them to place the packs on.

"Say, what's that behind you," Dan asked. "It looks like a pipe."

Merckle looked past Selvin and Miller. There was indeed, what looked like a curved copper pipe, just above the surface of the water. Merckle squinted. He peered at the object.

With the same suddenness it had appeared, the pipe disappeared below the water.

"That's damn strange," Dan said. He pulled in the packs off the wooden keel pole and placed them in the boat.

"We're coming in," Selvin said.

"The hell you say. You ain't been down for more than fifteen minutes," Dan replied. "Bully said those rebreathers have enough oxygen to last three hours."

"The hell I DO say and I don't give a good damn what Bully says. Drawing breath ain't an easy task in this contraption. I'm lightheaded and primed to purge my guts. We done our bit. It's your turn to swim with the fishes for a while."

Miller extended an arm to swim to the boat.

His arm halted in mid stroke.

"S-Something's got me!"

Selvin jerked to his right. "Me too!"

Merckle's eyes widened. Both men suddenly plummeted beneath the water.

A jolt of fear washed over Merckle. He drew his pistol. Wary eyes scanned the lake's surface.

"What in holy hell?" Dan said. He aimed his rifle, and swept the water.

An eerie silence fell across the lake. The only sounds were the quiet lapping of the water and the cry of a loon.

Without warning, Selvin and Miller erupted from beneath the surface. Lungs gasped for air, and coughed out lake water. The two river pirates thrashed violently against the surface, their rebreather masks absent.

"Shoot it! Damn it all! Shoot the monster!" Selvin screamed.

"Shoot what? I don't see nothing!" Dan looked down the iron sights of his rifle, searching for a target.

Merckle didn't wait to see one. The double action revolver boomed deadly lead at the water around Selvin.

One shot ricocheted off the water. Selvin cried out and grabbed his belly. Blood seeped out into the water.

"Damn Merck, you just don't learn, do you?" Dan chuckled.

Miller screamed. The two river pirates plunged beneath the water, surfaced a second later on their backs, and darted across the lake, towards the shore.

"Something's pulling them!" Merckle said. Dangerous Dan took aim and fired, alternating between shooting to the rear and just in front of Miller and the wounded Selvin. Merckle reloaded his pistol.

Unseen by the two river pirates, the water directly to their rear, began to stir.

* * * * * *

Kierian kicked his legs and swam towards the rowboat, like a shark closing in on its prey. Beneath the surface he breathed effortlessly through Dr. Waatt's Underwater Breathing Apparatus.

The good doctor's habit of over preparedness had surely saved their lives. Within moments of being thrown into the water, RA-7 had sped to the rescue, deftly attaching the WUBA to Kierian, and Dr. Waatt. Along with a WUBA, RA-7 attached a rescue harness to the unconscious Emma, and towed her along beneath the surface.

They had heard the machine gun bullets ripple into the water, while their gear sank to the bottom of the lake. Swimming below the water until they reached the cover of the brush and bramble near the shore, they had surfaced, keeping their eyes just above the water line. RA-7 had examined Emma and announced she was not badly injured. They left her resting comfortably against a tree and waited for the Ironclad to leave.

217

Kierian glanced to his right. Balthazar was keeping pace. It was amazing how spry the doctor was in the field. His snow-white hair, lean build, the limp and the cane, often gave the impression of a man on the physical downward slope of life.

Kierian knew better.

While not particularly athletic and lacking both great speed and great strength, Balthazar routinely outlasted men much younger than himself. Once in the field, like an old warhorse, he just kept on going.

They were close to the target. Kierian could hear the muffled sound of splashes and gunfire.

RAY must be fully engaged in his game of dunk and smother.

Balthazar had assured Kierian that when they made their attack, any screams or gunshots would be drowned out by the noise of the ship's steam engines. Kierian wasn't so sure. Normally, it would not have worried him but with only their knives and pistols, a firefight with a gunboat was ill advised.

Damn, I wish Emma was by my side. I would not have to worry about coordination, or if Balthazar will understand my damn hand signals. I can just act.

Emma was an absolute Godsend; bold beautiful with an indomitable spirit, she seemed able to read his mind and do just what was needed during a mission in exactly the way he needed her to do it.

"A strong woman, 'tis a blessing from on high, me boy. 'Tis like, wishing for your medicine to be whiskey and havin' the good doctor prescribe the same," his Uncle Seamus would have said.

He shook Emma and Uncle Seamus from his mind and focused. A rifle cracked; its report muted by the water. Kierian slowly surfaced, just enough to verify the location of the pirates.

Perfect! Their backs are to us and they are looking out at RAY, not down at the water. Time to perform some derring do's!

He submerged and swam beneath the rowboat. The two river pirates were standing and firing their weapons, already tipping the boat starboard. Kierian was about to surface and engage the pirates, but stopped. Emma was not with him. Additional communication would be necessary. He turned towards Dr. Waatt and pantomimed his intended action. Balthazar nodded his understanding.

Shoulders and backs lightened, as they detached the WUBAs. Kierian broke surface and reached for the side of the boat.

Dr. Waatt was only a half second slower. With a

mighty downward heave, the boat tipped, pitching both river pirates into the water, their weapons falling from their grips.

Arms and legs splashed in desperation to stay afloat.

Kierian dove. Rapid kicks of his athletic legs darted him towards the flailing pirates treading water.

He pulled his Bowie knife free from its sheath and surged out of the water, like a knife wielding Poseidon. Cold combat steel plunged into neck and chest. Blood spurted skyward and stained his field vest red. Contemptuously, Kierian wiped the dripping Bowie knife on the pirate's mangy shirt and shoved the dying body away.

The pirate sank to his watery grave.

Kierian spun. The second pirate was swimming towards him, his blade between his teeth, murderous intent in his eyes.

Dr. Waatt surfaced directly in front of the second pirate, a small knife in his hand. He made a single thrust into the surprised pirate's chest.

The pirate writhed in pain, clutched his chest, and his eyes rolled back. The dead man pancaked, splashing and sinking beneath the waters of Raquette Lake.

Kierian swam to the rowboat, looped one leg over

and effortlessly rolled in. Dr. Waatt pulled the two backpacks behind him. Kierian offered assisting hands, and hauledBalthazar and backpacks onboard.

"That is a cute little toy you have there, Balthazar," Kierian said. "Upon first seeing it, I thought it would do no more than scrape the pirate's knee."

"I call it the Yellow Jacket," Dr. Waatt said. "The knife holds 1.5 cubic feet of compressed CO_2 at one thousand Psi in a compressed air pellet. The gas ejects out a hole in the blade when the user pushes the button near the handle."

"Ah yes, very clever, to be sure. But I did not see any blood. Are you sure he did not just have a heart attack?" Kierian grinned, took hold of the oars and began rowing towards shore.

"Do you really think that pirate just *happened* to keel over dead at the precise moment I stabbed him?" Dr. Waatt shook his head. "Your attempts to disparage the usefulness of my technology get more and more desperate each time, Kierian. There was no blood because the Carbon Dioxide instantly freezes the wound, thus, eliminating a blood trail."

"Be that as it may, Balthazar, I believe I will stick with my Bowie knife."

"Do as you wish, Kierian, but I can assure you, the

221

internal damage caused by the compressed air does significantly more harm than that ox cutter, you wield."

Kierian chuckled, pulled back on the oars, and scanned the lake.

"I do not see any black smoke rising into the air. It appears you were correct about the commotion and shots going unheard."

Dr. Waatt nodded. "Of course I was. It is just a question of understanding the dynamics of sound waves, and the acoustical effect the environment we are presently in, will have upon them." Dr. Waatt opened both backpacks and examined the contents. "The waterproofing I applied to both packs seems to have done its job. Our gear seems to be all in order."

"*Both* packs? You mean one is still at the bottom of the lake?"

"Indeed. Miss Dareheart's is missing, I am afraid. I was hoping to be able to present her with it upon our return, to boost her spirits."

Kierian raised his binoculars and looked across the lake, towards the shore. RA-7 was on the small beach, happily playing with his yo-yo, the two river pirates sprawled on the sand, motionless at his feet. Emma sat on a log nearby, her head bowed and held in her hands.

Kierian frowned. Emma's morale was not what

worried him. She had a spirit that never stayed depressed for long and when it didn't rise, he was always able to lift it for her. It was the blow from Balthazar's boot to her head, as he righted himself after falling into the lake that concerned him most.

"I am sure her gear will be as undamaged as ours," Dr. Waatt said. "I will send RA-7 down to retrieve it once we regroup with the two of them on shore."

Dr. Waatt looked down at his boots, and Kierian heard him sigh softly. Te inventor tapped the top of his knee with nervous agitation but remained quiet for several minutes.

"I should have been more careful, Kierian. I should have controlled my fall better or at least, fallen in a way that no one besides myself was injured."

"It is not the first time Emma has taken a knock to her noggin, Balthazar. She will be fine." Kierian placed the binoculars back in their case and pulled back on the oars.

Were his words spoken to comfort Balthazar or himself?

He hoped they turned out to be true. He had not liked the way Emma looked, or how confused she seemed to be when they left her on the beach

"You told me she was struck by one of the Dunn's

with a lead sap, just yesterday," Dr. Waatt said. "Cumulative blows in so small a time period, can sometimes have lasting effects, but I suppose you are right. Such happenings are an occupational hazard in our line of work."

Cumulative Blows. Cumulative Missions. How many bullets, bombs and bad men can that girl survive? Two days, we are together, and two blows to her beautiful head is what she receives for the pleasure of my company.

Kierian pulled back on the oars; the soothing sound of the silent lake, peeled away the years in his mind to that night in 1893.

The lake and the smell of pine disappeared, replaced by the cobblestone of Rochester streets and the smell of wet pavement outside the Red Lion, the renamed saloon the John Bulls so often frequented.

He was slipping through the alley, on his way to meet a contact who had agreed to sell the resistance heavy Gatling guns when he first heard her screams.

They were not screams of horror, nor did he hear any begging or pleading, only a stream of cusses and curses filled with promises of death and the dismemberment of male anatomy.

Two John Bulls on top of her, ripped at her clothes. Three others stood by singing crude lyrics to the tune of

224

Yankee Doodle.

All laughed like jackals, at her futile resistance. She kicked, punched, scratched, spit, and struggled with all her strength.

But it was not enough.

So he intervened. He did what a good agent should never do. He sacrificed the mission to perform some chivalrous act for a girl in trouble, he did not even know.

He shot the first three before they even knew he was there. The fourth managed to raise his rifle before his head exploded from Kierian's fourth .45-caliber bullet.

The last raised his hands and begged for his life.

Kierian shot him down like the British dog he was.

He scooped up Emma, threw his coat over her and spent the rest of the night running through back alleys, with her in his arms, dodging British patrols and collaborating Metropolitan policemen before reaching the Resistance's safe house.

"Teach me to shoot, Piper. Teach me how to defend myself so what happened to me that night, can never happen to me again," she asked him a month later.

How could he say no? The Occupation was brutal and a fine looking girl like Emma, with a defiant spirit that would never tolerate the catcalls and insults the enemy tossed at her, was sure to end up back in another alley on another rain soaked night.

So he trained her as requested. Emma was a natural, her shooting eye even better than his. She soaked up everything she was taught; asking questions when the moment permitted, imitating his movements when it did not and always, *always* fiercely defending him.

She would not tolerate a critical word about him from anyone, and rarely would she question his decisions and never with anyone else around.

Her youthful allure and her ability to flawlessly imitate a working class British-Canadian accent, often allowed her to gain access where others could not. In June 1894, she crossed the border and gained employment in the household of the Canadian Secretary for Colonial Affairs, as the new scullery maid. On 4 July, 1894, she purloined with documents showing British troop movements and switched the sheet music of *Rule Britannia*, with *America Forever*, at Lord Walmsely's fancy dress party; the inadvertent playing of which the Canadian papers felt positively scandalous.

Captain Stark, their cell's leader had been none too pleased with her sheet music shenanigans. "That was a risky, maneuver, Miss Dareheart and could have easily

226

led to your capture."

Kierian had defended her. "It was our Independence Day, Captain, and they were going to play that dreadful song. How could our American Maid, let such stand?" She had beamed at his compliment and asked him to stitch *American Maid* on the Balmoral cap she had taken to wearing.

Not long after he was stitching *Banshee* on the cap, as she became the assassin the John Bulls never saw coming.

She had flourished as an operative and survived the war because of her training, though with a price on her head.

He had tried to fix that too. He thought if he left town the Brits would leave her be, and she'd settle down, maybe become an actress like Josephine and marry some respectable fellow. Instead, she'd begun dare deviling, going over falls in a barrel, performing skywalks, and leaping gorges with two rockets, tied to her back.

Not exactly the effect he had hoped his leaving would induce.

Maybe I should have said no to her, just put her on a train to one of the states untouched by the war. Maybe in the end, all I did is add years to one end of her life and take them off the other.

The boat scraped the shore, as they reached the beach and his thoughts returned to the present.

Kierian opened his cigar case; his eyes momentarily fell on the sheet of paper Theodore Roosevelt had given back to him. He plucked a cigar free, and hastily shut the case, placing it back in his pouch. He patted his pockets for a light. "Damn it to hell! My matchbook must be at the bottom of the lake."

Balthazar took his naphtha lighter from his pocket and handed it to Kierian. "I am confident, Miss Dareheart will be ship-shape and ready to sail, in no time Kierian." His voice was gentle and sympathetic, absent its usual intensity and curtness.

Kierian nodded, lit the cigar and tossed the lighter back to Dr. Waatt. Balthazar was probably right. Emma always was quick to recover from injury, but how long would that continue to be true?

The more time she spends with me, the shorter her life will be. That girl deserves much better. I got her into this life. It is my duty to somehow, get her out.

CHAPTER THIRTEEN

Emma adjusted her Balmoral cap. Her head no longer ached and the confusion had faded.

She was glad for that. It had been strange to suddenly be sitting on a log on some tiny beach, and not be able to remember how or why you arrived there.

Kierian had briefed her on their rescue by RA-7, the abduction of the professors and the sports, and his derring do's in defeating the four river pirates, with minor assistance from RA-7 and Dr. Waatt.

She had wondered, though, why she was left behind and not along on that mission.

"We already had this discussion, Banshee, do you not recall?" Kierian said, a look of concern on his face.

"I do not recall any conversations. The last I remember, I was in the water, about to swim to your aid."

"Temporary loss of memory is a symptom of a… concussion," RA-7 said. "You also failed the verbal cognitive…test. Thus confirming my original… diagnosis." The rescue automaton pulled out his yo-yo, bobbed it up and down and turned to Kierian. "That means I was...right."

"Yes, I understood you, RAY."

"Dr. Waatt says I need to explain things to you in... simple terms."

Kierian shot a look of annoyance at Dr. Waatt from the corner of his eyes. Emma spoke up before a renewed argument could begin.

"What verbal test are you referring to, RAY?"

"Accessing memory files... August 28, 1901 10:57 A.M:

Kierian McKenna: Balthazar is correct. You have a concussion... Miss Dareheart.

Emma Dareheart: Do not be silly. Please stop fussing. I am... fine.

Kierian McKenna: Very well. Let us put you to the test: What is my... name?

Emma Dareheart: Piper.

Kierian McKenna: Well, I will give you half a correct answer for that...one. What is the... date?

Emma Dareheart: It is August 28... 1901.

Kierian McKenna: Where are... we?

Emma Dareheart: Charlotte Beach by the Sea... Breeze. Now, can you take me on the damn Ferris Wheel like you... promised?

230

Kierian McKenna: Hardy har har… har.

Kierian raised an eyebrow. "RAY, I most certainly did not and do not say 'hardy har har."

"You… laughed." RA-7 replied.

"Yes," Kierian nodded, and straightened his slouch hat, "but not like that."

RAY had subsequently retrieved her pack and gear from the bottom of the Lake. It was good to have her things back. She was particularly pleased that her beloved Electromagnetic Rifle Model 2 was undamaged, and she lovingly wiped it clean of grit and grime, a satisfied smile on her face.

A girl likes her familiars with her. Granted instead of hairpins, handbags and hats, my familiars are guns, grenades and gear, but they are still mine all the same.

"So now what? Off to rescue the professors and the sports?" Emma said.

Dr. Waatt shook his head. "Your desire to aid the others is commendable my dear, but I must remind you, our mission is the rescue of Gladys Vanderbilt, not the professors and the sports."

"I think we should at least try, Balthazar. Leaving your comrades- in-arms behind is a poor habit to start."

"I agree, *if* it can be helped. Keep in mind we are on a clock. Our plan was to arrive one day prior to the deadline, so we could study the terrain and formulate a stratagem to deal with the Anarchists and their battle bot. I think it is ill advised to depart from the mission blueprint."

"We have two days, before that deadline expires. Surely, we can rescue the others and still beat the clock."

"My dear, those river pirates possess a steam powered ironclad, and all we have now is one rowboat. How exactly do you suggest we catch up to them?"

"Piper will think of something. He always does." Emma slid Kierian an imploring glance. The fact he was not taking her side in the conversation strongly hinted he agreed with Balthazar. Even so, Emma was confident he would rise to the occasion. Failing to live up to his self-proclaimed status of swashbuckling adventurer supreme was unthinkable to Kierian.

The Piper let out a small sigh, pulled a map from his equipment belt, unfolded it and spread it out on the beach.

"If we are to have any chance of rescuing the others, we need to know where they are headed." He traced his finger along the map. "Raquette Lake looks very long, with plenty of small little coves and landings dotting its shores. Checking them all in the limited time we

232

have would be impossible. However, if Lady Fortunate is smiling upon us, their pirate hide-out will be close by."

"They were lying in wait around that bend. Perhaps, that is an indication their hide-out *is* near-by," Emma offered.

"Wishful thinking, I am afraid, my dear," Dr. Waatt replied. "That simply may have been the best place to ambush travelers, not a sign that their home port is in close proximity."

"Why do we not ask, Mr. Pirate over there?"

"Which one?" Balthazar asked.

RA-7 sat on a log near the two pirates, playing with his yo-yo. "Only one is still…alive."

"Well, since we killed his shipmate I think it is unlikely, he will now cooperate, my dear."

A mirthless smile graced Emma's lips. "Oh, I am sure we can get him to be cooperative. What do you say, Piper? Time for a ten-fingered talk?"

Balthazar cast wary eyes at both Emma and Kierian. "What, pray tell is a ten-finger talk?"

Kierian picked up the map and walked over to the pirate.

The pirate sat unsecured in the sand. Any attempt at escape would instantly be halted by RA-7, who towered over him, smiling and playing with his yo-yo. The pirate hugged his knees. Eyes, wide in terror, never left the tall automaton that had dunked him to near unconsciousness and then, pulled him roughly across the water, like some ancient lake monster absconding with his prey to his bone covered lair.

Kierian squatted down in front of the pirate, spread the map out on the sand and smirked. "Time for a tete-a-tete."

"A wh-what?" the pirate stammered. His eyes alternated back and forth, between RA-7 and Kierian.

"A tete-a-tete. A heart-to-heart. A conversation." Kierian drew his Bowie knife. A stern look spread across his face. "RAY, hold his hand and splay his fingers."

Ray-7 grabbed the pirate's hand and fanned out the fingers, holding each by the knuckle, so they could not be bent or retracted.

"Kierian!" Dr. Waatt yelled and limped resolutely forward.

Emma stepped into his path, held up her palm, and shook her head.

"Do not interfere Balthazar. We need information and we need it now."

Dr. Waatt shook his head. "Not this way, my dear.

234

Torture is often ineffective, as the person will tell you anything he thinks you want to hear, just to stop the pain."

Emma smirked and lowered her voice to a whisper. "Perhaps, but the threat of torture, often makes the actual inflicting of pain unnecessary."

Kierian placed the edge of the big knife just above the knuckle of the pirate's thumb. "Now, I am going to ask you some questions. Each time you lie, refuse to answer, or do not reply fast enough to my satisfaction, I am going to chop a finger off."

"Oh dear God!" the pirate yelled.

"Desist with your requests of intervention from the Almighty, for He does not hear the pleas of murderous and villainous river scum." Kierian pressed the edge of his knife on the pirate's thumb. RA-7 covered his eyes.

"Wh-Why is that thing covering its eyes?"

"This is about to get…bloody. I hate the sight of… blood."

"Pl-Please! For the love of God, don't do this. I…I just—"

"You just tried to kill all three of us, and you did manage to injure my partner over there, who not only is exceedingly beautiful, but who I am also quite fond of."

"I believe he means you, my dear," Dr. Waatt elaborated to Emma.

Emma rolled her eyes. "Yes, Balthazar, thank you for the clarification."

Kierian locked his cold blue eyes on the pirate. "How many men are on your ship?"

"Pl-Please, I...I don't want to die. I—"

"That is not an answer. Goodbye to your thumb." Razored steel rolled into calloused flesh. A trickle of blood slid down the pirate's hand.

"NO! Eighty-two! There are eighty-two men in our crew."

Kierian nodded. "You are sure that is the correct number?"

"Oh wait! Eighty-seven! Eighty-seven! I mean, if you want me to include the five we just captured."

Kierian chuckled. "Question two: What kind of armaments does your ship carry? How many cannons? How many machine guns?"

"The *Vulture* has two cannons and two machine guns."

"Locations?"

"There's one set of each fore and aft."

Kierian nodded. "You are doing very well. You see? All you have to do is give honest answers and you get

236

to keep your digits. Now, question three: Where was your ship headed? Where were you supposed to ren-dezvous?"

"Rondy who?"

Kierian rolled his eyes. "Rendezvous. Where were you supposed to meet your ship?"

"Raider's Roost."

"Point it out on the map with your other hand."

Shaky pirate fingers pointed to a spot near the end of the lake.

Kierian smiled and sheathed his knife. "RAY, tie him to the tree."

"Aye,…Aye," the robot secured the pirate's arms around a nearby pine. Kierian rejoined Dr. Waatt and Emma, a self-satisfied smile on his face.

Dr. Waatt frowned. "Very good, Kierian, your bar-baric interrogation method gleaned information well enough, but we have no way of knowing if that infor-mation is accurate."

"I can go chop off a few digits and see if he changes his tune, if you like, Balthazar."

Dr. Waatt shook his head. "Fortunately, that will not be necessary." He limped over to the pirate, leaning heavily on his silver-headed walking stick. "RA-7, could you please provide me something to rest my weary bones."

"Bones do not grow…weary. Weariness is perceived due to senescence of the musculature, connective tissues, and supporting viscera in your… body."

"RA-7," Emma said, "Bone weary is a figure of speech, expressing that a person feels exhausted. Dr. Waatt wants something to sit on."

"I…understand." The robot picked up a large over turned tree stump and placed it directly behind Dr. Waatt.

"Thank you, RA-7." Dr. Waatt sat down on the stump and smiled at the pirate. "Allow me to introduce myself. I am Dr. Balthazar Waatt. And you are?"

"A-Amos Miller."

Dr. Waatt pulled his silver watch from one of the pouches on his equipment belt and checked the time.

"I apologize for my colleague's brutish methods. He is a former freedom fighter, and accustomed to treating enemy prisoners with gross brutality when he needs quick and accurate intelligence."

"I told them everything I know."

"I am sure you did. Please try to calm yourself. There is no cause for alarm. I shall inflict no evil upon your person." Dr. Waatt held up his watch. "This is a beautiful watch, is it not?"

Amos Miller nodded.

"No, sir, I mean, it is *exceedingly* beautiful. Look at it, closely. Observe the intricate carving of the master watchmaker."

The pirate glanced up. Dr. Waatt gave some slack to the watch chain, and let it swing back and forth.

Dr. Waatt's deep voice was gentle and calm. "It *IS* a beautiful watch."

"It is a beautiful watch," The pirate repeated.

"Follow the watch as it swings. Embrace the comfort of its motion. You cannot take your eyes off the beautiful watch. Or refuse the sound of my voice."

The pirate's eyes swung back and forth, following the watch's every movement.

"I cannot take my eyes off it or refuse the sound of your voice."

Dr. Waatt nodded. Dark, wide, unblinking eyes burrowed into the pirate from beyond the swinging watch. "The power of my voice compels you to cooperate. You will answer all my questions, truthfully. It is your desire to aid me as much as you can."

The pirate sat as still as a statue. His eyes continued to follow the watch. His jaw moved up and down, like a marionette; his voice an emotionless monotone. "I will answer all your questions truthfully. I desire to aid

239

you, as much as I can."

"Good. Very good. Now, Amos Miller, tell me everything you can about your ship and your fellow river pirates."

* * * * * *

Emma lay prone in the bottom of the rowboat. The barrel of her EMR-2 rested just above the starboard gunwale, pointing into the moonlit Adirondack night.

Across from her on the port side, Kierian held a similar position. His pump shotgun, loaded with double aught buckshot, ready for action. Dr. Waatt knelt at the stern of the vessel, his heat ray rifle covering their rear guard.

RA-7 silently pushed the oars through the water. His physiology made it unnecessary to employ the traditional rowing stroke humans used. The robot's motion reminded Emma of a dog paddle more than anything, but there was no denying its effectiveness and efficiency. Facing the bow rather than the stern, his automaton eyes, augmented with battery-powered image intensifiers, penetrated the darkness with ease.

The wind picked up and water from the choppy waves slushed over the side of the boat.

Emma had not known Balthazar could hypnotize someone like he had. She could think of at least a dozen

240

times in the past where his extraordinary skill could have come in handy and yet, he had not employed it. Kierian had even said as much.

"The old dog learns a new trick. Eh, Balthazar?"

"More like, remembering an old trick, Kierian."

"We could have used that trick on at least a dozen previous occasions. A pity you choose to leave it in your magician's bag all this time."

Dr. Watt glared at Kierian. "It is not magic, Kierian. It is science and I told you, I just remembered it. Emma is not the only one who has holes in her memory."

Balthazar said no more on the matter. The information he extracted from the river pirate included everything from the names of his fellow pirates, the personality of their leader, Bully Browne, their dining habits, experience in raiding, what they would probably do with the professors and sports, and the vital strategic fact that while the boat was an ironclad, the stern was in fact, made of wood.

All the information Kierian learned from the pirate was confirmed as well. Most importantly, the ship was headed for Raider's Roost seventy miles away, at the other end of the lake. Balthazar estimated they could only cover fifteen to twenty miles a day, far too slow a pace to rescue the others and Gladys Vanderbilt.

241

Kierian, however, had not disappointed and had come up with another cunning plan.

"We can rescue Gladys sooner than we planned. Then we go back for the others," Kierian had announced.

"I commend your strategic thinking Kierian, but to accomplish what you propose, we would have to row all night without any rest, and with our arms heavy with exhaustion, carry our weapons through the forest. We then, would have to slip into the anarchists camp, rescue Miss Vanderbilt, take her along with us back through heavy brush, row the length of the lake and then, perform a second assault on the pirates." Balthazar shook his head. "The odds of success would be quite low, I am afraid."

Kierian shook his head, puffed on his cigar and blew a smoke ring towards the lake. "We will shoulder our arms without trouble, Balthazar. Nor will there be any need to cut our way through wilderness brush."

"Oh? Pray tell, Kierian how you plan to manage that?"

"It will be my pleasure, Balthazar. No one will be tired because RAY will row the boat. There will be no need to bushwhack through the forest because once we rescue Miss Vanderbilt, you will use your wireless telegraph to call in the *Excelsior*. It will extract us, and fly the length of the lake in minutes. Then we shall use her Gatling guns for close support on the pirate vessel, while our ground assault is augmented by Mr. Singh and his Sikhs."

Balthazar nodded, pondered the new plan and ultimately raised no objections. The three of them had agreed the night before, that using the *Excelsior* to liberate Gladys was too risky. The moment the anarchists saw the airship they were liable to panic and execute the heiress. However, once she was rescued, there was no reason not to bring it in and put its awesome firepower to good use.

Emma smiled. *That's my Piper.* There was a lot to admire in Kierian's plan, especially its well-reasoned simplicity and there was also no denying Kierian's tactical brilliance.

Those who underestimated him as some shallow-minded dapper dandy, did so at their own peril.

"Ahoy! *Vulture* seventy yards ahead, off the... starboard side," RA-7 suddenly announced, pulling Emma's thoughts back to the present.

"RAY, are you sure?" Kierian said in a low voice.

"Affirmative. The *Vulture* has run aground, and is listing hard to ...starboard."

243

"Scan her decks, RAY. Is anyone manning the stern cannon and machine gun?" Kierian asked.

"Two bodies are lying next to the stern deck... weapons. Neither is showing any signs of...life."

"This is most peculiar," Balthazar said. "This is a lake, not an ocean. There are no unseen reefs lurking underneath the water that ships wreck upon."

Emma resisted the temptation to turn and look at the *Vulture* for herself. Instead, she kept her eyes glued to the far shore for signs of ambush.

"Ray, keep your distance and scan the rest of the ship especially those deck weapons."

"Aye, Aye, Captain...McKenna."

RA-7 initiated his dog paddle stroke and adjusted his course. The rowboat moved swiftly through the water. Emma scanned the opposite shore but the only movement she saw belonged to a white tail deer, visiting the lake for a nighttime drink.

"The *Vulture* is in visual...range. No signs of life... on deck. Bow weapons are... unmanned."

"Ray, keep us in the blind spot of those deck weapons." Kierian commanded.

"Aye... Aye."

"Banshee, move to the bow. Doctor, please hand the grappling gun to her."

Dr. Waatt shot a reproving glance at Kierian, reached into RA-7's giant backpack, retrieved the device and passed it to Emma. "The Compressed Air Vertical Ascension Tool, as requested, my dear," Dr. Waatt said, iterating the proper name for the device. Emma grinned, nodded her thanks, took the grappling gun from Dr. Waatt, and dropped to one knee. With an expert hand, she snapped open the brass hinges, unfolded the wooden stock, and pressed the stout wood and brass weapon snug against her shoulder. She gazed up at the listing ironclad, picked out the top of the pilothouse as her target and took aim through the rubber eyepiece of the brass scope.

Before she could fire, Kierian softly touched her on the shoulder. "Once you are on board, make sure you keep that pretty little head of yours down, Banshee. Balthazar and I will cover you from the rowboat if you come under fire."

Emma raised her head and nodded, a streak of annoyance shot through her.

Why does he feel the need to remind me to keep my head down. I know how to board a damn ship of war.

She pulled her head from the sight, and glanced at the Ironclad. Boarding a crippled vessel was dangerous work. Often times, the enemy would stay hidden until

245

the first wave boarded before emerging from ambush and opening up with a deadly volley of machine gun and rifle fire.

Their location would then be known and other waves of boarders would counter attack viciously, but that was faint comfort for the first wave who by then, were dead or dying on a blood- soaked deck.

Emma's ears perked for any sound of enemy movement but the only sound was the lapping of the water and the cry of a lake loon. She sighted again, through the scope, tensed her muscles, willing them to be as rigid as a corpse, and steadied the grappling gun. She inhaled and held the breath for three seconds, slowly, exhaled, moved her finger from the stock to the trigger, and fired.

CHAPTER FOURTEEN

The compressed air sent the grappling hook soaring towards its target. The hooks wrapped around the edge of the gun deck. Emma gave it a sharp tug, making sure the hooks would not slip and that the cable would support her weight.

She signaled to Kierian. Without delay, he pulled the pins of the smoke bombs and lobbed them onto either end of the main deck.

Emma stood, unfolded two wooden handles from the barrel of the CAVAT, and pressed a button. The cable retracted and hauled Emma skyward towards the ironclad. Once she cleared the edge of the ship, she swung her legs forward, released the button, and dropped softly to the main deck below.

White smoke billowed from the canisters at the far ends of the vessel and enveloped Emma. She lowered her goggles, drew her revolvers, and threw herself

247

prone, upon the wooden deck. Any pirates, who were hiding in ambush, would now have to content themselves with blasting away with un-aimed and inaccurate fire.

She aimed her pistols at the center of the cloud. Her eyes scanned the smoke just above deck level, for any sign of moving feet. Seconds passed, but it seemed like an eternity, as she waited for the maelstrom of deadly lead to pour through the air

Her heart rate increased, a spike of adrenaline ripped through her body. She took a deep calming breath, and fought back the temptation to blast away into the cloud to draw fire and initiate battle.

Patience, Prudence. Force the fight, your funeral pyre they will light.

A minute passed with agonizing slowness. The loon, once more, softly sang its eerie nighttime lullaby.

I can't wait forever. The smoke will dissipate soon and I need to get Kierian and Balthazar on board.

Emma stood, holstered her pistols, snatched the CAVAT, and tossed it back down to the rowboat. Moments later, Kierian and Dr. Waatt boarded. RA-7 stayed behind in the rowboat. The Rescue Automaton was about as useful in combat as a wooden frying pan was for cooking. There was a good possibility blood would yet be shed, and RAY hated the sight of the stuff. Anytime he saw a sufficient quantity he would fly into a screaming panic, throw his arms in the air, and run off in the opposite direction as fast as he could. Emma shook her head. She understood why Balthazar had created RAY with a "learning mind" but why he thought including emotion prudent, she could not fathom.

Kierian took the lead, his Winchester pump at the ready. He climbed up a small ladder to the gun deck, and trotted directly to the stern weapons where the two bodies RA-7 had seen, laid sprawled upon the deck.

"Neither of these are the sports, or Professor Boaltt."

"What is the cause of death?" Dr. Waatt asked.

"A gunshot to the head on this one," Kierian turned the second body over on its back, "and a knife wound to the chest on the second."

He rose and motioned with a hand signal that their next target would be the pilothouse perched atop the armored citadel. They quickly located a ladder, scampered up without incident, and took up positions around the pilothouse's solid oak door. No light emanated from any of the three pilothouse windows. Of course, that didn't rule out the possibility of the enemy hiding within but to peek a head up to the window to find out, was just asking to have a third eye carved into your forehead.

Emma pushed on the door. "It is locked, Piper."

"Hostile entry," Kierian announced. He pulled back the action on his pump shot gun. A shell ejected. He deftly caught it in mid-air, and replaced it with a deer slug.

"Ready with your party favor, Doctor?"

Dr. Waatt retrieved a brass apple-shaped, perforated device, crowned with a metal key, from his equipment belt.

"If I ever have the time, which is highly unlikely, I sorely need to author an index of the proper names of my devices, for you, Kierian."

"What is this one called again?" Emma asked.

"The MANED. It stands for Magnesium Ammonia Nitrate Explosive Device."

"I thought you told me before it did not explode."

"No, my dear; I said it did not *detonate*. Instead, it produces a subsonic deflagration. Deflagration is different from detonation as it—"

"Doctor, can you postpone the science lesson until a more appropriate time?" Kierian asked.

"Very well, Kierian. If you are ready to proceed,

please equip your ears with your plugs, and I will acti-
vate the MANED."

Emma extracted her plugs from her belt and
popped them into her ears. Kierian did the same. Balthazar had told her the device emitted '180 decibels of
sound and a blinding flash of more than one million
candela.' She had not known what he meant until she
saw the devastating effects it had on the minions of the
fiendish Ming Fang Fu. Balthazar had tossed it into a
small room, where ten Xi-Fen assassins waited ready to
practice their devilish craft. The explosion instantly
rendered the elite assassins blind, deaf, and staggering
about, with the balance of small children who had just
played several rounds of Twirl O' Whirl. A simple push
to the chest was all that had been needed to incapaci-
tate them.

Dr. Waatt turned the key in the top of the MANED.

Kierian aimed his shotgun and fired. The top hinge
blew apart. He worked the pump action loaded a second deer slug, pushed the action forward, fired, and
obliterated the lower hinge. He raised his boot and delivered a crushing kick. The door swung open, and Dr.
Waatt tossed the MANED inside.

BANG!. Blinding White Light flashed inside the
cabin. Kierian spun into the pilothouse, his shotgun

poised to fire. Emma followed; her extended right hand gripped her Colt and rested atop her left wrist, which now held her magnesium torchlight. The room was bathed in blazing white illumination.

The pilothouse was deserted.

Emma shined her torch into the adjoining room. The sign on the door read: CAPTAIN'S QUARTERS.

The room looked like a tornado had struck it.

Charts of Raquette Lake, topographical maps of the central Adirondack region and an assortment of other papers carpeted the wood floor. A half filled goblet of wine sat on a small wooden table next to a half-empty bottle. A second over turned goblet rested on its side. An overturned chair lay near by. In the corner next to a bed, an open chest over flowed with American and British-Canadian paper money.

Emma shined the torch to the windows. The left side window was completely shattered, broken glass, and a long brass telescope laid strewn on the floor below.

Kierian sniffed the open bottle and curled his nose in disgust. "If there was any doubt we are dealing with boorish lake trash, this should dispel it. Imagine being able to afford the finest wine available and yet, being content to drink this vile swill."

Emma grinned. "A nightmare of a thought, to be sure, Piper."

Dr. Waatt entered the room, a terrier on the scent. He scanned the quarters, strode to the table, and picked up the over turned crystal goblet. Holding it at eye level, his torch illuminated the object. Balthazar nodded once to himself and promptly began crawling on the floor. His long slender fingers patted beneath furniture and papers alike.

"Lose a cufflink, Balthazar?" Kierian asked.

Dr. Waatt ignored Kierian's quip and continued his examination. Sprawled on the floor, he moved inch-by-inch, reminding Emma of a slithering snake. Lanky fingers probed beneath the pirate captain's bed.

"Eureka!" Dr. Waatt raised his hand.

Between his fingers, was a brass button.

"Does that hold some significance to our mission, or were you just attempting to save a nickel at the tailors?" Kierian asked.

"Frugality is a virtue, Kierian, not something that should be mocked. You should attempt it sometime, and perhaps, you would not have to risk life and limb at the gaming tables so often."

Dr. Waatt pushed himself to his feet, withdrew a dog whistle from his pocket, and blew it once.

"You are calling in RAY?" Kierian asked. "We have not swept the entire ship yet. We could still encounter the enemy, and I doubt you can sell him on any combat we engage in being a game as you did on the lake." Kierian said.

"True enough, and if your powers of observation were not limited to fashion and fancies, I might not need him. As it is, his analytical expertise of the evidence I have discovered is essential."

RA-7 ducked his head to enter the room and remained crouched under the low ceiling. "You rang... Doctor?"

Dr. Waatt handed the automaton the brass button. "RA-7, what do you make of this?"

"That is a brass... button. It belongs to the beautiful Professor Veronica...Stonechat."

"How do you know that, RAY?" Emma asked.

"Professor Stonechat's buttons on her field coat were monogramed with AIA just as this button is... monogrammed."

Dr. Waatt handed RA-7 the wine glass. "Do the fingerprints match?"

"Accessing files.... Fingerprint on the glass is an exact match of Professor Veronica Stonechat."

"So Professor Stonechat was here," Emma said. "I

wonder what became of her?"

"She engaged in a struggle with Bully Browne, delivered a terrific blow to her captor's head, and escaped out the window." Dr. Waatt replied.

"How did you—?" Kierian began.

"It is a simple matter of observation and reasoning, Kierian. The wine stains on the chair, no doubt, came from the overturned glass Professor Stonechat held when she tossed the drink into the Captain's face. Not being the type of man who would quietly absorb such an insult, he rose from his chair and seized Professor Stonechat, causing her to knock over the chair she was sitting in."

"Ah I see, so—"

"He then grasped her field coat, which is when the button was ripped off. The Captain flung her upon the bed, with the most wicked intent in mind, sending the button to the location whence I discovered it."

"But what about the blow to the head?" Emma inquired.

"You will note the nightstand next to the bed is covered in dust, save one area where a long cylindrical object was removed. I deduce that object to be the telescope lying under the windows. Professor Stonechat no doubt, grabbed it from the nightstand and smashed the captain with it."

"Maybe she just threw it at him and missed," Kierian said.

"Then why is there blood on the edge of the brass ring?" Dr. Waatt shook his head. "No. That spyglass was wielded like a club. I surmise it was then used to break the window and clear it of glass to allow Professor Stonechat to escape."

"Your powers of deduction are astounding, Balthazar," Emma said.

Dr. Waatt tipped his campaign hat and bowed. "Thank you, my dear."

Kierian rolled his eyes. "Is there any chance you can divine what happened after she crawled through the window, Balthazar?"

Dr. Waatt's lanky strides carried him out of the pilothouse and outside the broken window. "There! Blood drops. RA-7 take samples. We shall analyze them when time is convenient." The Automaton obeyed, scraping the blood into a couple of test tubes retrieved from his equipment belt.

Dr. Waatt glanced up at the broken window. "I have little doubt, Professor Stonechat and possibly Bully Browne, cut themselves on the shards of glass still remaining in the window."

"How do you know he pursued her out the window and not out the door?" Kierian asked.

"The door was locked from the inside," Emma offered.

Dr. Waatt smiled. "Very good, my dear." He climbed down to the main deck and followed the blood drops. They ended at the closed hatch to the lower decks. A box filled with iron canon balls, laid on top of the hatch.

"I do not see anymore blood. She must have entered the lower deck and was closed within," Dr. Waatt said.

"But why?" Emma asked.

"Unknown, but I am confident the answers lie below. RA-7, remove the ammunition box, please."

"Belay that order, RAY." Kierian said.

Dr. Waatt turned to face Kierian.

"You have an objection to continuing our investigation?" Dr. Waatt asked.

"I have an objection to rushing below deck and acting as if we are on a scientific investigation rather than boarding an enemy ship with a crew twenty times our numbers. Why would they put a box of munitions over the hatch door, just to close Professor Stonechat within?"

"Maybe they were trying to keep something out?" Emma offered.

"Or keep something in."

"We will never know until we go down there," Dr. Waatt said.

Kierian nodded. "I agree, but we should be ready for trouble. The locked hatch may explain why we have not been attacked yet. The pirates could be down there in force, waiting for us."

"Your point is well taken, Kierian," Dr. Waatt replied.

"Very well, then. Banshee, draw your pistols and look sharp. Balthazar, another of your party favors may well be necessary."

Dr. Waatt nodded and pulled another MANED from his equipment belt. Kierian stood to one side, aimed his shotgun at the hatch, and nodded to RA-7. "*Now*, we proceed."

The automaton removed the munitions box and opened the hatch.

CHAPTER FIFTEEN

The hatch lifted and a wave of apprehension washed over Emma. She expected a volley of shots to rise from below, but the only thing that rose was the awful, unmistakable stench of death. All three members of STEAMCAPP raised their bandannas over their mouth and nose.

"Ray, let there be light," Kierian said.

High intensity beams of magnesium-powered light blasted from RA-7's eyes and lit the way. Kierian aimed down the barrel of his shotgun, took the lead and descended down the stairs. Emma followed two steps behind, giving him room to retreat if it became necessary.

A cold worm of fear gnawed at Emma's spine, as Kierian reached the bottom steps.

Kierian wheeled his shotgun to the right. "God almighty!"

Emma leaped off the final two steps, landed next to

Kierian, swung her pistols in the direction of the next room, and dropped to one knee.

"Mother Freedom's bell!"

A shroud of crimson carnage, carpeted the ship's hold. Bodies, or what was left of them, littered the blood soaked deck.

The crew of the *Vulture* had been ripped to pieces.

Arms, legs, intestines, and decapitated heads were strewn everywhere. Greasy red gore draped over boxes and barrels. Walls and rafters were painted with splashes of crimson and human remains.

She had seen worse only once before, when they liberated the camps.

These bastards are a villainous lot for sure, but no one deserves to be ripped apart like this.

A wave of nausea swept over her. Just as quickly, she willed it away, raised her pistols, and focused down the sights.

Keep it together. Focus on what you cannot see, what may be lurking. Watch for the threat.

"AHH!" RA-7 let loose a high-pitched bone chilling scream. The rescue automaton, threw his hands in the air, waved them in frantic distress and spun towards the staircase.

The room darkened into shadow. "Damn it, RAY,

get back here! We need that light!" Kierian yelled.

"RA-7. I recommend you engage your Courage Protocol, "Dr. Waatt said.

"Affirmative... Courage protocol... engaged." RA-7 stopped his ascension in mid step, calmly turned, dropped his foot, and walked back to his former position; once more, illuminating the butcher's yard of death.

"Doctor, the visual record of this is utterly repulsive to my memory... banks. I do not wish to see it...anymore. Activating Pure Blind...mode."

"A wise decision, RA-7," Dr. Waatt said.

"Vision now impaired one hundred... percent."

"How is it wise to blind himself?" Kierian asked.

"We all have ways of dealing with unpleasant sights, Kierian. Be thankful he cannot vomit."

A faint smile in spite of herself, played across Emma's visage. A fleeting image of nuts and bolts retching out of a nauseated robot provided a gallows humor respite.

"Besides," Dr. Waatt continued, "At present, you are using him merely as a walking floodlight. I see no degrade in our mission capabilities because his vision is temporality de-activated."

"Wide angle illumination, RAY." Kierian said. The

automaton complied, dispelling shadows from every corner of the hold. "Banshee, watchtower."

Emma's boots sloshed and squished beneath the grizzly remains and gushing horror that swam across the deck. She ran to a set of stacked crates and clambered up. Her perch provided excellent oversight to protect Balthazar and Kierian from any enemies playing possum, who decided to go out in a blaze of gory glory.

Kierian moved along the left side of the room, his shotgun scanned each body and crate he passed. Balthazar on the right side, did the same.

"There are bullet holes in the walls and crates. From the patterns, it looks like they were firing in all directions," Kierian reported.

"I concur with your analysis, Kierian. A very strange battle took place here."

"W-Waatt," a voice uttered.

Dr. Waatt spun, his finger slid onto the trigger of his heat ray rifle. A man slowly arose from a pile of corpses.

"Mr. Kaplan!" Dr. Waatt knelt down, and gently helped the sport to a sitting position. Emma kept her pistol aimed, but quickly saw there he could be no threat; half his face was torn away; his stomach ripped open, exposing his guts and revealing his doom.

Kaplan extended a ghastly, ripped, bone-exposed hand toward Dr. Waatt. "Ho-Ho-M-Ur-Ur-sus Arc-tos." Kaplan's jaw stuck open. He stared past Dr. Waatt, gurgled droplets of crimson, and joined the reaper's tally.

"A Bear did this? How did a bear get on board?" Emma asked.

"There was no bear, Banshee. No doubt, just the ravings of a dying man," Kierian said.

Dr. Waatt stood. His keen eyes scanned the deck of the hold with intense concentration. "Eureka!" He bounded over a headless body, and dropped to one knee. "RA-7, I need more light."

"Understood." The light beam in RA-7's left eye narrowed to a bright focused beam and illuminated a small area at Dr. Waatt's feet.

Emma climbed down from her crow's nest, warily stepped thru the gore, and looked down where Balthazar knelt.

Bathed in the circle of light, was the clear bloody print of an enormous bear.

"More often than not, Kierian, the dying, knowing they are about to meet the Creator face-to-face, utter truths rather than falsehoods. Hence why confessions of the dying are given considerable weight in a court of law."

"Be that as it may, there were no bear claw prints on the top deck. How do you explain how a bear boarded this vessel?" Kierian asked.

"Unknown at this time." Dr. Waatt tapped a gloved finger on the bloody print, "However, clearly, one did."

"That must have been why the hatch was sealed, to keep the bear from reaching the upper deck, but what of Professor Stonechat?" Emma asked.

"I saw no evidence of a female body, though the way they have been dismembered, that alone proves nothing. I suggest we proceed forward."

Kierian nodded.

"My dear," Doctor Waatt said, "would you please take RA-7 by the hand and lead him through this ghastly scene?"

"Of course." Emma trotted back to the automaton and took his metallic hand in hers. "Come along, RAY. It will be alright."

"Thank you Emma…Dareheart."

They weaved their way through the hold and entered the crew quarters. Like broken, discarded mannequins, more bodies laid scattered across the deck.

The door to the engine room was ripped off its hinges. Inside, the gory remains of six pirates greeted

264

them amongst the pistons, boilers and oily gears.

Dr. Waatt activated his magnesium torch and moved amongst the machinery. Quick glances of various instruments and gages informed him the status of the engines.

"The drive shaft has been completely severed from the steering mechanism," Dr. Waatt reported. "The rudder is jammed in the port position. Once that occurred, the pilot had no control over the ship and it quickly ran aground."

"Balthazar!" Kierian called, pointing at an unarmored section of the hull. "I think we know how your bear gained access."

Emma, RA-7 and Dr. Waatt joined Kierian. Wooden planks, smashed and splintered, opened into a massive gaping hole, wide enough for two grown adults to stand side by side.

Only a few yards beyond, lay the open grassy shore, dotted with wooden sentinels of pine. The moon-drenched sky gave an eerie glow to round circles of stone, suggesting former campsites.

"That entrance is certainly large enough for survivors to have escaped. Perhaps, Professor Stonechat, Professor Boaltt, and the other two sports made it out alive," Emma offered.

"It is possible," Kierian said. "We waded through a large number of bodies back there, but it did not seem like even close to eighty–seven."

Dr. Waatt peered through a magnifying glass at the edges of the smashed planks, retrieved a penknife and forceps from his equipment pouch, and began scraping at the broken planks. "RA-7, the gore is gone. I would ask you disengage your Pure Blind mode and assist me with my examination."

"As you wish... Doctor. Pure Blind... disengaged. Visual functionality fully... restored."

Balthazar held out the penknife and forceps to RA-7. "Hair and blood samples, most likely from Horribis Urtus Arctos."

RA-7 held out two test tubes, and Dr. Waatt deposited the evidence in each.

The first report of gunfire rolled in on them like thunder.

Kierian shoved Dr. Waatt away from the opening. Emma dove for cover. Bullets buzzed like angry hornets, slicing through the unarmored hull, sending splinters into Emma's left arm.

Kierian's shotgun roared. A man cried out in pain. Kierian racked the action on the shotgun and fired again. Another blast of buckshot sizzled into the night, another voice uttered a painful shriek. Kierian ducked back inside, just as a slug whistled by his ear and slammed into RA-7's chest.

"If I had pain receptors that would have…hurt."

Kierian slid two rounds into his Winchester Pump. "Balthazar, are you hit?"

Dr. Waatt lay on his back. His eyes gazed upward.

"I am uninjured Kierian, save for a cramp of muscle in my left leg." He rolled to his stomach and unslung his heat-ray rifle.

Kierian nodded. "RAY, illuminate the shore."

Brilliant light flooded out of the automaton's eyes, exposing every inch of the shoreline.

"Banshee, what size force are we facing?"

Emma peeked her head out and pulled it back, all in one practiced motion. A dozen figures rose up from behind the pines and advanced, guns blazing.

"I count at least a dozen, Piper, and they're on the advance."

"Now that they have lost the element of surprise and no longer have the cover of darkness to conceal them, we should be able to fend these lake brigands off easy enough," Dr. Waatt said.

"Not if they board the ship and attack us from two directions," Kierian replied.

"With limited visibility rendering it impossible to see if there is a second group and assuming the surviving pirates are eager to regain possession of their vessel, that may, in fact be a distinct possibility," Dr. Waatt admitted.

Kierian rolled into the opening, came up on one knee, and hip fired. He held down the trigger, pumped the action, and another pirate went down. He pumped and fired again.

The enemy threw themselves onto the ground to avoid the rain of buckshot and returned fire. A hail of lead splashed water and wood chips into Kierian's face. He rolled back from the opening.

"That was exemplary shooting, and a valiant effort, Kierian, but it would be ill advised to attempt such again," Dr. Waatt said.

Kierian pulled a splinter from his cheek and reloaded his shotgun. "You do realize, Doctor, if we do not keep them at bay and they move close enough, one grenade toss will spell our doom."

"Precisely why I propose we withdraw into the armored section of the ship."

"If we do that, they can board whenever and where ever they like," Emma replied. "They will hit us from two sides, for certain." She reached around the opening and blasted her six-guns blindly, emptying them at the enemy, hoping the torrent of lead would give them second thoughts on making a charge.

"We have to do something, my dear. Sitting here exchanging shots with a numerical superior enemy is folly. Sooner or later, one of them are bound to get lucky."

Emma reloaded her pistols.

Balthazar was right, but she was confident Kierian would come up with some clever and cunning plan.

He hated losing too much not to.

* * * * * *

Bully Browne peered through the binoculars, his cruel mouth twisted with hate.

Bastards. Son of a bitch, black souled devils.

They had to be the ones responsible for releasing that mechanical beast inside his ship. And it had to be mechanical, right? It moved too damn fast to be nature's kin and neither shot nor shell slowed it down.

One of the bastards spun into the opening of the *Vulture* and slam fired a pump shotgun, with extraordinary speed. The buckshot tore through the chest of one of his crew like tissue paper. The others halted their advance and threw themselves down to the ground.

"Keep up your fire, you mangy river rats!" he yelled at his crew. Bulging, hate-filled eyes watched two slugs slam harmlessly into the bronze metal man, kneeling in the opening of his ship's hull.

Anyone with the learning to make a metal man had the learning to make a metal beast. So these had to be the bastard whore-sons who wrecked his *Vulture*.

He rubbed a dirty hand at his temple. Throbbing spider webs of pain, laced through his head. He glanced at the unconscious blonde woman lying on the ground behind him.

Mother always said: yellow hairs beware. I should have listened to the old hag.

He kicked the blonde in the stomach and she moaned in pain. She was a feisty bitch, and ungrateful too. He had offered her a full glass of Falls Folly wine to make her more agreeable and how did she respond? By throwing it in his face. He had delivered two well-earned backhands across both the bitch's cheeks and threw her violently on the bed, but she grabbed his spyglass off the table, smashed it into his head and escaped out his cabin window.

He gave chase. Only the shuddering crash of the ship running aground had knocked him from his feet. It

270

was seconds later that he raced down the stairs after her.

That's when he saw the beast.

It stood on two legs, bellowing in rage, its yellow eyes promising death. Fangs and claws, dripping blood, carved and cut his men to ribbons, sending fountains of fatal red spraying across his ship.

He emptied his pistol into its head, but it only enraged the beast. He raced back up to the main deck, closed the hatch, and ordered his gunners to weigh it down with boxes full of cannonballs, damning most of his crew to a grisly and gory fate.

Better their sorry hides than mine.

He grabbed a bag full of gold coins, ammunition, supplies and abandoned ship. Twenty-two others soon joined him ashore, including the woman. Somehow, she had been fortunate enough to survive the beast. When the beast ran into the forest, hotly pursuing three of his men, her luck ran out. She ran past the pine he was hiding behind, and he knocked her unconscious as she passed.

Shrieks of horror commingled with a sinister roar, tolled the fate of the three men the beast had pursued.

Bully adjusted the focus of the field glasses. Two pistols appeared in the opening of the hull and blazed a hail of lead. Curse and cuss, flew from wicked lips as dirt and stone kicked into cheek and scalp.

Bully scowled at his river rats.

Damn their skulking skins. They're doing more flinching than firing.

He raised the bolt-action rifle and fired into the middle of his prone pirates. "I said keep up your fire, you damn shitbirds!"

He was well out of rifle range himself, but he did not consider that cowardice, simply good leadership. A captain's job was to direct the fighting not engage in it, after all.

Bully glanced towards the ship's bow, where ten pirates waded unopposed. It wouldn't be long now. Soon, they would board the *Vulture*, rush below deck and hit the bastards from behind.

CHAPTER SIXTEEN

RA-7 frowned, and his metal shoulders trembled. "I do not like this cunning...plan."

Emma rested the barrel of her EMR-2 on the automaton's right shoulder. She did not like it either. Kierian's cunning plan was for RA-7 to sit in the opening and act as a metal shield while she and Balthazar sniped away at the group of pirates, firing at them from their front. Meanwhile, Kierian would race up to the pilothouse locate any other pirates and deal with them accordingly.

"Fret not, Ray, I will be fine," Kierian reassured.

"I believe he is worried more about his own self preservation than your well being, Kierian," Dr. Waatt corrected.

Kierian offered a confident smile. "The chances of any of these freebooters scoring a damaging hit on you RAY, is minimal."

The automaton dropped his head to his chest. "They have already damaged my... buckskins. After this plan is implemented, they will be torn to...pieces."

Kierian patted RA-7 on the shoulder affectionately. "I will employ Saul to custom tailor you a new set *after* we have completed the mission, but to accomplish *that,* we must recover Professor Stonechat and to do *tha*t, we need to deal with the lake scum shooting at us."

Two bullets bounced off RA-7's chest. The robot cringed but held his position.

"Just think how impressed Professor Stonechat will be when we tell her how brave you were," Kierian offered.

"She will be impressed with... me?"

Kierian grinned, as he took the safety off his pistol. "Of course. The ladies always love a brave and courageous man. Do they not, Banshee?"

"We like them alive, too, Piper." Emma cast a pained look at Kierian. Confident blue eyes twinkled back at her, accompanied by a swaggering grin. "You should know by now, that I'm a hard man to keep down, much less kill."

"You don't even know the numbers you will be facing. I should be watching your back."

Dr. Waatt rested his heat-ray rifle on RA-7's other

shoulder flicked a few switches, and looked through the scope. "Perhaps she is right, Kierian. I can keep the enemy at bay well enough by myself."

Emma began to stand up.

"Stand fast, Banshee! You're staying here. That's an order."

Emma was taken aback how resolute Kierian's voice was. Years of obeying his commands in combat, instinctively stopped her in mid-rise. Hurt filled eyes, pleaded up at him to take her with him.

Kierian smiled, kissed her on the cheek and began to walk away. Emma spun, and took hold of his arm. "RAY, do you still have that bouquet of red shamrocks?"

"Affirmative."

"Please hand me two," Emma said, keeping her gaze on Kierian. She held out her hand and felt the automaton place the flowers in her palm. She rested her rifle against RAY's back, pulled a pin from her hair, and held it in her teeth. Nimble fingers speedily pinned both flowers to Kierian's upper vest.

"Protection to the daring, right, Balthazar?"

Dr. Waatt nodded. "That is correct, my dear."

Emma smiled at Kierian. "Do not dare get yourself killed."

* * * * * *

A lick of flame spit from the barrel of the bolt-action rifle. The bullet whistled by Kierian's right ear. He leveled the shotgun from a kneeling position and squeezed the trigger. A fist size pattern of buckshot slammed into the pirate's chest sending him slumping lifelessly, to the deck.

The shotgun *ca-chakked* in Kierian's hands. More pirates swung over the bow of the *Vulture*. Pistol and rifle fire cut the air around him. He slam fired the shotgun from left to right, peppering the enemy with double aught. The pirates dove for cover.

Kierian grinned. *Ha! These lake trash outnumber me eight to one and yet they still cower and hide!*

He pulled a smoke canister from his belt, tugged the pin fee, and tossed it onto the deck. White smoke billowed forth, blanketing the enemy in a ghostly shroud.

Kierian rose, raced across the main deck, and scampered onto the gun deck. He reloaded his shotgun, swung it up to his shoulder, and waited for his targets to emerge from the smoke.

* * * * *

With a blood-curdling yell, the river pirates charged

276

Emma and Dr. Waatt.

Emma rested the barrel of her weapon on RA-7's shoulder, sighted thru the brass scope, and pulled the trigger. With a crackling hum the EMR-2 fired, sending its aluminum projectile at super sonic speed, through the head of a river pirate.

Dr. Waatt took aim and pulled the trigger on his Maser rifle. A red beam of amplified energy sliced thru the air, blistering through flesh and bone, and yielded instant death to one of the charging buccaneers.

But on, they came.

"They're coming too fast, Balthazar!"

Dr. Waatt reached into his pouch and retrieved another MANED. "This should slow their advance to a crawl if not stop it entirely." He turned the key and swung his arm back, prepared to make an underhand throw around RA-7.

As the stun bomb left Dr. Waatt's hand, a bullet smashed into RA-7's left eye, shutting off the flood of light from that side. The automaton brought his left hand up to the damaged socket and the long bronze fingers, deflected the MANED skyward.

End over end, it tumbled toward the upper deck.

* * * * * *

Double aught death, dropped the first and second pirates to emerge from the white curtain of smoke. Kierian shoved two shells into the shotgun.

Klink!

He glanced towards the metal on metal sound and saw an apple shaped device bounce off the top of the armored wheelhouse.

Even as he tucked his shoulder and dove away, his mind already screamed to him, *TOO LATE!*

The MANED exploded.

Blinding white light flooded, Kierian's vision and his world went silent.

He had been shell shocked before, when the British fifteen pounders opened up atop Cobbs Hill, and he knew trying to stand would be futile.

I have to get to cover and fast. Can't fight blind and deaf.

He no longer held his shotgun. He patted around for it, but only for a second.

No time to locate it. Get to cover.

He drew his M1900, but it was his mind that would now be his most effective weapon.

He knew where he was, and where he had to go. Safety was within the pilothouse.

The smoke was slowly dissipating. No shots had come his way yet. If he could make it into the Captain's quarters, he could conceal himself until the stun bomb's effects vanished. He switched his pistol into his left hand, freeing his right to feel for the open doorway that would lead to safety.

Hand over hand. No fear.

He crawled across deck. Eyes blinked, willing the blindness to depart. He pushed off with his feet, and pulled himself forward with his elbows

Hand over hand. No fear.

His right hand found the doorway. He turned and crawled his way over the opening.

Two bullets slammed against the wall above him and ricocheted away.

They have found me. Have to move fast now. No choice.

He opened his eyes. The blindness had left him but his vision was doubled. He pushed himself up, ran a few steps, and lurched into the Captain's quarters, diving behind the table.

Running footsteps, across the deck told him the enemy was near. Kierian kicked over the table. The cheap wine smashed to the floor.

Ha! At least that swill will never be imbibed again. The world should thank me for that alone!

Two pirates swung around the opening and fired their pistols. Two shots blew through the table, and

279

whistled into the wall, above and behind Kierian.

Kierian spun around the table's edge and unloaded his Colt, firing in a spread pattern at the four images. The sound of two bodies striking the floor, as he ducked back behind the table and reloaded, announced his success.

More shouts and oaths of murder. More running feet.

The enemy was closing in.

They will either come for me or hit Banshee and Balthazar from behind. Damn! I should have brought her with me. Now, I have put all of us in danger. Never treat a civilian like a soldier or a soldier like a civilian. He shook his head. *I should have brought her with me.*

He pulled Balthazar's heat ray pistol from his belt, gripped it in his left hand, and waited for the overwhelming charge, determined to go out in a blaze of glory as he made his final stand.

* * * * * *

With a practiced hand, Dr. Waatt tossed a second MANED into the middle of the rushing river rats and averted his eyes.

Phrock-boom!

The explosion stopped the rush dead in its tracks.

280

Nausea, imbalance and vertigo, overwhelmed the pirates, incapacitating the entire strike force.

Dr. Waatt turned to tell Emma to begin the turkey shoot, but she was already on her feet and dashing down the corridor.

"My dear Emma, I implore you — "

She never heard the rest of Dr. Waatt's sentence.

Bright light beamed from her magnesium torch. She raced back through the lower deck, pivoting and leaping through the crimson carnage. She saw the stairwell and exchanged the torch for a pistol, in each hand.

She rushed around the corner, taking two steps in one leap and collided into three river pirates.

The surprised pirates hesitated.

Banshee did not.

She stuck the barrel of her Colt into the guts of the first pirate, pulled the trigger, and gave him a second navel. Flames from the barrel set his clothes afire. Banshee spun to her right, shoved the barrel of her other pistol under the chin of the second pirate and painted the ceiling with his brains.

The third pirate leveled his rifle.

Banshee roared with a shriek worthy of her name and kicked it away. Her Colts thundered .45-caliber death.

281

She shouldered her way past the bullet riddled corpses and bolted up the steps. She dropped to one knee at the top of the stairs, reloaded and scanned the decks. Six pirates were climbing up the ladder that led to the Pilot House, screaming vulgar and vile oaths that involved cutting out someone's liver and frying it up in a pan for din-din.

Only Kierian could make someone that angry.

She raced towards the ladder. The last of the six pirates heard her footsteps. He spun, and in one hasty motion, leveled his pistol, and fired.

His shot went wide.

Banshee's unflustered aim fired a single shot into the lake raider's head.

The other pirates spun to face her.

From the base of the ladder, Banshee's six guns spit out leaden death. Like wheat before the scythe, the pirates twisted and fell. Banshee climbed the ladder like a cat and made for the Pilothouse. A pirate groaned and raised himself to his knees. Banshee shot him through the back and coldly stepped over his lifeless body.

She took up a position next to the door, careful not to charge in and create some God-awful tragedy.

The barrel of her smoking Colt rapped thrice against the wall. "Knock, knock, knock, Mister Piper, I

282

am home."

Her heart sang, as she heard Kierian's charming chuckle. Gracefully she spun into the pilothouse and entered the Captain's quarters, stepping over the bodies of three dead pirates. Kierian stood, weapons in hand. The walls behind him were pock marked with bullet holes.

"I apologize the place is such a mess," Kierian said, "But as you see, I had some rather rowdy guests."

"Good thing I stopped by to lend a woman's touch."

"Your timing was impeccable. If I could determine which one of the two Banshees I see before me was real, I would give you a kiss."

"Fortunately, I can see fine for both of us." Emma leaned forward, her hands softly cupped Kierian's cheeks. Blood stained boots perched on tip toes to reach her Piper's lips. Brown eyes closed ready to meet—"

"Emma! Kierian!" Dr. Waatt called.

Kierian abruptly pulled back. Emma glanced behind her. Balthazar stood in the doorway leaning on his cane; his heat ray rifle shouldered. RA-7, his chest pock-marked with dozens of impact dents, smiled and waved from behind him.

"RA-7 and I have sealed the pirates in the lower

deck but only temporarily. We must evacuate the ship at once."

"Why? We wiped out the entire upper deck boarding party," Kierian replied.

"Because, if my calculations are correct, and I am positive they are, we have less than two minutes before all three boilers explode."

Kieran nodded. He stumbled past Dr. Waatt. "RAY, give me a hand, if you would. I am still seeing double"

Emma watched as RA-7 took Kierian by the arm and helped him down the ladder, to the main deck.

Chestnut globes glowered up at Dr. Waatt. "Balthazar, you really need to work on your timing."

Dr. Waatt cocked his head and pondered for a moment. "I do not see why that is so. RA-7's coal shoveling at enhanced speed, and a sustained blast from my MASER rifle, allowed me to rapidly re-heat the boilers. Furthermore, I have sabotaged the safety valves. The rate of steam pressure build up in the boilers will therefore, increase at a quantifiable rate. Uninterrupted, the explosion should take place, in—" Dr. Waatt glanced at his pocket watch— "One minute and thirty-two seconds."

Emma nodded and patted Dr. Waatt on the arm, as she walked past.

284

Relationships can be like boilers too, Balthazar. Keep them simmering too long and you can ruin everything.

CHAPTER SEVENTEEN

Lantern lights danced across the main deck of the *Vulture* like fireflies, as the river pirates swarmed across.

Bully smiled. There had been no gunfire for at least a minute. The bastards and their metal man must have been destroyed. If most of his crew had been slaughtered retaking his ship, so what? Violent, shit-bird goons willing to rape and pillage, were easy enough to find these days. It was the ironclad that was irreplaceable. It would need repairing, but a good mechanic would have his lovely steaming down the lake in no time, committing mayhem and murder to any who dared oppose him.

He took a swig from his canteen, swirled the water around in his mouth, and spit the rest into the face of the blonde. She jerked to a sitting position.

"On your feet bitch." Bully grabbed the blonde and pulled her by her shirt to her feet.

"My boys have re-taken the ship, and you and I have some unfinished business back in my cabin." Transparent evil lined his cackle, but the blond simply stared back at him with vacant eyes.

Bully scowled at her. He liked to see fear in his victims.

Blondie was denying him that.

Brutal hands slapped her hard across the face, reddening her pale cheeks.

No response.

"I didn't hit you so hard before as to scramble your senses, so you can quit playing the crazy. It won't help you none, anyhow. Mad or sane, I'll be taking my pleasures with you, shortly."

A deafening boom and a massive shock wave washed over Bully, knocking him off his feet. Horrified eyes stared towards the lake. Two more explosions followed. An angry orange cloud of flame rose into the sky. Flying chunks of metal, wood, and human limbs rained down where the *Vulture* once had been.

"My *Vulture*! My Lovely!" Bully pulled Blondie up and swung her around. Brutal hate blazed in his eyes, his hunting knife tore from its sheath.

"YOU BITCH!" white knuckles of rage shook the knife in her face. "You're the cause of all this! I would have been easy on you! You could have even enjoyed it, but not now!" Empty vacant eyes blinked back at him but Blondie made no other response.

"I'm going to take my pleasures, but it'll be in cutting and gutting now!" Bully pulled back his knife and slashed it in a brutal arc.

* * * * * *

From the cockpit of his Gryphon, Chaney glowered daggers of hate at the large white tent. It was made of double layered canvas. Inside, mosquito netting was hung to keep any insects from biting its occupant. It was perfect to keep the demon bees away from him, and as the only member of the brotherhood trained to drive the Gryphon, Chaney felt he damn well had earned it as his lodging place.

Instead, the Duchess now occupied it.

Damn her to hell! And Damn Barnabas Blackwell, too! Even in this wretched wilderness, she still gets the best of everything!

He had said as much to Barnabas yesterday.

"Whose fault is that, Chaney? You're the one who burned down the cabin and tents," Barnabas had replied.

"That don't excuse you giving her the big tent.

288

Duchess ain't worth spit and she sure as hell, ain't worth more than the rest of us, Barnabas."

"Right now, she is worth about one million in silver more. Without her, we have no leverage to get Professor Stonechat here, and without Stonechat we can't breach the inner chamber and if we can't breach the chamber, we can't get the artifact."

"You want the damn chamber breached? I'll blast it open with my Gryphon. That way, we don't need Stonechat and don't need to keep Duchess."

"Blast it open? And run the risk of bringing the whole structure down and dooming the mission?"

"I was just thinking—"

"Well, don't! Keep your Gryphon operational, soldier like you're supposed to, and leave the planning and thinking to me."

Knuckles knotted, his blood boiled with the foulness of hate. Bloodshot eyes glared at the big white tent, where Gladys Vanderbilt slumbered.

Duchess probably sleeps like a baby, while I'm lucky to get 3 hours sack time in this tin can.

The Gryphon was the only place besides the white tent where he felt safe from the demon bees. Each night, he secured himself inside. Each morning, he awoke with aches and pains coursing through out his body, while Duchess always looked fresh as a daisy.

He rubbed his bandaged shoulder. He'd damn well had enough of Duchess's lip this morning and would have finished his carving on her had Barnabas not intervened. He'd gone to see Dr. Neil, like Barnabas had said, and bitched enough that the Doc had given him a few ounces of laudanum for the pain.

But he hadn't used it. He'd endured the pain, waited for darkness, and slipped the laudanum in the wine bottle of Duchess's guard.

Vengeful lips spread into a Cheshire cat grin. Right about now, Knobbs should be peacefully visiting the land of Nod.

It was time to make his move.

Chaney popped the cockpit, grabbed the canvas bag at his feet, and climbed out of the Gryphon. Inside, the Timber snake squirmed and sounded its threatening rattle. A wicked grin played across Chaney's brutal face. Duchess's demise would be agonizingly slow, and also slow enough that Barnabas could still exchange her tomorrow for the silver and Stonechat.

With a confident and hate filled heart, Chaney stalked towards the large, white tent.

* * * * * *

Strong hands pulled Gladys from slumber and forced a dirty rag inside her mouth. Her eyes widened in fear and shock. Her attacker tied the gag securely around the back of her head. Already bound hand and foot, she could offer no resistance.

"Time to die, Duchess," a voice hissed from behind the mosquito netting.

A match flared, lighting the kerosene lamp on the wooden crate next to her cot. The instrument of her demise dropped inches from her face.

Gladys screamed into the rag; her green eyes widened in terror. The serpent slithered across her chin; its cold reptilian skin, brushed across her cheek, its forked tongue searching for her scent.

Sadistic laughter erupted from behind her.

Gladys shot a desperate glance towards Mr. Knobbs.

The guard lay sprawled and unmoving on the ground, a broken bottle of hooch inches from his open hand.

The timber snake traced an "S" across her chest, and onto the cot near her right side. Its threatening rattle informing her, death was imminent.

Gladys barrel rolled.

Twin fangs flashed in the lamp-lit dark.

She crashed to the ground. Shockwaves of pain radiated along her collarbone and shoulder.

"Oh no you don't Duchess! This time, there ain't going to be any escape for you!"

Gladys rolled onto her back in time to see a stick flip the serpent to the ground by her feet.

Its fangs flashed again. Gladys yanked her feet back toward her chest, avoiding the death bite by inches.

She jerked herself to a sitting position and scooted back.

The snake slithered forward.

Gladys scooted again. The hard canvas of the tent against her lower back informed her there was no more room for retreat.

Outside, a thunderous explosion rattled the sleeping camp. Feet ran against hard ground. "...Under attack..." someone shouted. The sadistic voice behind her cussed and she heard him run off.

If the camp is under attack, then Mr. Blackwell will come for me. I just need to buy time.

But there was none left.

The timber snake slithered forward. Its coiled body rattled out its song of death and raised its fangs for the kill.

Gladys swung her feet. Her boots smashed into the

292

crate sending the lamp crashing to the ground.

Fire instantly ignited the kerosene and the laudanum laced alcohol, creating a stream of fire between her and serpentine death.

Flames licked at her feet, like hungry devils of hell.

* * * * * *

Barnabas bolted up from a sound sleep.

Had that been thunder? He cocked his head and listened. Two more thunderclaps told the tale, eliminating the possibility of the sound being natural.

Explosions! They're a few miles away but definitely man made.

Barnabas attached his holster around his waist, and rushed out his tent. The brothers were awakening, some gripping their rifles nervously and pointing towards a glowing fire, about three miles away, near Raquette Lake.

How can there be fire on the lake?

Someone yelled fire. Barnabas nodded, thinking they were talking about lake.

The smell of burning canvas proclaimed the terrible truth. Barnabas spun about. His eyes widened, and failure clutched a vice hold on his heart. Fire sheathed the front flaps of Gladys Vanderbilt's tent. Flaming fingers reached out quickly, spreading their fiery touch to the rest of the tent.

Barnabas raced around the back, drew his hunting knife, slashed away at the ropes holding the tent edges, and ducked his head inside. The Vanderbilt girl huddled in the corner. Barnabas dove inside, as the flames rapidly spread. He grasped under the heiress's shoulders and yanked her from the burning tent.

"What happened Miss Vanderbilt?"

The girl responded with a mumble. Barnabas realized her mouth was gagged. All thoughts that an enemy had done this left him. "Chaney?" he asked, removing the rag from her mouth.

Gladys nodded. "It sounded like him....I-I could not see. Whoever it was they... threw a snake into the tent. I had to knock the lamp over or it would have bitten me for certain."

"You're a very resourceful young lady, Miss Vanderbilt." Barnabas slashed the ropes at her feet and closed his arm tight around hers. He pulled her into the center of the camp. A handful of his men tossed buckets of water on the tent, quickly extinguishing the fire.

"Barnabas, Knobbs is dead," a brother named Sadorwitz informed.

"Damn fast for a fire to have cooked him," Barn-

294

abas replied.

"He didn't look none charred, but he's deader than a door nail, sure."

Barnabas glanced toward the lake. The explosions had been massive, almost like artillery firing. But who would have artillery? What would they be firing at? Had Alfred Vanderbilt managed to sail some heavily armed gunboat up the lake and deposited a rescue team? They had instructed the party, delivering the ransom, to come by land along the common trails used by hunters and picnickers but maybe they hadn't listened. Maybe whoever was coming had gone by water.

"Barnabas," Sadorwitz said, "Are we under attack? What should we do?"

"If we were under attack, bullets would be flying by now. Still, it doesn't make sense to stay put. It's almost light. We'll break camp and head to Reese Lake, directly."

"No breakfast?"

Barnabas shook his head. "No breakfast. Break camp, and make sure we have a few scouts watching our backdoor when we get marching."

"Alright, Barnabas. If you say so." Sadorwitz dashed off, shouting out Barnabas's orders to the others.

The anarchist leader glanced once more, towards the lake. He had no doubt Chaney had been the one to try and kill his hostage. For now, there was little he could do about it. Chaney knew how to operate the Gryphon. Kill him, and he eliminated the biggest advantage he possessed in any firefight.

No, he still needed Chaney but he would damn sure keep the Vanderbilt girl with him at all times, until the exchange. After that, it didn't matter what happened to her. By then the whole country would be turned upside down.

* * * * * *

"Well done, RA-7, your rowing was exemplary," Kierian said, as he exited the rowboat and walked onto the beach.

"Thank you Kierian…McKenna," The automation answered.

Dr. Waatt limped ashore, pulled his binoculars from his equipment belt, activated the image intensifier, and scanned the beach. "By the stars and stripes! Look up on the bluff!"

Emma unslung her EMR-2, brought it up for action all in one smooth motion, and peered through the scope. "My God! It is Professor Stonechat, and the scum is holding a knife in her face!"

296

"Turn his lights out, Banshee," Kierian said.

"She is too close. Even if I hit him the shot will most likely plow through his body and strike hers."

He peered through his spyglass. "No choice," Kierian said. "Look at his face. He is going to kill her, for certain. You have done this before. Take the shot."

It was true this would not be the first time she would have to shoot to save a hostage, but it was also true that she had missed before. The logic told you after the deed had been done, that the person would have perished anyway, and you should give yourself an 'A' for effort. The truth however, was that you damn well still knew it was your bullet that had killed an innocent and that was a fact not easily lived with.

"RA-7 illuminate the bluff so Miss Dareheart can have a better view," Dr. Waatt said.

"Belay that order, Ray."

"Kierian, if she has more light to see by, she—"

"It will spook that pirate. He will simply move down the trail out of our sight and gut Professor Stonechat." Kierian kept his eye to the spyglass. "Banshee, shoot for the apricot. Professor Stonechat is out of time."

Emma swung her EMR-2 up, and sighted down the scope at her target. She watched as his knife arched upward. She took a deep breath, slowly exhaled and pulled the trigger.

With a crackling hum, the EMR-2 fired.

Apprehension knotted in Emma's stomach. Like puppets whose strings had been cut, both target and hostage collapsed to the ground.

CHAPTER EIGHTEEN

"Professor Stonechat! Professor Stonechat!" Dr. Waatt uncorked a flask of ammonium carbonate and waved the smelling salt beneath the archeologist's nose.

RA-7 ran his fingers over her head. "I detect No bumps or… contusions. Concussion and brain damage…unlikely."

With a sudden jerk, Professor Stonechat sat up. terrified green eyes stared at Dr. Waatt.

"The roar of the mighty bear, the cry of the lake wet loon; submit to the way and the where, at the rising of the moon."

Immediately, she collapsed. RA-7 reached out his arms and prevented her from crashing to the hard ground.

"She is in a catatonic state, I am afraid," Dr. Waatt informed.

"I concur… Dr. Waatt."

Emma adjusted her Balmoral cap. "What is wrong with her? You don't suppose my bullet went thru the pirate and struck her, do you?"

Dr. Waatt shook his head. "I do not. There is no obvious wound that I can see. Clearly, the good Lord guided the bullet's trajectory my dear."

Kierian patted her on the head. "A first rate shot to be sure, Banshee."

Emma smiled and nodded.

Damn right it was first rate!

Dr. Waatt walked to RA-7's giant backpack, which contained his equipment and the ransom. He retrieved several poles, each about three feet high.

"If your eyesight has returned to normal, Kierian, would you be so good as to place my Movement Awareness Devices in the appropriate locations. I doubt anyone can scale the bluff, and bushwhacking from what I could see, would be extremely difficult; so, I would advise you focus on the trail that led up here and directly, to either side."

Kierian, without argument, activated his magnesium torch and walked down the trail to set up MADs.

Back in the day, they would string pots, pans and empty cans between trees, to alert them of interlopers. Of course, tin pans didn't emit an ear-piercing shriek, momentarily disorienting the trespasser as well as alerting STEAMCAPP to their presence like the MADs did.

Even Kierian saw the superiority in the devices over the old ways.

Dr. Waatt rolled out his sleeping bag by a large boulder, unzipped it, and motioned to RA-7. The automaton carried Veronica Stonechat, gently laid her down inside, zipped it closed, and patted her kindly on the head.

"If she was not struck by my bullet, what *is* wrong with her, Balthazar?"

Dr. Waatt drew his heat-ray pistol and fired an extend blast into a large boulder, instantly providing a heat source for the unconscious archeologist.

"Professor Stonechat's mind is reacting to the shocking events she witnessed. From the poem she recited, that would be the brutal slaughter of the *Vulture* crew by the Grizzly bear. Unable to deal with the chemical reaction in the brain caused by the emotional shock, her mind has shut down all functions, save those absolutely necessary for life."

"Will she recover?" Kierian asked.

"In time, yes. I do not see any physical injuries save, for some bruising around the jaw and cheeks."

"How much time? We do not have a lot of it left," Emma replied.

"Understood, this has been a most exhausting day and we all are in much need of rest. I suggest we camp here, and if by morning Professor Stonechat has not sufficiently recovered, I will employ ECT."

"ECT?" Kierian asked.

"Electro Convulsive Therapy. I will literally shock her out of her Catatonic state."

* * * * * *

Thursday
August 29 1901
STEAMCAPP'S Campsite

Golden rays shined down from a clear blue sky, slicing through tall evergreens, and bathing Emma in a warming glow.

She awoke with her head lying on Kierian's chest and her pistol gripped in her right hand. His arm was draped around her and his hand gripped his M1900.

She slipped out from his embrace and gently rolled up right, careful not to wake him. Sitting up, she holstered her pistol and rubbed the sleep from her eyes.

Old habits die-hard. During the war, the dream terrors came every night, and being close to Kierian was the only thing that kept them at bay.

But that was then. This was now and the night terrors had not come in a long, long time nor did she recall any last night. So, why had she sleepwalked over and laid down on him like it was 1893 all over again?

Why did I do that? I'm not a little girl. I do not need Kierian thinking I need a snuggle to feel safe. Thank God he didn't wake and find me there.

She retrieved her Balmoral cap, and slung her EMR-2 over her shoulder. Lowering the Binoggulars over her eyes, she gazed down upon the lake.

Twisted sections of the bow and stern were all that remained of the ironclad. Body parts floated in the lake, a grim testament to the fate of all the souls who so recently crewed her.

Damn! When Balthazar wants to, he sure knows how to blow something all to hell.

She glanced around the campsite. Balthazar was sleeping peacefully on his back, a sleeping mask over his eyes. Professor Stonechat remained in the same position she had been placed the night before.

Emma frowned. She had hoped the Professor would come out of her stupor with a good night's rest.

303

While she was confident Balthazar knew what he was doing, she was not looking forward to watching him use the 'wonders of electricity' to shock the archeologist back into sanity.

Using the heat ray pistol to ignite a few twigs and brush grass, she started a fire, brewed a pot of coffee, and cooked up some bacon, rice and beans. Kierian awoke as the bacon began to sizzle.

"Awakey, awakey, Coffee and Bake-y," Emma said.

Kierian's blue eyes beamed at her. He holstered his pistol, stretched his arms, reached into his pack, and handed Emma a red shamrock from RA-7's bouquet.

Emma smiled. "What is this for?"

"For coming to my aid on the ironclad so promptly." Kierian grinned and dug his grooming kit from one of the compartments in his equipment belt. Dexterous fingers opened the leather pouch and carefully spread out its contents on a satin cloth.

"Groom before the doom, Piper? Some things never change."

Kierian slid his engraved brass comb from its silk sheath. "Why should they, Banshee? Just because a person sleeps under the stars instead of under silk sheets is no excuse not to look one's best."

Emma took a sip from her coffee. "How did you

sleep?"

Kierian ran the comb through his dirty blond hair, and deftly maneuvered the vanity mirror, carefully looking over each area of his head. Precise strokes combed any patch of unkempt hair.

"I am no longer seeing double, I was not stabbed, or shot by a vile river pirate, nor torn apart by a wild bear. All in all, well enough I would say. And you?"

"Like a baby."

"No nightmares, then?"

Emma took another sip of her coffee and shook her head. "No. Why do you ask?"

Kierian poured a splash of Dashing Drake's Hair Shine into his hands and fingered it through his hair.

"I awoke in the middle of the night with you laying on my chest. I thought after what you saw in the hold, maybe—"

"I have seen worse. You know that."

Kierian poured some water into his shaving mug. His ivory-handled silver-tipped badger hair shaving brush, dipped generously into the tin of Tayler's Lavender Luxury Shaving soap. Practiced strokes smoothed a creamy lather onto his face. "Just because you have seen worse, does not mean that seeing a human slaughterhouse will have no effect on you, Ban-

305

shee."

"I am fine. Sights like yesterday's come with the job."

Kierian effortlessly snapped open the straight razor with a flick of his wrist. "There are other occupations you know. Occupations that don't involve wading through human remains and rivers of blood."

"I have another job."

Long, precise, well practiced strokes of the razor, sculptured Kierian's face. "I meant something respectable, that does not involve risking life and limb, or going over water falls in a thimble."

"Barrel," Emma corrected. "There are also respectable jobs for a man too, Piper. Ones that do not involve clandestine missions to Cuba to rescue beautiful nineteen-year old female revolutionaries."

Kierian smirked. He glanced at the mirror and slowly shaved the other side of his face. "I am simply pointing out that there is no need for you to be in an occupation that brings back the ghosts of missions past every night."

Emma's eyes narrowed over the top of her coffee mug. "I was just cold. Stop fussing about me. I am not fifteen anymore. I can take care of myself."

Kieran nodded. A few practiced strokes of the

straight razor completed his shave. He wiped off his face, and turned, locking his blue eyes on her. "I know you can, Emma, but you should not have to."

"I'd rather take care of myself than be dependent on some gent. Besides, exactly how long do you think you would you last without me as your partner?"

Kierian choked a laugh. "Me? Why, I would be good as gold. After all, I would still have the genius of Balthazar Waatt by my side."

"Ha! You and Balthazar? As field partners? Without me to play peacemaker?" Emma scoffed. "If you two didn't kill each other five minutes into a mission, it would only be because you were too exhausted from your pre-mission pissing match."

"Well, I would excel solo, then. The point is —"

"Solo? Like yesterday when you nearly got yourself killed charging a strike force of river pirates without me watching your back?"

An audible sigh escaped Kierian's lips. "I should have coded you Brick, because sometimes there is no getting through to you."

Emma shrugged. "Maybe yours should have been Burro because sometimes, you can be such an a —"

A 125-decibel shriek bleated alarm through the peaceful Adirondack forest.

Kierian snatched up his shotgun and raced down the trail. Emma followed, breaking into the brush, and veering right as Kierian broke left. She ran parallel to Kierian; athletic legs leaped over logs. She ducked under low hanging branches, ignoring the wooden fingers swiping across her flesh. They neared the alarming MADs. Emma sighted two men ten yards away, their rifle barrels extended in her and Kierian's direction.

Kierian took cover behind a large cedar, racked a round into the shotgun chamber and took aim.

RA-7 emerged suddenly from the brush, stepped onto the trail and held his hands up.

"RAY get down! You are in the line of fire!" Kierian yelled.

"I recommend you hold your fire,… Kierian McKenna. Intruders identified as Mr. Henroff, Mr. Leslie… and Professor Boaltt."

Henroff and Leslie stood up from behind their log. "Mr. McKenna? You are alive! We thought you dead and drowned, sir," Henroff said.

Emma stepped out into the trail. "And we thought you sliced and diced apart by a grizzly bear."

Mr. Leslie smiled. "Miss Dareheart! It is good to see no harm has befallen you either. We did not see any of you surface. How did you manage to survive?"

308

Dr. Waatt suddenly emerged from the brush behind the three sports.

Balthazar was a crafty old dog. Emma had not seen him or heard him as she raced through the brush, but he must have been working his way all along to a rear position. If it had been an enemy, they would have had them dead to rights in a lethal crossfire.

Dr. Waatt shouldered his heat ray rifle. "We survived through the use of my under water breathing apparatus which RA-7 carries for just such emergencies."

"And yourselves," Kierian asked. "How did you survive those river pirates, exactly?"

"The pirates took Kaplan and Professor Boaltt below deck, and poor Professor Stonechat was escorted to that lecherous Captain's cabin," Henroff related. "Shortly thereafter, the ironclad made a turn at a bend in the lake. There was a sound of sheering metal. The vessel careened hard to the right, and ran aground."

Dr. Waatt nodded. "The drive section separated from the rudder. That was the sheering sound you heard."

"There was an awful shudder," Leslie said, continuing the tale, "our guards were knocked from their feet. We jumped them, killed the machine-gun gunner and the cannoneer, leaped into the water and swam ashore.

Once there, we headed inland. During the night we heard the most God-awful shrieking and screaming. A few hours later, the shooting renewed and concluded with a massive explosion and fireball, which must have been the ironclad exploding."

"Yes, that was our doing," Kierian said proudly.

"Your doing? You three defeated that entire crew of pirates?"

Glowing pride covered Kierian's face. He puffed out his chest. "Of course! River pirates are no matche for the likes of STEAMCAPP."

"In point of fact, we did have some assistance," Dr. Waatt said. "A Grizzly bear smashed its way into the ironclad and slaughtered a good deal of the crew, but Mr. McKenna is correct that our expertise, and my scientific acumen, were able to overcome the pirates and destroy their vessel."

Henroff nodded. "Have you seen any sign of Mr. Kaplan, Doctor?"

Dr. Waatt nodded. "I am sorry to inform you that Mr. Kaplan is dead. He was slain by the bear."

"You are sure? Did you see the body yourselves?" Leslie asked.

"Indeed. It was Mr. Kaplan who, with his final words, told us of the Bear. Shortly after, I was able to

310

confirm his statement by finding a giant bloody bear print."

Henroff dropped his head to his chest. "George was a good man, Doctor. I pray I get a chance to avenge him and slay this killer bear."

"You did not see the bear yourselves, then?" Emma asked.

"No Miss Dareheart, but we heard it, and I do not exaggerate when I say it was the most terrifying and horrifying sound I have ever heard," Mr. Leslie said.

Henroff nodded. "I must agree. I have heard all manner of sounds in these forests, sounds that would frighten a tenderfoot to the grave, but this one raised my neck hairs just as certain."

"In any case, come morning we headed back to the lake and saw the destruction. We scavenged rifles, ammunition and supplies, and headed up the trail. That is when we encountered Professor Boaltt."

"And he is exactly where?" Kierian asked.

Henroff turned around and looked behind him. "I-he was right behind us just a few moments ago. Professor Boaltt? Where are you, sir?"

"Professor Boaltt changed his position forty-five seconds ago. Probable destination our... camp," RA-7 informed.

Henroff and Leslie headed up the trail. Emma began to follow.

"Emma, Kierian," Dr. Waatt called. "Please tarry behind. I have something of importance to tell you."

CHAPTER NINETEEN

"You do not recall anything at all?" Dr. Waatt asked.

Veronica shook her head, wiped the sweat from beneath her pith helmet, closed her eyes, and tried again to remember. She recalled nothing from the night before. The last memory she had before waking up, moments ago with Professor Boaltt kneeling over her, was of running down steps to the lower deck of the ironclad, as she tried to escape the vile captain Bully.

"You do not remember the bear attacking the ironclad?" Dr. Waatt asked.

The notion seemed absurd, and for a moment Veronica thought Dr. Waatt was either suffering from sunstroke or trying and failing to make a joke. "A Bear? On a ship? Dr. Waatt surely, you jest."

Professor Boaltt nodded. "It is true, Professor Stonechat. A bear, the most fiendish looking I have ever laid eyes upon, smashed its way in through the stern of

313

the ship and slaughtered most of the crew. I myself only escaped death by the most narrowest of margins."

"Your torn and bloody clothing testify to your truthfulness, Professor," Veronica replied "But I do not recall any bear attack."

"You certainly are rough on your apparel Boaltt," Kierian said.

"Ha! Once again you are mistaken, McKenna." Boaltt pointed to his torn and bloody clothes. "These are not mine. I exchanged clothing with a dead pirate so I could slip in amongst them and better make my escape."

Kierian nodded. "Of course you did."

"Professor Stonechat," Dr. Waatt said. "You awoke briefly before and recited a poem about a bear. You do not recall that either?"

"No, Doctor, I am afraid I do not. A poem you say?"

"Indeed. RA-7, please repeat it for Professor Stonechat."

"As you wish...Dr. Waatt." The automaton's good eye bounced back in forth in his metal socket. "Accessing memory... files. *The roar of the mighty bear, the cry of the lake wet loon;...submit to the way and the where at the rising of... the moon.*"

Green eyes widened in surprise. "I said that?"

"Affirmative….and in a very lovely voice might I… add." RA-7 smiled and batted his one good eye at Veronica.

She shook her head. "No, I do not remember anything about a bear, reciting that poem, or even how I got here."

"How curious," Dr. Waatt said.

Veronica dropped her head to her chest. "I am afraid it is not all that curious Dr. Waatt. The truth is psychogenetic disorder is not alien to my family line, especially after a traumatic event. You recall that I was delayed from arriving at the dig site for several days after I received the telegram from Professor Bridgewater?"

"Indeed, I do."

"Well, I shall not hold back the reason now, for I see it is essential you know what a weak vessel travels with you on this mission of mercy." Veronica sighed. "I was late because I was forced to admit my father to the Buffalo State Asylum."

"My dear lady, I am so sorry," Dr. Waatt said, taking her hand in his.

"Thank you Doctor. Father was a missionary in China, a member of the United Society of American Missionaries. You perhaps have heard of them?"

315

Dr. Waatt nodded. "A very worthy Christian organization indeed. They are unjustly vilified by other missionaries for dressing and speaking Chinese as they minister to the Chinese people and spread the Good news of the Lord."

"You are correct, Doctor," Veronica replied. "However, despite *going native* and being beloved by the local people, my father and the other missionaries were abducted by a Secret Chinese Society known as the Xi-Fen."

At the mention of the name, the members of STEAMCAPP exchanged solemn glances with each other.

"You have heard of them?" Veronica asked.

Kierian nodded. "Our paths crossed last January."

"Then you know both of their zealotry and their savagery. They tortured and murdered the other missionaries in unspeakable ways. Father was rescued by United States Marines from the gun boat *USS Liberty,* before such evil befell him but he was never the same."

"I am sorry that happened to your father, Professor," Emma said.

"Thank you Miss Dareheart, but I fear my own response to the horrors I apparently saw prove we Stonechat's have rather delicate mental states. I had hoped that by training my mind in the pursuit of an intellectual field such as archeology, I could avoid my father's fate, but now, after my mind's shameful response to the events you have related, I see there is no avoiding my unlucky destiny."

"Oh tut, tut, my dear! The Good Lord provided us with free will. Therefore I am certain that there is no fate save that which we ourselves create."

"Thank you Doctor, but how else can you explain my lack of memory except that my mind is weak, and unequal to the task of dealing with what I saw, shut out all memory of the event."

"I do not disagree that is what most likely, happened, but it does not mean you will end up losing your wits and living out your days in bedlam."

"Everyone responds differently to horrors, Professor," Kierian remarked. "I have seen people traumatized by an initial attack who thereafter, are the picture of calm in whatever storm they find themselves in." Kierian smiled at Emma. She beamed back at him

Dr. Waatt reached into his pack and retrieved his bible. "The Lord's word has brought great comfort to me, in many a dark hour, Professor. You have passed through an ordeal and come out in one piece. If however the ghosts of ordeals past return, I encourage you to trust in His Word rather than lean on your own understanding."

Veronica smiled and graciously accepted the Holy book. "Thank you, Doctor. You have been most kind."

"Professor Stonechat," Kierian said, "are you well enough to travel?"

Veronica nodded. "Yes, Mr. McKenna, and I pledge not to be a further burden to you, nor slow you down from your mission of mercy, as I have thus far."

Kierian nodded. "Very well. Then I suggest, we shoulder our arms and quick-march to the rendezvous point without further delay."

They moved out a half hour later. Veronica was supplied with food, water and a .38 caliber sidearm. Kierian, his face painted, as it had been the first day of the adventure, explained the order of march. He, Henroff, and Leslie would scout ahead, while Emma would lead the rest of the group about a mile behind.

Dr. Waatt would bring up the rear, while Veronica and Professor Boaltt would march in the middle of the formation. Emma, her face also covered in the hues and shades of the forest, looked none too pleased she was not accompanying Kierian, but like a good soldier, she fell obediently into her role as shepherdess of the group.

Banshee moved them forward at a deliberate pace. The mature forest they traveled through boasted a high canopy of trees, with little underbrush. A browse line, testified to the over population of deer. Veronica noted it would have been prime hunting grounds for natives who lived in the area through out recent history.

Squirrels darted from tree to tree. Chipmunks ran for the cover of logs and brush, as the party made their way through the creature's natural abode. At times, the trail was wide, level and easy to traverse, but just as often they encountered long stretches of rocky, narrow, and steep ascents.

They approached a freshwater stream that cut across their path and Banshee raised her fist, signaling for the group to halt. With effortless grace, the adventuress hopped from one boulder to another, quickly crossing the stream. Immediately, she took cover behind a large boulder that sat amongst giant pines, took aim down her rifle and scanned the trail ahead for any sign of the enemy. Satisfied none were in sight, a gloved hand motioned for Professor Boaltt, Dr. Waatt, Veronica, and the Rescue Automaton to cross the stream.

Veronica carefully stepped from a rock and reached with her opposite foot, towards another. Her foot slipped on the wet round stone and she teetered. A bronze metal hand darted out and caught her arm, gently pulling her back on balance. Veronica nodded her thanks. The Rescue Automaton responded with a lovesick smile and gently held her hand until she had safely crossed the rest of the stream.

Veronica approached the boulder Emma had used for cover. Inquisitive eyes carefully examined the rock and her slender fingers scratched at several groves, within the stone.

"You chose an interesting erratic to take cover behind Miss Dareheart."

"An erratic?" Emma answered. She did not look at Veronica, but continued to intently scan the forest ahead.

"Yes, a glacial erratic. They were transported by glaciers millions of years ago and give us information on pre-historic glacial ice flow."

Emma shrugged. "It looked like it would provide good cover and had a few notches in it where I could level my rifle barrel."

Veronica nodded. "Those notches indicate the rock was quarried for soapstone. Would you not concur, Professor Boaltt?"

Boaltt shot an annoyed glance at both the boulder

and Veronica. " I—yes, I suppose."

Dr. Waatt crossed the stream and joined the conversation. "What exactly *is* soapstone, Professor Boaltt?"

"Soapstone?" Professor Boaltt swiped the sleeve of his shirt across his sweaty brow. "It is a—stone that the native tribes used, um for many, um purposes in their daily living activities and so forth."

"Like what exactly?" Dr. Waatt inquired.

"Well—"

Veronica was surprised Dr. Waatt was ignorant on the subject. His kind words from before prompted her to return the favor and happily add to his knowledge of Earth sciences. "Mainly, it was used to make bowls, plates and utensils by the indigenous peoples of the Late Archaic period, prior to the production of pottery in the Woodland period."

"Thank you, Professor Stonechat," Dr. Waatt responded.

Veronica pointed a slender finger at several other boulders. "The nicks and cuts on the erratics, also may indicate the presence of cert."

"Um, yes, and before you ask Dr. Waatt, cert was used by the natives peoples to make tools, such as knives," Professor Boaltt added.

Dr. Waatt nodded. "Cert knives I understand could

321

be incredibly sharp. It is fortunate you were not stabbed with one of those, Professor Boaltt as you would not have recovered as quickly as you seemingly have from your bayonet wound."

"Yes, quite," Boaltt responded, annoyance reflected his tone. Veronica had noticed Professor Boaltt no longer kept his arm in a sling but had not thought much of it as he still kept a bandage over the wound. There had been a hint of accusation in Dr. Waatt's words, and he now held a stern, fixed gaze on Professor Boaltt. Clearly, there was tension between these two men but what it derived from, she could not say. Had something happened last night to cause it?

"Desist with the chatter, people," Miss Dareheart said. "And do not bunch up so much. One well tossed explosive and we'd all be headed to the happy hunting grounds."

They marched on. Half an hour later, they passed a trail coming in from their right that ascended sharply.

Emma called for a halt and disappeared up the trail, returning a quarter of an hour later.

She whispered something to Dr. Waatt before rounding up the group and continuing down their previous path.

Fifteen minutes later, the trail opened up into an

area covered in tall grass and devoid of any trees save a single gigantic pine in the center. Kierian and the two sports appeared on the other side of the clearing; Veronica concluded Mr. Leslie must have taken a fall because he was covered in thick, black mud.

Kierian waved and signaled the group to bush-whack around the clearing.

"We're close now," Emma said once they had reached the forest trail on the other side. "Rest up, eat, drink some water, and check your weapons. It might be the last chance you have to do so." Veronica sat down on a large log, ate some of the jerky Dr. Waatt had given her, and drank down several mouthfuls of cool refreshing water. With cautious steps, and one hand full of branches, Kierian and Emma began traversing the grassy plain. Both tapped the ground in front of them, with a long branch, reminding Veronica of a blind woman she had seen at the Asylum tapping her cane as she walked. Occasionally McKenna and Dareheart would plant one of the tall branches in the ground and tie either a red or blue ribbon to the branch

"What are they doing?"

"Planting explosives, snares and....trip wires," RA-7 replied.

Veronica watched them with a mixture of curiosity

and admiration. On the hike through the woods she had been mesmerized by the old growth forests, glacial erratics, evidence of ancient floodplains, and ancient trees that gave testimony to the region's forgotten past. Interesting facts, to be sure, but not the type that would aid in the recovery of an abducted fifteen-year-old heiress.

McKenna and Dareheart, on the other hand, saw possibilities for ambush, the best routes for escape, and where they could make a stand if needed.

They must have been holy terrors to the British during the war. No wonder they put a price on their heads.

One thing was certain: Alfred Vanderbilt had chosen well, when he had employed STEAMCAPP to recover his sister.

The respite lasted a quarter of an hour and then they were on the move. Veronica soon began to see the lake below, through the trees. A dark shroud of tension quickly descended over the entire group. Dr. Watt unslung his rifle. Emma slowed her pace, frequently dropping to a knee, and holding up her fist; a signal for everyone to halt while she intently scanned the forest. The fifth time this occurred, Kierian, Leslie and Henroff appeared. Moments later, STEAMCAPP held a private counsel of war. Kierian pointed down the trail, and said something to Emma. She nodded and disappeared down the path towards the water. Veronica watched her as she scampered up a tree, as fast and graceful as a squirrel.

"Professors, please join us," Kierian called.

Veronica and Professor Boaltt stepped over large tree roots and joined Kierian and Dr. Waatt.

"Well, Mr. McKenna?" Veronica asked, "What did you see?"

Kierian took a swig of water from his canteen. "They are there. I counted seven anarchists on that small island, including two snipers up in the trees."

"Any sign of the mechanized battle bot?" Veronica asked.

Kierian shook his head. "Negative. They probably could not transport it to the island, but I am sure it is close by, as will be the rest of their army of thugs."

"Speaking of transport, how are we to get to the island?"

"It has been provided. There is a rowboat on the beach. It is large enough to fit four persons into it."

"What about RA-7?" Veronica turned around, but the robot was gone.

"Where has he run off to?" Boaltt asked.

"Ray is where he needs to be," Kierian replied.

"And where is that?" Boaltt demanded. He has the damn ransom, McKenna! These anarchists are not to be trifled with."

"Neither are we," Kierian said.

"If you do not meet their demands, if you try and play one of your games with them, they will not hesitate to kill that girl."

"RA-7 will be where we need him to be when we need him to be, Professor Boaltt," Kierian replied. He lit a cigar, took a few puffs and blew a smoke ring past Boaltt's left ear. "And that is all you need to know."

* * * * * *

Veronica glanced up from the center of the rowboat and craned her neck at the tree she had watched Miss Dareheart ascend.

Thick branches, leaves, an Eagles nest, but no Miss Dareheart. Incredible. Where is she?

"Professor Stonechat," Dr. Waatt tapped her lightly on the shoulder from the rear of the rowboat. "I would ask you to keep your eyes front. Miss Dareheart's ability to remain hidden from enemy eyes is indeed remarkable, and while it is highly unlikely these anarchists will detect her hiding place, it is still, best not to give hints to the enemy of her location."

Veronica blushed. "Of course, Doctor. How foolish of me."

Small waves lapped at the sides of the boat, as Kierian McKenna rowed towards the small island in the center of the lake. Red paint peeled away from rotting wood and ancient oars. Water leaked in from the bottom, soaking Veronica's boots.

"This boat has seen better days," she remarked.

"Indeed," Dr. Waatt said, "however, it should remain seaworthy enough for us to get to and from the island."

"This was a clever place to make the exchange." Professor Boaltt said.

"Why do you think it is so clever, Professor Boaltt?" Veronica replied.

"You can see anyone approaching from any direction for miles and it is well out of rifle range. The anarchists can be confident of no one aiding us once we are on their island. I would suggest therefore, that we do exactly as they say."

"It is true that we can expect no aid once on the island, but then again, neither can they," Kierian remarked.

"What do you mean?" Boaltt asked. "I hope you you do not plan to effect a rescue and take Miss Vanderbilt by force?"

Kierian pulled back on the oars and grinned.

"We would prefer a peaceful exchange," Dr. Waatt replied, "but once we hand over the ransom and Professor Stonechat translates their tablet, they will have no reason to keep any of us alive."

"Two to one, it ends in a firefight of some kind," Kierian said.

"Good Lord! I hope you are wrong, Mr. McKenna!" Veronica said.

Dr. Waatt patted a reassuring hand on Veronica's shoulder. "Fear not good lady, if after the exchanges are made they do not see a reason to keep us alive, we shall endeavor to provide one for them."

* * * * * *

"Barnabas Blackwell, I presume," Kierian said.

Surprise momentarily stretched across the face of the man standing a few feet across from Kierian, on the tiny circle of land, at the center of Reese Lake.

"How do you —" he glanced at Professor Boaltt and smirked in understanding. Confident eyes turned back to Kierian.

"I would ask who *you* are, but I don't really give a good damn." Blackwell tapped the handle of an exotic

328

looking pistol holstered on his right hip and sneered at Kierian. Four hard looking men standing behind him cradled rifles, and serenaded Veronica and the others with grim cackles. "What I do care about," Blackwell continued, "is where the ransom is. I don't see you carrying a large chest, and I doubt you have a million in silver coins stuffed in your trouser pockets."

"Where is Miss Vanderbilt?" Kierian replied.

"You'll see her when I see the one million in silver."

"I am not in the habit of making transactions sight unseen. Proof of life is required before I will show you the coin."

"You're in no position to make demands, mister. Let's get something clear: You do as you are told, or I shoot the heiress and then all of you. It is as simple as that."

Kierian grinned, pulled a cigar from his pocket and lit it.

A crackling hum and high-pitched whistle, cut through the late afternoon air. Pine bark chips spit into Blackwell's face as an aluminum projectile plowed into the tree next to him.

Blackwell swiped a hand across his cut cheek. Astonished eyes gazed at a finger dotted with blood. The anarchist leader flashed hot at Kierian.

Kierian grinned. "I know, I know. We all should be well out of rifle range, safe from scoping snipers. Professor Boaltt thinks that is why you cleverly choose this location for the exchange and the fact is we *ARE*, out of range, at least in regard to *your* henchmen."

Kierian smiled. Blue eyes twinkled threatening charm.

"However, there is a creature that inhabits these woods called the Banshee. The Banshee is distinguished by its chameleon like ability to blend in with nature making it impossible to be located by enemy riflemen and also, as you just saw, by its proficiency with the Waatt EMR-2."

"An abbreviation for Electro-Magnetic Rifle Model Two," Dr. Waatt informed. "The weapon is powered by a magnetic field coil and uses aluminum munitions. Its range far surpasses any contemporary rifle in the world, thus, why you are now imperiled even though over a mile away from shore."

Blackwell glared at Kierian. "Tell your 'Banshee' to stand down, raise his weapon over his head where we can see him, or I'll kill the girl."

Kierian calmly shook his head and took another puff on his cigar.

"No. Neither of those things are going to happen

330

and let me explain to you why. ANY aggressive action by you, or your henchmen will result in Banshee plowing one of those aluminum projectiles through *YOUR* head. After that, what happens won't really matter too much to you, but in order to forewarn your confederates I will indulge you with the sequence of events."

Kierian tapped the stock of his pump shotgun slung over his shoulder. "I am surprisingly quick and deadly in a firefight, Mr. Blackwell. I guarantee I will get both of your snipers hiding up in the trees above our heads before they can swing their nine pound Martini-Henry rifles down and get a shot off at me." Kierian pointed to his left. "The good doctor will simultaneously and literally melt the heart of one of your three thugs with his heat ray weapon and Banshee will probably get at least two of the others before they get off anything more than a hurried shot."

"That leaves one man free to shoot you or Miss Vanderbilt dead," Blackwell snarled.

Kierian nodded. "True enough. I have no illusions of all of us coming out of a firefight unharmed, though I will trust in Good Lady Fortune to see I am not slain outright, as you will undoubtedly be. In any case, one of us would eventually finish off your remaining thug. It would no doubt be, all around, a very bloody affair,

331

but my team would emerge victorious."

Veronica watched Blackwell as his contemptuous eyes glared at Kierian McKenna.

Apprehension tied a knot in Veronica's stomach. She wondered if Dr. Waatt would have been a better choice to handle the negations. Kierian McKenna had a way of striking a man's pride, and like a man lighting a match inside a hydrogen-filled airship, his words and tone seemed to court utter disaster. He seemed determined to make the other man choke down his words when a teaspoon of humble pie might be more productive.

It seemed a most dangerous path to tread when dealing with murderous abductors.

"What my long winded colleague is trying to say," Dr. Waatt interjected, "is that it is in all our interests to make a peaceful exchange, rather than throw threats at each other and let our pride lead us into an unnecessarily bloody and lethal encounter."

Angry, prideful eyes blazed at Dr. Waatt and then Kieran McKenna. Blackwell's hand gripped the butt of his pistol. Veronica brought a hand to her mouth and gasped. *My God! These men are going to do it! They're going to shoot it out and kill us all!*

"Mr. Blackwell," Professor Boaltt said, "should we

not get onto the business we have all come here for and avoid bloodshed?"

Blackwell glanced at Boaltt, held his gaze for a moment and then nodded. Self-control suddenly drained anger from his face, and his hand moved off his weapon. Blackwell snapped his fingers. "Bring Miss Vanderbilt forward."

Two of the thugs walked behind a large boulder and hefted a bound and gagged Gladys Vanderbilt to her feet. A purple knob decorated her left eye. Cuts and scars announced the rough treatment the fifteen year old had endured, yet the girl's eyes flashed defiance rather than fear.

Kierian looked over Gladys Vanderbilt. He shook his head. "You Bastards."

"You have seen the girl. Now let us see the ransom," Blackwell said.

Dr. Watt nodded. "Very well. I implore you however, not to be alarmed by the deliverer of the coins."

"Deliverer?" Blackwell asked.

Dr. Waatt retrieved a whistle from his vest pocket. "Indeed. Professor Boaltt, if you would explain."

"He has a metal man in his service, Blackwell. An automaton, but it is an annoyingly silly thing and incompetent in combat so do not be alarmed."

Dr. Waatt blew the whistle. RA-7 instantly emerged from the bottom of the lake, holding a large wooden chest and walked ashore.

A shot rang out and slammed into RA-7's chest.

Kierian swung his shotgun into his hands in one fluid motion. Dr. Waatt drew his heat-ray pistol and leveled it at the thug who had fired.

"HOLD YOUR FIRE!" Blackwell screamed. He spun towards his men behind him "Dammit, lower your weapons!"

Frightened henchman eyes ping-ponged from Kierian to Blackwell to the automaton. Blackwell drew his weapon but instead of firing at STEAMCAPP, he aimed and fired at the man who had pulled the trigger.

Deadly current burned, as lethal electric agony played over every inch of the anarchist's body.

Blackwell pointed his weapon in the direction of his men as the blackened body fell to the ground. "I said lower your goddamn weapons!"

His command was followed without hesitation.

Kierian shouldered his shotgun and clicked his tongue. "A word of advice: When you have to start killing your own men to accomplish your mission, Mr. Blackwell, it is time either to get a new mission, or new men."

Blackwell's eyes glowered daggers at Kierian. "I have had enough of your jibes, mister. Bring the ransom over and show us the silver."

Dr. Waatt nodded and RA-7 deposited the chest at the doctor's feet. Waatt dropped to one knee, and turned the three numbered dials that sat above three locks, to the chest. Silver coins shined bright. Blackwell and his men smiled contently.

"I assume the woman in your party is Professor-Stonechat?" Blackwell asked.

"She is," Boaltt replied.

"Send her over."

"Send her over?" Dr. Waatt said. "There is no need for that. Hand her the tablet and she will translate it for you."

Blackwell chuckled. "The tablet is part of the temple door. Professor Stonechat will be coming with us to perform the translation to grant us access."

Dr. Waatt kicked the chest closed, rose to his feet and pointed an angry finger at Blackwell. "That was not part of the deal! You have one million in silver currency. Be on your way with it and leave Professor Stonechat alone!"

"I am afraid you have misunderstood," Blackwell said. "The silver is not the primary ransom. Professor

Stonechat is."

"We will not trade one hostage for another! We never would have brought this dear lady along if we knew these were the terms," Waatt said.

Blackwell glanced at Boaltt and grinned. "Quite. Exactly why we abducted Miss Vanderbilt, so you *would* bring Professor Stonechat." He grabbed Gladys by the elbow and pulled her in front of him. Swift hands yanked a fragmentation explosive from his belt. He pulled the pin with his teeth and spit it out on the ground.

"I'm damn well done playing with you people, and if your Banshee shoots me, this bomb will go off and kill Miss Vanderbilt, sure as sunrise."

Dr. Waatt's eyes blazed red-hot fury at Blackwell.

Veronica Stonechat stepped forward. "Stop! Stop this at once! There is no need, Mr. Blackwell. I will come along and translate your inscriptions for you, so long as you promise safe conduct to the shore for Miss Vanderbilt and the others."

A victory grin played across Blackwell's face. "Agreed."

Dr. Waatt grabbed Veronica's arm. "Professor Stonechat, I cannot allow that!"

"It is not your choice to make, Doctor. I came here

on a mission of mercy, and up to this point, I have been nothing but a burden to all of you. Now it seems I am the only one who can bring this mission to a successful conclusion without bloodshed, and so I shall." She pulled her arm free and walked a few steps, bent down, retrieved the bomb's pin and carefully inserted it back into the explosive device.

"I shall go with you, Professor Stonechat," Boaltt said. "I will ensure no harm comes to you and perhaps be able to aid you in some small way." Boaltt stepped forward. Blackwell cut the ropes at Gladys feet but left her hands tied and mouth gagged. He shoved Gladys hard in the back, towards Dr. Waatt and the girl stumbled into his arms.

"RAY, Retrieve," Kierian said in German.

RA-7's right arm hyper-extended from his body. Metal fingers closed around Boaltt's arm and yanked him backwards as his arm retracted.

Blackwell drew his weapon, aimed at the automaton, and then hesitated.

Kierian pulled a smoke bomb from his belt and tossed it. A shroud of white smoke obscured Veronica's view.

Blackwell grabbed her arm and jerked her towards the opposite shore of the island.

Behind the wall of smoke, a shotgun roared twice. The three remaining thugs aimed their weapons and aimed at the expanding cloud.

"Hold your fire you fools!" Blackwell yelled. Violent hands pulled Veronica over a sandy beach and shoved her into a canoe.

"Keep your head down, Professor Stonechat," Blackwell said, as the three thugs piled in and took up the oars, "lest your violent friends shoot you by mistake." She shot a final glance back at the island but all was obscured by smoke.

"Take heart dear lady," she heard Dr. Waatt yell though the cloud. "We shall not abandon you!"

Veronica prayed Dr. Waatt was a man of his word.

* * * * * *

"McKenna! Are you mad!" Boaltt bellowed.

Kierian answered him with a smashing blow from the oak stock of his Winchester pump across Boaltt's neck.

The Professor fell back unconscious. More roughly than necessary, Kierian tossed him into the rowboat.

Balthazar drew his knife, and cut Gladys free. He stepped over the bodies of the two snipers, helped her into the boat, and threw himself into the stern, aiming his heat-ray pistol into the expanding cloud of smoke.

"RAY, do you have the ransom chest?"

"Affirmative," RA-7 replied.

"Then row like the devil and get us to shore!" Kierian said.

"Aye, Aye Captain McKenna." The automatons gears whizzed, pistons pumped, and his arms moved like a blur propelling the small boat across the lake in record time.

Henroff, Leslie, and Emma rushed out from behind two large boulders and helped pull the rowboat ashore.

"My God," Henroff said. "We saw the whole thing through our binoculars. I thought for sure, they would shoot you to pieces as you attempted escape, but they did not even fire a shot."

"There was no chance of that, Mr. Henroff," Dr. Waatt said. He pointed to Boaltt. "They did not wish to risk hitting their boss."

CHAPTER TWENTY

"How long have you been privy to this knowledge Doctor?" Leslie asked.

"From the beginning. It was very obvious to any one with an observant eye, when we interviewed Boaltt in Vanderbilt's study. As soon as I checked his arm, I knew he was lying. A steel bayonet did not make that wound. It was too jagged and most likely, made by stone, possibly a cert knife, which are quite common at archeological dig sites."

"Then why not call him out on it?" Leslie asked.

"While it did imply he was stabbed by a worker at the site, as I doubt the anarchists were carrying stone knives, it was *not* definitive proof. It was possible, after all, that he could have fallen awkwardly on jagged stone and cut himself and that his deception was simply to cover the lie of his *valiant defense* of Miss Vanderbilt."

"Valiant defense? Fiddlesticks!" Gladys Vanderbilt said. "That horrible man attacked me for exposing him as a fraud. You are correct about the wound Doctor, for it was I who stabbed him with the cert knife."

Dr. Waatt smiled at the confirmation of his theory. "I did attempt to expose Boaltt at the interview when I asked him to explain Professor Bridgewater's theory on St. Brendan's journey. However, Professor Stonechat, in what I now see as a case of over exuberance, answered in his stead."

"What you *now* understand?" Henroff asked.

Dr. Waatt nodded. "I must confess, that for a time, I suspected Professor Stonechat was in league with Boaltt, but I am now convinced that is not the case."

"I assume then, there was more evidence of deception you uncovered, Doctor?" Leslie asked.

"Indeed. Mr. McKenna detected Boaltt was not wearing the suit he *'borrowed'* from Mr. Ambrose Russ. For once, my intelligence and intellect gladly bowed to Kierian's vanity."

Kierian beamed. "Thank you for admitting so, Balthazar."

Dr. Waatt curled his lip at Kierian and continued with his explanations.

"Shallow of character, as it might be, to know more about fashions than the master tailors of the world's major cities, in this case it was decisive. Boaltt was not

341

wearing the suit Mr. Russ gave him, and being that it was so finely cut, it must have belonged to Boaltt himself."

"I do not see why that is so important," Leslie said.

"Mr. Leslie, why would a man stumble out of the forest half naked when he had a perfectly good suit in his pack he could wear?" Kierian offered.

Dr. Waatt nodded. "More over, why would a professor on an archeological dig, have a dinner suit with him at all? Unless of course, he planned on being at Sagamore all along."

"Ah. He knew he would be the one delivering the ransom note," Leslie said.

Henroff pondered the information. "That seems rather an arrogant risk to take, bringing along a dinner suit, I mean."

"Black tie, means Black tie, Mr. Henroff," Kierian replied. "Just because one is engaging in a criminal conspiracy does not excuse one from dressing fashionably."

"The criminal mind is an arrogant mind," Dr. Waatt shot a glance at Kierian, "which is often their undoing. As for being caught, even Mr. Russ failed to notice it was not his own suit. To most, including myself, black tie dinner wear is all the same."

Kierian retrieved a Mozart and lit it. "Fortunately for you, I was around to save you from your ignorance."

Emma chuckled. Balthazar was never going to hear the end of how Kierian's fashion sense exposed treachery lurking within their midst.

Dr. Watt frowned. "Yes, I suppose in this *one* instance, Kierian, that is technically true. However, you still did not interpret the information to mean he was working for the enemy. If you will recall, I surprised both you and Emma with my theory."

Kierian blew a smoke ring in Balthazar's direction. "I cannot be expected to do everything, Balthazar. This is a partnership after all."

"Why go to all this trouble?" Henroff asked. "I mean, why not send one of their underlings with a ransom note?"

"If the men on the island were representative of the rest of their gang, I doubt any of them would have had the intelligence to pull off the deception of being one of the victims and holding up under questioning. I suspect, Boaltt came along to make sure everything went as they had planned, that Professor Stonechat came along on the journey, and to assure the rescue party could not pull off any heroics."

343

" Yes but-"Henroff began.

"I am afraid further explanations of Balthazar's brilliance, will have to wait, Mr. Leslie," Kierian said. He glanced up. Grey storm clouds had begun to darken the sky. "We need to move out on the double."

* * * * * *

Chaney's eyes bulged with hate. Angry hands gripped the controls of the Gryphon. "All for nothing! You let the Duchess go home and healthy for nothing!"

Blackwell stood amongst the giant pines, on the shores of Reese Lake and glanced up at Chaney, aware the battle bot's machine gun was aimed his way. He took a few steps to his left and watched to see if the arm would move with him.

It did not, but it didn't mean it wouldn't if Chaney got even hotter than he already was.

"Calm down, Chaney. We have Professor Stonechat. Now, we can proceed with the next phase of Operation Atlas. That is what is important."

Drizzling rain tapped atop hat brims and tin plates. Watery impact points dotted the lake water, like so many tossed pebbles. The weather had turned and so had the men of the Brotherhood of Labor, who were acting anything but brotherly.

344

"We don't give a damn about Sir John or that Stonechat woman. As for this plan of yours, maybe it works, and maybe it's just all some tall tale," Chaney said.

"It's not a story. Lilith Grimm herself assured me of the artifact's existence. That is why we need to stop this arguing, get to the dig site, secure it, and retrieve the artifact."

"Maybe Grimm got it wrong," Chaney replied. "She ain't some all knowing Goddess, Barnabas. All *we* know is the ransom *is* real. Davis and the others saw it, that is, before you let it slip through your damn fingers!"

Cold flinty eyes stared back at Chaney. The back of his head tingled oddly. Intense outrage streaked fire through his brain. How dare he refer to Lady Lilith simply by her last name, as if she was one of his grubby dock pals!

How dare he doubt her words and wisdom! And she *was* a Goddess! A beautiful, human Goddess. But Chaney wouldn't know that. He had not been granted the privilege of being in her very presence, hearing her strong, hypnotic voice, or feel the electric charge race through his body at the touch of her slender fingers. He hadn't looked into those green eyes that bore into your

345

very soul, opening your own eyes to the truth of the world, and holding you enthralled, as the voice ripped away the veil of deceit that had held you prisoner your entire life and gave you new found purpose in her holy crusade against the ruling elites.

Outraged, his hand tapped the handle of his electricity pistol, as he began to calculate if a quick draw could fry Chaney before he could swing the battle bot's gun into play.

No, for Lady Lilith, I must check my temper. I must complete the mission. I must not fail her.

His hand moved away from his weapon, to his vest pocket, where he kept the signed photograph of his Goddess.

Worshipful fingers tapped it three times.

He had almost allowed that smart mouth on the island to provoke him into rash action that would have caused him to fail Lady Lilith and ruin the entire mission.

He could not let that happen again. Chaney and his Gryphon were no longer vitally important, but Chaney's use of *we* for the first time was not lost on Barnabas. A good many of the brotherhood had moved around the Gryphon in a show of solidarity.

Chaney was no longer alone in his troublemaking.

"Those people aren't going anywhere. They know we're heading for the dig site and Miss Vanderbilt knows the way. We will exchange Professor Stonechat for the ransom and Sir John when they show up tomorrow."

"You think they'll risk Duchess by going there? I bet they're getting paid a damn king's ransom to return Duchess to her lordly brother and his country castle. Why would they give a good damn about Stonechat or Sir John Boaltt? They probably already put a bullet in his brain and left him for the wolves."

"You weren't there Chaney. You didn't see and hear the fire in that doctor's eyes, when he realized Stonechat was coming with us. Mark my words, they'll be along tomorrow, sure as sunrise."

"I ain't waiting, Barnabas. Grimm might have charged you with this Atlas mission and beguiled you into obeying her every command, but the silver was for us, for our wives and children. Those people have it. They're still close by, and damn it to hell, we're going to go get it!" Chaney pushed a button and the cockpit slowly closed. Barnabas thought about taking a quick-draw shot but stayed his hand. He still had a few loyal brothers and having Chaney elsewhere while Stonechat worked painstakingly to make sense of the inscriptions

347

that would gain them access to the temple, might not be such a bad thing.

Besides, maybe Chaney would succeed. Maybe he would kill the smart mouth, the doctor and the unseen Banshee. Maybe he'd even save Sir John.

The drizzle had turned into a soft but steady rain. The Gryphon's motors turned over and the battle bot stomped angrily down the lake trail with all but seven of the brother's following behind.

Barnabas walked in the opposite direction, back to the tree Stonechat was tied to. He cut her loose and shoved her forward.

"Come along Professor, you have some inscriptions to interpret."

* * * * * *

Leslie rushed down the muddy forest trail towards the grassy plain and skidded to a stop in front of a gigantic fallen pine.

"Report, Mr. Leslie," Kierian said. He leaned against the pine, his pump shotgun cradled in his arms. Nearby, RA-7 played joylessly with his yo-yo; a sad frown upon his face at the loss of Veronica Stonechat.

Leslie bent over at the waist, sucked in heavy breaths of mountain air and stammered out his report. "They're coming...Mr. McKenna. They're... about a mile… and a… half back and that…that mechanized beast…it's leading the way."

Kierian nodded. "Understood Mr. Leslie, thank you. Take a quick rest, eat some food, and drink down some water. Just because it is raining does not mean you cannot dehydrate yourself."

"You were right about them coming after us Kierian," Dr. Waatt said. "Perhaps, it was a mistake to take the ransom with us."

Boaltt leaned against a small tree, his hands bound in front of him. "You are damn right it was a mistake and so was taking me!"

"The mistake was yours, in presuming you could outwit us," Dr. Waatt replied.

Raw contempt glowered from Boaltt's eyes. "You think you are so damn clever, Waatt, but so did Miss Vanderbilt, and look what happened to Bridgewater and the rest of those fools when she crossed me."

"Gunning down unarmed workers with a mechanized battle bot is nothing to brag about," Kierian said. "Your band of merry murderers will find we are tougher nuts to crack than those they have previously encountered."

"Your confidence in your toys is most amusing Mr. McKenna, but there's too few of you, and you possess

349

nothing that can destroy a Gryphon."

"It will not be the first time, Mr. McKenna and I have faced long odds, Mr. Boaltt, and we always found a way to triumph and persevere," Emma replied.

"Times change, Miss Dareheart."

"Indeed, these days we have the genius of Doctor Balthazar Waatt with us to enhance our chances."

"Mark my words, you will all die, some slower than others. Behold Miss Vanderbilt," hungry eyes leered at Gladys, studying her from head to toe. "They already beat her soft tender skin black and blue. What do you think is next on the menu when we no longer have a reason to keep her alive?" Sharp teeth gleamed. Boaltt cackled wickedly.

Gladys involuntarily took a step back.

Emma recognized the fear.

She remembered trying to be strong when you felt weak, trying not to show the bastards they had gotten to you when you knew they had, trying not to show the fear but realizing it would always lurk somewhere deep within your soul, no matter how hard you tried to hide it.

Thankfully, Gladys had not yet been so fearfully damaged. She was young and could be protected by the Vanderbilt fortune. She would heal.

Emma decided to make damn sure.

She sauntered over to Boaltt. Strong gloved hands cupped the tree trunk Boaltt was leaning against. Emma braced herself, grinned down at Boaltt, and without warning drove her right knee hard into the lech's jaw.

"You bitch!" Boaltt roared. He sprung up to his feet with surprising strength and quickness. Emma dropped and swept his leg, sending him crashing to the forest floor. Boaltt pushed himself up to a sitting position. "I'll-"

Emma spun on one foot and snapped her boot across his face. Boaltt crashed face first into the mud.

"Miss Dareheart! Control yourself!" Dr. Waatt implored. "We need him alive."

Kierian cupped his hands, lit a cigar, and blew smoke in Boaltt's direction. "I would stay down if I were you, Mr. Boaltt. Miss Dareheart does not tolerate lecherous villains who look at fifteen year olds like they are a porterhouse steaks."

"You do not have anything to fear Miss Vanderbilt. Not from those vile anarchists and certainly not from this piece of horse shit," Emma said.

Boaltt turned over on his side, and spit blood. "You'll pay for that, Dareheart." He pulled himself back up to a sitting position and glanced over at Balthazar.

"Waatt, you seem to be the only reasonable one here. Cut me loose, and leave the ransom. I'll order the men to leave you be and you can be on your way. You can even take Miss Vanderbilt along with you."

"We are not leaving without Professor Stonechat," Dr. Waatt said.

"Then you doom your entire party to destruction. Stonechat is a dead woman."

"You would do well to pray that is not so, Mr. Boaltt," Dr. Waatt said. "The only reason you are still alive, is because we need to exchange you for the Professor."

"You will not live that long, Waatt. The only exchange you will be making is this life for a handshake with the devil!"

"My eternal soul is safely in the hands of the Lord, Mr. Boaltt, but since you are so confident we shall be slain shortly, there is no reason to resist enlightening us on your plans. For example, why is Professor Stonechat so important to you that you must silence her after she has interpreted those inscriptions?"

"Ha! I shall tell you nothing Waatt, and I warn you not to waste your time attempting to hypnotize me. Your robot told me all about that, and I assure you, my mind is made of much stronger stuff than that of some river thug."

"I wager RA-7 also informed you of Mr. McKenna's ten-finger talk. Perhaps, I was too quick to dismiss his methods of interrogation."

"Go to the devil, Waatt!" Boaltt held his bound hands up. "Do your worst. I shall tell you nothing!"

"Dr. Waatt," Gladys Vanderbilt interrupted, "Professor Bridgewater believed the inscriptions explained how to access the temple safely. He was also certain lethal traps aplenty would be set off by anyone forcing their way inside. That is why we cabled Professor Stonechat to assist us."

Dr. Waatt nodded. "What is inside that is so valuable that lethal traps were set to protect it?"

Gladys shrugged. "I cannot say. Professor Bridgewater believed the temple contained proof of Brendan's voyage. It is a ritual and religious site, so it could be Celtic artifacts the natives considered sacred, are buried within. However, I cannot fathom there is anything worth killing for or that anarchists would be interested in possessing."

"Pah! Those anarchist fools are nothing more than pawns in a greater game. A pity you will not live long enough to know what that is. I shall savor the looks of utter despair on your smug faces when your world comes crashing down around you."

"Doctor," Kierian said, "I think we should save Boaltt's interrogation for later. Right now, we have a more immediate concern to deal with, namely the mob of murderous anarchists and the battle bot headed our way."

"Yes Kierian. You are quite right. One problem at a time."

"RAY, keep an eye on our prisoner," Kierian said. He motioned for everyone to join him and walked a few yards away to stand under a large pine tree, its gigantic roots over hanging an enormous boulder.

Henroff spoke first. "Dr. Waatt, it's clear you have some feeling towards, Miss Stonechat, but-"

"If you are implying I harbor romantic intentions towards Professor Stonechat, you are in error, Mr. Henroff. I do, however, regret suspecting her of being in league with that monster Boaltt. Perhaps, if I had not been so suspicious, I would have applied more thought to assuring her safety, as a gentleman should. Instead, I let my distrust color my actions towards an innocent woman."

"Be that as it may, Doctor, and as much as I hate myself for saying so, I think we need to consider

Boaltt's offer."

Emma shot a disapproving glance at Henroff. There were times when try as you might, you just could not bring everybody home alive, but you did not cut and run until there was absolutely no other choice, and you certainly never left someone in the clutches of the enemy without at least attempting a rescue. It was an appalling suggestion, but Emma tempered her response, reminding herself the man was a civilian. "*Nemo resideo*, Mr. Henroff."

"I am afraid I never learned Latin, Miss Dareheart," Henroff replied.

"It means, leave no one behind," Kierian replied, "and I must agree. Leaving your compatriots behind to save your own skin is a God-awful habit to start."

"I suggest it not to save myself, Mr. McKenna, but to insure that no harm befalls Miss Vanderbilt. We were sent here, after all, to rescue her, and we have accomplished that task. Is it truly wise to endanger her on a second rescue mission?"

"Probably not, but what other choice do we have?" Emma said.

"Leslie and I could escort her out of the forest while you make the exchange for Professor Stonechat," Henroff offered.

"If the anarchists had stayed put or moved to the dig site, I would take you up on that offer, Mr. Henroff," Kieran said, "unfortunately, the die is now cast. The enemy is on the march and we need all hands to win the day."

"You do not mean to give battle to them. Do you Mr. McKenna?" Leslie asked.

"People tire, Mr. Leslie, machines do not. If we run, the battle bot will catch up to us eventually, and by then we'll be too exhausted to fight. If we split up, they'll just wipe us out and then run you down an hour later."

"The only question now," Emma said, "is, what ground do we choose to fight upon?"

"I propose we fight upon the mountain, Miss Dareheart located on the way up here," Dr. Waatt said. "It should be high enough for me to get a message to the *Excelsior*."

"Will the wireless work in this weather?" Emma asked.

Dr. Waatt squinted his eyes and peered into the rainy, darkened sky. "I cannot be sure. The atmospheric disturbances could disrupt communications, but *if* the message was received and *if* they arrived in time, the *Excelsior* could easily destroy the Gryphon, re-supply us, and evacuate Miss Vanderbilt, while we rescue Professor Stonechat."

Kierian shook his head. "That is too many ifs to rest our survival upon, Doctor. If the message did not get through or the Excelsior was late in arriving, we would have our backs to a cliff with nowhere to retreat."

Emma nodded her agreement. Kierian never believed in letting himself be gulled into fighting some glorious last stand. He was too cunning a fox to fall into such a trap. He always made sure whatever den they were in, had at least two ways out.

Kierian glanced up at the sky, took a puff on his cigar, and looked over the grassy plain in front of them.

"These anarchists still have a mile and a half to march. By the time they get here, they'll be tired and soaked to the skin, unless they thought of bringing along rain ponchos as we did."

Kierian took another puff on his cigar and continued to think aloud.

"They'll be angry, impatient, and the Gryphon will make them over confident. We have already set trip wires and traps, so preparation on our part should be minimal."

"All things considered, I think we could not ask for a better place to make a stand." Blue eyes twinkled in the rain at Emma. "What do you say, Banshee? Care for an afternoon of mud fighting?"

Emma grinned. "You know me, Piper: I always love a good mud bath."

* * * * * *

Chaney swerved the Gryphon hard right, avoiding grinding a brother named Sadorwitz into hamburger by mere inches. The battle bot stomped off the mud soaked trail, crashed through underbrush, up rooted small trees, and pulverized rotting logs into mulch before Chaney could turn the iron beast and steer it back onto the trail.

"Keep your damn feet Sadorwitz!" Chaney yelled from within the dry, confines of the cockpit. It was the third time it had been necessary to swerve off trail because one of the brothers couldn't keep their clumsy feet from slipping out from under them.

Inside the Gryphon, it was hot as pitch. Outside the weather was equally miserable. Rain turned the dirt trails slick with mud. Tree roots, lurking deceptively beneath the undergrowth, caught careless feet, twisted ankles, knees, and sent men sprawling.

Twice the procession had grounded to a halt, and Chaney had been forced to stop, raise the cockpit and take the dangerous risk of becoming a target to snipers.

He urged the brothers forward.

They bellyached and bitched.

He didn't have Barnabas's gift for speechifying, but he reminded them of the fortune in silver that awaited them down the trail and that back or forward it made no never mind: the rotten weather was the same in either direction.

Chaney accelerated the Gryphon. The battle bot stomped angrily down the mud path. Anarchists leaped into pine sentinels to avoid being crushed. Sharp needles pierced cheeks and arms. Fists shook, and lips mouthed silent curses at the battle bot's operator.

The damn fools! Why won't they get out of my way? All they need do is trail along behind and let me bring the hell and the victory. Sure, it ain't no picnic breathing in coal-fueled exhaust, but it ain't like it'll kill you, like being stomped will.

The trail curved and a steep incline taunted already tired legs. Chaney powered the battle bot forward to crest the hill, passing those who had dashed ahead.

Stacked logs, five feet in height, blocked the trail's entrance to a grassy plain.

Chaney idled the Gryphon to a stop. The logs

looked recently cut, but Chaney couldn't fathom Duchess and her rescuers hacking and stacking so quickly. He could see the brothers milling around the logs. They were talking and looked none too happy, but he could only catch a few words from inside the cockpit.

"Maybe, was the metal man that done it," Sadorwitz suggested. He was standing close by the Gryphon, his face, hair and most of his clothing caked in mud. "That robot probably has the strength of a hundred men!"

Chaney scoffed. Ever since Blackwell had returned from the exchange, the brothers had been prattling on and marveling at the robot who emerged from under the water like some aquatic automaton god.

Damn ingrates! Never a word said in praise of me or my Gryphon and after all the killing we've done for 'em. But some walking watery bag of bolts shows up, captures the great Sir John Boaltt and they act like he's some ancient deity returned from on high. Next, they'll probably lay offerings at his feet and bow down in worship like savages.

Chaney wiped the sweat away from his eyes. Now, they were admiring the metal man's lumber jacking skills. He revved up the battle bot's motors. A single charge from his Gryphon should smash open a path, reduce the logs to kindling, and undo the Bunyan Bot's hard work.

"Hey! Found another way around," a brother shouted excitedly and pointed to the left of the logs. Others joined him. They pushed aside a pine branch and hastily rushed down the newly discovered trail.

None of them ever heard the fateful click when the tripwire snapped.

CHAPTER TWENTY-ONE

A miniature volcano erupted. Razored shrapnel, fragged the anarchists to shreds. The few who survived the initial explosion were fed a steady leaden diet of double aught death, from Kierian's Winchester pump.

Kierian withdrew behind a boulder and fed shells into the shotgun's magazine, as a shower of rifle and shotgun fire peppered mud and stone. He peeked his head around the boulder and drew it back all in one motion.

Three more anarchists rushed down the trail, firing from the hip.

Kierian dropped to a prone position and extended the shotgun around the edge of the boulder. The Winchester belched smoke and fire. Buckshot pellets tore and pulped organs.

The three anarchists collapsed, dotting green pines and mud with savage red. Kierian rolled back behind the boulder and reloaded. The narrow trail had forced the enemy to bunch and rush. The tripwire should have taught the anarchists that the trail was a death trap.

Should have.

A confident smirk played across Kierian's face. The second rush had shown these villains needed extra teaching. It also marked them as thuggish amateurs.

Tack-a, Tack-a, Tack-a.

A stream of British .303 rounds ripped into the rock face of the boulder and chipped away at Kierian's smugness.

Well-armed amateurs, especially those armed with a Maxim machine gun, could fill the reapers bill just as thoroughly as well as armed professionals. With a practiced hand, he lobbed a smoke bomb into the trail.

Mr. Maxim responded with a storm of gunfire, cutting down branches and sending geysers of muddy earth into the air.

Rifles cracked in the air. Winchester .30 WCF's whistled towards the anarchists and slammed into the stacked logs. As instructed, once they saw the smoke, the sports had opened fire. Kierian counted to ten. Mr.

363

Maxim sounded off once more but not in his direction. Piper dashed from one boulder to another, withdrawing to his next firing position in good order.

* * * * * *

Pine branches, smashed against the Gryphon's viewport. A cloud of smoke obscured everything else.

Chaney tried to charge down the trail but it was too narrow and forced him to stomp into the thick brush. He fired blindly into the cloud, hoping he would hit the shooter but doubting he would.

The Gryphon was slow to respond. Chaney cursed as he tried to get back to the main trail. Gryphons were not designed for forest fighting but for open field combat, and that grassy plain beyond the stacked logs was as open a space, as an Adirondack forest would ever provide.

Chaney sneered as he turned the battle bot around. Duchess's mercenary lackeys had made a mistake attacking them here. He would smash thru those logs, charge across the open field, and fire and fry them all to hell.

* * * * * *

Emma laid prone on the wet ground, right knee drawn up, body weight resting on her left side, and the

EMR-2 tucked high into her shoulder, close to her neck. The front of her rain poncho repelled the ground water, keeping her body dry while a shield of overhanging pine boughs filtered rain from overhead. The barrel of her EMR-2 extended between two logs, and the small ridge she occupied just above the others, provided an excellent overview of the grassy plain below.

"Anything moving across it is yours to reap, Banshee" Kierian had told her.

Emma tapped her rifle. "I have sickle in hand, Piper. I shall reap us a plentiful harvest of death."

Kierian had held up two smoke canisters; one with a red band around it and one with a green. "Red for retreat, green for go."

Emma nodded. "Red I retreat, Green I go."

Kierian had smiled at her, stowed his smoke bombs, and ruffled her hair thru her cap before running off to set up his death trap.

Emma had watched it all transpire from above. She almost felt sorry for the anarchists as they blundered down the trail to their deaths. Like the John Bulls and the Dunns, and countless others, they learned the hard way of how brutally efficient Kierian McKenna could be once you chose to engage him in a fight.

And the ambush had been nothing if not efficient.

After the foolish second charge, nine anarchists had been eliminated from the fight and if Mr. Leslie's count had been accurate, that was nearly half their number.

When on the defense, it was seldom necessary to kill the enemy to the last man. Usually you just needed to make the cost of their butchering not worth the price they had to pay. Then the enemy usually broke and ran. Had they not had the battle bot, Emma figured the anarchists would have done just that. But they did have it and it remained a serious problem.

Balthazar had identified the mech as a British made Gryphon, a clumsy coal powered weapons platform that was designed for open field fighting, urban combat and holding strategic positions like bridges, cross roads, and railway yards. In a forest setting, its lack of maneuverability would be a disadvantage.

That analysis had been spot on. Once it encountered the thick Adirondack brush as it pursued Kierian, it began to lurch around worse than a drunken sailor on leave, firing blindly towards his location. By the time it got turned around and found the trail again, Kierian was safely back to the tree line on the other side of the plain.

She wiped a drop of rain from her cheek, popped open the cap of her brass scope and peered through.

She could see the Gryphon's head as it smashed into the logs RA-7 had cut and stacked with marvelous speed and efficiency. It had truly been an impressive display of lumber jacking.

Caribou Jack would have been jealous. Who needs Mr. Choppy when you have RA-7.

A loud crack reverberated across the plain. The first charge fractured the logs. The Gryphon might be unwieldy and clumsy, but its brute power could not be denied. The battle bot stomped backwards, charged again and shattered the wooden wall. A cheer went up from the anarchists. The Gryphon led the way, marching with heavy stomps, firing its Maxim into the air, and belching flame from its flamethrower like some champion boxer flexing his muscles as he stepped into the ring. The anarchists swarmed through the tall grass, firing rifles and shotguns as they rushed across the plain.

* * * * * *

Rifles cracked from the tree line at the far end of the plain. Bullets pinged and ricocheted off the Gryphon. Chaney's cruel mouth twisted with hate.

The overconfident fools! Their shitty little trap on that narrow trail bloodied the brothers, sure, but we still have the numbers, and now that my Gryphon is on flat land and has

367

room to maneuver. Duchess and her robot can measure what's left of their lives in minutes.

Chaney sneered and stitched the tree line with a volley of machine gunfire. The rifles went silent. He pushed the Gryphon forward, never noticing when the Gryphon crushed the stick with a blue ribbon upon it beneath its iron right foot.

* * * * * *

Emma grinned, as the Gryphon sank up to its upper thigh in thick black swamp mud.

"Swamp mud, Banshee. It is quicksand's forestry cousin and the entire plain is covered with the stuff," Kierian had revealed to her.

The tall grass had hid the mud perfectly. Earlier she and Kierian had placed shooting ribbons on sticks through out the plain to mark the location of the larger pools. Good fortune continued to bless Kierian's cunning plan when the Gryphon stomped dead center into the largest pool. The anarchists on foot suffered similar fates: some sank waist deep, others, only ankle deep but all were now immobile.

Emma lowered her eye to her scope, took aim, and began the turkey shoot.

* * * * * *

The awfulness of the situation slammed into Chaney full force. Shocked eyes stared out the view port. All around the plain, trapped brothers pulled at legs and flayed desperate arms to escape the swamp mud.

All to no avail.

Terrified faces turned to their champion and pleaded for deliverance. He pushed the throttle to full power, confident he could power out of the mud's suction.

The right leg moved but only just. He tried the left, and managed to straighten the Gryphon.

Red rain splattered on the view port window as a near-by brother's head exploded. Chaney watched in horror, as the trapped brothers were shot down one by one. A defiant scream burst from his lips. He held down the trigger on the Maxim, emptying half a drum into tree line.

The slaughter continued unabated.

A red beam of energy sizzled out from the tree line, striking his Gryphon's right leg. The beam held steady, slowly boring its way through the iron armor. He traced the line of the beam and let loose with the Maxim. The beam disappeared. Chaney ground his teeth. Helplessness and despair gripped his cruel heart as he watched his brothers die. The thought never crossing his rancorous mind, that the innocent workers of Adirondack site 403b must have felt the same despair as he and the brothers gleefully gunned them down.

Curse your privileged hide Duchess! This is all your goddamn fault!

He pushed and pulled the throttle controls. The Gryphon rocked back and forth. Slowly, it began to break free.

A wave of white-hot hate washed away the feelings of helplessness. Hatred burned his bitter heart black. Once free, he would backtrack out of the plain, find the small trail, and stomp his way around. Then he'd scorch Duchess and her friends to ash, even if it meant burning the entire forest down with them.

* * * * * *

Green smoke billowed out from the smoke canister. Emma rested the EMR-2 against a tree trunk and slowly stood. A final check assured her all was in order. She turned a gauge on her rocket pack, pressed the ignition button, and soared into the air.

* * * * * *

With a giant sucking sound, the Gryphon broke free of the swamp mud. Chaney's lips curled contemptu-

370

ously as he retreated, retracing his steps back towards the narrow trail.

Then he saw it. It streaked into the grey sky from off the ridgeline like a roman candle.

A Rocket! They're firing a Goddamn rocket at me!

He elevated the Maxim, aimed, and fired.

* * * * * *

"Dammit Kierian!" Dr. Waatt exclaimed.

The expanding green smoke cloud blocked his ability to acquire the Gryphon through his Maser's scope.

Even switching to the infrared selection had not been affective and trying to change his firing position was both dangerous and would take too long. Without the Maser's super heated cutting beam, the Gryphon could not be permanently disabled and would be free to unleash all its hellish weapons on Miss Dareheart.

Emma was flying straight into a hailstorm of leaden death.

* * * * * *

A stream of bullets sliced through the air, barely missing Emma.

She was in trouble.

Moments after taking flight, the Gryphon had freed itself from the swamp mud. Now it was on the move forcing her to alter her landing target.

Better I overshoot than land short in front of his weapons.

Emma fired the rockets and streaked forward, consuming precious fuel. The pack was extremely heavy, and to reduce the weight and give her more control she had filled her tanks only half full. Now, her margin for error was zero.

The Gryphon retreated backward. Its Maxim fired. Bullets swarmed past Emma like angry hornets. She soared over the Gryphon, momentarily out of its weapons arch.

The rocket began to fail. She glanced at the gauge. It read empty. She was flying on fumes now.

There was no choice. She had to land.

The Gryphon was directly below her under an enormous pine tree, but unless something stopped its backwards march, she would land directly in front of the iron beast and its guns.

A solid and steady red beam of microwaved energy sliced into the right leg of the Gryphon. Iron armor melted under the super heated thermite powered weapon. Emma stole a glance over her shoulder and smiled. Balthazar was standing on RA-7's shoulders, his magnetic boots holding him in place firing over the green cloud of smoke, and giving him a perfect angle to fire on the Gryphon's legs.

Sparks flared off the Gryphon as the Maser beam sizzled. Whatever Balthazar had hit, slowed the Gryphon to a crawl. She pumped the ignition several times sending her into a controlled dive. With a soft thump, she landed on the battle bot's right shoulder. The pilot scowled at her with a mixture of shock and hatred. Emma twiddled her fingers in a faux friendly wave, drew a bomb from her hip pouch, and lit the fuse.

The desperate pilot swung the Gryphon's right arm at her.

She sidestepped.

The arm smashed into the cockpit, cracking its view port. The impact knocked Emma off balance but she righted herself instantly. Keeping her balance on the iron hulk was child's play compared to sky walking on ice. With a practiced hand, she tossed it down the Gryphon's exhaust pipe and hit the ignition on her rocket pocket.

The silent click tolled the emptiness of the fuel tank. Rapidly she worked her fingers, unbuckled the rocket pack, and leaped towards the towering pine. Hands extended, desperate for a saving branch. Pine needles burrowed into her palms as slender gloved fingers, clutched solid wood. Emma used her momentum and swung her feet forward, leaped again, and grasped yet another branch. Strong arms pushed—

The bomb ignited like liquid thunder and blew the Gryphon in half. Huge chunks of metal rained down around the tree.

The shock wave cost Emma her grip and slammed her into the pine's trunk. She plummeted. In desperation she threw out her left hand and caught a branch.

As she hung by a single hand, something stirred below.

Out of the Gryphon's mangled cockpit the pilot emerged. Half his face was skeleton. A bloody hand slowly raised a pistol and took aim at Emma.

Emma's right hand darted for her Colt.

And scraped an empty leather holster.

Skeleton face pulled the trigger.

Nothing happened.

Dead eyes realized the mistake. Failing strength forced a double handled cock of the pistol's hammer. Desperate buckshot and rifle fire blistered the burning wreck of his Gryphon but missed Skeleton Face.

Emma winced at a sudden stinging pain in her right arm. She shot a glance and saw it. Ignoring more stings she grasped the small hive nestled between branch and trunk and chucked it.

Horrified skeleton eyes went wide as the hive smashed full in his face. Angry bees swarmed and took their revenge delivering blistering stings too numerous to count. Skeleton Face stumbled back, dropped the pistol, slammed against the Gryphon's cockpit, and slumped down to the ground, as the bees delivered savage stinging strikes.

An iron spike slammed into the tee trunk six inches above her head. Emma saw RA-7 standing at the end of the narrow trail. The Automaton smiled and waved his metal fingers in greetings. She grabbed the attached rescue rope and shimmied down to the safety of the muddy earth. Dr. Waatt and Kierian dashed over.

"Thank the Lord you are unharmed, my dear," Dr. Waatt said. "For a moment, your survival was surely in question."

Emma glanced at the burning wreck of the Gryphon. Bumble bees continued to buzz around the dead corpse of the pilot.

Emma grinned. "No Balthazar, to bee or not to bee, *THAT* was the question."

CHAPTER TWENTY-TWO

Dr. Waatt glanced up from his wireless telegraph at the setting sun over Braxton Mountain. The elevation and the clearing skies bolstered his confidence that a message could get through to Sagamore.

If all went as planned, the *Excelsior* would rendezvous with them in them at the dig site, in the morning. Once it arrived, with its awesome firepower and Mr. Singh's reinforcements, the mission would be all but over. The Anarchists, now without their battle bot and superior numbers, would acquiesce to STEAM-CAPP'S terms and exchange Professor Stonechat for Boaltt.

As for the ransom, they had decided it was now forfeit. If by some quirk of fate the anarchists did get their hands on it, they would be in for a nasty surprise. Kierian had turned it into what he called "Jacks-in-a-box." Opened incorrectly, it would set off the explosive

376

devices he had planted within the silver, turning the coins into thousands of pieces of deadly "jacks."

Balthazar grasped a metallic cylinder off the broad flat boulder where the transmitter sat, placed it on the ground and raised the antenna up a bamboo pole. A copper wire extended from the cylinder to the antenna, assuring the wireless telegraph's connection with the earth. He shot a quick glance over the mountain's peak. The setting sun hung in the sky, like a fiery hellish ball of flame. Clouds streaked with hues of pink, red, purple, and blue, partially cloaked the floating fireball.

Emma stood near by, one boot balanced on a large boulder near the overhang and one hand looped around Kierian's left arm. "Is it not absolutely gorgeous, Mr. McKenna? A pity the civilians are too exhausted to join us and enjoy its beauty."

Kierian peered down the mountain path where about thirty yards away, their main camp was located. He took a puff of his Mozart, blew a smoke ring over the mountain and watched it float in mid-air before it quietly dispersed. "I am not surprised. After all, I doubt they are used to campaign travel."

Dr. Waatt scoffed. "We did cover a considerable amount of ground today, Kierian. By my estimate, our boots tread around twelve miles, including the two-thousand two hundred and seven foot hike up this mountain."

"Be that as it may, Balthazar, it is still a shame they are missing this sunset," Emma said.

Kierian nodded his agreement. "Ball of fire, stretched forth to admire; Scarlet sky so pleasing to the eye; Like a love's true heart, mourns its depart; But rises anew upon morning's dew."

Emma beamed. "That is beautiful. Who wrote it?"

Blue eyes twinkled down at Emma. "I possess other talents, Miss Dareheart besides my derring-do's."

"*You* wrote it? Why have I never read any verse or prose from you before?"

"I have not exactly had the time to put pen to parchment, Miss Dareheart, though I have considered hiring a writer to chronicle my many rousing adventures."

"Perhaps, Mr. Edison could use them for, his moving picture stories," Emma said.

Kierian cocked his head and nodded. "Miss Dareheart, that is a capital idea, though poor Edison would be hard pressed to find anyone to adequately portray me on his sliver screens."

Emma smiled and laughed softly. "There is but one solution then: You *must* portray yourself, for no one could possibly duplicate your dash and derring-do's, Mr. McKenna."

Kierian puffed on his cigar and nodded his agreement. Balthazar scowled. Kierian was insufferable enough without Emma stroking his ego with dreams of fawning fanatics crowding nickelodeons to watch his embroidered blarney. Why she took such delight in his over embellished accounts, or found his dandified strut and swagger so captivating, he never had understood. He had met them both the same day in 1895, when their resistance cell rescued him from the ruins of a crashed airship in the forests near Black Creek, the same crash that had cost him most of his memories of his earlier life.

Emma was eighteen years of age then, and already showed signs of becoming an impressive young woman. It was understandable that a young girl during wartime, would be beguiled by Kierian's dash and daring, but Balthazar had always figured she would out grow all that. And for a while, after the war ended, he had thought his prediction was spot on. Emma had become a sensible, pragmatic and unflappable young woman, a true credit to her sex. While Kierian was recklessly gallivanting in Cuba, rescuing Evangelina Cosio, she had exhibited a curious and studious mind regarding the sciences and mathematics, and had even borrowed some of his scientific volumes to study regularly, so she could better manage her dare deviling stunts. However, as soon as Kierian reappeared the volumes were returned, the studying stopped, and the fawning idolization began anew.

Heart over mind. What a damn shame. How could someone so sensible and with such pluck make such an irrational and illogical choice?

"It is a pity sunsets end so quickly," Kierian said. "It appears so warm and close, I dare say, you could almost touch it." He reached into his pack, pulled out a fresh red shamrock from RA-7's bouquet, and handed it to Emma.

Emma beamed.

"If you touched it Kierian, you would be incinerated instantly," Balthazar snapped. "Fortunately for you, and unfortunately for the burgeoning moving picture industry, there is no chance of that. Far from being near, it is actually ninety-three million miles away from earth." Dr. Waatt returned to his wireless and attached two wires to the brass rods of the spark gap.

"Is it really so far, away?" Emma asked.

"Indeed, though that is on average. Earth does not travel around the sun in a perfect orbit. Instead its orbit

380

is elliptical, which means the Earth and sun change distances during the year. At its closest, the sun is ninety-one point four million miles away. At its farthest, ninety-five point five million miles away."

Balthazar peered to his right. Precisely twenty-five yards parallel to his position, RA-7 sat on a boulder next to the wireless's receiving unit, playing with his yo-yo.

"RA-7, is the receiver ready for operation?" The automaton smiled, and nodded. Balthazar threw the transmitter switch and began to tap out a message in Morse. The machine buzzed with power, while a ragged stream of purple electricity flowed between the spark gap. Almost simultaneously, the electric bell on the receiver unit rang, indicating the coherer's detection of the signal. The attached Morse Code machine, tapped out Balthazar's message.

"It would appear both units of the wireless are functional. Now, we simply wait for the *Excelsior* to respond."

"You are confident the message will get through?" Emma asked.

"As confident as one can be in the mountains. It is always problematic communicating with so many peaks and obstructions between the sender and the receiver." Balthazar waved to the rescue automaton. "RA-7, would you please join me and retrieve my microscope and the hair and blood samples we took from the ironclad?"

"What do you want with those?" Emma asked.

"Simple, scientific curiosity, my dear. By looking at the blood and hair samples I should be able to determine and inform the local Game Warden, if indeed, a Grizzly bear has somehow migrated into this region or if it is just a rogue black bear wrecking havoc."

RA-7 arrived, carefully set up the microscope on the flat boulder and prepared a glass slide of the hair samples.

"Do you require illumination…Dr. Waatt?"

"Not at present. The remaining solar light and the full moon is sufficient." Balthazar peered thru the microscope and adjusted the magnification. "Now, let us see if…." Slowly the secret microscopic cellular world came into view.

That cannot be correct.

Balthazar pulled his eye away, shook his head and took a second look.

"This…cannot be right."

"What is it, Balthazar?" Emma asked.

"The cells… they appear to be… mutated."

"In what way?" Emma asked.

Balthazar took the slide off the microscope and set it down on the ground. Impatient fingers snapped at the rescue automaton. "RA-7, the blood samples." RA-7 held out the next slide in his bronze fingers. Balthazar snatched it and hurriedly put the slide under the microscope.

"My God... how can this be?" Balthazar sat back against the boulder, his mouth ajar. Synapses blazed. Pieces of a puzzle he had not even known existed horrifyingly began to fall and fit into place.

RA-7 cocked his head to one side. "Dr. Waatt, are you... ill? Your face has suddenly become quite...pale."

Dispassionate monotonous words ignored the automaton's question. "The slides show a combination of human and bear cells."

"How can that be?" Emma asked.

Puzzle pieces fell and fitted.

"The opening...Kierian, the opening in the hull of the ironclad's stern...the way the timber fibers were bent...."

"What about them? Doctor, what is wrong?" Kierian said. Sensing Balthazar's apprehension, he reached down and grabbed his shotgun. Emma followed his action and snatched her EMR-2 dexterously into her hands.

Balthazar's stomach knotted. A pained expression spread across his face. "I have been such a fool! I am no more a scientist than Boaltt is an archeologist! I fitted the data to my own prejudices, rather than accept what the data actually was!"

"Balthazar," Emma said, "tell us what is wrong."

"That was no entrance on the ironclad, my dear. God forgive me; I should have realized. It was an exit!"

"Then how did the bear get aboard?" Emma asked.

Dr. Waatt removed his campaign hat and ran a hand through his long snow-white hair. "Do you not see, my dear? Do you not see? There is but one answer. The bear was already on board!"

Puzzle pieces fell and fitted.

Dr. Waatt looked up at Kierian. "Kaplan's last words... He was not trying to say, 'Horribus Urtus Artos.' He pronounced the phonetic 'M' but I dismissed it as a mispronunciation of a dying utterance."

"What do you mean?" Kierian asked.

"My God, Kierian he was trying to tell us, trying to warn us, trying to say Homo Urtus Artos."

"That translates to human bear, Balthazar."

Dr. Waatt nodded.

More puzzle pieces fell and fitted.

"Professor Stonechat! She was not in a catatonic state. She was in a *hypnotic* state! No doubt placed into one when she encountered the bear. Do you remember her poem? 'The Roar of the mighty bear, The cry of the lake wet loon; Submit to the Way of the *were*; At the Rising of the Moon.'"

More puzzle pieces fell and fitted.

"W-e-r-e not w-h-e-r-e... The great thirst, the mode swings, the rapid healing of that arm wound, the blistered hands-probably from running on all fours-it is Boaltt. Boaltt IS a were-bear!"

Kierian raised an eyebrow. "Balthazar, have you lost your senses? That is just a legend. There are no such creatures as were-wolves or were-beasts."

Balthazar shook his head and tapped the slide. "The data says otherwise. Lycanthropy has been theorized to be an actual condition by some of the world's foremost cryptozoologists. The Roman courtier, Gaius Petronius wrote about it and later, Gervase of Tillbury and then there is the well documented and curious case from Germany of the diabolical Peter Stump."

"Ancient folklore and nothing more, I would wager," Kierian said.

Balthazar ignored the remark and continued. "More recently, the British scientist Sir John Talbot wrote sev-

385

eral monographs on the subject, after traveling to Tibet and Transylvania to conduct his research. He was considered the foremost authority on the subject until he reportedly perished onboard *HMAS Black Prince*, when you two blew it to kingdom come."

"SJ Boaltt is a possible anagram of Sir John... Talbot," RA-7 said.

A bone chilling woman's scream from the direction of the camp, ripped through the air.

"Miss Vanderbilt!" Kierian exclaimed and rushed off down the trail, chambering a round into his Winchester pump. Emma followed directly behind.

"Wait! Kierian, Emma, firearms will be useless against such a creature!"

But they were already gone, and even if they heard him, the insufferable dandy and the foolish lovelorn dare deviless would not have stopped. An innocent was in trouble, and honor and duty required them to fly to the rescue.

They are correct. There is a time where one must forgo careful planning and charge directly unto the breach.

Balthazar turned and looked at Ra-7. Determined arms extended outward.

"RA-7, fit me with the S.A.M.S.O.N."

CHAPTER TWENTY-THREE

Birthed anew by maximum lunar radiation, the mighty beast was loosed.

And Sir John Talbot reveled in it.

The pompous fools at the Royal Academy of Science had laughed at him, mocked him, and scorned his work. Lycanthropy, they said, was the bastard child of cryptozoology; itself a bastardized field of pseudo-scientific study, populated by imbeciles and lunatics. They had made him look foolish and weak and refused to even give his work a proper hearing.

But the Legion of Cain had listened.

They had furnished him with funds, a first rate laboratory, and most importantly, a tooth from Ursus Arctos Tyrannous, the great bear of the Pleistocene era. The potion he and the Legion's brilliant chemist, Dr. Henry Jekyll had created, replicated the effects of a Tyrannous bite. Combined with his unique heredity, and the proper amount of moonlight, it had transformed him not just into a bear but MORE than a bear. Now, *he* was mighty. Now, *he* was strong!

And all would fear the dread roar of Bearamore!

Bearamore padded forward. The Vanderbilt heiress had undone his original scheme, and exposed his subterfuge. How fitting that she be the first to have her skin ripped from her bones. How delicious her tender flesh would be!

A rifle roared. A bullet slammed into his shoulder, a second into his ribs.

Bearamore rose and bellowed in rage. Regenerated cells instantly closed both wounds.

More shots slammed into him. Bearamore turned to face the authors of his pains. Dread eyes fell on the forms of the two sports.

Vanderbilt's Lackeys. Henroff and Leslie. Very well, the heiress will have to be the third to die.

Bearamore stalked forward.

Leslie raised his rifle.

Bearamore's right claw ripped the rifle from the sport's hand. The werebear's left claw slashed open the sport's ribcage, exposing meat and bone.

Leslie stumbled back, his chest a ruin of red.

Bearamore bounded forward. A brutal barrage of tooth and claw turned the sport into nothing but grizzle and gore.

Henroff fired. A bullet slammed into Bearamore's left shoulder.

Bearamore turned from his butchery and roared.

The sport worked the lever action frantically, hip-firing shots in rapid succession, sending a hail of lead into Bearamore's chest.

Bearamore ignored the bullet impacts and stalked forward.

"Your feeble attempts to stop me are most amusing, lackey," The werebear growled. "You are naught but a night's nourishment. Fodder food for the great bear-god Bearamore!"

Henroff pulled the trigger again. The firing pin clicked on an empty chamber. Desperate hands swung the rifle like a club. The walnut stock slammed hard into Bearamore's shoulder.

Monstrous claws carved bloody furrows across Henroff's face, ripping flesh from skull.

Henroff screamed. His hand clutched the mangled ruins of his face.

Bearamore dug his claws into Henroff's shoulders. Sharp, pitiless teeth, closed around the sport's neck and tore it asunder.

The beast took control momentarily and began his feast, but Talbot remembered Gladys and regained control of the warring natures.

Henroff's actions had broken his hypnotic hold on the girl and she fled up the trail. Four powerful legs gave chase and cut her off from the path leading to the mountain's summit.

Frantic Vanderbilt eyes darted left and right.

Bearamore roared as he watched the awful truth dawn on the heiress's face; hemmed in on either side by the mountain's ledges and its 700-foot drop, Gladys Vanderbilt had nowhere to go.

Bearamore slowly advanced. Blood coated fangs bared, savoring the moments of anticipation of a long awaited kill.

* * * * * *

Emma sped down the trail, just behind Kierian.

His shotgun roared. A spread of buckshot slammed into the shoulder of the enormous werebear facing Gladys Vanderbilt.

Kierian angled to the creature's right, firing as he ran, his shots finding purchase in the monstrous hide.

The werebear turned, rose up on two legs, and roared in defiance.

As soon as Kierian was clear of her line of fire, Emma dropped to one knee, toggled the magnification on her riflescope down to 1x, sighted, and fired.

390

Iron-cored aluminum blew a gargantuan hole through the werebear's skull.

The beast stumbled and staggered backward. Astonished brown eyes watched, as brain and bone instantly grew anew.

Kierian slam-fired his Winchester. Buckshot tore flesh and muscle. Instant regeneration repaired the damage. The werebear lumbered towards Kierian. A fearsome swipe lunged for his face.

Kierian ducked, shoulder rolled under the massive paw, speed loaded a deer slug into the shotgun, and blasted a round into the werebear's side.

The werebear howled. A massive backhand, crashed into Kierian, smashing the Winchester from his hand and sending him sprawling amongst the sleeping bags, packs and ransom chest.

Emma aimed another shot. Gladys Vanderbilt drifted into her line of fire. Thundering steps to Emma's six o'clock caused her to glance behind. RA-7 rushed down the trail towards her.

Kierian pushed himself up to one knee and drew his M1900. "RAY, get Miss Vanderbilt the hell out of here!"

A streak of bronze flashed by Emma. The rescue automaton snatched Gladys Vanderbilt into his arms without breaking stride and dashed for the mountain trail.

With surprising agility, the werebear pivoted, swiped a razor sharp claw at the Rescue Automaton's raised leg, and sent the bronze giant toppling over.

RA-7 twisted as he fell, assuring his metal back absorbed the shock of the hard, rocky ground, rather than the soft skin and breakable bones of his human charge.

The werebear pounced.

RA-7 pitched Gladys as softy as he could, over his head, sending her into a somersault.

With a sickening thud, the werebear landed on the automaton. Razor sharp claws ripped away at RA-7's chest and shoulder panels. Sparks filled the air like tiny lightning bugs.

Emma adjusted her aim and fired.

The shot ripped a giant hole in the werebear's shoulder. The creature leaped to its feet, spun, howled, and stalked towards Emma as the shoulder wound instantly healed.

Kierian dashed in front of her and raised his pistol. "Go Ray, and do not stop until you reach Sagamore!"

RA-7 staggered to his feet, his left arm, all but severed, hung uselessly at his side. He reached down and scooped Gladys up under his right arm. Like a thief fleeing a bakery with a loaf of bread, he plodded down the moonlit trail.

The werebear growled and charged.

Kierian slammed a stiff arm into the beast's chest and emptied his pistol point-blank into the beast's heart.

The werebear bellowed, and took a step back.

Then its right claw raked down Kierian's shoulder, and upper chest.

"Kierian!" Emma cried. Heart-wrenched hands hip-fired the EMR-2, as blood soaked fangs closed towards Kierian's neck.

Kierian's Bowie knife sprang from its sheath and plunged through lower and upper werebear jaws, denying a killing bite.

The werebear staggered back.

Kierian collapsed among the packs.

Horrified, Emma hurdled over the packs, stood between him and the werebear, and raised the EMR-2.

With a mighty crunch the werebear snapped the Bowie knife in half. Furious yellow eyes hypnotized Emma.

Her finger froze at the trigger. Her mind suddenly ordered her motionless.

Pull the trigger, Amelia, pull the damn trigger!

The werebear stalked forward. Sharp, hungry fangs bared for the kill.

"TALBOT!"

The creature roared and spun around.

Dr. Waatt stood in the center of the campsite, leaning on his walking stick, his limbs, shoulders and upper back encased in a Titanium exoskeleton. "If it is a fight you desire, you monstrous abomination of nature, then come face S.A.M.S.O.N!"

Powerful werebear legs charged across the stony mountain ground straight at Dr. Waatt.

With the hypnotic hold broken, Emma raised her EMR-2.

The werebear closed the distance on Dr. Waatt quickly.

Balthazar stood as still as a statue and continued to lean on his walking stick.

Emma aimed for the legs. Any higher and she risked the projectile cutting thru the beast and striking Balthazar.

Fangs bared, the werebear's massive shoulders lowered.

Balthazar sidestepped.

The werebear charged past and towards the edge of the cliff.

Emma fired. Another massive wound erupted in the leg of the monstrous beast. For a second, Emma thought it would topple over the mountainside, but it skidded to a stop, the wound closed, and the werebear wheeled around.

Now, it was Balthazar who charged. Gears ground and whizzed. Steam hissed from twin pipes on the back of the exoskeleton.

The werebear reared up and bellowed. Razored claws swiped at Dr. Waatt's head.

Balthazar raised his left arm and parried the blow. His walking stick's silver head slammed into the werebear's cheek, ripping open a jagged wound.

A trickle of blood flowed down its jaw.

Kierian rallied and pushed himself up into a sitting position. "Banshee," Kierian pointed a finger at the werebear. "The wound Balthazar made with his walking stick, it is not closing."

"I guess it is not just silver *bullets* that can harm this monster. A pity my projectiles are made from aluminum."

The werebear bellowed. A frenzy of swiping claws, raked at Dr. Waatt.

Titanium arms darted up, crossing in the shape of a metallic 'x' in time to absorb the onslaught.

395

The werebear bellowed again and rained a flurry of powerful blows down upon Balthazar's armored shoulders, driving him to one knee.

Balthazar held his 'x' block and absorbed the hammer blows.

The werebear took a step forward.

Balthazar raked the walking stick head into its shoulder.

The werebear bellowed, but it was now inside Balthazar's guard. Mighty paws wrapped around Dr. Waatt's back, hefted him off his feet, and squeezed.

Emma heard a crack.

Violently the werebear threw Balthazar. He crashed to the ground, rolled over, landed on his stomach and sprawled motionless on the rocky slope of Braxton Mountain.

* * * * * *

Bearamore roared in victory.

Waatt learned my secret but like the fools on the ironclad, he learned it too late. All his fancy toys and advanced weaponry were no match for the power of Bearamore!

He heard the round whistle through the air. Pain seared in his side as it found its mark. He bellowed and spun around.

Dareheart!

396

The adventuress fumbled, patted pockets and her equipment belt.

The bitch is out of ammunition! Time to feast!

Bearamore stalked forward and bared his blood-stained teeth.

Dareheart threw down her rifle, drew her Colt, and blazed away.

Behind her, McKenna, his shirt soaked in blood, drew one of Waatt's toys, the heat-ray pistol. He struggled to raise it.

Bearamore roared.

I shall kill McKenna, feast on Dareheart and then, return to my temple, where the Algonquins worshiped my kind like the gods we truly are.

McKenna shoved the ransom chest forward with his legs.

Fools! Do they think they can buy their lives with coin?

Bearamore gave a final roar and stalked in for the kill.

* * * * * *

"Banshee, my right shoulder… assist."

Emma ducked under Kierian's arm, placed one hand on his elbow and wrapped the other around his wrist.

Together they raised his right arm and aimed the

heat-ray pistol.

"Well, you know what they say, every ransom chest has a silver lining."

Emma steadied Kierian's arm. "I thought that was clouds that had silver linings."

"Clouds, ransom chest; Po-tate-o, Po-tot-o."

Kierian's fingers squeezed the heat-ray trigger and held it down. The gun crackled, hummed, and fired.

A red beam of energy burned a quarter size hole through the ransom chest, igniting the explosives inside.

One million dollars worth of silver coins exploded out of the chest like a giant shotgun, catapulting silver shrapnel in a deadly arch, peppering the werebear's upper body.

The beast staggered backwards. Silver coin edges embedded in its body, stuck out like footholds of a cliff.

The creature bellowed, unsteady legs staggered forward, crimson teeth and razor sharp claws remained bared.

Dr. Waatt struggled to his knees.

"Balthazar! Thank the Lord you are alive! I thought I heard your spine snap!" Emma exclaimed.

"The snap you heard, my dear, was the exoskeleton being damaged. As for my health, an analysis of such must wait until this abomination is utterly destroyed!"

Balthazar, reached down, toggled a switch on each boot, sprang forward and charged.

Gears spun and whizzed. The exoskeleton propelled Balthazar Waatt forward, and he plowed into the wounded werebear like a wild boar, driving it back toward the edge of the cliff.

The werebear bellowed and wrapped its arm around Balthazar.

But Balthazar did not stop. His legs kept moving, driving the werebear to the precipice.

For a moment, they both were silhouetted against the eerie glow of the full moon.

Then they toppled.

And plunged over the side of Braxton Mountain.

CHAPTER TWENTY-FOUR

"BALTHAZAR, NOOO!"

Emma dashed to the edge of the cliff and peered into the shadowy gloom of the Adirondack forest.

"He is gone! Balthazar is gone!"

Kierian did not reply.

Emma spun and darted back. Kierian was doubled over. His shoulder wound bled profusely. Wide brown eyes stared at the wound in alarm. In all the engagements he had been in, in all the battles they had fought together, Kierian had never once been seriously wounded. Even after the charge up Cobbs Hill with the Rough Rangers, though she had counted over fifteen bullets holes in his frock coat, not a single one had so much as nicked him. Good Lady Fortune had indeed, watched over him like a mother bear over her favorite cub.

The jagged wound and his blood-soaked shirt froze her heart with despair. Tears welled up in her eyes.

Save the tears for the cemetery, she thought. Do what needs doing.

400

"Save the tears for the cemetery, Banshee, and do what needs doing," Kierian gasped.

Emma nodded. "You are bleeding bad, Piper."

"I am aware." He pulled a shotgun shell from his belt and held it out to Emma. "Cauterize the damn thing, at the double time!"

Emma snatched the shell from his hand, cut it open with her knife, poured out the shot, and tore open his shirt.

Kierian winced. "Another Sinclair-Hodge ripped to shreds."

"I shall make an appointment with Saul for a new fitting as soon as we return from the mission."

Kierian nodded. "I will hold you to that promise."

"Do you want a shot of whiskey, first?"

Kierian shook his head. "I am about to pass out, no sense wasting good whiskey. Best get on with it, Banshee."

Emma nodded. Steady hands poured the gunpowder into the gruesome wounds.

Kierian reached across his body with his hand and fumbled in his pocket for his lighter.

"I will get it, Piper."

Kierian nodded.

Emma retrieved the lighter. She did not bother to

401

ask him if he was ready. How could anyone be ready for such a *treatment?* She flicked open the lighter, thumbed down the button, and lit the black powder.

In the fading light, the five rows of powder sparked, sizzled, and burned down Kierian's upper chest.

Kierian cried out, and flopped back unconscious. The bleeding stopped, but Emma did not like how he looked. Beads of sweat dripped down his ghostly pale face. His forehead was so hot, you could fry an egg on it.

Death was written on his face.

Despair twisted inside her. It was usually not the wound that killed, but the infection that followed. She held his head in her lap, poured cool water over her bandana, and dabbed Kierian's forehead with it.

She felt so damn helpless. RA-7 might have been able to assist but he was dashing back to Sagamore with Gladys Vanderbilt. Balthazar would have thought of something too. He probably would have known some nearby plant with healing properties, or invented some potion on the spot that could at least bring down Kierian's fever.

But Balthazar was at the bottom of Braxton Mountain with the were-bear he had taken with him.

402

She was alone.

Alone, and unable to help the man who had saved her, the man who had taught her she could be strong as steel and still laugh and smile at the world and its ever-present hypocrisy. Hot tears spilled down her cheeks as she stroked Kierian's sandy blond hair.

The pages of her mind, turned back the years.

* * * * * *

After the Tommies had assaulted her, she had woken up in the bedroom of a farmhouse. Strangers brought food and water, stroked her cheek, brushed her hair, and asked how she was feeling in the gentle voice that people used when speaking to children, lunatics and the dying.

The damn Pity Voice. God I hate that voice.

Outside her door where they thought she could not hear, they uttered phrases like "Poor dear, She'll never be the same," and "What kind of life will she have now?"

What kind of life did I have before? Scraping and scheming to survive. Smiling and looking pathetic to get a handout from some well-to-do sir, and trying to figure how to cut the sexual strings that they always expected to be attached. Being reminded every day that I was worth less than the milk-

403

man's carthorse. That I was weak, and merely prey for the strong?

On the fourth day a doctor even stopped by to treat her injuries. That was an unusual kindness. Proper doctors rarely examined people like her. Most people would probably have taken it as a sign they were safe and the people around her meant her no harm.

But Emma was no one's fool. Fifteen years of street living had taught her the hard cold truth that no one was ever *that* kind, unless they wanted something from you. So she held her tongue and played the traumatized victim until she could figure out what was what.

When she woke up on the fifth day, there *he* was, sitting with a smile on his face, dressed like he was going to dinner at the Executive Mansion.

"Good morning, girl. How are you faring?"

The twinkling blue eyes gave him away. She did not remember much about the features of her rescuer but she did remember his eyes. Yes, this was the man who had saved her and she figured that earned him a response.

"I am fine. Thank you for saving me."

"Ha!" he slapped his knee, grinned, and tipped so far back on the legs of his chair that she thought he would topple over. "You see?" He cocked his head back and shouted over his shoulder " Josephine, I told you she would talk." He slapped his knee again, chuckled and turned his head back to her. Blue eyes twinkled down at her. "Just waiting until there was someone worth talking to, I wager. Right, Miss…?"

Emma simply stared back. Was this really the same man who had saved her? The man who had ruthlessly gunned down five John Bulls, then carried her through the streets of Rochester, dodging British patrols, stealing a hansom cab and bluffing his was past a checkpoint?

That man had been all business and brutally efficient in combat.

"Who are you?"

"You can call me… The Piper."

Piper? The man sitting before her now seemed more harlequin than hero. Yet there was no denying those eyes that were so blue you could just drown yourself in them. "Well then, you can call me Street Urchin"

The Piper laughed. "No, I said THE Piper."

"Is that suppose to mean something to me? You say your name like you expect heavenly trumpets to sound."

"Trumpets?" He cocked his head and seemed to

consider her words as a suggestion rather than deri-
sion. "No, too British. I would prefer something more
American, like a folk song, sung in the music halls, or a
poem recited on stage about my derring-dos. Yes, I
think that would suit me fine."

Emma raised an eyebrow. "Your derring-dos?"

"Of course! You must not be from around here or
you would no doubt have heard of them, and me." He
brushed back his sandy blond hair from his handsome
face.

She shook her head. *Who is this arrogant Alan?*

"I am from around here, Piper. I was born in
Rochester."

"In the West end no doubt and to a middle class
family. You are too good looking a girl and too well
spoken to be anything but a West ender."

"I am not a Westie and I am not middle class. I was
born in a shit hole on Third Street, in the eastern part of
the city."

"And where do you live, now?"

"Under a bridge, in an abandoned building, with a
friend in their shit hole hovel if I am lucky. Who gives a
good damn?"

Usually after her litany of dwellings she got the
'poor dear' look.

The Piper just smiled.

He did not tell her he was sorry, or lecture her on the wisdom of staying at a workhouse, or tell her he knew good Father Feeder or Sweet Sister Charity who would help her out, and make her a respectable young lady.

"Well, regardless, your parents and relations did a poor job of informing you on local folk heroes."

"My parents did a piss poor job on just about everything. I never knew which of the gents who rodgered mother regularly, was dear ol' daddy, and mother was too interested in her gin bottle to feed and clothe me, much less have story time."

"What a shame, but never fear, now you have me to educate you first hand, Miss..."

What a clever Clive this Piper is.

It was then she realized that despite being on her guard she had just told him where she was from, where she was born, that she had no family relations and lived on the streets.

Now he wants to know my name.

She did not want to tell him her name. Your name was all you really had on the streets. People who knew it could use it for good or for ill, it always being easier to trust someone who called you by name. A person should have to earn an introduction, not just ask for one like they were ordering dinner.

The Piper placed two glasses on the nightstand by the bed, poured her a glass of brandy, and one for himself.

Emma stared suspiciously at the drink. "I am not going to drink your hooch."

"God forbid, I ever serve a lady, hooch!" he said. The smile dropped from his eyes and he stabbed a well manicured finger at her. "Trust me, Miss Urchin, I would rather kiss that old hag Queen Vick, than be known as a man who drinks and serves hooch in a lady's company."

He seemed genuinely insulted and for some reason, that bothered her.

"I... I did not mean to offend you, Mr. Piper." Emma picked up the bottle and looked at the label. A smiling old lady hoisted a glass of a black liquid. Blackberry vines decorated her portrait. "However, Granny Simmons' Blackberry Brandy? That is not exactly what President Blaine drinks, I wager."

The Piper smiled, the lyrical lint of his voice returned. "President Blaine is safely ensconced in Fortress Washington where the wine and whiskey flows unabated. You and I must do with what we can procure." He pushed the glass towards her then stopped and pulled it away. "Unless you are too young to drink. I hazarded a guess of eighteen, though Josephine postulated you to be older than you appear."

"Sixteen," she corrected. A second later she realized her mistake.

Damn it. Just told him my age!

"Ah, it must be your mature attitude and proficiency at cussing, that makes you seem older." He pulled a deck of cards with a four-leaf clover on the back, from his pocket and began to shuffle. Dexterous hands gracefully blended and cut the cards.

"Are you some kind of card shark?"

The Piper grinned. "If I was, I would not have revealed my expert shuffling skills to you, now would I?"

"No? What would you do?"

"I would throw them on the bed and mix them up like little Jack Horner before he was sent to his corner."

She felt the corner of her mouth begin to stretch into grin.

Damn but he is easy to talk to.

"That would be a bit obvious I think."

He grinned again. "You know how to play rummy, Miss..?"

Clever Piper. You do not give up do you?

409

"I am not playing rummy with you."

"Why not?"

"Because you want something. You are trying to put me at ease with your charm. That is why they call you the Piper, correct? Like from the poem? You are like the Pied Piper of Hamelin who plays a hypnotic and serene song and gets people to follow him to their destruction."

She threw her arms out wide, and dramatically. *"Please your honors, said he, I'm able, by means of a secret charm, to draw all creatures living beneath the sun, that creep or swim or fly or run; after me so as you never saw! And I chiefly use my charm, on creatures that do people harm; the mole and toad and newt and viper; And people call me the Pied Piper.''*

The Piper clapped, laughed softly and his blue eyes twinkled. "An excellent rendition, Miss Urchin but the Pied Piper *saved* the children, remember?"

The Piper's voice was soft, pleasant and the lilt seemed more intoxicating than even before. He looked into her eyes with his blue orbs and quoted another section of the poem.

"*A wondrous portal opened wide; As if a cavern was suddenly hollowed; And the Piper advanced and the children followed; And when all were in to the very last, the door in the mountain-side shut fast.* "

She stared back at him, and was fairly sure she fought back a contented sigh, but failed to prevent a smile. Miss. Ferris had told her that the first time a man read poetry to her would be like her seeing her first sunrise. Assuming the limerick, "There Once Was A Man From Nantucket" did not count, the prissy old matron of Miss Ferris's School For Wayward Young Ladies, had been damn right!

The Piper took a sip of his brandy and smiled, his twinkling blue eyes never left her.

Despite herself she ran a hand through her brown mane. "Yes, well , one interpretation is he was just some slick con man who abducted the children away from their parents."

The Piper shrugged. "Maybe the parents were worthless and neglectful. Maybe those children needed

411

someone who gave a good damn, and was willing to take them away from the squalid lives they were forced to live." His eyes twinkled and he took another sip of brandy. "In any case, I am impressed. You are well read Miss Urchin. I was not aware Robert Browning was read much on 3rd street"

"I spent two years at a reformatory for young ladies, after Smilin' Jim framed me for a pinch. The matron and her ladies taught us how to walk with books on our heads, how to sew and crotchet, how to set the table, and how to serve insipid, snobby bitches. However, they did have a nice library."

"One never can be sure when education may come in handy."

"Indeed," Emma replied. Sarcasm dripped from every word. "I am sure knowing the difference between a soup spoon and a bouillon spoon will serve me incredibly well in life."

"You never know. Perhaps you will one day gain employment in the household of a New York Fifth Avenue robber baron, or as a maid to some British Canadian lord."

"Too much bowing and scraping. I'm not a by-your-leave, Sir, or yes-my Lady Priss, kind of girl."

The Piper nodded. "No, I would guess you are

not." He began to deal the cards but Emma held up a hand. "No cards. Remember?"

The Piper smiled. "Very well. It is probably for the best you forgo playing rummy so you can focus entirely on my tales of derring-dos, Miss...."

Emma stared at him. His persistence was becoming annoying.

"Bertha."

"Bertha...?"

"Bertha Boxcar."

The Piper laughed and shook his head. "No, you are not a Bertha. I knew a Bertha once. In fact I was hired to find her by her father. A very unlovely girl she was, in both spirit and countenance."

"I suppose you cannot always be rescuing beautiful fair maidens from the castle. Did you find her?"

"Of course! The mission is the mission regardless if you like it or no. Bertha had run off with the first male suitor who told her she was pretty. Alas, he was only after her fortune. It fell to me to convince her of her folly and safely return her to the loving and watchful eye of her dear father. In any case, you are not a Bertha."

"Matilda. That is my name, Matilda Mudpie."

The Piper chuckled. "No, I think not."

"Sophia Soppysow? Geniuve Gingeller?"

The Piper chuckled. His blue eyes twinkled as he laughed. She wanted to smile and laugh along with him.

Stop that! There is nothing to laugh about. This is just jam on the bread but the bread is still moldy and stale.

"So, no brandy and no cards. Fair enough, then on to my tales!"

For the next three hours he told her one fantastic story after another, all with himself as the swashbuckling hero, saving damsels in distress, and defeating a variety of Rochester street thugs, Genesee River pirates and despotic British-Canadian officials across the border, as part of some secret organization called the Hunters Lodge.

The Piper was a natural storyteller. His voice was lyrical and his tone almost musical. He flawlessly imitated street accents. Body gestures accompanied the story but were not overly intrusive. Despite herself, Emma became immersed in the tales. Suddenly, it was vitally important to know if the heroic Piper rescued Thomas Tucker Sr. so Tommy Tucker Jr. could make ice cream with his rescued father on his tenth birthday, or if he recovered the incriminating and indiscreet letters Miss Elizabeth Newcastle had written, that if made

414

public, would surely ruin her dream of marrying her true love.

Emma could never quite tell what parts of the story were embellished and which were unlikely but true events. One story about 'Nasty' Nick Kress, a local pimp who had recently met his end after being run over by a train, especially drew her attention.

She knew Nasty Nick. He had tried to make her one of his girls and gave her a black and blue shiner around her right peeper when, in answer to his nasty offer, she had spit in his nasty face.

From what she had heard, she had gotten off easy.

Word was, Nasty Nick enjoyed tying girls to train tracks who displeased him. He would twirl his handlebar moustache and make them beg for their lives.

Sometimes he untied them.

Sometimes he did not.

In a wonderful case of poetic justice, Nick had become drunk, fallen asleep on the tracks, and was subsequently sliced in half by the midnight special.

At least that is what the papers reported.

Whispers on the street said different.

Someone had tied Nick to the tracks, guaranteeing his grisly fate. The Piper explained he was that someone, and that he had been hired to find a twelve-year

415

old girl by the name of Catherine Burleson, who had run away from her middle class home. Nasty Nick got her hooked on the opium pipe and turned her into a street whore. When the Piper had come to rescue her, she was tied to the tracks and Nasty Nick was telling her she was a worthless piece of horse shit that no one would ever love and would never make him 'no dough' on account of her ugliness and it was the railway to hell for her.

The Piper's eyes became intense and his tone stern. It was only justice that Kress take her place, the Piper explained. In great detail he described the type of knot he had used and even the name of the train that had sliced Nasty Nick in half.

"He would have just done the same thing to the next girl. I figured it was time for him to —"

"To… pay the piper?"

The Piper grinned.

Emma allowed herself a half smile.

Was it true? Dozens of woman had no doubt prayed the rosary for Nasty Nick's demise over the years. As far as she was concerned, the person who sent him to the devil's dinner deserved a statue in St. Paul's Square and the key to the city, but was the Piper that person? Or maybe he just heard the details on the street and turned it into a self-glorifying tale?

Emma could not tell, but most of the stories were less grizzly and they made the corners of her mouth twitch as suppressed smiles attempted to bust free.

I have nothing to smile about. Why does this devilishly handsome, insanely arrogant stranger who kills so easily make me want to grin and chuckle like a silly schoolgirl?

Halfway through the Adventure of Blue Blaze, she could take it no more and burst out laughing.

"You did not out run a race horse! Now, that I know is not true."

"I most certainly did. I am quite fleet of foot."

"If you are that fleet of foot they should call you Mercury not Piper."

The Piper laughed and took a sip of his brandy. "Shall I tell you how I did it?"

"You did not do it. So there is nothing to tell. No one is fast enough to win a sixty-yard race against a Thoroughbred, race horse"

The Piper smiled. "If I tell you how, you must tell me your name."

"Why should I? You have not told me yours?"

The Piper nodded. "Fair enough. You tell me yours and I shall tell you mine."

"Only if how you beat the racehorse is true. I am

417

not giving up my name for a bunch of blarney."

Blue eyes twinkled at her and he extended his hand. "Deal."

She shook his hand and nodded. "Alright, how did you beat Blue Blaze and win back the horse for little Annie pain-in-the ass?'

"Annie Paninsas," the Piper corrected.

"Whatever the little brat's name was. How did you beat Blue Blaze?"

The Piper smiled. "I set up a course where we ran thirty yards up and thirty yards back. Mr. Garrison Crittenden, who had swindled Blue Blaze from the Panisas's, desired not just to defeat me but to humiliate me by winning by the largest margin possible."

"Oh Mr. Piper," Emma said sarcastically, "You do not mean to imply that your confidence and cocksure attitude birthed a desire in someone to see you humbled and humiliated?"

The Piper nodded. "Hard to fathom, I agree, but it is the truth." He took another sip of his brandy before continuing. "When the gun went off Crittenden dug in his spurs and went directly to the whip, putting Blue Blaze in a full gallop. Unfortunately for Crittenden, I possessed information about his mount that he did not. Blue Blaze, you see, was a spirited horse and once he was in full gallop he yielded slowly to the reins. He subsequently over ran the thirty-yard marker by a significant margin. By the time Crittenden got Blue Blaze turned around, I was home free."

The Piper leaned back in his chair and smiled a self-satisfied smile. Proud blue eyes twinkled.

Emma pondered the solution.

Damn it, if that is not… plausible!

She looked up at him and laughed softly.

"And my name is Kierian McKenna, Miss…."

"Emma."

"Emma…?"

She was not going to tell him her Christian name. Why should she? It was a nobody's name, a name that had caused her nothing but pain. It was an unimpressive name, and she wanted to impress the Piper.

"Dareheart. Emma Dareheart."

Kierian McKenna smiled and extended his hand again. "Now that is a name that befits you! It is my great pleasure to meet you…Emma Dareheart."

* * * * * *

The uncaring moon slid behind a bank of clouds, causing inky shadows to emerge. Emma softly ran her fingers down Kierian's feverish face. Anguish stabbed

419

at her heart like a hot knife. She leaned over and embraced him. The Red Shamrock he had pinned to her
vest earlier, pushed flush against his face. She held him
tight for several minutes, pushed aside the flower,
kissed him softly on the lips and quietly quoted the end
of the poem:

"*And in years after, she used to say; It's dull in town since*
my playmates left! I can't forget that I'm bereft.

Of all the pleasant sights they see; which the Piper promised
me. For he led me, to a joyous land; Joining the town and just
at hand; Where waters gushed and pine trees grew; And
flowers put forth a fairer hue; And everything was strange
and new.

And just as I became assured my heart would cure; the music
stopped and I stood still.

And I found myself outside the hill; Left alone against my
will,

To go now living as before, And never hear of the Piper
more"

Emma hugged Kierian tight.

Come back to me Piper. I do not want our story to end just as
it is really beginning.

CHAPTER TWENTY-FIVE

The awfulness of Boaltt's transformation had paralyzed Gladys with fear. Terrified eyes had watched as clothes ripped to shreds; bones disjointed, elongated and re-shaped; muscles ripped, bulged, and expanded; Jaw-bones cracked, transmogrified, and razor sharp fangs grew where teeth once sat; fur replaced skin.

The horror became too much. Gladys had closed her eyes, hoping she would wake up from the night-mare but knowing it was all too real. She had wanted to scream, but something had seemed to take over her mind and compelled her to remain silent. Only when Mr. Leslie had fired on the beast and it had turned away from her, had the spell been broken, and she had been able to give voice to the horror within.

Now, as the rescue automaton cradled her against his metal hip and raced down the mountain trail, she could feel her very soul shiver with fear.

She peeked behind and tried to peer into the moon-lit darkness but she could not see much.

Her heart pounded heavy in her chest. She wanted to speak to the robot but her lips trembled. Terror still held its icy controlling grip.

Gladys closed her eyes, deeply inhaled the pine air, and despite the fear, willed herself to speak.

"Are...Are we s-safe. Are..w-we being chased." The words came out rough but they came out all the same. The sound of her own voice not shrieking in abject terror, made her feel more at ease.

The automaton lurched to a stop. His neck gears, clinked and clanked. His head slowly rotated around, and his single good eye scanned the forest. "I detect no indications of...pursuit."

"Are you sure? How can you see much of anything in this dreadful darkness?"

"My optical fixtures are fitted with night vision... intensifiers."

"But you have only one good eye," Gladys countered.

"Indeed, but if we were being pursued I would detect the sounds of...pursuit. A creature of that size would create a lot of noise as it crashed through the... brush."

The automaton continued his mountain descent.

Gladys felt a spark of relief ignite. The controlling

422

fear began to melt away. "Mr. Seven, I thank you for rescuing me, but since I am now out of danger, may I not walk unassisted? Being pressed against your metal side is quite uncomfortable."

"I apologize for your...discomfort, but we can move at a brisker pace if I carry...you."

"Perhaps, a repositioning then?" Gladys asked hopefully.

The automaton pondered on this for a few seconds before coming to an abrupt stop and setting Gladys on her feet. He pulled a canteen from his equipment belt and handed it to Gladys.

Gladys gripped the canvas container with both hands and chugged down the water. "My goodness!" Her face contorted in disgust. "Why does this taste like rusted metal?"

"How do you know what rusted metal tastes... like?"

Gladys snorted. "Brothers revel in making their younger sisters taste all manner of disgusting things."

"The water is treated with iodine tablets in order to destroy any bacterial... organisms. The metallic taste is due to the numbing of your taste buds by the...iodine."

RA-7 slowly dropped to one knee. Metal gears, pulleys and pitons, scraped, screeched and clunked.

"Mr. Seven, are you injured? The manner of noises escaping from your limbs seems most unnatural?"

"Diagnostic evaluators are not responding but I do seem to be experiencing system wide...impairment."

"How bad is your impairment?"

"The Diagnostic Evaluators, report the level of functionality of all my systems but since they are not responding, it is difficult to...say."

RA-7 motioned to his back. "You may climb up on my... shoulders. Please strap yourself to the foot and hand... grips."

Gladys did as instructed. RA-7 slowly stood. The parts that made up his legs, scraped, screeched and sang a distressing tune.

"Perhaps, we should return to assist your friends. I am sure Dr. Waatt could fix whatever is wrong with you."

RA-7 shook his head. "Negative. I am not a combat...automaton. I would provide little...assistance. Besides, Kierian McKenna ordered me to get you the hell out of there and not to stop until we reach... Sagamore."

"Yes, but surely he would not wish you damaged beyond repair in the process."

"My continued functionality is not important. I am...expendable."

"Nonsense! No one is disposable." As the word escaped her lips Gladys thought back to Chaney's words: *...Just tossed her aside like a disposable part of a machine and replaced her with a new one.*

She brushed away a stray hair that had fallen across her forehead. *If we make it back to Sagamore, I shall speak to Alfred about our workers and the conditions under which they labor. We must make certain, those who labor for Vanderbilt industries are treated with dignity, and fairness.*

"Sacrifices must be...made," RA-7 said. "The mission must always come...first. The mission was to rescue you, and return you safely to your brother...Alfred. I will assure successful completion of the...mission."

They traveled in silence for an hour. The steepness of the mountain path soon leveled off, and the decent became more gradual. The horror and fright had departed, replaced by a guarded calm.

At some point fatigue overwhelmed Gladys and she nodded off. A sudden sensation of swaying violently to the left and right awoke her, and she quickly realized the Rescue Automaton was staggering.

"Mr. Seven, what is wrong?"

RA-7 staggered to a stop and teetered. For a moment Gladys thought he would topple over, and she began to loosen the bindings that secured her to his back. Suddenly, RA-7 caught his balance, dropped to one knee, and allowed her to dismount from his shoulders.

"What is wrong?" she repeated.

"I am winding...down."

"Winding down?"

RA-7 nodded with a herky-jerky motion of his enormous bronze head. "I am a clockwork Automaton. I must be wound every four to seven...days. Depending on the amount of power...exerted."

"But surely, Dr. Waatt wound you up before the mission began and that was but three days hence."

"Indeed but I previously engaged my Courage Protocol which used up more power than...usual."

"So much so, that you cannot function? That seems a bad trade off."

"Using the Courage Protocol should not have depleted me so...quickly. "Therefore I must conclude that my winding mechanism has been...damaged."

She probably should have been scared. If the Rescue Automaton could not continue on, she would be stranded in the middle of the deep dark woods of the

Adirondacks, possibly with a monster on the loose.

But Gladys was sick of being frightened and sick of being a victim. It had been her own stubbornness that had made it necessary for STEAMCAPP to place their lives in danger in the first place, and so far she had contributed nothing at all to the mission. Here was her chance to be something more than be a burden. Here was her chance to stand tall, pitch in and be part of a solution rather than be part of the problem.

"We must get you help Mr. Seven."

"But the mission, I must — "

Gladys held up a defiant hand. "I am afraid I must insist Mr. Seven. I will hear no more about you being expendable. Now, I assume you have maps?"

"Affirmative. Your brother supplied us with some prior to our...departure." RA-7 pulled a map from his equipment pouch and handed it to Gladys. It was hand drawn in meticulous detail by the Adirondack League's Chief Cartographer and very easy to read.

"Please indicate our location."

The rescue automaton did so. Gladys scanned the map and quickly found Sagamore.

"I do not think you will be able to make it to Sagamore, Mr. Seven. Not in the condition you are in. It is too far away."

"I…concur. However I could get you…close. Perhaps, you could make it the rest of the way on…foot."

"Perhaps, but that should only be our last resort. We may not be able to make it to Sagamore but perhaps we can bring help *from* Sagamore."

"I do have signal flares I could…fire. However I would suggest, we be both closer to Sagamore and in a more open…area."

"And so we shall." Gladys jabbed her finger down on a hand drawn cluster of buildings. "Can you make it another two miles?"

"I shall do my…best."

* * * * * *

Vivian Castleberry, Headmistress of Silver Oaks Academy, sat in the hand crafted oak chair in the middle of the Academy's stone amphitheater and dabbed at the corner of her right eye with her kerchief. Tongues of flames from the annual farewell bonfire licked the night air. Wood crackled and snapped, and the combined voices of 75 teenage girls, singing with well-practiced harmony, serenaded the surrounding Adirondack forest.

"Is the smoke irritating you, Mrs. Castleberry?" Daphne Pembroke, one of the senior girls inquired.

428

Mrs. Castleberry nodded. "Yes, Daphne," she averted her gaze from the eighteen year-old and, hurriedly wiped away the evidence of a small tear forming under the lines and wrinkles of her right eye, "It is just the smoke."

Daphne nodded and went back to singing *The Silver Sisterhood Forever* with the rest of the Academy's girls. The song was the camps anthem and usually was sung as the final song of the semester.

But this year, it would be the final song of the *final* semester.

Silver Oaks had been the first all-female summer camp where young girls learned how to be young ladies, where studies of Latin and Greek intermingled with classes in archery, horseback riding, tennis, and canoeing. It was where friendships forged in youth, lasted a lifetime.

But what often was the first to be, sadly was often the first to go. Silver Oaks facilities were outdated and in need of repair, and the small fortune her dearly departed and much beloved Harold had left her was insufficient to compete with the newer camps, built and financed by wealthier benefactors than she could ever hope to attract. Attendance and tuition had fallen and thus the camp would have to close.

Mrs. Castleberry gazed with pride at her girls. She had done right by them. They were good girls. Well, most of them were. A few bad apples like Pandora Dippledross and her partner in crime, Penelope Wentworth challenged the time tested traditions and rules that Vivian and the staff had labored so hard to uphold. The combination of the two girl's wealth and viciousness garnered them a small following of equally mean girls, but most of the others avoided their corrupting influence and simply tried to stay out of their way.

Heavy cracking of tree branches from behind the far side of the amphitheater, roused her from her thoughts. At first she thought it to be just a deer, but when small trees began to teeter and topple, she knew it was something larger.

Like a herd of cattle threatening to stampede, the nervousness among her girls started slowly. Heads turned, individual voices quit the song in mid verse and then, entire sections went silent. Heads twisted and peered into the forest. A girl yelled, "Bear!" Another screamed.

And then it appeared and brought Vivian leaping to her feet. A giant, gleaming, metal man, one arm hanging uselessly at his side, staggered wildly towards the fire.

430

Vivian's eyes stared in astonishment. Her girls were yelling excitedly; the younger ones clinging to the older ones for protection.

The metal man raised his good arm, waved and incredibly began to speak. "Please, do not be...alarmed. I mean no...harm"

The report of the double-barreled shotgun startled Vivian. Buckshot slammed into the metal man.

"Two in the center ring and it nay even scratched the paint," Mr. Farnsworth, the caretaker said as he reloaded his weapon.

"Mr. Farnsworth, please do not fire again. You may hit one of the girls," Vivian ordered.

"It's a monster! Kill it!" Pandora yelled. She charged down the steps of the amphitheater, with Penelope right behind her. The two girls snatched two of the iron pokers Mr. Farnsworth used to stoke the fire and began smashing them into the metal man's legs.

"No girls stop! Stay away from that thing." Vivian lifted the hem of her long skirt and hurried down the stone steps. She had just reached the ground when the metal man tottered and crashed to the ground.

"Die monster! Die!" Penelope yelled, smashing the poker into the robot's head.

431

"Penelope stop!" Vivian wrapped her arms around the teen and ripped the poker from her hands.

Pandora continued the assault.

"Please…s-stop." The metal man pleaded. He held up his good arm to protect himself, but Pandora slammed it away with the poker.

"Die metal monster!"

"Mr. Farnsworth," Vivian yelled, "stop her!"

"Stop her? Seems to me she's got the right idea. My pap always said, once you have a bigun' down, you keep him down."

Suddenly another girl, a strange girl wearing brown trousers, dashed forward and tackled Pandora to the ground.

Pandora pushed the new girl off and made the mistake of leaping to her feet. The girl cracked Pandora with a solid right cross to the chin, knocking her back to the ground.

"Down goes, Dippledross!" cackled Mr. Farnsworth. The caretaker clapped his hands, slapped his knee, and cackled as an eerie silence blanketed the amphitheater.

The strange girl picked up the poker and brandished it like a club. Vivian rushed over and stood between Pandora and her attacker. "Pandora." Vivian shook her.

She did not respond.

Doctor Franklin rushed over with his medical bag and examined Pandora. "There is no need for alarm; the girl is simply unconscious. She will be alright."

Vivian stood and turned. The new girl had dropped the poker and was cradling the metal man's head in her arms.

"Mr. Seven," she said, "Are you alright?"

"Please....sit me...up. I am almost...out of....power. We...must...fire the...flares."

"What is it?" Vivian asked, "And who are you?"

"*He* is RA-7. He is a Rescue automaton and he is my friend."

Pandora responded to the smelling salts and jerked awake. Immediately she stalked, fists balled toward the new girl. "I do not know who you are," Pandora began in her snottiest and snobbiest of voices, "but my father is Osgood Dippledross, president of the New York Central railroad, and I am his little princess and if Princess wants someone ruined Princess gets someone ruined."

The new girl helped the metal man sit up and shot a calm but seething look towards Pandora. "My name is Gladys Vanderbilt, and my brother OWNS the New York Central railroad, which means he is your father's employer, so unless Princess wants father to be unemployed and find herself taking another fire-side snooze, I suggest she sit back down and exercise several long moments of contemplative silence."

Pandora's jaw nearly hit the ground in shock and surprise, but Vivian noticed her fists unballed, and while she did not sit down, she took several wary steps away from the girl calling herself Gladys Vanderbilt. Pandora was not used to being stood up to, nor having the card of her family's power and status trumped but the new girl had already shown a willingness to back up her threats.

"Excuse me," Vivian said, "but do you have any proof of your identity Miss...Gladys, and can you explain why you suddenly emerged out of the forest, in the middle of the night with this....rescue robot."

"I was abducted. RA-7 and his friends rescued me."

"And where are these friends?"

"They were attacked by a....by the leader of the abductors."

RA-7 opened a panel in his side, pulled out a flare gun with eight rotating barrels, raised it and fired into the night sky. The flare streaked high, then exploded with fingers of what looked like lightning. He fired again and a red distress flare streaked high and then exploded. Small red lights floated down from above.

"What is he doing?" Vivian asked.

"Electrical distress... flare should... be... detected and the... red distress... flare will... hopefully be... seen."

He continued firing until the flares were exhausted.

"I do not know who you are Miss," Vivian began "but-

"Does it matter Mrs....?"

"I am Mrs. Vivian Casteberry, Headmistress of the Silver Oaks academy for girls."

"Very well Mrs. Castleberry. If you have a picture of my family somewhere you can compare my visage, otherwise you will have to await for confirmation from the authorities."

RA-7 fired the last flare and fell with a crash, onto the ground. Gladys softly stroked his metal head.

Vivian stared at the odd couple. "Clearly, you have some affection for that, metal man, Gladys but I must insist you give us some proof of your identity before, -"

"Why?"

"I beg your pardon?" Vivian replied.

Gladys let out a frustrating sigh. "Why is it important I prove who I am? That could take hours. If I am not a Vanderbilt, I will not receive assistance? We have traveled long and hard and barely escaped with our lives. Mrs. Castleberry, please, I and my friend need your help and we need it now, not hours from now."

Vivian looked at the girl once more. The way she spoke with an air of quiet, elegant authority and strength, spoke of upper class breeding. The girl's confidence and resolute action had made her seem older initially but now as the flames flickered and the wood cracked, Vivian heard the pleas of a younger girl.

A girl who had asked for *her* help.

Vivian looked around the amphitheater. All the Silver Sisters were watching.

Was this not what she was here for? Did she not teach the girls everyday to help each other? To be kind to strangers and do good when and where ever they could? She straightened her skirt and nodded as her motherly instinct came to life. She put her arm around, Gladys and smiled. "Come with me, Miss Gladys. We shall help you and your Rescue Robot. Mr. Farnsworth, bring the sled and horses enough, to pull the metal man

436

to the workshop."

"Thank you Mrs. Castleberry," Gladys said.

Vivian smiled and gently patted Gladys's back. "You are most welcome, my dear."

"If you have a wireless, I would like to send a message to my brother in Sagamore."

"Of course, my dear. There is one in my office. We shall contact your family and the authorities forthwith."

Gladys sighed and leaned into Vivian. "Thank you so very much. I and my family are in your debt."

Vivian smiled and gently patted Gladys's back. "It will all be alright, my dear. Yes everything will be alright."

CHAPTER TWENTY-SIX

Kierian's foot slipped atop the aluminum-coated cotton skin of HMAS Black Prince. The hydrogen filled air beast began its ascent, lumbering upward from its mooring birth at Durand Harbor.

A tapestry of blue sky contrasted with the scarlet dinner coat of Colonel Hyram Sterling. His massive Webley revolver pointed at Kierian's chest. "Hands in the air McKenna," the colonel commanded. "The game is up."

Kierian glanced over the side of the massive airship. Banshee was half way down one of the mooring lines that still swung free, the waves of Lake Ontario rolling beneath her.

"It's a long way down, McKenna. Give up the game. You have played your last card and I hold the trump."

Kierian faced Sterling. Slowly he raised his hands.

An arrogant sneer stretched beneath the Colonel's bushy mustache. "Lord Kitchener is safely ensconced in his stateroom surrounded by his Highland guards, your confederates have been repulsed, and you have nowhere left to trot off to this time. You have failed."

"You, John Bulls never learn," Kierian said. "It's that

cocksure arrogance that keeps dooming you."

"It is you Americans who never learn Mr. McKenna. You prattle around, fighting for your 'liberties, espousing the glory of the average man, and where has any of it got you?" Sterling shook his head. "Had you not rebelled against the mother country one hundred and twenty years ago, you could be a part of the British Empire, the greatest Empire the world has ever known!"

"You mean slaves of the Empire."

"Slaves? That's preposterous. So long as her citizens know their place, do not attempt to rise above their stations, give homage and recognize the Queen as their sovereign ruler, they are free to live in peace."

"That sounds like groveling, Colonel. Americans do not grovel."

"When The SSB boys get done with you, I dare say you'll be doing plenty of groveling McKenna and I pray I am there to see it!"

The airship's nose lurched upward. Its silver back arched and Sterling slipped. Instinctively, he threw his gun hand out to correct his balance.

Quick as a cat, Kierian dropped his hands, shook loose the Remington Model 95 Derringer from his right sleeve and raised his weapon.

Sterling spun and fired. His shot went wide.

439

Kierian's did not.

The .41 Short bullet slammed into the British officer's right shoulder, sending the Webley flying from his hands and over the airship's side.

"You scoundrel!" Sterling cried, as he gripped his wounded arm. "You have accomplished nothing! Do you hear me? Nothing! Your friends and colleagues have all died for nothing! Canada is still ours, Kitchener is safe, and once the brilliance of British science are set to the task of creating airships like your Excelsior, we will be back. The Sun will never set on the British Empire, McKenna. Never!"

"Buckem and Balderdash, my dear Colonel. The stone cold fact is your troops have been driven from the city and your Great Lakes fleet is now a smoking wreck at the bottom of Lake Ontario. As for Kitchener..." Kierian flipped open his pocket watch. "He has about one minute and twenty-three seconds of safety left. Then he and the rest of you, John Bulls, will have a most explosive end to your day."

Sterling's eyes went wide with horror. "You fool! We have signed an armistice. We are at peace!"

"The thousands of women and children who died in your internment camps, will be at peace. This is not India or the Sudan and you are not fighting Zulu's or Fuzzy-Wuzzies. You do not get to murder thirty thousand civilians and simply fly back to London for tea and crumpets with old queen

Vicky."

"Damn your blood, McKenna! We will hunt you and Dareheart down like the rabid dogs you both are! We shall hunt you to the ends of the earth!"

The fog of memory dimmed and the blue sky faded into swirls of grey. Kierian opened his eyes and blinked. The airship disappeared like a midnight apparition come the witching hour, replaced by an orange ball of flame.

For a moment he thought he was seeing *Black Prince* explode again, but there were no screams of the dying, no one burning alive and no bodies floating in the murky water by the harbor pier.

He shielded his eyes from the blinding morning sun. A canopy of pine trees swaying softly in the breeze replaced the dancing waves of Lake Ontario, and he saw a familiar face sitting by the embers of a dying campfire.

"Emma?"

Emma offered a weak smile. "Welcome back to the land of the living."

Kierian pushed himself up. Pain radiated through his right shoulder, now set in a sling. He ran his left hand through his sandy blond hair and glanced around.

441

The morning dawn revealed the horror of the night before, as his eyes fell on the gory remains of Leslie and Henroff.

"How...how long?" His voice sounded hoarse and garbled. He grabbed the canteen next to him. Refreshing water washed away the dryness. He took a second swig, swirled the water around his mouth, and spit half of it onto the ground.

"It is around eight in the morning," Emma replied. "You were with fever most of the night, but it broke around four."

Kierian nodded. Bits and pieces of memory knit a mosaic of the previous night: Emma patting his head with a cool compress, Emma setting his right arm in a sling, Emma holding him, and imploring him to fight to the last breath.

"Where is Balthazar? I suppose he cooked up some medicinal tea made from tree bark that broke the fever."

"Kierian, Balthazar is dead. Do you not remember?"

Broken memories returned like an unpleasant visitor to the doorstep of his mind. "That beast. He took it over the cliff with him."

Emma nodded, dropped her head to her chest,

pushed away a stray strand of hair, and absently chewed on the corner of her lip.

Kierian sat down next to her, arched his arm around her shoulder, and pulled her close.

"Balthazar was a good man, Kierian," Emma said, every word a melancholy note. "God knows, he was slow to trust and could be stubborn as a mule but there was a loving heart under that armor of intellect."

Kierian smiled. "I once told him he was being stubborn and he replied: 'I am not stubborn Kierian. It is simply that my way is the best way and all your arguments and metaphors to the contrary will not alter that fact.'"

Emma laughed. "He did not lack for confidence in his views and positions. That is certain."

"He was a remarkable man. He lacked my dash and daring, but he was solid as a rock in a fight. I did not think anything could bring down that old warhorse," Kierian said.

"Nothing did," Emma replied. "In his mind, taking that beast over the cliff was the only way to assure its demise. Dying in the process would just be a side effect of making the correct decision."

A strong burning odor wafted through the air. Kierian glanced at a wooden bowl sitting by the fire, filled with silver sludge.

"I have a vague memory of you cooking some God-awful soup last night. I presume that is it. You did not feed any of it to me, did you?"

Emma smiled. "That is not soup. I melted down some of the silver coins and covered what few remaining bullets we have in silver. If that beast somehow survived, I wanted to be ready."

Kierian nodded. He had taught her well. The best way to deal with the sorrow of loss was to keep busy. Sitting about focused on the hurt and the danger still to come, letting it paralyze you into hopelessness and inactivity, was a recipe for disaster. He was glad Emma was still thinking, still fighting.

"What *is* our weapons situation exactly, Banshee?"

Emma pulled a small notebook from her pocket and motioned to the long guns stacked barrel against barrel in a neat circle. "Twelve rounds of .45 caliber ammunition, two buckshot shells, and four deer slugs for your shotgun. We have 40 rounds of .30-30 ammunition that Leslie and Henroff were carrying. My EMR is empty. The heat-ray pistol's thermite is used up but Balthazar's heat-ray rifle still has a few charges left in it."

"And our mission status?" Kierian asked.

"More than likely, Ray has reached Sagamore by

now, with Miss Vanderbilt. The Anarchists still have Professor Stonechat, and since Werebear-Boaltt is dead at the bottom of the mountain with Balthazar, we have nothing to exchange her for."

Kierian nodded.

"In all honesty Piper, I think we should consider aborting."

Kierian raised an eyebrow in surprise. "Abort? That is not a word I think I have ever heard you say on a mission, Banshee."

Emma shrugged. "We accomplished our mission. We rescued Gladys Vanderbilt, and at a damn heavy cost. You are hardly in condition to perform your usual heroics. It cuts against me to leave Professor Stonechat behind but–"

Branches snapped and cracked. A tree limb swung into another branch with a thud.

Something was coming up the slope.

Emma drew her Colt and handed it to Kierian. She snatched one of the rifles from the stack, worked the lever, chambering a round, dropped to one knee, and took aim. "Only your first two rounds are silver coated Piper, so make them count."

Branches swayed. Twigs snapped. Kierian saw a bushy balsam pine branch sway backwards. He cocked the hammer and took aim.

"By the stars and stripes! I do not believe my eyes!" Emma exclaimed.

Dr. Balthazar Waatt limped from behind the branches, brushing off the coat of pine needles, leaves and twigs with an annoyed hand.

A deep purple bruise marred his forearm just above the left wrist and a trail of dried blood extended from his right temple, down his cheek.

All things considered, he looked remarkably well for a person who had plunged over the side of a cliff.

Emma dropped her rifle, and bounded forward. Jubilant arms encased Balthazar in a warm embrace. "I thought we had lost you, Balthazar. I should have known it would take more than a were-bear and a seven-hundred foot fall to kill you."

Dr. Waatt allowed his lips to stretch into a subdued smile. He patted Emma softly on her back. "You are correct that I survived the were-bear, but as for being hardy enough to survive a seven-hundred-foot plunge off Braxton Mountain, I am afraid you are in error, my dear."

"Oh? You seem fairly solid for a ghost," Emma relied.

Dr. Waatt smirked. "Clearly, I survived my dear, but

446

I survived precisely because I did *not* plunge seven hundred feet to the bottom of the forest. My estimation is I fell about one hundred feet. It was at that point that my magnetized boots attached to the nickel deposits within the stone strata of Braxton Mountain, slowing me enough that I was able to establish a foothold."

"How did you avoid breaking every bone in your body?" Kierian asked.

"The S.A.M.S.O.N took the brunt of the impact, saving me from devastating injury, though sadly, it is now beyond use."

Kierian shoved the pistol into his belt. His blue eyes twinkled, and a jubilant smile graced his face. Warmly, he shook Dr. Waatt's hand. "The old warhorse survives to fight yet another day. It is good to see you, Balthazar."

"I have told you before Kierian I am not old. My hair is prematurely grey and while I do not remember my exact day of birth I theorize I am about three and fifty years of age and even then, I would confidently say that I am spry for that age. In addition–"

"Balthazar," Emma interrupted. Dr. Waatt shot a glance at Emma's admonishing face and turned back to Kierian. "I am glad to see you are still alive too, Kierian."

Kierian grinned. "Thank you, Balthazar, very good of you to be concerned."

"In truth, I must say I am shocked. You were clawed by a were-bear, and with the lunar radiation at its height last night I thought you would have turned."

"Turned?" Kierian asked. " What? Into a creature?"

Balthazar nodded. "Indeed. Lycanthropy is highly contagious if a person comes into contact with a beast's blood or saliva. Most likely, the cells of the body mutate at an extremely advanced rate, altering the genetic structure of the person and transforming them into a were-beast."

"Well, the McKenna breed is indomitable. No doubt they and Good Lady Fortune's blessing, put the were-bear infection to chaotic flight!"

"Ha!" Dr. Waatt scoffed. "While I have given up trying to reason how you continue to waltz through life unscathed, defying the laws of probability as often as you do, I sincerely doubt it is the cause of you surviving a were-bear attack." Dr. Waatt turned and looked at Emma. " What did you do for him my dear?"

"I did nothing, but cauterize the wound with gunpowder, tried to cool his fever, and set his arm in the sling." Emma replied.

Dr. Waatt shook his head. "No, you did something.

448

You must have. Did you make some tea from the bark of these trees or attempt any natural remedy?"

"I told you all I did Balthazar, except that I kissed him."

Kierian grinned. "Stealing kisses when I am unconscious. For shame, Banshee."

"Magical as I am sure your kisses are my dear, unless your true name is Princess Charming, I doubt it played any part in_" Dr. Waatt glanced back and forth from Kierian to Emma. "The height would be about right...my dear, you were prone when you kissed him, were you not?"

"Why, yes I was Balthazar but-"

Dr. Waatt grabbed the flower pinned to Emma's blouse. "The Flower! I would wager anything, he inhaled its spores."

Emma cocked her head to one side. "Now that you mention it, the flower was pressed flush against his face for several moments. I had to push it away to kiss him."

"Of course!" Dr. Waatt slapped his knee. "It all makes sense now!"

"What does? Balthazar, what are you talking about?"

"*Trifolium Pratense*, or Red Shamrock is native to

Ireland, *not to* the Adirondack region, and yet, directly outside the church of the Twelve Apostles, is an entire field of the species."

"And that indicates what exactly?" Kierian asked.

"That it was brought here from Ireland and purposely planted as a medicinal crop, very possibly to act as an antidote against Lycanthropy."

"I thought the church was founded by the Jesuits?" Kierian said.

Balthazar shook his head. "No, it pre-dates the Jesuits. I now believe that church was founded by Brendan, hence why the designs on the stained glass windows were so unconventional and why Professor Bridgewater took such a great interest in them. They were not representations of our Lord's twelve apostles but of Brendan and his Monks, the twelve apostles of Ireland!"

Kierian nodded, beginning to follow Balthazar's reasoning. "If that is true, the close proximity of the church, to the dig site where Professor Bridgewater thought confirmation of Brendan's Journey rested, cannot be mere coincidence."

Emma joined the boys with her own thoughts. "The Anarchists needed Professor Stonechat to gain them access to the Temple, which means there is something

450

inside they want very badly, something perhaps the monks themselves buried there."

"What could Irish Monks bury eleven-hundred years ago that militant anarchists would want in the 20th century?" Kierian asked.

"Unknown," Balthazar replied, "but I fear it may have something to do with Boaltt-Talbot. You will recall he is the foremost expert in the world on Lycanthropy, and as we now know, a were-beast himself. Further, you will recall Mr. Leslie mentioned fifteen people had been killed in the region by a bear that was suspected of being a grizzly. That was almost certainly Boaltt."

"He was looking for something." Kierian said. "Something he knew was in the region but not sure exactly where."

"Like the Temple site?" Emma offered.

"I think that likely," Balthazar said. "When Professor Bridgewater discovered it and announced plans to excavate it, Boaltt and whoever is the true power behind the Anarchists, set this infernal plan in motion."

"But what could the monks have buried there and what use would it be to anarchists?" Emma asked.

"The answers to those questions reside at the temple." Balthazar stood and pounded his walking stick hard into the rocky ground. "We must, with all haste, proceed there at once!"

"Balthazar, we are in no condition for battle," Emma pointed out. "We need to re-group, re-supply, and get Kierian immediate medical attention."

Dr. Waatt nodded. "Ask and it shall be given unto you; Seek and ye shall find. For everyone that Asketh recieveth, and he that seeketh findeth. Matthew, chapter Seven, verses seven and eight." Balthazar lifted his cane and pointed into the sky. "A most relevant and comforting verse to our present situation. Behold!"

Kierian and Emma turned and followed his gaze.

Speeding across the blue morning sky was what looked like a large silver whale.

Emma smiled.

The *Excelsior* had arrived.

EPILOGUE

Abraxas Mansion
Somewhere in the Thousand Islands Archipelago

Octavious Bitterwood, Grandmaster of the Legion of Cain, gazed at the giant circular stained glass balcony door and ran a pensive finger around the circumference of his brandy snifter.

Victory was so close he could taste it.

He was well aware, however, that over its two thousand year existence, the Legion had been close to victory many times, only to have it snatched away at the moment of triumph.

This time will be different. This time the enemy does not even know we are operational.

He gazed at the scene painted on the glass, portraying Cain executing the usurper Abel.

You were the first born, and the secrets from the Tree of Knowledge were rightfully yours, not the usurper's. Yet they marked you and casted you out.

Octavious took a sip of his brandy and glanced at

453

several of the other stain glass window scenes; Nimrod, whose Tower of Power would have brought the world under their control had not Eber sabotaged it and caused The Great Confusion; Korah, who had bravely led a rebellion against Moses; Achol of Akrod, who had the Ark of the Covenant in his possession but understood neither its technology nor its operation.

How close the ancient Magus had come to victory. Yet, close was just another word for failure. Was it not? And now it was his turn to attempt to succeed where all others had failed.

The door to his private study opened without a knock and someone entered.

He knew it was Lilith Grimm. No one else would have been so bold to enter without begging his permission. He resisted the desire to turn and gaze at her beauty, at the fiery red hair, the smooth alabaster skin, and the alluring green eyes.

He did not fear the mesmerist's power. Octavious knew many of her secrets, and his study of the ancient defenses against mind control gave him a confidence most others lacked in her presence. Yet, he was still a man, still susceptible to her womanly charms and there was no reason to show weakness and let Lilith begin dreaming of the Legion having a grandmistress, instead of a grandmaster.

He heard her soft steps and could smell her intoxicating scent, enhanced by a chemist's customized fragrance of frankincense, turkish rose, bergamot, jasmine, and amber.

"I have a message." Lilith trilled.

Her voice was soft, husky, and Octavious was aware of a slight oscillating of his right eardrum when she spoke.

He took a sip of his brandy. "From Sir John?"

"No. It is from Barnabas Blackwell."

Octavious took another sip and waited for her to continue but she did not. One of Lilith's games was to hold onto whatever it was you needed from her, for as long as she could. The more time you were in a state of dependence to her, the more time her charms had to sink their hooks in, good and tight. Even now he knew she would give her report a dribble at a time.

"What does your pet have to say?"

She placed a soft hand on his shoulder and squeezed. The perfume from her wrist wafted alluringly upwards. "The Stonechat woman has opened the temple. Barnabas expects extraction of the artifact to take place on schedule."

"Good, very good." He took another sip of his

455

brandy and kept his back to her. "Everything is proceeding as planned. America's elites are all gathered at Sagamore, including the Big Four and once we have the artifact, there will be nothing that can stop us or save them."

"Not everything has gone according to plan, Octavious." Lilith's arm swept off his shoulder. In spite of himself, Octavious turned and looked. Lilith was dressed in a sleek fitting green dress that accented her lovely form. She walked with a practiced sultriness to the table with the brandy decanter, poured herself a glass, and looked at him with those captivating green eyes.

The Grandmaster waited patiently refusing to show any sign of irritation.

"Sir John has been captured," Lilith reported. "His cover as Professor Boaltt was exposed."

Octavious nodded. "When did the capture happen?"

"Late yesterday afternoon, when they made the exchange of the Vanderbilt girl."

"The moon was full last night. I am confident that by now, Sir John will have disposed of whatever lackeys Vanderbilt sent."

Lilith sipped her brandy and with a slow motion of

456

her hand brushed back part of the mane of red hair that had fallen across her left cheek.

"The team Vanderbilt sent was STEAMCAPP."

Octavious finished off the remains of his brandy, steepled his fingers together, and nodded.

"Is that not, Dr. Waatt's team? The one who stopped Operation Dragon Gate?"

"Indeed."

"His interference in two of our operations, in so short a period of time, would seem to indicate we have been exposed. Perhaps your security measures were not as thorough as you thought," Lillith said.

"I disagree. Dragon Gate took place in his hometown. As far as we can ascertain, that is the only reason he became involved."

"Octavious, the Adirondacks are not his hometown."

"I am aware Lilith but that means nothing. His team may have simply been the one Vanderbilt called in to rescue his sister. It does not mean he is hunting us."

Octavious ran a hand through his coal black hair. Only after he had done so did he realize the motion he had used to be the exact one Lilith had used on her own locks.

Was it a suggested action of hers? A test? He looked at Lilith. The enchantress smiled and sipped her brandy.

"Waatt and his associates are flesh and blood. I am sure by now, Sir John has disposed of them all."

Lilith shrugged a milky white shoulder. "If not, they could cause trouble. They have a powerful airship as I recall."

Octavious opened the stained glass door, beckoned for Red Lilith to follow, and walked out onto the balcony.

"So do we."

Below, moored at their stations were two enormous airships, armed to the teeth with cannons, machine guns and rockets. They were painted red and black and flying the Legion Flag: The great serpent, coiled around the world they would soon rule.

In front of each airship, 1000 legionnaires, including the 400 volunteers from the Nimrod Clan, dressed smartly in their black and red uniforms snapped heals to attention and saluted the Grandmaster and the Red Queen.

"Air Marshall Von Hellwig," Octavious said, projecting his voice through the balcony's bronze voice trumpet, "Are your airships and their crews ready?"

"Jawohl, Grandmaster! We await your order to commence Operations."

"The order is given, Air Marshall. Retrieve the artifact, initiate the final phase of Operation Atlas, and bring an end to the United States of America."

"As you command, Grandmaster!"

Octavious's right hand balled, his left hand covered it and he raised it above his head as Cain had raised the rock that smote down Abel. "As Cain was victorious over Able," he brought down his fists in a striking motion and in unison, the legionnaires responded, "So shall we be victorious over America!"

The Air Marshall dismissed the crews, and they rushed inside their airships. Moments later, the heavily armed vessels rose into the air, headed for Adirondack dig site 401B, and the Temple of The Bear.

TO BE CONCLUDED IN:

S.T.E.A.M.C.A.P.P

THE ADIRONDACK AFFAIR

BOOK II: AIR LORDS OF THE ADIRONDACKS

If you enjoyed STEAMCAPP: The Adirondack Affair: Book 1: The Rising Of The Moon, I would be very grateful if you could take the time to leave me your thoughts in a review at :

https://www.amazon.com/dp/B07HM9PBZ5

I am always very interested to know what my readers liked, and enjoyed, what questions they have, and even what they may think will happen next. Someone once said to me: "if you knew no one would ever read your book, you would still write, correct?(actually they said "right" but I changed it so it would be easier for you all to read.)

I said no I wouldn't and that is the honest truth. Without my readers, for me, the hard work, the research and the time invested isn't worth it. Without my readers, the stories and characters stay in my head, and X-box gets a lot more play time.

But with my readers support, I am inspired. With my readers, it is a joy to write, because I know I am bringing some pleasure to my fans, making life wherever you strive to live it, a bit more enjoyable as you escape into the world and adventures of Emma Dareheart, Kierian McKenna, Dr. Waatt and RA-7.

I'm currently hard at work putting the final

touches on STEAMCAPP: Phantasmagoria. It's a halloween 100 page story. I plan on making that free to anyone who wants to be on my mailing list.

AIR LORDS OF THE ADIRONDACKS, is nearly complete. I hope to have it out by spring of 2018 but perhaps if you inspire me with the hue and cry for it faster in reviews, my inner muse will feel obliged to provide.

Thank you to all who read, and God bless .

Below, so you know I am working on it hard, is a preview from Air Lords.

Book II: Air Lords Of The Adirondacks Preview

****

Taka-taka-taka-taka

The flying machine's Maxim machine gun, strafed the starboard hull of the *Excelsior* with a deadly stream of British .303s.

"Where in thunder did they come from?" Henry Brandt, the tall, imposing, Master-At-Arms of the *Excelsior* exclaimed.

Half way to the dig site where they hoped to extract Professor Stonechat, fifteen machines that looked like flying bobsleds had suddenly emerged from beneath *Excelsior* and attacked without warning.

"Unknown at present, Mr. Brandt," Dr. Waatt replied, from his captain's chair, located in the center of the airship's bridge. "The rotor blades atop their vehicles, no doubt allow for vertical ascension. They therefore, could have risen out of any of the forested areas we are flying over."

"Or from another airship," Emma offered, standing next to Dr. Waatt and Kierian. "Just because they attacked from below does not mean they originated from below."

Dr. Waatt steepled his fingertips and nodded. "Mr. Gorman, are there any aerial contacts on the PARA besides the flying sleds?"

The twenty-two year old blond haired operator studied the round display screen of the Waatt Waves Projection And Receiving Apparatus. The device sent out electromagnetic waves that when reflected back gave both range and size of any metallic object that the waves struck. Presently, several small green blips denoted the sleds but no larger blips appeared. "Negative, Doctor. No, other contacts in range."

Dr. Waatt nodded and turned to *Excelsior's* wireless operator Fathiyah Hajji. "Miss Hajjii, have you picked up any unusual wireless communiqués?"

The beautiful dark haired Moroccan gracefully turned in her chair, one gorgeous leg crossed over another and shook her head. "No, Doctor I have not."

"Who gives a good damn, where they came from," Kierian said as he stood next to Balthazar. " Master-At-Arms, return fire, and knock those flying bobsleds out of the sky!"

Brandt glanced down at Dr. Waatt from his Operations station. Balthazar nodded to him then shot a disapproving scowl at Kierian.

While they had all agreed Kierian would serve as STEAMCAPP's field commander on missions, when onboard *Excelsior*, since after all it was his airship, it was Balthazar who gave the orders.

The Master-At-Arms swept his hand down a column of switches. Inside *Excelsior's* twelve glass ball turrets, a green light flicked on signaling the gunners to open fire.

Brrrrrrrrt.

Excelsior's Gatling guns simultaneously opened fire with a ripping report.

Emma glanced out one of the tall oblong glass windows that encircled the bridge and saw an enemy flying machine explode. Another, hissing steam, tumbled towards the forest of pines below.

"Three, enemy contacts dead ahead!" Mr. Gorman shouted.

Three flying sleds in a triangle attack formation streaked towards *Excelsior*. Emma's eyes darted to the glass ball turret of the heat ray cannon, located just forward of the bridge. Inside, the gunner's mate gripped the handles of the heat ray weapon and rotated the gunnery chair. He turned a dial on his control panel, flicked a switch and the massive concentric coils

465

around the weapon glowed red hot. Calmly he aimed the main heat cannon as the flying machines made their attack run. With an almost pleasant hum, the weapon fired and a powerful beam of red microwaved, amplified energy obliterated the middle sled.

But the other two sleds continued their attack.

Their rotors were a blur as they unleashed a volley of machine gun fire directly into the glass window of *Excelsior's* bridge.

Emma and Kierian instinctively hit the deck.

Balthazar sat still as a statue in his chair as the flying machines finished their attack run and soared over *Excelsior*.

"There is no need to seek cover," Dr. Waatt explained. "I took the liberty of reinforcing the *Excelsior's* windows with several layers of ballistic glass just prior to receiving the letter from Alfred Vanderbilt. We should be quite safe from small arms fire."

Emma glanced at the windows. The bullets had failed to penetrate the glass but did manage to cause a few small fracture lines.

"Perhaps we should deploy the shield, Balthazar, just to be safe?" Emma suggested.

Dr. Waatt, his fingertips still pressed together, quietly observed the flying machines buzzing around his

466

airship like an entomologist studying a new species of insects. "I do not believe that is necessary just yet, Miss Dareheart. From what I see, these gyro sleds are lightly armed. Only a very lucky hit would penetrate the *Excelsior's* spider-silk skin."

"Yes, but why take the chance?" Emma asked.

"The power drain from using the shield will slow us to a crawl, Miss Dareheart," Brandt explained.

"Indeed," Dr. Waatt said, "and it is apparent that whoever this enemy is, and wherever they came from, they were sent to delay us from reaching the dig site and Professor Stonechat. Raising the shield would do naught but allow them to complete their mission."

Emma nodded. Outside *Excelsior,* one, two, then three flying machines exploded as the Gatling gunners found their range.

"Balthazar," Kierian said. "Who exactly *is* our adversary? Were-beasts and armed gyro sleds seem a bit above the capabilities of simple anarchists."

"I concur, Kierian," Dr. Waatt said. "You will recall, Boaltt said as much when he referred to the anarchists as pawns in a much greater game."

"Then who is the true master gamester behind all this?" Emma asked.

"Someone, with technology that matches our own

and who clearly possesses superior resources."

Butterflies with wings of anxiety knotted in Emma's stomach. Ever since they had pulled Balthazar from the wreck of the crashed airship they had enjoyed the advantage of superior technology over every foe they had faced. In many cases it had been the difference between victory and defeat. Now, that advantage, even by Balthazar's admission, was gone.

"Contact! Airship at 4000 yards and closing," Mr. Gorman said.

"Maintain present speed but take us up to 8,000 feet, Mr. Perry," Balthazar said to the pilot.

"Aye, Doctor. 8,000 feet." A small bell rang as the pilot pulled the lever on the Altitude Order Telegraph, a dial about nine inches in diameter, and set it at 8,000 feet. Seconds later the bell rang again, signaling that Chief Engineer Keltz had received and executed the order. Instantly the air inside *Excelsior's* envelope superheated and the airship rapidly rose.

"We may lack, a technological advantage, Banshee," Kierian said, "but I doubt there is anyone more experienced in handling their airship than Balthazar is at handling his."

"Thank you for your vote of confidence, Kierian," Balthazar said.

Emma smiled up at Kierian and he gave her a reassuring wink.

Outside another gyro sled exploded and Emma watched the rest of them suddenly break off their attacks and fly off to the west.

As *Excelsior* rose into the blue sky, her butterflies increased. If Kierian was shooting compliments to Balthazar it meant it was not just herself that was having doubts.

Even the Piper was worried.

HISTORY NOTES

The world of STEAMCAPP is set in an alternate reality where events occurred slightly differently than in our own timeline. Below are some notes on OUR actual history, the differences in the SC timeline, as well as some of the inspiration for the Alternate timeline that some of my fellow history nerds may enjoy.

The British-American War

I grew up in a time when the United States and Great Britain had been close allies starting back in WWI, then in WWII and through the cold war, so I was surprised to find out in my research that this was not always so.

After the America Civil War there was a lot of Anti-British sentiment due to the British aiding the Confederacy and nearly going to war with America during the **Trent Affair**.

Further back, I discovered the **Carolina Affair**.

On December 29,1837 Captain Andrew Drew of The Royal Navy crossed the international boundary, seized the American ship *Caroline,* killed an African American crewman by the name of Amos Durfee, set the ship on fire, set it adrift and cast it over Niagara falls.

America Was outraged. President Martin Van Buren protested to London and was ignored. On May 13, 1838, "Pirate Bill" Johnston retaliated, capturing, looting and burning the British Steamer *Sir Robert Peel* while she was in American waters. Skirmishes continued on both sides but eventually cooler heads prevailed.

But what if they had not? And what If similar events happened the 1890s when every major nation , including the US and Great Britain were jockeying for Imperialistic advantage and the weaponry was much more lethal? What if James G. Blaine, a well known anti-British Republican who in our timeline ran for President in 1884 and lost, was President at the time? In the world of STEAMCAPP the what if became reality and for the third time in 125 years, America and Britain were at war.

Billy Lush and The Rochester Bronchos.

The Rochester Red Wings are the beloved minor league baseball team of my home town but in 1901 they were known as the Bronchos.

Billy Lush, the player Emma was celebrating with after her skywalk was an actual player. He hit .310, stole 50 bases, led the Eastern League in Triples and scored 137 runs in only 132 games. The Bronchos won the league tile in 1901 with a 89-49 record.

George Armstrong Custer

In February 1866 after being mustered out of the volunteer army, Custer was offered a command by Benito Juarez and 10,000 in gold to be adjunct general of the army. Secretary of State William Seward opposed it and did not want an American general commanding foreign troops.

In the SC timeline, Custer survives the Battle of Little Bighorn, is court-martialed and THEN is offered a Mexican Command by Maximillian. He successfully defeats the rebels, and then turns on the Maximillian, orchestrating a military coup and becomes Emperor of Mexico himself.

British Internment Camps and Lord-Kitchner

During the Boer war, the British under Lord Kitchener began a scorched earth policy to defeat the Boer guerrillas. The systematic destruction of crops, live-stock and the burning of homes caused a massive refugee problem. Over 45 "internment camps" were set up. Most of the occupants were woman and children and over 26,000 perished in these camps.

Since in the SC timeline neither the Boer war or the Spanish-American war has occurred, I moved the atrocity to the British-American War.

German-American Relations

Did you know that there was a possibility, before Germany began their unrestrictive submarine warfare in WWI, of American coming in on THEIR side?

Tis true. With a large population of Germans in the US joining the allies, was no sure thing.

In the SC timeline the British-American war has moved the United States and Imperial Germany closer. This is a major concern for the Brits as a marriage of German Zeppelin building and American Helium stores could tip the air power advantage decidedly in a German-America way.

Acknowledgements

This book would never have been completed without the support and assistance of many people.

First I would like to thank my wife Gwen, who lovingly read through, helped proofread the story, and constantly encouraged me that my writing was good enough for publication.

My sister Maura, read the entire story when it was in beta and therefore has read much of the sequel. I am grateful for all her heartfelt encouragement and for cheering me on so passionately.

I would also like to thank my wonderful friends for all their help and support. Kurt, provided the techy plausible science behind the gadgets and equipment in the S.T.E.A.M.C.A.P.P. world and Jeff was largely responsible for Emma's tightrope tech. Jan believed in me as a writer so much, she insisted on referring to me as her "author friend" even before the book was completed.

My thanks to the Critiquers on Scribophile.com, particularly Evie L. Noelle who helped with all things Stonechat and archeology and especially to Katia Hart whose editing and suggestions on scenes and word choices were a great help.

My deep gratitude goes to my writing partner and fellow author M.P. Shelford who shepherded me through the formatting process and has been by my side through the twisting journey of self-publishing a first novel, providing encouragement and support wherever and whenever I needed it.

Finally I would like to thank the readers, whose interest in the Adventures of S.T.E.A.M.C.A.P.P. make all the hard work worthwhile.

26805506R00277